girls like her

Pam Stone

STONE'S THROW PUBLISHING

Girls Like Her
by Pam Stone

Copyright © Pam Stone 2017

ISBN 978-0-692-81996-8

Published by Stone's Throw Publishing. No part of this publication may be reproduced, stored in a retrieval system, or transmitted in any form or by any means, electronic, mechanical, photocopying, recording or otherwise without written permission of the publisher.

This is a work of fiction. Names, characters, businesses, places, events and incidents are either the products of the author's imagination or used in a fictitious manner. Any resemblance to actual persons, living or dead, or actual events is purely coincidental.

To the memory of my mother, Joan,
who knew these cliffs well.

Acknowledgements

Writing a work of fiction is dependent upon many things with unflagging support and encouragement being paramount. I express my heartfelt appreciation to Merri Mayers, for her ardent optimism and devoted reading of each line of the manuscript. Bobbi Sommer gave greatly appreciated creative confidence, and my agent, Anita Haeggstrom, provided both her savvy eye and enthusiastic assessment. Maggie Pagratis created the cover art and Rachel Richardson contributed a most helpful proofing. Finally, Paul Zimmerman, as always, was enormously helpful in all things technological, and patiently walked the streets of Asheville with me so that I might authentically create the haunts of my characters.

against their bodies and nod or shake their heads, Leigh felt with a sudden start that never had she even possessed the aplomb to be self-assured enough to engage in such an activity that was so run of the mill normal for any other girl. She would, she remembered, pick carefully through stacks of sweaters or jeans and, holding them self-consciously against her chest, disappear into the changing room to despise the image that greeted her in the mirror: baby fine bangs rising absurdly into a halo of static electricity as she pulled her sweatshirt over her head, glasses sliding down her straight but rather stubby nose, jeans that were too loose in the waist but straining in the rear and the hips, and heavy breasts in an ill-fitting bra that did absolutely nothing for the taupe and cream sweater she'd struggled into.

"You found nothing *again*?" her mother had queried from the kitchen, noting the absence of shopping bags when she had banged the back door upon returning home, silent and sullen. "Surely there's something in that mall that you like."

"Nothing fits, everything looks awful. Everyone else can wear what's in style except me!" Leigh had blasted, not stopping on her way to her room.

"Why do you care what everyone else wears?" her mother called after her in that exasperating manner of one who resides firmly within a world of pragmatism. "It's the beginning of a new school year—why not start a trend of your own?"

Typical, Leigh had fumed with a snort, closing her bedroom door heavily behind her. Not a word of comfort, not an effort to understand...always with her mother, *always* it was more important to pick yourself up, square your shoulders, and not only face an obstacle but pole vault over it. Seething with self-loathing, the last thing Leigh wanted was to take an initiative to stand out and "start a new trend." Emotional survival at that fragile age of fifteen meant blending in with the pack and essentially disappearing.

"All right," came Tracy's voice from behind her. "I only ordered a medium Coke but it came in a cup as big as a silo, so I'm amped up and rarin' to go. As a matter of fact, not only am I ready to do more shopping, but I might just jog beside the car on the way home."

Leigh cracked a smile that didn't include her eyes and nodded. "Yep," she said. "Let's find my mother her birthday present. And it's got to be useful, you know."

Pulling the caramel liquid through a straw, Tracy replied mischievously. "Oh, yes. Useful. You know, maybe we should go shopping for your mom at the hardware store. Instead of getting her a purse to match her shoes, we could get her a Leatherman."

Leigh stopped, turned, and faced her. "Honest to God," she said flatly. "She already has one."

In a flash, Tracy's left hand flew to her mouth to prevent spraying her friend with her drink as she burst into laughter. "Are you *serious?* I mean, I was *kidding!*"

Leigh nodded and resumed walking. "Oh, yeah. I saw it clipped to her belt loop when she was outside putting a new hinge on the garden gate."

"Your mom," Tracy mused, "has to be the most self-sufficient woman I've ever known. She's like a pioneer woman. When you think of everything she's been through, I don't think I've ever even heard her complain. And unbelievable energy—I can't believe she's going to be seventy! You remember when she led our Girl Scout hike through the state park when we were kids? None of us could keep up with her. And I'll bet none of us could, now."

"Well," Leigh said somewhat tonelessly as she entered the bookstore, "I lost interest in trying to do that years ago."

Chapter 2

ANYONE WHO WOULD HAVE found an empty table near the back of *The Winery on Market* might have noticed the couple sharing a bottle of pinot and a platter of fruit and cheese. It would also be only natural that a stranger's eye be drawn first to the woman, her glossy dark bobbed hair tucked unselfconsciously behind one ear and displaying a simple pearl stud. She sat with one hand placed in her lap, emerging from the sleeve of a hip-length black cashmere sweater, and leaned slightly over her plate as she forked a wedge of pineapple into her rather small mouth.

A pleasant enough looking fellow, her companion's age was impossible to determine owing to an unlined face but slightly peppered and somewhat shaggy hair—he could have been anywhere from his late twenties to forty—watched the woman with interest. Anticipation. When no utterances were made he filled the void himself.

"It's odd, isn't it?"

Laying her fork on the table and carefully blotting her lips, her eyes rose to his and she gave rather a wan smile. "Pretty surreal," she replied.

"I can't tell you," he began, then faltered. Leaning back in his chair, he looked upwards to the ceiling as if searching for guidance and blew his breath out slowly before continuing. "I can't tell you how much I appreciate how considerate and amicable you've been through this entire ordeal. I mean, we've both witnessed friends

9

going through the same thing and it turning out to be a nightmare: pettiness, hostility."

"David," she replied, her head cocked to one side in that gesture that always touched him, "I'd like to think neither of us ever possessed those traits during our marriage, so at least to me, it's not surprising those aren't a part of our divorce."

"Yeah," he agreed, sighing. "But it does tend to bring out the worst in people. I'm just relieved it hasn't with us."

"Well." She smiled, and said with a genuineness that unintentionally hurt, "I guess that's one thing we got right."

There were a few awkward moments of silence that followed and David motioned to the waiter for the check. As it arrived, the woman reached for her purse.

"No, no," he said, retrieving the billfold from his jacket. "This one's on me."

"David—" Her hand extended to the check.

"Denise," he said firmly. He covered her hand with his. It was warm. Delicate. Bare of any ornamentation. "Let me. Please."

She acquiesced and pulled her wool pea coat from the back of her chair and waited for the charge to be completed. Together, they then rose and walked through the bistro to the front door.

The hostess, a pretty college-aged girl with her hair in a loose braid over one shoulder, smiled to them as they prepared to step into the street. "Was everything all right?"

Denise smiled politely and glanced at David, who, returning her look, said, "Everything was fine."

Stepping out into the sharp February air, they turned and faced one another. He took both her hands in his and she didn't resist.

"I guess this is it."

Unexpectedly for both of them, her eyes suddenly brimmed with tears.

"Yes." She nodded. "I guess it is."

He leaned forward, meaning to give her a quick kiss, but instead lay his cheek softly against hers for a few moments. "Bye, Denise," he murmured.

"Bye David," she echoed. Then, mustering the practicality that he knew all too well, she drew back stiffly as she pulled her hands free. "Best of luck."

"Yeah. You too."

He watched her turn and stride purposely away, the heels of her suede boots clicking down the sidewalk. She would meet admiring glances, he knew, as she made her way to where her Audi was parked off the street. She would never once check her reflection in a window, a confident trait he'd always found attractive. Before reaching her car, she withdrew her phone from her pocket to check messages. Just moments after the dissolution of her marriage, Denise was checking in with work. Nothing illustrated the failure of their relationship more poignantly, David thought. A brisk wind ruffled the top of his hair and seemed to spur him to action. Shoving his hands deep into the pockets of his jeans, he wheeled around and began to walk to his car.

"Time to get on with your life, boy," he said aloud.

Chapter 3

A STEADY STREAM OF birthday greetings had begun arriving daily in Lissie's mailbox for the past two weeks. Among them, the obligatory *On Your 70th* emblazoned in gold, a couple along the not-so-funny lines of "You know you're old when..." and a religious one, soft focused and serene, with the scene of an ocean and lighthouse. Nothing yet from David or Leigh, but, of course, they lived locally and would be presented at the big to-do.

Lissie removed her gardening gloves as she retrieved the day's mail and flipped quickly through the envelopes. They ranged from fire engine red to a soft mauve, and with a smile on her face, she tucked the grocery store circular under her arm and made her way down the gravel drive to the antebellum farmhouse where she had resided and raised her children for over forty years. Mounting the old stone steps that led to the sprawling front porch, she hesitated as her eyes swept over the dormant flowerbeds, making quite sure she had thoroughly cleared and raked the areas. She gently fingered the gay faces of the pansies she had installed during the late autumn in the two massive planters that stood like sentries on either side of the top step. Never a fan of what she considered to be the gaudy purple and orange varieties of the species, she had instead chosen soft buttery yellow and cream and was pleased with the result.

It was a sharply crisp afternoon but she relished being outdoors—probably a trait acquired from her parents who had been stout believers in growing as much of one's own food as possible. Even as a child, she had not complained of the routine chores of weeding and digging, not even in midsummer with bothersome gnats and bees. It seemed as normal as waking, eating, homework, and sleeping. No one was more concerned about the lack of connection with nature that modern children seemed to have than Lissie.

"Does she ever take that thing out of her hand?" she had asked Leigh while observing Kirsten over lunch a few months ago.

"It's part of their body," Leigh retorted. "And it's not just her, it's the whole culture. Generally the only conversation we have is by text."

Lissie pushed her half-eaten chef's salad aside, clasped both hands together, and leaned forward towards her granddaughter.

"Kirsten?" she asked.

The girl, with the same fine hair as her mother but with the firm set jaw of her father, looked briefly away from the screen she held into the pale blue eyes of her grandmother and replied, "Mmm?"

"Must you?"

"I just want to finish sending this one text," she said and returned her attention to the screen of her phone.

Leigh met her mother's questioning expression with an 'I told you so' shrug of the shoulders, and began to twirl the ice at the bottom of her glass with her straw.

"Yes, but prior to 'this last text' has been several other texts, and, frankly, dear, it's quite rude."

Leaning back heavily against her seat in the booth, Kirsten lay down the instrument and sighed.

"There," she said flatly. "OK, Nan?"

"It's not that I'm trying to be a killjoy," Lissie replied lightly. "But the point of this lunch was to take the opportunity to chat, to catch up with one another. I haven't physically seen you both in nearly two months. So can you tell me how you are and what you're doing?"

"How I am is fine," Kirsten said dully. "And what I'm doing is school."

"And how is that going?" Lissie pressed.

"We just started back," Kirsten said. "So, it's not really going."

13

What followed was an uncomfortable silence. In an attempt to fill the void, Leigh reached for the laminated menu housed between the table condiments and mumbled, "Anyone want dessert?"

Lissie reached for her purse and pulled out a twenty dollar bill. "I don't think so, dear," she said, placing the bill next to her daughter.

"You're leaving?" Leigh asked, surprised. "We've barely been here half an hour. You haven't even finished your salad."

"I enjoy a lunch out," Lissie, rising, explained with her trademark forthrightness. "I stay quite busy at home, so to find the time to get away for an hour or two is a treat. But what I don't enjoy is a lack of common courtesy with no attempt at pleasant conversation. Kirsten, your sullen nature is not an attractive one and Leigh, dear, you're not doing her any favors by allowing it to continue. So if you will excuse me, I shall take my leave and return to my chrysanthemums."

"Fine," Leigh snapped. "Sorry I've let you down *again*, mother."

"All I ask," Lissie replied calmly, gathering her things, "is for a little common courtesy. This isn't an attack on you, Leigh."

"Well, that's not what it feels like."

"I'm sorry you feel that way," Lissie said, looking down at her daughter's flushed cheeks. "And I look forward to seeing you—*both* of you—for a real visit." Shrugging into her anorak, she added, "If that's something you think you'd enjoy."

"Don't worry," Leigh said hotly, not taking her eyes from the menu. "I'll make sure we all play 'happy families' should we get together in the future."

"Leigh," Lissie sighed, making one last effort of civility before returning to her car. "This is the third lunch that we have had where the atmosphere was exactly the same: Kirsten giving the impression that she's been dragged along on some sort of community service, you, after the initial greetings, saying very little that isn't negative or with some sort of complaint about Wes, or home, or life in general, and really, dear, I have bitten my tongue during those instances, but I made a vow with myself that I wouldn't let it continue for a third time. It's frustrating for me, and quite honestly, darling, it's draining."

It had been a good two weeks before they had spoken again. Lissie broke the silence by calling her daughter to inquire whether or not Leigh might like a flat of the pansies that she had left over from her planting. The conversation was courteous but stilted, and from there, the uneasy relationship had continued to lurch forward between the two women.

Opening the heavy, wide front door, Lissie took note that there were chips of glossy dark green paint missing from around the lock and added the touch-up to her to-do list. Most of the women in her neighborhood referred to it as their "Honeydew list," i.e. their "Honey do this," and "Honey do that" list, but Lissie, divorced for thirty-five years, couldn't imagine not being self-sufficient enough to take on such little—and even big—tasks. She was satisfied with the gate she had built and hung to enclose the vegetable garden last summer and had no fear of ladders and gutters that needed cleaning out repeatedly each fall.

Assisted by the bootjack in the front hall, Lissie pulled her white-socked feet free from her Wellies and padded across the wide plank floors en route to the kitchen and kettle. Placing the unopened birthday cards on the well-worn farmhouse table, she picked up the kettle and filled it at the sink, glancing out the window between a pair of glass-fronted cabinets. The view was a quiet one: the apple orchard, bare-limbed and dormant, interrupting the swath of land that ran gently downhill towards the empty stable that used to house Leigh's pony and David's mini-bike.

John had so carefully planned each and every view, Lissie recollected, thinking fondly of the man she had married in her mid-twenties. An architect, he had transformed the rambling dwelling from the decaying abandoned farmhouse it had been to the structurally sound and charming home it was to this day.

"I am lucky," Lissie whispered aloud, placing the red kettle on top of the gas stove and firing up the front ring.

She meant it. Certainly not about the brooding silences that she had naively interpreted as emotional complexity and had found wildly

15

attractive upon first meeting and falling in love with her husband, and certainly not the ensuing depression that was beyond her grasp to recognize and alleviate. But before the despair of his illness had taken its toll on their marriage, John had been consumed with creating a safe and inspiring environment for their children, just little more than toddlers at the time. It was this house that she felt so grateful for: no mortgage, no concerns other than the periodic new roof or hot water tank. John hadn't been capable of being generous during the divorce— he had lost his job at the firm and Lissie, seeing the warning signs, had studied in the evenings, dishes cleared away, for her real estate license. She dove into the property market, earning enough over the years to pay off the house early, and, living on a shoestring, save substantial amounts towards tuition fees for the children.

The whistle of the kettle eased her back to the present. Pouring the boiling water over a teabag of Earl Grey, she took her mug—a favorite that Leigh had given her as part of a chintz set last Christmas—and pulled back a chair from the kitchen table, its heavy oaken legs scraping across the old pine boards. With a soft smile, Lissie inserted a butter knife to slice open the envelope of each birthday greeting. After reading nearly every one, she lined them up like soldiers in a row before her.

She hadn't noticed the final one within the stack, a brown envelope with *Air Mail* stamped beneath the postage stamps of Queen Elizabeth and addressed to 'Ms. Felicity Merriman.' Now she took a slight pause as if to prepare herself, cut cleanly through the top of the envelope, and snapped open the floral tribute. What she read caused a sharp intake of breath, and with a face that radiated joy, she placed the card at the front of the queue on the table. Lissie rose from the table to the kitchen phone ("so retro," Kirsten had described it) archaically mounted on the wall. In moments she had dialed from memory her former colleague and still rather close friend.

"Peter?" she breathed, nearly unable to contain her excitement. "It's Lissie. Can we meet for lunch?"

Chapter 4

WHEN LEIGH RETURNED HOME after her failed birthday shopping excursion, she was surprised to see Wes's late model Taurus already tucked safely into the garage. Removing a glove to touch the hood as she walked past, she felt that the warmth from the engine had long dissipated, revealing he had been home for quite some time. Odd. April 15th was less than two months away, and Leigh couldn't imagine the company giving Wes any time off when stacks of tax returns had been piling up since January. Entering from the garage into the kitchen, she heard him before she saw him, coughing and blowing his nose from his recliner in the den.

Perhaps if they were still dating or newly married, she would have clucked over him a bit, and asked if she could bring him a hot drink or fetch him some cough drops. Twenty years on and lately, more exasperated with him than not, Leigh's opening remarks were, "You sound terrible. Shouldn't you be in bed?"

Wes blew his nose thoroughly, polished it, and dropped the tissue into the wastepaper basket he'd brought in from the bathroom. "I'm all right," he began hoarsely before spluttering into a coughing fit. "There's something going around—I started feeling pretty rough after lunch and came home. I'll go lie down in a bit, I just wanted to answer a few emails from the office."

"Can't you do that from bed?" Leigh asked. Her request was far less from a place of concern and far more from the distaste of watching him hack all over everything. She was quite certain that he was going to infect the entire household.

"In a minute," he replied, his fingers pecking over the keyboard of his tablet.

"And the guest bedroom, please," Leigh said, returning to the kitchen. "I really can't afford to catch whatever you've got with mother's party coming up."

Wes, compliant in most of her requests, retired without a word to the overtly feminine guest bedroom, closing the door behind him. Leigh's mood lifted a moment, realizing she would have their master bedroom to herself for at least a night or two. Indeed, she would be only too glad to have separate bedrooms, but had yet to bring that up to her husband.

It wasn't that they didn't get along, she justified to herself as she began to unload the dishwasher and before thawing a chicken breast for dinner. The sudden idea to make chicken soup from scratch would be a sympathetic offering that was at odds with her deepest truth: she enjoyed avoiding her husband. They rarely argued, and there was rarely any real animosity that resided within the dated split-level ranch in which they lived. However, their conversations were as flavorless and uninspired as this bleak February afternoon. Now in their forties, they simply had what might be expected when a couple marries at the age of twenty: very little in common. And for Leigh, that was what felt so discomforting about sharing a bed with her husband. Simply sleeping together was such an intimate occurrence that sharing a bed when not sharing anything else— thoughts, dreams, disappointments—seemed disingenuous and forced, really.

Wes had always been a decent guy, Leigh would readily admit, removing the chicken breast from the fridge and placing it in the sink. Neither was it his fault that her achingly low self-esteem, as a slightly stodgy girl of nineteen, made her enthusiastically agree to marry him after ten months of courtship and against the silent yet disapprovingly set mouth of her mother. Girls like her, Leigh believed, had better marry the first man who might show interest, because girls like her weren't pretty with a stream of suitors from which to choose. Girls like Leigh were hard workers who got good grades and, in her case, became a nurse, while Wes, in his third year at the state college where they met, also chose the sensible route to become an accountant, greatly relieving his parents who had watched his short lived stint in a garage band with horror.

Only to Tracy had Leigh ever admitted that her decision to become an RN had nothing to do with any sort of heartfelt calling to heal, but, rather, because it was recession-proof: no matter what happened with the economy, nurses would always be needed. Plus, the pay was good and benefits provided. And truthfully she had enjoyed her early years assisting in a doctor's office until she took a higher paying job at the local hospital where the industry standard dictated that she work twelve-hour shifts. Heavily pregnant with Kirsten, she suddenly found herself incapacitated and on bed rest when her back went out, the first of several occurrences which led to Wes's suggestion that she could become a 'stay at home' mom if she liked. If they lived frugally, his salary could justify it.

That, thought Leigh, now leaning over the stainless steel sink with her weight divided over each hand and her eyes fixed on the plate rack before her, was the beginning of her disappearing into the suburban hausfrau she had become. To be honest, it wasn't as if she'd experienced any dreams being shattered, she told herself grimly. The truth was she hadn't really *had* any dreams. The fact that a boy had placed a ring on her finger was breathtaking enough. Marrying Wes so quickly was the only reckless thing she had ever done. They would have kids, she had supposed, because that's what couples did, but she hadn't planned on getting pregnant just three years later. She had disliked every bit of the pregnancy (she had never lost the weight, afterwards) and truly struggled to feel a connection with the red-faced, screaming infant that had been placed in her exhausted arms after a twenty-seven-hour labor. The only time she had been truly happy, she thought, or at least content, was as a child in the expansive farmhouse in which her mother still lived.

Even Kirsten, a difficult baby, would stop crying when they went "back home" (as Leigh never failed to refer to it as) to visit her mother. As large as the house was, with its sun-drenched, airy rooms and center staircase, it somehow retained a sense of coziness and intimacy. There were two fireplaces, one of which was now boarded-up to prevent drafts, and Leigh's favorite place in the world was on the floor beside her father's feet, beside the well-worn sofa (oh, how she had cried when her mother had sent it to the Goodwill after the divorce) in front of a roaring log fire in the living room. When not overtaken by his illness, he would occasionally read aloud to her amusing snippets from the newspaper. Not particularly close to her younger brother, David, these were the times Leigh could pretend she and her father were the only two people in the house.

Funnily enough, she realized with a start, the state of her parents' marriage then hadn't appeared much different than her own. At least to Leigh, there had been no warning signs: no heated arguments that she could recall, no stony silences from her mother. Her father often went quiet for long periods of time, and when this happened, especially after he had lost his job, or as her mother had put it, "having a rest," he would disappear to his office or the bedroom for what seemed weeks. Sometimes he even left home. On those occasions, she had remembered hearing her mother pleading over the phone and muffled behind closed doors, only to reappear red-eyed until she caught sight of either Leigh or David. Then she would smile brightly before giving them a little chore to do, or suddenly pull them close and ask if they'd like to help her bake a batch of cookies. But most of the time, Leigh simply remembered her mother as being busy. Always busy: rushing to get them to school, rushing to clear the table, rushing to leave for work at the real estate office. With the rushing came not a lessening of affection, but certainly shorter displays of it, and an almost obligatory approach towards birthdays and holidays, as if they had to be scheduled in.

Leigh mused before pulling down a recipe book devoted to soups from a stack of a half dozen others jammed into the end of the plate rack: that house was the only tangible thing on which she had ever pinned any dreams. One day she would return to live in the place that she liked to believe needed her, as well.

"After all, it stands to reason, doesn't it," she had remarked to her husband after it was clear there simply wasn't enough savings to remodel the twenty-year old kitchen and bath that she detested in their present house, "that one day, David and I will inherit our old home, and I can't see David possibly wanting to live there, especially now that he and Denise are divorcing, and by that time, if we keep saving, we should be able to buy him out."

"Maybe," Wes had replied. "But we'll be empty nesters by then, and it's a helluva big house to keep up for just two people. Most people downsize."

"My mother lives there all by herself and is perfectly content," Leigh had countered firmly.

"Well, your mother isn't most people, is she?" Wes said before taking his coffee and leaving the room.

No, thought Leigh, as Kirsten banged in through the back door, dropping her backpack on the kitchen table before heading up to her room. No, she isn't, but that was beside the point. While it had never occurred to Leigh to inquire where Wes might like to move after retirement, his unenthusiastic response in regards to her dream of moving back home had felt like a betrayal. How could he not appreciate what was so enormously important to her? It was if he didn't know her at all. She shoved the book back into the plate rack. Dinner would be baked chicken and rice.

Chapter 5

FAR FROM BEING A pleasant reaction to have, whenever David saw Leigh's name appear on the screen of his phone, he would cringe inwardly. It wasn't that he disliked his sister. He simply dreaded what often felt to be a pervasive wave of negativity emanating from her. Especially lately, he thought as he continued to let the phone ring, there always seemed to be another disappointment or frustration in which she needed to vent or assign blame. For a moment, David was tempted to let her call go straight to voicemail, but with his mother's birthday this weekend, he assumed her call would be about that, and so he touched the screen instead.

"Hi Leigh," he began with a brightness he didn't feel. "How's it going?"

"Hi," she replied. "Do you have time to get together to figure out what we want to do for Mother's birthday?"

David leaned back in his office chair and said, "Sure. I'll need to check my schedule but yeah, when did you have in mind?"

"How about today?" Leigh said. "I need to drop the car off at the dealer's so they can figure out why it keeps stalling out, and I figured I could kill time with you instead of waiting there."

"Oh, today?" David hesitated for a moment then added, "I have a shoot today."

Leigh's distinctive heavy sigh was clearly audible from the other end of the phone. David, wary of such tactics but anxious to get the visit over and done with, offered, "But it's not until two, so if you can get here well before then..."

"I could head up now, which should get me to you around ten, and then I could just hang out until your shoot arrives." she suggested.

The thought of having Leigh, and, as Denise had so aptly described it, her "wet blanket" personality fill his studio for four hours was unappealing at best, so David, feeling no guilt whatsoever, replied untruthfully. "I'm afraid I'm having lunch with a client at noon."

Another sigh. Smaller, but still begging the query, *what's wrong?* David refused to bite.

"OK, that's fine," she said flatly before hanging up. "See you at ten."

David remained leaning back in his chair and began drumming the top of his desk with a pencil. Staring out the barred window of his studio, he could catch a glimpse of the mountains, coldly blue and bare of leaf this time of year, arching above the rooftops of nearby buildings. He normally had some sort of music playing, bouncing off the exposed brick walls, but for some reason he had been working in silence the last couple of weeks. Leaning forward and placing the pencil upon a folder, it was as if, he suspected, any distractions might prevent him from keenly feeling the grief that should be coming from the demise of his marriage. The truth was he didn't seem to be feeling anything.

"That's not terribly uncommon." His mother, on whom he could always count to be direct and honest, had replied to his confession over a cup of coffee when they had met for lunch a few days after the proceedings. "The finality may not have fully sunk in. Looking back," she admitted, stirring in another little tub of creamer, "I think I felt completely numb for months after divorcing your father. And I was the one who initiated it. I suspect it's different for everyone, darling. There's no right or wrong way to feel."

23

He continued this rare indulgence of self-exploration: you would think that he would surely be feeling something, *here*. His eyes swept to the back of the studio where he had set up the obligatory mottled blue background cloth (companies always chose the mottled blue), where he had begun lighting the subject of that afternoon shoot five years ago: a slender, quite serious-looking yet comely brunette, newly-acquired by King, Dean, Harrison and Shaw, there to have her photograph taken for the firm's website.

"Are you allowed to smile?" he had teased, adjusting the softbox, "Or are we after the *I'm a serious attorney* attitude?"

She had looked at him frankly, not dropping her guard.

"I would say an appropriately professional portrait for an appropriately professional woman."

This was going to be a nightmare, he had thought, excusing himself and walking over to the shelf which housed his Bose and turning on a local indie music station. White-collared types were always so stiff, so awkwardly animated for these sort of sessions, and he was still considering, as he strolled back, whether or not he was willing to put in the effort to relax his subject or simply let her portrait reveal the humorless icy prig she actually was.

"Do we have to listen to that?" Denise asked, still sitting primly with her hands in her lap, knees together, and ankles crossed.

"No, we do not." David wheeled back around to turn the radio off.

"It's not music in general," she had suddenly said. "It's just that particular one. It's Bright Eyes, isn't it? The band? That song is such a heartbreaker."

"You win the award for not only knowing the name of that band, but knowing the song," David declared, impressed. He lowered the volume considerably.

"And what do I win?" she wanted to know.

Without thinking and completely against character, David impulsively replied, "Dinner."

Her shoulders, which had relaxed somewhat, returned stiffly straight and she asked, "Do you always hit on your clients?"

David deliberately averted his eyes as he crossed in front of her and adjusted the softbox a final time.

"Who said I was hitting on you? I just said dinner. Not dinner *together*. I've got a coupon for Burger King that I was going to give to you. But not now," he said, shaking his head. "Not with that attitude."

Denise regarded him for a moment, then said, "Show me the coupon."

"I'd have to look for it," David replied. "I think it's in my other pants."

"Of course it is," Denise said. "Along with your wallet, probably."

"Ouch," David gave a little grimace before turning to face her with folded arms. "So, now I'm trying to weasel out of paying for a dinner we're not even having? What kind of modestly successful photographer do you think I am?"

Denise had allowed herself a quick smile that looked as though she had pulled a string to create. She checked her watch, prompting David to pick up his camera and get to work.

"So here's the deal, Miss, Miss..." He searched for her name.

"Bradley," she offered, then amended, "Denise."

"So here's the deal, Miss Bradley," he said, rejecting her offer of informality. "We can either start shooting now with you feeling very stiff and uncomfortable, resulting in you looking very stiff and uncomfortable, or we can find a way to help you relax and feel more comfortable, resulting in you looking more relaxed and comfortable."

"And let me guess," she shot back. "Some sort of alcohol is involved?"

Taking quite a large risk, David had countered, "Jeez, get over yourself. I was going to suggest playing some Sinatra. But if you need booze to loosen up, there's a package store next door and you can go get yourself a nice big can of malt liquor."

Thoroughly thrown, Denise allowed herself to be amused. Hers was not the giggle he had expected but a low, throaty laugh that he found intensely attractive. And she kept laughing throughout the shoot as David baited her with, "Yeah, you think you're something; you should have seen the Jack Russell I shot, yesterday. I'll have you know she asked *me* to dinner. Drop your chin."

Denise complied, and asked, "Did you go?"

"What, and cheat on my ferret? What kind of person are you? Now, turn a little to the left. *Left*."

"You don't have a ferret."

"And you," said David, stopping to turn his camera around and show her the digital images, "will never know." Resuming his professional demeanor, he asked, "What do you think? Like any of these?"

"It's not really up to me," Denise replied. "It's up to the firm to choose. But that one," she said as she pointed a perfectly-manicured finger, "is nice. I don't think I've ever seen that expression on my face before."

"For what it's worth, I like it too," David offered. "Smiling, alert, but relaxed, and dare I say it, an expression that borders on mischievous. But I don't know if you want that sort of persona for a law firm."

Denise shrugged and rose to her feet, gathering her purse. "Like I said, it's up to them to decide which picture they'll put on their website."

David had expected her to depart his studio as breezily as she had entered, however she remained for a few minutes, looking at the framed poster-sized photographs on the wall behind his desk.

"I have a magazine at home with that on the cover," she said, gesturing to a still life of summer flowers spilling over the mason jar into which they had been thrust. "You shot that?"

"Yep," he replied, hands shoved deeply into his pockets. "It's just a regional magazine. It's not like I'm shooting the cover of *Vogue* or anything."

"You're selling yourself short," Denise declared firmly. "I think it's beautiful, especially the way the light pours through the glass. It's says everything about what I'd like summer to be."

David wondered if it might have been his imagination, but it felt as though she was stalling. Waiting. As tempting as it was to ask for her number, he wasn't going to risk the lucrative contract with the firm in case his suspicions were off and he offended her a second time.

"Nice working with you," he said, reaching out his hand to shake hers. "Hope you like whichever one they choose."

And that was that. Then, six weeks later, a festive red and gold-bordered invitation to the law firm's Christmas party arrived on his desk. He had attended the year before, strictly out of professional courtesy, and found it deadly dull, but this year, he had mused, there was perhaps an intriguing reason to attend.

Arriving nearly a half hour late, David had time as he stood in line at the bar to discretely observe Denise, confidently mingling with ease, without appearing the slightest bit showy. While a couple of the wives and the flirty office receptionist, Mia, tried a bit too hard with too much makeup and too much flesh on display, Denise blended comfortably into the background with a simple yet form-fitting dark green velvet dress until she turned her attention upon whomever her subject might be. Then she smiled genuinely with her deeply set grey eyes, luxuriously fringed with thick lashes as dark as her ebony hair, and perfectly even smallish white teeth. He had remembered her as attractive. However, now, David thought, her beauty hit him like a slow-moving train.

"Hello, again," she had approached upon noting him moving from the line with his hand firmly clasping a glass of single malt.

"Hello," he smiled.

A year later, they were married.

Chapter 6

WHILE HIS FRIENDS, NAMELY a college roommate named Eli who bunked the remaining two years of his education in order to busk his way through Europe, had decried marriage as confining and even 'life sucking,' David was joyfully drifting along in what seemed to be an extended honeymoon. What initially attracted him the most to Denise was her complete self-sufficiency. Unlike any other woman with whom he had been involved, there was never the need to explain any late hours he might keep, whether it be on a difficult shoot or a night out with friends. Never had Denise implied any obligation from him to keep her entertained or secure. Two years into their marriage he had never received a single text tersely requesting what time he would return home, nor anything even approaching a cold shoulder should his plans for the day or evening not include her. And she, in return, thought nothing of going out on her own to see a film, or grab a bite by herself at a local bistro.

"Dude," Eli admitted, peeling away the label of his beer bottle, "you got lucky. You're the only guy I know who's happily married."

"Not luck," David replied, leaning upon his elbows at the bar. "I was a confirmed bachelor before meeting Denise. But she made it pretty clear she didn't need me as her babysitter; she's very much her own woman." He drained the last of his beer and motioned to Eli to see if he wanted another.

"Yeah, that'd be great," his friend replied gratefully.

"It's your round," David reminded him.

Eli's explanation that he was "a little short this month," was expected as David observed aloud it had appeared he had been "a little short" all last year as well. He gestured to the bartender to bring two more beers from yet another microbrewery, one of dozens in the area, with silly names and flamboyantly illustrated labels.

"What's this one?" asked Eli, turning the bottle around to read it. "*Twelve Cylinders*. Pretty ridiculous."

"That's what you pointed to," Stephanie, the bartender, reminded him before setting down a dish of peanuts and turning away.

"If you had a brewery, what would you call it?" David wanted to know. "*Eli's Bitchin' Bitter?*"

Eli grabbed a handful of peanuts. "Nah, I could do better than that. I'm an artist, remember." He gestured to the peanuts. "Want some?"

David shook his head. "No. You don't wash your hands after you pee."

From ten feet away, they both heard Stephanie's grimacing, "Eww."

"How about *Hoppy Whores?*" Eli blurted, then nearly did a spit-take laughing at his own joke much to the annoyance of the clutch of young women gathered behind him. He made a pained face as he and David clearly heard "assholes" murmured throughout the group before they departed to a safer part of the pub.

"They want me," Eli said. "They all want me."

David scratched his stubble and remarked, "They all want you to shut up. Face it, you're old."

"Didn't we used to be hip?" Eli frowned.

David nodded.

"And cute?"

"Well, I still am."

"You're too skinny. Chicks dig a man with some muscle."

David rose and looked pointedly at Eli's burgeoning beer belly. "Is that what you're calling it? Anyway, I'm taking my cute ass home to my cute wife. See ya."

Eli patted his stomach with something that approached pride. "Keeps me warm on these cold nights. That, and a couple of," he purposely raised his voice, "*Hoppy Whores!*" Glancing quickly at his intended targets who returned his look with disgust, he added to David, "Go on; don't mind me. Go home and ravish the beautiful Denise and don't think once about leaving me here on my own."

"Oh, I won't," David smiled and rose to clear the tab and head home. "Watch him, Steph, will ya?"

Stephanie glanced over her shoulder and retorted, "Sure. I love watching train wrecks."

David laughed and stuck a few folded bills in her tip jar.

When he eventually arrived home, Denise, as usual, could be found in front of her laptop, either reading or answering email, and only occasionally in front of the television with a glass of wine. She would shut down her work and lift her face to be kissed as she felt him saunter up behind her.

"Mrs. Merriman," he would murmur into her ear. "It's time to come to bed."

"Mrs. Bradley-Merriman," she corrected, leaning back in her chair, stretching and arching her back.

"Oh, no, we're hyphenated?" he groaned, massaging her neck. "You didn't tell me we were going to be a hyphenated couple."

Denise rose and wrapped her arms around her husband.

"This way you can think of having *two* women: your mistress *and* your wife," she smiled seductively, nibbling his lower lip. "Two in one."

From the beginning David had felt somewhat taken aback by how intensely attractive Denise found him to be. She loved it when he didn't shave. She loved it when his hair began to spill over his collar. He had never been with a woman so assertively sexual, yet he had to admit that despite his own confidence and ability, there were times when he felt slightly intimidated by his wife's intellect and flourishing success. Money was never an issue. The subject had been brought up only once when he had raised an eyebrow as they began to search online for a home together, when Denise casually mentioned they

30

could look at something much nicer as she could easily put down thirty percent.

"I'm beginning to feel like a kept man," he said, only half-joking.

"Don't be silly," Denise replied, her eyes glued to the screen as she clicked upon the house they would in fact purchase and move into within three months' time. "I'm lucky enough to be earning a good living right now and if we add that to what you can chip in, think how small our mortgage will be. It just makes good sense."

"Just wish I could contribute a bit more," David said, shrugging. "Maybe I can valet park your car for you when you come home each day."

Denise removed her hand from the mouse, sat back and stared at him.

"Please tell me this isn't a problem for you," she said, with just a touch of exasperation. "I've tried to make it abundantly clear that I could care less about how much you make. What I care about is *ambition*, which you have in spades. It would be one thing if you were sitting around and not putting forth any effort, but you work every bit as hard as I do and you're doing really, really well. I'm hugely proud of you. I'm proud to go to your openings, proud to hang your photographs in my office and I love bragging about my hunky..." Here she leaned in and punctuated each word with a kiss, "...artsy, talented husband."

After that, the matter had been dropped, and David willingly, and, truth be told, happily accepted the perks of their combined income with weekend jaunts to Martha's Vineyard, New York, and summer holidays in Tuscany and Barbados. He was well aware that Denise was indeed a cosmopolitan woman and with that came cosmopolitan tastes. Never did he find that pretentious. He admired greatly that, unlike her older brother, Brendon, she had declined working for her father's law firm in Boston, instead striking off on her own and eventually accepting the offer from Richard King in Asheville. It seemed important to her to prove her self-worth, whether to herself or her family, David wasn't sure. Denise worked hard as she had a passion for the law and all it represented, and she enjoyed the rewards her income provided. There was nothing wrong with that. He loved when during their engagement she suggested that they keep separate accounts so they could each save or spend what they pleased without answering to each other. As long as they assumed joint responsibility to monthly expenditures, there would be no issue.

As David's reputation as a creative and talented photographer began to reach a larger appeal, it wasn't unusual that he needed to shoot on location, resulting in more time away than he would have liked. However, Denise had urged him to seize upon every opportunity and he knew full well that not only were there a dozen capable photographers behind him that would be more than happy to grab his assignments, but that Denise, toiling through even longer hours with an increased workload, would not once whine or moan that she didn't see him enough. Frankly, if he was honest, he sometimes wondered if she missed him at all.

And so they worked at a feverish pace together, coming up for air and much needed breaks. As these breaks were unfailingly spent at a resort or on a plane destined for a resort, David began to chaff slightly at the idea of leaving home.

"Can we not just spend this weekend here?" he had asked, wearily, seeing his wife scouring last minute deals online for an approaching three day weekend.

"We spend every day here," she countered, clicking on a package offered on Sanibel Island.

"Not really," David replied. "Not together. We're always working. It'd sort of be nice to just hang out and do nothing, don't you think? See a movie, go to the farmer's market?"

"I get so bored of Asheville," she sighed, her back to him. "It's nice to come home to, but it's really nice to get away from."

Thinking back, this was the beginning of the first strains on their marriage. It was more than just these getaways. It was the crowd they would unfailingly encounter: the Botoxed, exceedingly wealthy white collar demographic that they found themselves seated next to at the pool or spa or restaurant. David didn't care for them. It was one thing that his wife was from that world. This he could overlook, as he had never once heard her utter the phrases or sentiments that peppered conversations that seemed to surround them in close quarters. He began to bristle at both the superficiality and the sense of entitlement that followed in their wake. He knew very well had it not been for Denise, he would have never set foot in Wellington to watch a polo match Richard's nephew was playing, or felt the compulsion to try a talented young chef's new restaurant in Manhattan because a friend on Facebook had raved about it. He could care less and suddenly he felt as if he were running with a crowd that he was quite sure would not be graciously inclusive if he were on his own. Sure, he shrugged, it had been quite fun playing the role of young jetsetters now and then, free from responsibilities and living an extravagant life of spontaneity, but it lacked substance. David was wary of being defined by it, whereas Denise seemed to embrace it headlong. It was important, she pointed out, to give the impression of being successful, and "network," in regards to her career. This he understood, albeit grudgingly. In his own career, he let his work speak for itself and was profoundly grateful, especially now, to be self-employed. He thought longingly of Tuscany and the delicious tawny light in which he had captured his wife idly strolling through a vineyard, straw hat in hand, white cotton dress billowing behind her, the evening sun catching glints of garnet through the windblown strands of her dark hair. However, after just a few days she had grown restless. She wanted to return to Florence and immerse herself within the buzz of the congestion of tourists, drinking in more museums and restaurants. She wanted to do some shopping. She remarked how fun it would be to hop to Milan for a couple of days to see what was being offered this season by Italian designers. She was a woman, he began to think with some discomfort, that needed constant diversion, distractions...the complete opposite of himself.

Chapter 7

IT WAS WITH AN odd start that Leigh became aware of a little pang of envy as, miracle of all miracles, she found a parking spot near David's studio, and glanced at the simple white lettering over a burgundy background that hung above the door, spelling out 'Merriman Photography.'

David was still, of course, a Merriman, and even her mother had remained a Merriman. When Leigh had asked her, a few years earlier, why she hadn't chosen to return to her maiden name, Lissie had replied, somewhat surprised, "Why would I change my name from my children? It would be as if I didn't acknowledge your father's contribution to our lives."

Leigh, however, was married and went by March. Leigh March. Bland, she thought, as she strode closer towards the front entrance of the studio, nothing attractive or lyrical about her name whatsoever. Two syllables, plain, forgettable. Whereas Leigh Merriman flowed beautifully. She might be an actress or an interior designer with a name like that. She sighed. Leigh March was who she was, and she couldn't help but to feel excluded from those who retained the name of her father.

David looked up as his sister entered, and waved a hand as a gesture of welcome.

"How's it going?" he asked. "How's Wes, Kirsten?"

"Sick and difficult," she replied, sinking heavily onto the chair opposite his desk and placing her handbag on the floor beside her.

"Both?" David asked.

"Well, Wes's got what looks to be a virus and Kirsten is at that age where I, evidently, know nothing, and she, of course, knows everything."

"I guess this is the part that mother meant when she told us, 'Just wait until you have kids,'" David replied.

"Yes, but you never did," Leigh countered.

Whether or not she was aware of it, the comment stung. David, rising, asked, "Do you want coffee? We can either go around the corner to get it or stay put and have it here. I can make us a cup."

Leigh, not yet making a move to take off her coat or gloves, said, "I vote we stay here. It's freezing outside, although not much warmer in here. Why is always so cold in here?"

David kept his back to her as he brewed a couple of cups of hazelnut, the last of the selection Denise had purchased and brought in, months ago, thinking his clients might like something different than his 'molten cups of mud.'

"I suspect because it's just a big, open space. Concrete floor. Hard to heat these old buildings and I can't afford to have the system ripped out and replaced. You take cream, right?"

"Sweetener," she corrected. "Whatever you've got over there in a pink packet."

David returned to his seat and they sipped quietly for a few moments but it was not what he thought might be called a companionable silence. Conversations with Leigh tended to be stilted and one-sided. If there was a query to his welfare or what might be going on in his life, it seemed to serve only as a platform for Leigh to then discuss or compare what was going on in hers. It was something he had noticed for the last few years but only recently had it become an effort not to be irked by it.

"So, Mother's birthday..." Leigh began.

"Mother's birthday," David echoed. "It's a big one, isn't it?"

"Hard to believe," she replied. "Seventy."

David placed his coffee mug on his desk and leaned back in his chair, clasping his hands behind his head. "I think she's going to live forever. She's got more energy than women half her age. She just never slows down."

Leigh nodded, then added, "I think after her cancer, she went out of her way to adopt this sort of *carpe diem* attitude. It never slowed her down. Even with the chemo, when it was obvious she was so ill, she just refused to admit to it. I don't know why she has to be that way."

David pulled a face and shrugged his shoulders. "There's doctors that will tell you that that kind of fighter mentality is often pretty successful in beating cancer. I think she was just intending to bulldoze her way straight through it and, you know, she did. It's been ten years, no recurrence. So," he thought, as his voice trailed, that he might change the subject. "Are we taking her out? What's the plan for Friday?"

Leigh looked surprised. "Take her out? We always have birthdays and holidays back home. I thought we'd either cook her a nice dinner or even have it catered, as she's got a few friends who would like to attend."

David hesitated for a moment then said, "Given that it's a pretty big birthday, don't you think she might like to do something different? Because if we have it at her house, she's the one who's going to be doing all the cleaning and straightening up beforehand. That hardly feels like a treat, having a bunch of people arriving on your doorstep."

"She's never mentioned that before," Leigh said with a slight edge to her voice.

"Well, she never would, would she?" David replied. Trying to defuse the tension, he offered, "There are a lot of really nice restaurants in town and I'm happy to pay for her meal, as well as my own, and even yours, if you like. I think Mother would love that. She rarely treats herself to that sort of thing."

"The thing is," Leigh said, looking down at what remained in her cup. "I've already told a couple of her friends. You know, Frances, and that guy she used to work with, Peter? I've already told them we're having something at the house."

"Ah, I see," said David, feeling a tinge of resentment. As expected, this was less of a discussion of what they might do for his mother and more a confirmation of Leigh's plan, already in place.

"Then I guess you don't really need me for anything, right?" he said, removing his hands from behind his head and now hunching forward slightly, leaning on his elbows. "But I really think you should ask Mother what *she* would like."

"David, she's fine with this. When I mentioned it to her, she said 'that's fine.' And the nice thing is that the house is big enough for people to fan out and walk around instead of all being squashed together at a table in some restaurant. And look, I'll go over myself a day early and do the cleaning. I might even drag Kirsten over there."

David nodded. He had no doubt Leigh would be dutiful and see to anything that needed attention. She had inherited that work ethic from their mother, and truth be told, their father, in his earlier years. Which reminded him.

"Has Mother heard from any of her family?" he asked. "I don't suppose Uncle Hugh is coming?"

Leigh gave a wry smile, "Not from Australia, no, but I did email him and he has instructed me to buy her an enormous bouquet of flowers and a bottle of champagne, which I will pick up Thursday. Mother has a cousin in Savannah who apparently isn't well enough to attend, and another cousin in the UK, I think, but I don't believe they keep in touch." She rose and walked to the coffee machine to refresh her cup. As she stirred in the sweetener, she said casually, "I thought about contacting Dad..."

David sat up with a start.

"Why would you want to do that?"

Leigh hesitated for a moment, then clarified. "Not about the party. I didn't mean contacting him about the party, I just felt," she turned back around to face her brother and leaned against the table, "sorry for him. I mean, his seventieth birthday came and went and we didn't see him or make any sort of big deal about it—"

David cut her off. "Leigh, that's a completely different relationship. The last thing he would *ever* want is some sort of party."

"I know," she sighed. "But I still feel sorry for him. I just feel like he's been completely forgotten. And it's not his fault."

"Not his fault?" David cocked his head, as if wasn't sure of what he was hearing. "Do you not remember how you and I flew to Los Angeles—to *Los Angeles* for God's sake—to see him for Thanksgiving all those years ago? When he and his girlfriend—which one was it, Sabra? When she invited us, and when we got there, he sat with us for a half hour, disappeared into his study, and then we were told he couldn't see us, after all, that he just wasn't up to it?"

"That's because he's *ill*, David," Leigh replied, tersely. "He can't help it, he can't help suffering from depression."

"Yes," David began, exercising a patience he didn't feel. "He's ill. I realize that. But he chooses not to get help. He chooses to go off the meds he needs. I'm not saying it's easy, but it's also difficult to be sympathetic to someone who hasn't made a single overture to be a part of our lives. I mean, he's continued to function on some level; he's not destitute, he still worked for the last several years, he's just chosen not to get in touch."

Leigh said nothing, electing to keep her confession to herself. While David had accepted circumstances as they were, Leigh had indeed contacted her father. It didn't matter that he hadn't initiated a single call or email, but on the few occasions when she had spoken to him on the phone or sent him a chatty note, he had been cordial. She called him 'Daddy,' and fussed over him from a distance, worried that his slightly congestive nasal tone was turning into a cold or that he wasn't eating enough. He, in return, would ask vaguely how she was, marvel that his granddaughter could already be sixteen, and would generally end the call a few minutes after it began by asking her to give his best to everyone, followed by "Talk to you soon" but of course, he never did. Leigh was well aware that if she didn't pursue their relationship there would be none, but she pardoned his offenses with almost a maternal consideration. He wasn't well, and Leigh continued to feel that somehow, as long as she remained in touch, she could help him. These brief, stilted conversations must surely be a comfort to him. They certainly were to her.

"And it's not that I'm angry with him," David added, mistaking her silence for unspoken frustration. "I'm not anything about him. It's just the way it is. He's got his life, we've got ours and I wish him the best, I really do, we're just not a part of each other's life."

Leigh checked her watch and changed subjects abruptly. "Do you have any ideas for catering, if we go that route?" she asked. "Hors d' oeuvres first and then, I guess, a buffet?"

David smiled and nodded. "Sure, that's fine. Let me know what you need me to do."

Leigh pushed the strap of her handbag over her shoulder. "I think I've got everything under control. We'll ask people to arrive around six. Oh—I ordered a huge cake from Hanson's here in Asheville, so if you want to pick that up on your way down, that would be great."

"I can do that," David replied, walking her to the door.

"By the way, what did you get her?"

"Oh." David ran a hand through his hair. He really needed a haircut. "I found a first edition of '*A Shropshire Lad.*' She's always loved Housman."

Leigh nodded and said, "Great." However, as she said her goodbye and walked back to her car, hunching against the wind that had begun to whip over the mountains, she frowned. Who on earth was Housman? She recognized the rather disconcerting fact that she knew very little about what her mother actually liked, only what she didn't. How odd.

Chapter 8

"I THINK," SMILED PETER, raising his nearly empty glass of chardonnay towards Lissie in the gesture of a toast, "you may be the bravest woman I have ever met."

Lissie smiled warmly and ducked her head in a mock bow. "I don't see it that way, Peter, I really don't."

She signaled for the waitress to clear away their plates and ordered coffee for them both.

"I would bet that if you took a thousand women of your age," he began, then catching her eyes going a bit flinty, he quickly corrected himself. "Of *any* age, and asked them if they would consider moving abroad, by themselves, without knowing anyone, not a one, not a single one, would do it."

Lissie laughed. "And that's just fine! But you're not quite correct. I do know someone, my cousin, Nora. I'm going to live with her, at first. It was by her suggestion, actually. She's divorced, like I am, and living in a village in Dorset. You know how I feel about England—"

Peter chuckled as he interrupted, "Do I, ever! I remember asking why you always took lunch at your desk instead of going out with the rest of us, and there I was, thinking you were such a devoted workaholic that you insisted on typing in new listings during your lunch hour when all the time you were online investigating properties for sale in England! 'Window shopping,' you called it."

Lissie chuckled in agreement, her eyes smiling at the recollection. "That window shopping was my therapy, it really was. Just fantasizing

40

at the time, I suppose." She folded her hands together on the linen tablecloth and looked past Peter, past the other patrons, at a memory she alone could see. "Perhaps it's because my own mother was English, but I've always felt such a pull to return there. And even though I rarely had the opportunity to visit, Peter, each time I felt as if I were home. That I had come home." Her gaze returned to his. "And after the kids were out of the house and married, with their own lives, combined with this rather overwhelming birthday approaching, I thought, why ever not? What was holding me in North Carolina?"

The waitress arrived and placed two slender white cups of coffee in front of each of them. Declining an offer of cream, Peter waited until she departed, then leaned in and asked, "Not your children? Not your grandchild? Won't they feel terribly hurt?"

Lissie leaned back in her chair, took a sip of coffee and placed the cup carefully back into the saucer.

"I've considered that. For quite some time, really. But you know, Peter, they have their own lives and I have mine and what I think would work quite nicely is for me to remain in England for the current visa allowance of six months, then return here, then fly back to England six months later. And really," she looked at him, frankly. "I don't honestly see the children that often. Leigh and I try to have lunch once a month or so and sometimes can't even manage that, and David, with his schedule, is often traveling or terribly busy, so honestly, I can't say we'd see each other less if I were living abroad. And with Skype and email and telephones, why, it might just be possible we'd be in touch even more!"

Peter nodded, looked down for a moment as he deliberated over his next question. Taking the chance, his eyes met hers and he asked, quite candidly, "I don't suppose you might miss me?"

Lissie extended her hand and rested it upon his wrist for a moment. "Of course I would." She smiled, then added quietly, before taking her hand away, "as I would all my friends. But I don't think Elaine would appreciate your asking."

Peter grinned broadly and shrugged. "You wouldn't have me! I couldn't wait forever, you know." Eyes twinkling, he continued. "You know I'm kidding, right? Sort of?"

He was still a handsome man, Lissie thought, conventionally handsome with his all-American good looks. And still a full head of hair! Slightly jowly now, she noted, but then who wasn't at their age? He had worn well and would, like all men with such strong features, remain handsome until the day he died.

"Elaine is a wonderful woman and you're a very lucky man," Lissie replied firmly, but she returned the smile.

Peter glanced around the room, now quite empty, leaned in and murmured, "Yes, she is. And yes I am. But, oh, girls like you can break a guy's heart. Confident, self-assured, cute as hell... I understood, I always understood that you had no intention of an office romance or any sort of relationship, but you couldn't blame me for trying." He leaned back and raised his hand to signal for the waitress to bring the check. "So I admired you from afar! I still do."

"And you can continue to do just that," Lissie replied brightly, but her reply was not unkind. "From a couple of thousand miles away."

As the waitress approached, Peter shook his head slowly and raised both hands in a display of capitulation.

"You are amazing, Lissie," he said. "I think you're brave as hell and good for you for living your dream. Only a handful of people actually do that, and I'm not one of them. Well done. I'll always be your biggest fan."

As he helped her on with her coat and asked what time he and Elaine should arrive for her party, Lissie suddenly found herself feeling a warmth that began in her cheeks and flooded throughout her entire being. She gave Peter a peck on the cheek and stepped out onto the pavement, eager to experience this headiness alone. She had never stepped so lightly in years, she thought, despite her slightly heavy suede-shod feet. This isn't about being selfish, she thought, turning her smiling face to catch her reflection momentarily in a shop window. What she saw was a slender woman with chin-length silvery hair lifted lightly from her forehead as she walked briskly, hands shoved deeply into the pockets of her plum-colored coat, feeling to all the world like a girl of eighteen. This was about adding the final layer to who she was meant to be. Her eyes sparkled as she recalled Peter's parting compliment, *"I think you're brave as hell and good for you for living your dream."* By articulating her dream to Peter, she had taken the first step in transitioning it into a plan. This was happening. This was now happening.

Lissie ducked into her car and drove the relatively short distance home. She was startled to see Leigh's cream Toyota parked on one side of the garage. Concerned that she might have forgotten some planned event, she searched her memory but came up with nothing. Both children had keys to the house, so there was no irritation that Leigh was inside, but the fact that her daughter was there, unannounced, on this particular afternoon gave pause to Lissie. She remained inside her Volvo for several moments, tapping her gloved fingers upon the steering wheel. She had hoped to sit both children down whenever that could possibly be arranged to share her adventurous plans with them, and with Leigh now here, this might be a good opportunity. She gave a little sigh. There was no telling what sort of mood her daughter might be in, especially lately, and she couldn't bear the thought of tarnishing what had been such a golden afternoon. No, she thought, unsnapping her seatbelt and stepping out of her car, she would keep her excitement to herself, just for today, and tell the children soon.

Leigh was vacuuming the area rugs that covered the wide plank floorboards of the living room and humming, serenely in her element. With Kirsten in school, and discovering her mother not home, she had spent a rather blissful hour and a half on her own, simply going over what was already a clean and tidy home. She liked that about her mother, she thought, switching off the vacuum and plumping up the cushions resting upon the wheat-colored sofa and loveseat. She liked that her mother always treated the house with the respect it deserved. She had dusted and polished the furniture first, despite there being very little need, and as she did so, she had removed the silver-framed family photos from the sideboard and lingered over them. There was no single photograph of her father. That was to be expected, but Leigh felt a dull ache as she picked up a cherished picture of the entire family—she and David couldn't have been more than six and four—standing windswept in the surf somewhere south of Nag's Head. David was held securely in his mother's arms, Leigh leaning happily against her father's muscular thigh, towheaded and squinting against the sun. Her mother's gaze was obstructed by sunglasses, but her father's face—and this is what struck Leigh the most—was a completely open expression of self-assuredness revealed in a wide, laughing grin, his blonde, wispy hair blown wildly about his head, his eyes crinkling in amusement.

This was the father Leigh had known, the father she remembered. She would even admit that such a jovial emotion had been rare from him. However, as she placed the photograph carefully back amongst the others, actually pulling it forward to pride of place, she could not bring herself to believe that this man had fully disappeared. Surely, she thought, with enough love and encouragement, this man could somehow be resurrected into the father he was meant to be.

Leigh moved into the kitchen and had decided to use an application of lemon oil on the cabinetry to give the wood some needed luster. Her father had even designed the kitchen with her mother's blessings, sticking close to the original template. It was a true, rustic country kitchen, appropriate to the age of the house, with round, copper knobs to pull open the drawers and cabinets. The wood was maple and stained a reddish gold that was so wonderfully warm and glowing in the early afternoon light that eased in from the window. How many meals had they had around this table? she thought. She decided to give it a bit of a buff as well. She let herself dream, rubbing the saturated cloth languidly over its surface: And how many lovely quiet moments had she shared with her father, just the two of them, on Saturday afternoons as he sat with a cup of coffee and asked her to read from a library book her mother had chosen for her?

"Just sound it out," he had encouraged, as she had stumbled over words. "That's the way. See how smart you are, Bunny?"

Smiling at the memory, Leigh turned to begin on the cabinets and, catching sight of the refrigerator, gave a little laugh. The only mistake her father had made, she thought as she shook her head, was the harvest gold color of the appliances he had ordered all those years ago. When finally worn out, her mother had replaced them all with a no-nonsense white—"Imagine the finger prints on stainless steel!" she had replied to Leigh's protestations over such a boring choice. However, Leigh believed what would look terrific was the range of vintage 1940s reproductions now available—pricey, to be sure, but well worth the investment. And she was quite sure her father would agree. In fact, she thought, she might even broach the subject the next time she spoke with him to see if he shared her opinion.

"My goodness, what have we here?" said Lissie, entering from the back door and taking in the small army of cleaning supplies on the countertop.

"Hello, Mother," Leigh replied, looking up with a start. "I'm sorry—I had originally planned to stop by and offer help with the housework before the party Friday, but when I saw you were out, I just sort of dove in and started."

"How very kind," said Lissie, setting down her purse on the table and giving her daughter a kiss on the cheek. "But you needn't go to such trouble. I was going to give it a lick and a promise tomorrow, anyway."

"It's very clean," Leigh admitted. "I just didn't want you to get stuck with any extra stress, worrying about last minute details. Oh," she remembered, "I'm going to be calling the caterer today-"

"A *caterer?*" Lissie echoed, shocked. "Isn't that terribly extravagant?"

"Well, it's a big occasion, isn't it? David and I are splitting the cost, so don't worry. And it makes sense. This way we can all enjoy the evening and no one is stuck with cooking or a single dish to clean. Anyway, she gave me some ideas, but I wanted to check with you first. Are there any sort of things you'd especially like to have?"

Lissie smiled. "Heavens, I'm being so spoiled. Let me think about that for a moment. Would you like a cup of coffee?"

Leigh assented and sat in the chair she had always taken since childhood. As her mother placed a fresh filter into the machine and spooned in the coffee, they chatted back and forth quite easily. Lissie felt a distinct relief in how things were going. This was the sort of afternoon she wished every encounter with Leigh could be. She began to wonder if her daughter might be receptive to her plans should she disclose them. She would rather have both children present for that, of course, but these sort of relaxed conversations were rare with Leigh. Lissie continued to weigh the possibility. Hesitating, she instead made a point of telling Leigh how much she liked her hair this length, how becoming it was.

"It's so baby fine it's the only way I can wear it," Leigh sighed. "Kirsten's hair is fine, too, but she's got a ton of it, and I wonder where she got it from? Wes's isn't thick like that, and she certainly didn't get it from me."

"Sometimes traits can skip a generation," Lissie said, setting a pale yellow mug dotted cheerfully with daisies before them both.

"I guess I got mine from Dad," Leigh mused.

"Yes, I think you did," Lissie agreed matter of factly, "And his nose." Wary that this line of conversation could lead them into what had often become difficult territory, she changed subjects and asked, "Have you seen David, lately?"

"A couple of days ago," Leigh replied. "He didn't look so great."

"Oh?" Her mother looked surprised.

"Well, a bit unkempt. His hair has gotten pretty long, and I noticed his sweater had a hole under the armpit. I guess that's what happens to men after divorce. I'd never let Wes leave the house looking like that."

Lissie gave a small chuckle. "I don't think Denise ever had too much say so in David's appearance. He's always said that as he considers himself self-employed, he can dress for comfort. But he cleans up well. And he knows to be suitably attired should the occasion call for it."

"I never could figure those two out," Leigh declared flatly after taking a swallow of coffee. "They seemed like the most unlikely couple in the world."

Lissie gave a small sigh, realizing that her daughter had adopted a negative tone.

"Oh, I don't know about that," she replied, coming carefully to the defense of her son. And Denise. She had always liked Denise. She was smart, good natured, successful and very much her own person. Lissie's eyes swept over to the stack of mail that she had placed upon the countertop,. Denise had in fact sent her the loveliest birthday card. Written inside was a particularly dear sentiment of how she would always think of her with great fondness and Lissie hoped very much they would remain in touch, despite the divorce.

"David's kind of a bohemian and frankly, I always thought Denise seemed a bit...snobby."

"Did you?" Lissie asked, determinedly keeping her voice light.

"The shoes," Leigh pointed out, "the Kate Spade handbags...she sort of came across as a fashion plate. I don't know, it seemed whenever we were all together for a family function, she never appeared to be very interested in conversation. Just sort of coolly indifferent to everything."

Denise had indeed been guarded in conversation with Leigh, Lissie knew, but had suspected that was because there was little she could contribute when the usual point of view coming from her sister-in-law had more often than not been petty grumblings. Leigh had seemed if not downright unhappy, then certainly deflated for ages. At one point Lissie was even anxiously wondering if her daughter was showing signs of inheriting the depression from which her father had suffered. However, as the years passed from childhood to adolescence, Leigh had also made it very clear indeed that she remained quite conflicted about the divorce of her parents. More than once Leigh had openly accused her mother of abandoning her father when he needed them most. She had never been a particularly jolly child, Lissie remembered, but she had been a relatively quiet and compliant one. And regardless of how carefully and patiently Lissie had explained to both children why it was better for their father to live apart from them, she knew that when the divorce was final, it was the beginning of a jaundiced outlook on life from her daughter.

"I suppose," Lissie finally replied, "a woman in her field has to look a bit polished, don't you think? And perhaps she's just a bit more reserved than most."

"Women like Denise," Leigh began slowly, unable to resist the dig. "Have no idea what the real world is like: doing mounds of laundry, driving your kids back and forth to soccer, having the constant backtalk every time you ask them to pick up their room, hardly any time for yourself..."

"But she specifically chose *not* to have that life," Lissie reminded her daughter, choosing her words carefully. "It doesn't seem quite fair to compare the two. She has chosen to have a rather high-pressured career, and you have chosen to have a child and create a wonderful family. I think you're both very much, 'real world'—just different worlds."

Lissie recognized the familiar tension beginning to flare between them but couldn't say where it was coming from. Leigh acknowledged it as well and, as was her habit, assigned unspoken frustration toward her mother for not understanding her world wasn't actually 'a wonderful family.' Rather, as Leigh felt it, Lissie was siding with Denise.

"Well," Leigh replied, placing her hands on the table and rising. "At any rate, they didn't work out, so I'm guessing maybe David felt the same way." She began to pick up the bottles and jars of cleaner.

"Don't bother, dear," Lissie said, unwilling to respond to Leigh's last declaration, "I'll put those away. And again, I can't thank you enough for all you're doing."

"All right," Leigh replied, picking up her handbag and fishing for her car keys. "I told everyone to arrive around six. And you're going to have a huge bouquet arriving from Uncle Hugh, so you might want to think about where you'll want to put that. The caterers will probably want the sideboard and maybe even the dining room table to lay out the buffet." Her tone had turned businesslike and flat.

"I certainly will, thank you," Lissie said, walking her daughter to the door. She did not make a move to kiss her goodbye, less from a lack of affection and more from an uncertainty of how to approach her at the moment. "And I'll look forward to seeing everyone Friday."

Leigh closed the door behind her and walked over to her car. No one bothered to lock their cars in this driveway, in this neighborhood. She slid into the driver's seat, fastened her seatbelt and switched on the ignition. Before putting the car in reverse, she stared hard at her childhood home, its inviting flagstone path winding round to the front door, the beautiful symmetry of the fireplaces on either side of the clapboard exterior, the enormous magnolia to the left and the great pin oak to the right. Leigh felt something like an agonizing affection for it. This house was a constant in an otherwise changing world, changing life. She felt embraced by it, *understood* by it, and with that realization sudden tears sprung to her eyes. Abruptly, she backed her car out of the garage, turned round in the drive and headed home. Halfway there, she pulled over and impulsively phoned her father.

Chapter 9

THE MORNING OF LISSIE'S birthday dawned bright and clear and bitterly cold. The air, however, was completely still, and Lissie felt, as she often did, that she could withstand any freezing temperatures as long as there was no wind with which to contend. Knowing that the caterers wouldn't be arriving until after lunch, she stretched, then lifted the bedclothes away to greet the day. She intended to do a half hour's yoga, followed by a brisk walk—her regular morning routine— and then reward herself with a leisurely hot soak in the tub.

Padding into her bathroom, she stood before the etched antique mirror that hung above the pedestal sink, and greeted her own reflection: tousled hair and slightly sagging features that lifted immediately as she broke into a smile that was genuine in its display. The fine lines around her blue eyes creased deeply, and the apples of her cheeks seemed to defy gravity as her heart-shaped face radiated the happiness she earnestly felt.

"Hello," she said aloud. "This is what seventy looks like!" She stooped and splashed the cold well-water from the tap over her face. Patting it dry with a towel, she was pleased to see how pink, how lively, her complexion appeared.

"You're the only woman I know who isn't depressed about growing older!" Her friend Frances had chuckled down the line upon phoning her the night before.

Lissie had taken a sip of chardonnay and replied, " I intend to live a good, long, life, Frances, and I can't do that unless I grow older, can I? And you know something? In ten years, we'll both look back and say, 'Oh, if only we were just seventy!' I am blessed, my dear, to be fit and healthy, and I have quite a bit to look forward to."

"As always," Frances laughed, "you are my greatest inspiration, Lissie. You really are. Whenever I begin to doubt whether or not I can do something, I just think 'now, how would Lissie handle this?' and then I get that added push to see it through. Can't wait to see you tomorrow evening!"

Lissie had put the phone down and returned to her desk, grasping the mouse of her laptop to return to searching real estate listings near her cousin's residence in Dorset. She had set the mood for her internet excursion: a glass of wine, a small plate of cheese and fruit, and the beautiful strains of 'The Lark Ascending' lilting from the stereo. Nora lived not too far from Lyme Regis and, slipping on her reading glasses, Lissie realized that there was rather a small amount of rental flats from which to choose in that area. *"Don't be silly,"* Nora had replied when Lissie had written about her idea to take her own accommodation. *"I've got two guest bedrooms and I'd love to have you stay with me!"* However, as grateful as Lissie felt by the offer, she also knew that having a guest for a couple of weeks was one thing. Six months was quite another. And frankly, she thought, clicking on to a tidy two bedroom cottage described as 'walking distance to the beach and all amenities,' she wanted her own space to completely immerse herself in every aspect of her soon-to-be new life. Living alone was the way to do it. She would gratefully stay with Nora the first week or two and learn her way about the area, and then her plan was to live nearby, allowing for impromptu cups of tea or dinners together and as many outings as could be arranged.

Peering closely at the row of photographs beneath the main picture of the cottage, Lissie smiled approvingly. Inside, it was small to be sure, and exactly the sort of place she desired: cozy, with a fireplace in the lounge (were those Victorian tiles framing its perimeter?) and a beamed ceiling.

There was a modest fitted kitchen, slightly dated, with no Aga, on which her heart had been set, but inviting enough with its cream-colored cabinets and warm wooden countertop. The bedroom was large enough for the featured double bed, bedside table and wardrobe, plus an upholstered faded floral chair near the window through which a glimpse of rooftops could be seen. 'Located on Broad Street,' the advertisement read, directly in the heart of Lyme Regis. She would research exactly how far that was from Nora. Leaning back a moment, she took another sip of wine and relished the thought that through years of careful budgeting, she could easily afford the rents she was seeing displayed. For now, if she remained careful, she would be able to live abroad fully six months a year—even more, if allowed, although England wasn't presently too keen on seniors attempting to take up full-time residence—and not touch her capital. And later, she thought, popping a small triangle of Gouda into her mouth, there would be plenty of money to do as she liked, within reason. Weekends in Paris, perhaps! She could even treat Nora to a sun-kissed holiday in Spain. What perfect bliss, she thought, what perfect, sparkling, bliss.

Coming back to the present as she poured herself a strong cup of tea after her customary breakfast of yoghurt and fruit, she stepped into her tracksuit and tennis shoes, then zipped up her 'bubble jacket,' as she called it, and, with a nod to her bladder, remembered to pop back into the bathroom before grabbing her knit cap and gloves.

It was serenely beautiful outside. As Lissie swung down the drive, her shoes crunching along the gravel, her arms pumping, she could see her breath coming out before her. Turning right onto the quiet, country road, she waved hello to her next door neighbor, Carol, dashing down the front steps of her Cape Cod to snatch the paper,, quilted bathrobe clutched tightly together against the cold. Lissie was glad to see she wasn't the only one who still took an actual newspaper instead of reading it online. Even the resulting ink-stained hands were worth it, she thought, striding purposely. There was something comforting about a paper. She rarely watched televised newscasts anymore as she had reached a point of despair from viewing a constant barrage of violent images. But with a paper, she had declared to Frances one day over lunch, she could control what she did and didn't see. In reading about a flood or a terrorist attack, she could remain abreast of the news without her brain being flooded with horrific images. This, she concluded, was a much nicer way to live.

"You're crazy!" Carol called out to her good-naturedly before darting back inside the warm comfort of her home. Like Lissie, she was single, but Carol was widowed and, rather adorably, had her gentleman friend park his small van around the back of her house as he had moved in a few months ago. If she had worried about prying eyes, she didn't understand Lissie, who would have given her a hearty congratulations. Life was too short, Lissie believed, to even entertain such thoughts, but perhaps Carol had come from a different sort of upbringing than her own.

One of the few non-Baptists in her community, Lissie had been raised Episcopalian but found herself only attending for Easter and Christmas each year. She simply felt closer to God outside, in her garden or walking along as she was now, dazzled by the brilliant blue of the morning sky. But Lissie loved the formality and music of the services when she did indeed make the drive to St John's. Perhaps I'll attend church more often when I'm in England, she thought, puffing along, and imagined a rather idealized version of the area surrounding Nora's neighborhood: a small, Norman church, rolling hills dotted with sheep, charming shop fronts in the nearby village featuring a tea room, a real butcher, and the obligatory pub. She smiled to herself as she realized her fantasy was actually firmly planted within the twenty-first century: no place was immune to crime, not even a chocolate box village where Miss Marple might reside. There would also be, she knew, disappointments and frustrations (probably the weather) with her new life, surely, but not now, she thought, not now while I'm dreaming about it all.

She hugged the grassy verge as an SUV passed slowly by. Her walk would take her round the bend just ahead, where the view would open from deep woods on either side of her to open farmland and Foxhaven Stables, most of its occupants having left before sunrise to join the hunt near Briarpatch Farms, a vast thousand acre reserve twenty minutes away. Lissie wasn't a fan of blood sports but had argued the case that the area hunt had prevented large swaths of land from being developed which, in the end, was to the benefit of all wildlife. Admittedly Lissie felt relieved when she learned they were incorporating more and more 'drag hunts,' in which the scent of a fox on a cloth was dragged throughout the countryside before casting hounds. There had been an epidemic of mange, the local huntsman had told her when she had bumped into him at the grocery store still clad in his breeches and boots, that, despite the hunt's best efforts to put out medicine disguised in food for the foxes, had wiped out an entire colony this year. The drags were the only real way for the members to have a true gallop across country.

And how brilliant they looked, she thought, her eyes taking in a couple of fuzzy yearlings, their manes and tails filigreed by the morning light, picking at what little grass was left in the front field. As she walked past, she recalled coming across the first flight of the hunt just before Christmas. The 'pink' coats of the mounted staff had come sweeping down a hill and galloping into the woods, directly behind twenty couples of hounds in full cry. The rest of the field wore traditional black wool jackets, standing in the stirrups and bent over the necks of powerful, plunging horses, immaculately braided and turned out. Simply remembering the thundering hooves gave a thrill to Lissie's heart. In England, she had read, riding to hounds was now exclusively drag hunting and she wondered if there would be any fixtures in the area of Dorset where she would settle. She would like very much to see that. Perhaps she would even be invited, as she had been here, to the enormous breakfast afterwards, before the roaring fire in the clubhouse (an ironic name, she thought with amusement, for the rather dilapidated farmhouse that served as the hunt's headquarters), with a glass of whiskey and tales of the day's adventure from windblown and, depending upon who might have become unglued leaping over a creek, mud-splattered locals she had known for decades. Lissie herself had never ridden, but she appreciated anyone who embraced the outdoors with such gusto, especially the children. Lissie had always felt strongly that today's children spent far too much time indoors, and she grinned at the memory of seeing a five-year-old tyke bobbing up and down on a fat, furry Shetland as she trotted alongside her mother, astride a sleek bay Thoroughbred.

Well-known landmarks told her she had walked far past her usual half mile. Invigorated, she turned to walk home, still swinging her arms and looking very forward to the hot soak that awaited her. Entering the front door of her home, she nearly bounded up the stairs, and before shrugging out of her jacket, she began to draw a bath, turning on the taps. It would take some time to fill the deep cast iron steeping tub. She tossed in a handful of Epsom salts so that she would enjoy her evening with neither an ache nor pain, should she find she had overdone it a bit during her morning's constitutional, as she called it. She began to undress.

Standing once more before the mirror, her gaze fell from her flushed face to her chest and she unconsciously raised her right hand to touch the scar, faded but still present, from her mastectomy a decade ago. Had she had both breasts removed, she would have vetoed reconstructive surgery, but as she had joked to Frances, it was only her intense desire for all things symmetrical that led her to have an implant to match her remaining right breast. And she had such small breasts! It never failed to strike her as surprising, she thought, stepping gingerly into the hot water, that anyone with such small breasts could develop cancer. Intellectually, she of course knew better, just as she knew upon finding the lump and after the subsequent news that the odds were not in her favor. Both her mother and an aunt had succumbed to the disease. She had not once thought *why me* but rather *I suppose it's my turn*, and approached her treatment with tenacity and dogged determination. Settling back and closing her eyes, she allowed herself only a fleeting memory of losing her hair and refusing Leigh's offer of trying on wigs, instead choosing a series of caps or scarves only when the weather dictated a covering. She hadn't wanted to conceal her illness but to look squarely into the eyes of any curious glance with the unspoken resolve which made it very clear that she did not consider herself a victim. And chances were, she thought grimly as she soaped her left arm, that Leigh might very well receive the same diagnosis one day. Lissie had especially wanted to be a strong example for her. Nearly every significant thing she had ever done, she knew, had been done as an example for her children.

Lissie pulled a loofah mitt over her hand and began to lazily soap her knees and calves, still slender, still strong. *Seventy*, she thought. *Seventy!* She marveled how it sounded and couldn't yet relate to it. Had she suffered chronic ill health for years or been wracked with aches and pains climbing out of bed each morning, she might very well sigh and grudgingly accept the number. But with the exception of the occasional twinge in her left knee, or forgetting that her reading glasses were on her head, she genuinely felt like a woman half her age, if not younger. There was nothing, she thought, feeling slightly triumphant, she couldn't do at seventy that she hadn't been able to do before. While Frances had given up tennis, even doubles, owing to arthritic hands, Lissie could still take her beloved walks, garden an afternoon away or even ice skate, something she hadn't done in years but had been rather accomplished at as a young girl. When Kirsten was six, she had taken her to an ice rink for her birthday and was astonished how solidly confirmed she felt as soon as she had stepped out onto the ice for the first time in at least twenty years. Kirsten had watched her, open-mouthed, as Lissie gracefully glided away for a couple of minutes before returning, skating backwards, to take her granddaughter's hand and support her, stabbing, slipping, her childish wonky ankles collapsing inwards.

Seventy! And John would be, she mused, about seventy-three. It was always difficult to imagine how anyone, when unseen for decades, would look at such an age. Before she had married him, John had still retained his physique from a distinguished, if short lived, collegiate athletic career. He had been a diver. In fact, it occurred to her as she turned on the hot water again until her toes looked as red as cherries, anything that had interested him had been an individual pursuit. While he had the talent, he had chosen not to take part on the rowing team or any team activity. His decision to study architecture, from the beginning, had seemed to stem from a fascination regarding the technical aspect of the field rather than any sort of passion for structural aesthetics. He was keen on what was appropriate, nothing else. She could never tell, in the early days when he shared his blueprints with her, spreading them out over the kitchen table, if it was because he lacked imagination or if she was simply impractical and silly.

Even as a man of thirty-five when he descended into illness, she remembered, he did appear to age quite suddenly. His fair hair never grayed, but he began to look hollow-eyed, and when he moved into the guest room and remained there for a week or even two at a time, only coming out for a sandwich or the occasional shower, his once bronzed complexion began to resemble prison pallor: he grew pale, slightly hunched, with a haunted look about him. It was a terrible time, she thought with a slight shiver despite the steam rising from her bath, and there was simply no saving him. He refused counseling, he refused to be disciplined about his medication. And then her own mother became ill...

There had been no one, absolutely no one she could tell. Her brother was already working abroad. In the strangest way, looking back at it, caring for her mother and worrying about her father, seemingly helpless and suddenly frail, had been a bit of a blessing. She *had* to be strong. There wasn't a moment to think about anything else besides sitting at her mother's bedside in the hospital, before rushing home to cook and clean for her father, then managing to arrive to greet her children as they tumbled off the school bus at half past three. And when it became apparent they were going to lose the house owing to the mortgage being in arrears, Lissie had used the last bit of the only credit card she had, earned her real estate license, and gotten a job. Of all people, it was Peter that she finally confided in after acquiescing to his insistence of driving her home early during a winter storm. He had pulled up to her house just after lunchtime, his next rescue being her children at school, and had casually asked her out for the second time, only to receive the shock of his life when she began to convulse with sobs into her gloved hands. Lissie had allowed him to hold her close as everything she had kept pent up came out in floods of tears and hiccupping attempts at explanations. The wool of his grey overcoat was comforting to her wet cheek and she needed—she desperately needed—the strength of his shoulders and the arms that wound tightly around her. Finally she pulled away, accepted his offer of a handkerchief and blew her nose obediently, apologizing profusely despite his protestations. She thanked him for going to retrieve her children and said she would telephone the school to tell them to expect him while she began a huge pot of soup for all of them when they returned. He had never seen her cry in the nearly forty years since that day, and as he watched her square her thin shoulders beneath the shabby camel coat she wore, before stepping delicately yet determinedly through the snow towards her front door, his heart broke into pieces for her. However, he knew—he knew even then—Lissie would never allow herself to be rescued.

But oh, she thought, taking her mind back further, oh, there had been such wonderful times, and that, she decided firmly, was where she would return for the remainder of her bath. She traveled back to her favorite memory, so cherished, so protected that she had never told anyone...

For her twenty-first birthday, she had traveled later that year with her mother to England for the first time. It was 1967 and her mother, having left her homeland directly after the war with her new American husband and early in her pregnancy with Lissie, was somewhat horrified to witness the plethora of miniskirts and long hair on the youth that greeted them in London before boarding a train for the long journey to Plymouth. Despite her mother nodding off soon after they took their seats, Lissie shook off any feeling of jet lag and kept her eyes fastened on the towns and countryside that flashed before her like a green river. It was enchanting, every bit. Even as they pulled out of the city at the beginning, she was fascinated by the long, narrow fenced gardens behind terrace houses, comically painted different colors carefully up the seam that divided them in two. Some had treated their back gardens as nothing more than a trash heap, while others were tended and tidy, and each and every one was adorned with a metal freestanding umbrella clothesline. There were charming villages and industrial areas, and as they came close to towns, Lissie couldn't get over how *tiny* were all the cars! Like wind-up toys, she thought, thinking of their Chevrolet back home. But when they finally arrived in the West Country, from where her mother hailed, they were greeted by her kindly grandparents, the one and only time she would meet them. Squeezed together in the rear seat of her grandfather's ancient Morris Minor, they were driven back to their home in St. Jude's. And thus began Lissie's love affair for all things English. She was being properly immersed in what already felt slightly familiar to her: tea during breakfast and white toast in the silver toast rack, a soft boiled egg in a gaily painted cup, bottles of milk delivered to the door and stored in a small refrigerator in the kitchen. The memories tumbled over themselves...her grandmother pushing the tea trolley, bumping over the threshold from kitchen to lounge, cups and saucers clattering, the freshly-baked plum cake making her mouth water before she even saw it...walking out with her grandfather, dressed nattily each morning in tweed jacket and dark red vest, to the news agents to pick up a paper... a three day excursion to the seaside with just her mother, greedily picking at the last crunchy bits of a fish and chips supper wrapped in greasy newspaper.

It was on the North Coast of Cornwall that her heart began to beat wildly. In Padstow, it had been blazingly hot, exceptionally rare for middle June, and they donned their swimsuits to lie luxuriously in the sun at Treyarnon Bay. As they motored towards Tintagel, her mother entertaining her along the way with legends of King Arthur, Lissie's spirit began to soar as high as the gulls as they approached Trebarwith and stepped out of her grandfather's car, her mother, as radiant and youthful as Lissie would ever remember her, pointing out Gull Rock in the distance. They had packed a picnic and, dividing the load between them, spread out a blanket over the sunburnt grasses, high upon the cliffs. They set out the still warm Cornish pasties, bottles of cider, and a bowl of fresh strawberries. They sat, their bare legs browned, their noses and cheeks tipped with sunburn, and took in the glorious sea as the breeze lifted their hair from their temples and waved the wildflowers that tumbled over the cliffs.

It may have been the cider, but suddenly her mother, having trained as a dancer in her youth, was compelled to leap to her feet, kick off her sandals, and, giggling, walk briskly forward in allegro with arms extended to either side before flinging one shapely leg upwards, pushing off the ground with the other, leaping into the air above the cliff in what she later described as, "a feeble attempt at a petit jete'."

Lissie had never seen her mother, in her mid-forties at the time, so unabashedly effervescent and alive. Her russet hair spilled free from its combs and anyone, from even a close distance, truly would have mistaken them for sisters.

"This," her mother announced, pirouetting slowly, arms outstretched, "is where your father proposed to me!" She dimpled sweetly, and cried as if to all the world, "Have you *ever* seen anything more beautiful?"

Lissie, young enough to laugh at her mother yet old enough to recognize the poetry of the moment, rose wordlessly and joined her, linking arms, and stared out to sea.

In twelve years, stunningly, she would be gone.

Lissie opened her eyes and extended both arms towards the ceiling, in tribute to the memory of that treasured afternoon.

"I will return and dance on that cliff, darling," she whispered. "And I know you will join me."

Chapter 10

THE LAST NAME DAVID expected to see illuminated across the screen of his phone was Denise. Startled, he hesitated for a moment before sliding the bar to answer. He certainly had no reason to avoid speaking with her. It was simply that their last meeting ended with such finality that, unless he should bump into her somewhere in town, he had not expected to talk to her again. He picked up the television remote and lowered the volume on the morning newscast he had been half watching as he'd answered a few emails before heading into the studio.

"Hello Denise," he said, hoping to sound nothing more than casual.

"Hello David," she returned. "I wanted to run something past you, to see how you felt about it."

"Fire away," he replied, curious. He settled back into the cheap, but comfortable sofa he had picked up to furnish the apartment he had taken upon their separation.

"You know how much I love your mom," Denise began.

"I do."

"Well," she hesitated, as if gathering courage, then proceeded, "I sent her a card for her birthday, but I had picked up something a while ago that I thought she'd appreciate. I can easily mail it, but I would love to give it to her in person, if it's not an imposition." She began to falter. "I mean, I don't want to overstep any boundaries—"

"Denise," David interrupted, raising his hand as if halting her concerns. "We never set any boundaries, so don't worry. Mother has always been very fond of you and, of course, feel free to take it to her in person."

He could hear an audible sigh of relief on the other end.

"Thanks, David," she said. "I really appreciate it. Would this evening be all right? After I leave work?"

"This evening..."He hesitated a fraction too long and Denise sensed it.

"If that's too sudden, I can always wait. I just thought with it being her birthday—"

"The thing is," David began, "we're throwing a birthday party for her."

"Ah, I see," she replied. "So sorry. Tell you what, I'll just pop it in the mail, instead."

Emboldened, David found himself saying, "You know what, Denise? Just stop by. Really, it's not like we're acrimonious, right? Mother would love to see you. Come by and give her your gift and have a glass of champagne and some cake. There's no reason to feel awkward about any of it."

There was a short silence as Denise contemplated the offer.

"Sure," she replied. Her voice was light. "Why not? OK, sounds good. See you later, then."

"See you later."

David could almost see her hanging up from the tasteful peach interior of her carefully appointed office at the firm. *The firm*, he thought with a slight wince, from where he had nearly scuppered her hope of advancement. It had been the last crack—a chasm, really— in their marriage, and one he couldn't repair.

Funny, he thought, rising to fill his travel mug with coffee before heading out the door, funny how one casual remark could become two, then three offenses, all culminating in a final explosion from which there was no return. And no one had been more surprised than he was, when he first found himself bringing up the thought of having a child.

"Do you ever feel," he said, nuzzling into the back of her neck after a rather spontaneous session of lovemaking on a lazy Sunday afternoon. "That you might want something more?"

Denise had frowned, then rolled over, laughing at him. "More what? Sex?"

"Nah," David had replied softly, stroking her feathery bangs to one side. "More, I don't know...us?"

Denise cocked her head to one side. "What do you mean?"

David hesitated before continuing, "Maybe I'm having a sort of midlife crisis...it just seems that we both spend most of our time working like crazy and all of a sudden I turn around and I'm thirty-six, and I wonder if the next time I stop to think about it, I'll be fifty-six—"

"And?"

"And," he continued, stumbling to find his way, "have nothing to really show for it?"

Denise sat up in bed and draped her lithe legs over his.

"You already have lots to show, baby," she smiled. "You've got a ton of work lined up, we've been able to stash a good chunk of money away, and really, we're doing pretty great, don't you think? Mexico, Miami...I'm thinking maybe Paris this summer, how about you?" She leaned over and kissed him, lingering over his lips. "We could rent a little cottage in the Burgundy countryside and eat baguettes and drink red wine all day long. What do you think?"

"I think that's great." David smiled and chose his words carefully. "But I was also thinking how great it would be if, maybe, you know, if it wasn't just us going along on these trips. Maybe—" He took a deep breath. "One day, we could have a mini Merriman."

Denise pulled back, her delicately arched brows raised in surprise.

"A 'mini Merriman'?" She exploded with laughter. "You mean a *baby*? God, David, don't tell me you're getting broody!" she smacked him playfully on the rump and rose from the bed en route to the shower.

"No," she added, over her shoulder. "What we need is another getaway. You're right—we've both been working crazy hours and when things slow down at work, if they *ever* slow down, I'm going to tell Richard I've got to take a break—we'll grab a long weekend somewhere." And whether or not it was intentional, she turned on the water, drowning out any chance he had to reply to her final declaration. "Maybe Bermuda. Or Aspen! Can't do that with a baby in tow!"

Chastened, David had hoped he had chosen a suitable moment. Denise had swatted the idea away as if he had made an absurd observation—a joke, really, that didn't merit further discussion. He had meant to simply feel her out, test the waters of expanding their family and had thought, even while acknowledging Denise's laser-like career focus, that perhaps she'd at least consider the matter. So unnerved was he that he left the subject alone until a couple of months later when they had self-consciously waited in line, laughing, in early November, when the shopping mall had advertised Santa Claus would be in residence and they had thought a photo of them both perched upon his knee would make a funny Christmas card for their friends and family.

"We're being stared at," Denise whispered, as several children had looked up curiously at the two adults in the middle of the queue.

"We need a kid as a prop," David joked and gestured to a funny little boy directly in front of them, his hands clenched into fists of excitement, "What do you think of that little redhead in the green corduroy coat? He looks like he stepped out of a Norman Rockwell painting. Think we could rent him for a couple of bucks?"

"Stop," she had hissed at him, but couldn't contain her mirth. "Stop staring at them—we already look like weirdos, as it is."

One charming little girl, standing quietly between her parents in front of them, had pressed her face against her mother's thigh and peeped upwards at both of them, her enormous eyes taking in one and then the other before turning back and raising her arms to be picked up. Her mother obliged, and the child continued to stare at David and Denise both over the shoulder of her mother's quilted jacket.

"She's like a cherub," David said.

"She is," Denise agreed.

"Sure you wouldn't want a little girl like that?" he teased, digging her playfully in the ribs with his finger. "And if she looked like you, she'd be a stunner."

Denise, either not hearing him or deciding not to react, stepped out of the line for a moment to ask a sizable 'elf,' a rather tall, bored teenage girl, what the price would be if they purchased just the wallet sized photographs instead of the entire bundle.

It was when they were driving home that her first flash of annoyance surfaced. He had made the mistake of bringing up the subject once more.

"David," she asked impatiently. "Where is this coming from? We have always agreed that we were not going to be tied down by children. In fact, it's one of the things you said that attracted you to me. Your career has you traveling more and more, and my workload is way too much to ever contemplate having a child, even if I wanted one, which I don't. I don't *want* that lifestyle. I want to be free. I want us *both* to be free to go where we choose, when we choose, without dragging some kid along. Especially now, especially with Richard dropping hints about making me a partner."

Yes, let's not piss off Richard, he thought. He found it hard not to loathe the larger than life managing partner. Instead, he countered, "I know it's what we agreed," and glanced over at her, but she was staring out the passenger window. "But people can change their minds, can't they? People do it all the time."

"You mean *you* changed your mind," she replied, then turned her gaze coldly upon him. "I didn't."

"So you're not even willing to discuss it?"

"We are discussing it," she said, firmly. "And the case is closed."

"No more questions, your honor," he quipped sarcastically, as was his tendency, whenever he felt anger seeping into his chest.

The air had been tense between them for nearly a week, afterwards. By Thanksgiving, things had thawed and David made a deliberate attempt to keep their conversations casual, neutral. They had returned to their normal way of life which he couldn't help feeling was stifled, listless, defined by work. They shared scraps of conversation in the evenings before he turned to the television for company and Denise turned to answer 'just a couple of emails,' which kept her in her home office for an hour or so. The relatively recent musing to have a child was something he couldn't quite explain, especially when he was denied the opportunity to discuss his feelings. He had ruminated while staring up at the ceiling one night with Denise snoring lightly beside him: It wasn't because his other friends were having children. David smirked. God, his friends were mostly musicians and artists that had yet to commit to a cable provider, much less a relationship. He didn't even have any idea whether he would be a good father, but he suspected he might. He turned over and propped himself up on one elbow and stared at Denise, lying on her side, the indentation of her waist and delicious curve of her hip evident beneath the covers. He realized with a start that it wasn't about wanting a child for the sake of having a child. It was about wanting more *her*. More *them*. Starting a family would give them a path forward from the stagnation he felt they had been experiencing for some time. But Denise wouldn't see it that way, it occurred to him with a realization that began to settle in with a chill. Denise didn't feel a need for anymore them. She didn't desire anymore *him*. She was satisfied with the status quo, and David, who had admittedly been emotionally apathetic in regards to every other relationship in which he had been involved, suddenly realized that what had initially attracted him to Denise—her self-sufficiency, her ability to entertain herself—had now descended into the sinking feeling that came with the knowledge that his level of commitment far exceeded his wife's. For the first time in his adult life, he began to feel vulnerable, unsettlingly insecure—exactly what he had found irritating and claustrophobic in former girlfriends. Ironically, the only time he felt he had all of Denise was physically, during their lovemaking which was as frequent as it was intense. He devoured her and deliberately chose his moments late into the night because that way, when they were finished and lay in each other's arms, breathless, spent, he knew that she was too tired for anything else except drifting to sleep, her head cradled against his shoulder. It was then he could hold her close, stroke her hair, feel utterly complete. At any other time, she would pull away as she suddenly remembered an email that needed replying to or a trial brief proofread.

Two weeks before Christmas, David did, in Denise's eyes, the unforgivable.

"What do we have to wear to this thing tonight?" he had asked, standing in his boxers in front of his closet.

Denise snapped a diamond stud into her earlobe and looked over her shoulder. "What you wear every year—a suit. And don't look so miserable. You look gorgeous in a suit."

David dragged out his obligatory navy suit that had appropriately served him for celebratory functions as well as funerals. "I don't have to wear the tie with the snowmen on it, right?"

Denise chuckled. "Look, it's two hours out of your life. Richard always puts on a killer spread. And this year there's no cash bar, so you've got that to look forward to, within reason. You'll have a good time."

Forty minutes later they had pulled into the manicured grounds and circular drive of Chadford, Richard's country club. A red jacketed valet darted out and took care of their car, and they walked, clasping hands, beneath the hemlocks bedecked and twinkling with white fairy lights into the grand entrance of the building, hesitating long enough to remove their coats and exchange pleasantries with fellow revelers in front of an enormous Christmas tree.

"Two hours," David mouthed at his wife as he looked up to see Mia, who had never truly gotten over her crush on him, making a beeline in his direction. Denise had given him a saucy wink before approaching one of the firm's clients with an animated greeting.

The first half hour had been bearable despite Mia's detailed account of her recent breakup 'with that ass Jeff.' David had been able to enjoy two glasses of a very nice pinot noir and successfully made his escape by returning a nod to one of the firm's associates, Spencer, whom he had met the year before. As the young man stood before a polished sideboard with miniature copper reindeer flanking an impressive tray of canapés, he began to help himself to a glazed pear and goat cheese crostini, and David excused himself from Mia to join him. They chatted amiably for a few minutes when, with an inward groan, David saw Richard, signaling with an expansive wave of the hand, trying to catch his attention and beckoning him over. Draining his glass, David took advantage of a server who, with perfect timing, was striding past with a tray of champagne flutes held aloft. Without a break in his stride, David plucked one up with his right hand as he walked steadily towards Richard.

At least on the few occasions that he had run into Richard, it was difficult to get a bead on the man. When alone, as he had appeared last spring, exiting a sandwich shop with a ridiculous powder pink sweater tied around the shoulders of his turquoise polo shirt, David had found him to be tolerable, even affable. However, whenever he had an audience, no matter how small, it was as if Richard was compelled to resort to some sort of archaic alpha male behavior and make it very clear that he was in charge. In charge of what, David never knew, but having been on the receiving end of belittling barbs before, he remained wary in his presence.

"You're being overly sensitive," Denise had chided him. "He was only kidding."

"He told me he knew someone from *Olan Mills* and could get me a job with them!" David had shouted.

"David, old man!" Richard blared his usual greeting that David always found ironic, considering that Richard must be at least two decades his senior. "We don't see you enough!" He turned to his audience of partners, clients, and his overly-tanned, overly-blonde wife, Monica. "This is the lucky dog who landed our Denise."

David smiled tightly and carefully took a swallow of champagne, wondering, as he always did, why flutes never allowed enough room for anyone with an unconventionally sized nose.

"And the lucky dog who shot your firm's roster," David reminded him.

"Yes, yes," Richard nodded. "And a fine job you did. Now, tell me…" He stepped closer as if about to confide in him but instead clapped him on the back, causing David to jump involuntarily, "When are we going to get you on the golf course?"

"Oh, I don't think that I'm a golf course sort of guy," David replied, beginning to appreciate the buzz he was feeling from the considerable amount of alcohol he had consumed during a relatively short period of time.

"Well, hell," Richard guffawed, his accent becoming more pronounced as it tended to do after a couple of bourbons. "We all know that, but if you're with me, they'll let you in."

Before anyone could respond, David gave such a sharp bark of laughter at the condescension of this red-faced, beefy man whose oddly hollowed eyes told the tale of a recent surgical lift, that Denise turned her head sharply from the other side of the room. Seeing her husband with an empty glass in one hand and leaning in a little too close to her boss, she excused herself and nearly trotted over to join them.

"Denise!" David slipped his arm around his wife's waist and looked at her with comically widened eyes. "Richard just told me he could make sure I won't get kicked off the golf course."

"Well, that's nice!" Denise chirped. Eager to change the subject, she pointed to Monica's emerald and gold pendant and cooed, "How beautiful! Is that a gift from Richard?"

Feeling dismissed, David stepped back and seized another champagne from a server's tray, deliberately avoiding Denise's sideways glance.

"Got that for her last month," Richard answered for his wife, "as a little bit of an apology for so many late nights at work. Happy wife, happy life, you know. How about you, David? Or, should I say, *you, Denise*? Have you given David anything special for all the overtime that's been keeping you at the office?"

Denise shook her head and smiled a bit too brightly.

"David works an awful lot of hours, too, Richard."

"Do you?" Richard looked at David with what seemed to be genuine surprise. "What do you shoot mostly? Weddings? Kids? I would think you'd have far more free time than an up-and-coming associate attorney."

"Yeah," David replied sardonically. "Kids, pets, all that stuff. Trying just to make ends meet."

Denise felt the tension in his arm as she tucked hers through his elbow. "Don't be ridiculous, David," she scolded, then stated with some pride, "actually, my gorgeous husband just landed the account for Chateau Hivernaux. He's going to be up there all next week, shooting sexy blonde models on skis for their new brochure, and I have to pretend I'm not the least bit jealous."

"Well," Richard drawled. "I'd say he's a lucky guy, able to capitalize on a hobby, as well as having a wife who's both beautiful *and*—" He gave David an obnoxious, little wink. "—earns enough to be the breadwinner in the family."

"When we have a family," David shot back, "trust me, I'll be providing just fine, thanks." He felt Denise's hand tighten around his bicep, but ignored her.

Richard's eyes flicked to Denise, "A family? What's this? You're planning on having children?"

Before Denise could answer, David replied crisply, "We're talking about it."

"I can assure you," Denise laughed icily, dropping her husband's arm and placing her hand lightly upon Richard's wrist. "We are *not* talking about it, Richard. I'm far too busy and far too dedicated to the firm."

Richard smiled and said, "You might want to make a note of that, David. Sounds like there's been a breakdown in communication, old man."

The tension between the small group was pulsating. David stared directly into Richard's eyes and had a sudden revelation that his ridiculous eye lift, so obvious, so unnatural, was borne of the same fear that caused fading Hollywood stars to desperately strive for the same attempt at youthfulness as if no one would notice. *Richard is scared,* he thought with a flash of triumph, *he's a scared, vain little bully.*

"Oh, there's no problem with our communication," David replied, before adding pointedly, "I know exactly what I'm saying, *Dick.*"

The one thing that David had always admired about his wife was her ability to appear completely unfazed and collected, regardless of the situation. He didn't know if that was because she was a successful attorney, or if that attribute made her a successful attorney. Before Denise, he had had a string of girlfriends who, within a year or so, had bemoaned his level of commitment and had expressed their frustrations through what had seemed to be flammable rages or muffled sobs. Because the woman who had served as his lone role model, his mother, seemed always quietly in control and self-assured, a crying or overwrought woman left him nervous, uncomfortable, and eventually cold. However, Denise was cool under fire, calm, level-headed. And when she was particularly angry, as she was now, the only thing that snapped were her eyes. As she turned them, blazing, onto her husband, he knew she was livid as she made an attempt to inject levity.

"Well, Richard," she chuckled, turning to smile apologetically to Monica. "You see where your generosity got you this year? An open bar leads to open mouths, with no editing button!" She turned her attention back to David with a low voice that was as deadly firm as it was quiet. "I'll call a cab for you and I'll meet you home, afterwards." With that, she turned on her heel, linked arms with her boss and his gilded wife, and directed them across the room towards another group.

It was as graceful an exit that could be managed and David, humiliated in her abandonment, left without a word. When he arrived home, he poured himself a whiskey, then two, and found himself alone in bed the following morning, dry-mouthed and joined by a dull headache, with Denise nowhere to be seen. In fact, he realized, taking in the undisturbed side of the bed next to him, there was no evidence that she had come home. He rose, relieved himself in the bathroom, cringed at the sight of his bloodshot eyes and walked down the hallway, poking his head around the corner into the open planned dining room and kitchen.

"Denise?"

Silence. He tried to phone her but his call went straight to voicemail. His subsequent text went unread, unanswered. He began to worry. Surely if she'd had an accident, someone would have notified him? Or had they already tried? He checked his phone again for messages, and found nothing. He decided to take a quick shower to help clear his head as he felt himself on the verge of panic. It was when he emerged, five minutes later, with a towel wound around his waist that he heard her key turn in the lock of the door in the house they shared. He hadn't thought of what he might say. He had nothing rehearsed. He simply said what he felt.

"Denise, I was really beginning to worry."

Denise walked past him, still wearing the black skirt and chiffon blouse that she had worn to the party. Even her lipstick looked fresh.

"Denise?" he followed her into the bedroom, "Where did you stay last night?"

She pulled open her dresser and pulled out an oversized cowl-necked sweater. She walked towards him with such determination that he backed up a step, over the threshold and into the hallway.

"Excuse me, I need to change," she said tonelessly, and shut the door in his face.

David retreated to the kitchen, made himself the strongest cup of coffee he could manage and waited quietly for her. He could hear the shower running, then her hair dryer, and when she reappeared, a half hour later, he felt as if he had been sucker-punched as he saw her carrying her small wheeled suitcase and duffle bag.

"Denise?" was all he could think to say.

"I can't be with you," she said, her voice flat and devoid of any emotion. "I'm staying at a hotel." She started for the door until David leapt up and took her by the shoulders.

"What are you talking about? Look, I made a mistake last night, we both made a mistake—"

"We *both?*" her voice was incredulous. "David, you deliberately attempted to sabotage my career at the firm. You were drunk, insulting—I was utterly humiliated."

"What the *fuck?*" David dropped his hands and ran them through his hair as he turned to walk away. He attempted to compose himself, failed, then strode back as angry as he'd ever been. "Your boss stands there, in front of his little fan club, insults my career, insults me, and *you're* humiliated? Are you kidding me? And what's worse," he said as he stepped closer to her, "is that you made no effort to have my back, Denise. You apologized for me like I was a child and left with your crowd. You left me standing there. How do you think that made me feel?"

"You called Richard a *dick!*" Denise cried.

"He *is* a dick!"

"Yes," she fumed. "He is a dick, but he's a successful dick who is considering me as a future partner. Have you any idea how rare that is for someone who has only been with a firm for six years? I have worked my ass off in that job, David, you know I have, and then you stand there, before everyone, after I have made it very clear to you that I don't want children, I will never want children, and tell him we're 'talking about having children'—the last damned thing any managing partner wants to hear. Because now I'm dead in the water, do you understand that? Now, he thinks the next thing I'm going to ask him for are months of maternity leave, and time off because baby is sick and I can't get a sitter—*how could you do that to me?*"

They stood there limply and stared at each other.

"I feel like I don't even know who you are," she finally spoke, her voice barely above a whisper. "I feel completely betrayed and I don't think I can trust you anymore."

She picked up the duffle bag and suitcase and walked to the door. He made no effort to open it for her.

"Denise..."

His aborted plea made no difference. Without another word, she was gone.

Chapter 11

HAVING DECIDED UPON A suitable gift for her mother, Leigh was feeling rather pleased with herself as she tucked the gift certificate she had chosen into a "From all of us" birthday card she had actually signed for the entire family. She had called upstairs to Kirsten, warning that they'd be leaving in ten minutes regardless if she wasn't ready, after having rejected her daughter's first outfit of leggings and a cropped sweater.

"They're *new*," Kirsten had retorted, already irritated that taking her phone along had been forbidden.

"They're still leggings," Leigh had replied with dismay. "You've got more clothes than anyone I know—go put on something suitable. This is a special occasion for your grandmother and everyone's going to be dressed nicely."

Wes could be counted on to dress appropriately and she gave a nod of approval as he entered the kitchen in a turtleneck and sports coat. He watched her as she sealed the envelope.

"So, what did we get her?" he asked, pouring himself a glass of water from the tap.

"Honestly," Leigh sighed. "If it were up to men, no one would ever receive a gift, and if by chance they did, it certainly wouldn't be gift-wrapped. Just wadded up in newspaper."

"Actually," Wes replied, "I threw out suggestions but each one was shot down."

"Because your suggestions are always the same: a bottle of wine, a robe...she's turning seventy, Wes. It's a big deal."

"Fine, fine," came the reply Wes seemed to say more and more these days. "So, what did you get?"

"I got..." Leigh replied, deliberately dragging it out as she stuck a small bow on the envelope, "yoga classes!"

"But she already does yoga, doesn't she?"

"She does yoga by herself," Leigh turned to face him. "This is a class, taught in town, with a group of other women she probably already knows, so a good, social way to get her out of the house. The spring schedule starts in March, so I bought her three months of weekly classes. And who knows," Leigh mused, tucking the envelope into her purse. "I might even join her. It's supposed to be very good for you and maybe it'll help my back."

"And something you could do together," Wes noted.

"And something we could do together," Leigh echoed. "All right, let's get going. Kirsten!"

* * * *

David found himself feeling strangely at odds as he combed back his hair in front of the bathroom mirror, still steamed from his shower. He had gone from feeling quite numb, as his mother had suggested, focused intently on work and withdrawing from his small circle of friends, to a sudden nervous flip in the pit of his stomach at the prospect of seeing his former wife. It had been not quite two weeks, and so felt less as a divorce and more of a reunion of sorts. He had suggested it, he reminded himself, lathering up to shave the stubbly growth to which his mother tended to object but Denise had always loved. However, she had pleasantly agreed to his invitation. Surely, he thought, pulling the razor downwards towards his jaw line, surely they were cordial enough to each other that there shouldn't be any awkwardness. *So why*, he thought, rinsing the blade, *do I feel so nervous?*

Finished with his shave, he pulled a V-necked navy cashmere sweater over his head before remembering with a start that Denise had given it to him two Christmases ago. He checked his watch; he was running late. He really didn't have time to go through his chest of drawers and find something that was both clean and presentable, so he stepped into a pair of charcoal corduroys and reached for a black jacket at the back of his closet. He frowned at the pet hairs on the sleeves from God knew where and began to feverishly search for a lint roller. He cursed, pacing from room to room, throwing open drawers before catching sight of himself in a mirror.

"Calm down," he ordered his reflection. "Just calm the hell down. She's not coming to see you."

The admonishment was effective. He exhaled slowly and, failing to find the lint roller, used strips of tape instead. That would do. He patted his pockets for his keys, remembered he had left them on the hook by the door, seized the gift bag on the counter that contained his mother's book, and left.

Snow flurries flitted across the windshield of his Jeep as he drove the familiar back roads to his mother's house, standing like a bastion of grace and carefully guarded memories. He paused before killing the ignition, the headlights trained on the home of his youth. He had inherited his mother's artistic eye, his father's sense of proportion, and he still appreciated the rustic elegance of this rambling farmhouse he knew so well. His eyes caught sight of the caterer's van, parked off to the left and he pulled up alongside so as not to block anyone or be blocked himself, and strode quickly across the front yard, tapping lightly upon the front door before letting himself in.

"Darling!" His mother had smiled, looking up from fingering the blossoms of the extravagant bouquet sent by his uncle that now adorned the primitive hickory table in the foyer. "How good to see you!" She walked towards him, arms outstretched, and kissed his cheek.

"Happy Birthday, Mother," David returned the kiss and handed her the bag. "You look wonderful."

He meant it. David had always loved that she had never made any attempt to color her hair, striving to look younger. Her chestnut hair spent years being naturally streaked with grey until finally turning completely silver, which flattered her pink complexion. She looked particularly vibrant tonight, he thought, younger than usual. Like him, she was in a navy sweater but with black cigarette pants and velvet flats. He also noted, with a loving warmth, that she wore the birthday brooch he and Leigh had purchased for her together at the local drugstore when they were children. It couldn't have cost more than a couple of dollars, and one of the green glass eyes of the gold tone cat was missing. How like her to mark the occasion with such aplomb, he thought. No sedate pearls or twin sets for his mother. She much more enjoyed the lark of spontaneity.

"I can't believe you still have that," he said, pointing to the ornament.

"It's my most treasured possession," she smiled.

"I wanted to tell you before anyone else arrived, and I hope you don't mind." He found himself speaking quickly as the headlights of Wes's car flashed through the front windows. "Denise has something for you and I told her to bring it by tonight. Are you all right with that? If not, I can call her and—"

Lissie took her son's hands in hers and looked at him in that direct way he had always felt to be so reassuring. "David," she said, her voice low, "I've always thought of Denise as a second daughter. Not only is it all right, it is very, very touching to me that she would go to such trouble. I am delighted she is coming."

David gave her a grateful smile and they both turned as Leigh and her family could be heard coming up the front steps.

"Shall I take your gift to the living room?" he suggested. She nodded in reply and walked briskly to the door.

It seemed as if the other guests arrived en masse: Leigh, Wes, and Kirsten were followed within minutes by neighbors who had simply walked over. On their heels came Peter and Elaine, along with Frances, as well as Leigh's friend, Tracy. The house was ringing out with the din of animated conversation, punctuated with hearty laughter. Lissie tapped a wine glass with a butter knife to get everyone's attention that they were all to help themselves to seemingly endless platters of hor d'oeuvres placed throughout the living and dining rooms. David found himself contentedly playing bartender as he stood behind the dining room table with the antique, copper tub that normally housed kindling for the fireplace, now filled with ice and bottles of wine, beer, and champagne to be uncorked for the birthday toast.

Leigh, he noted, was overseeing the catering crew, making sure glasses were topped and plates refilled, not really mingling or visiting with anyone, but she looked more relaxed and more serene, he thought, than he had seen her in ages.

He was right. Leigh found herself absorbing the life and energy the house was emitting, filled as it should be with family and friends. She paused outside the kitchen entrance, drinking in the polished woodwork and carefully arranged furniture, the floral linen draperies back just in time from the cleaners...what a pleasure it was to see the few items of family silver, the candlesticks and serving pieces reflecting the glow of the fire roaring in the grate, the crystal stemware sparkling, the festive arrangement of pink and white balloons suspended from the chandelier. She couldn't even imagine, she thought with a dart of pain, returning to the dated 1970s split-level she abhorred. This was where she belonged, she thought, tears suddenly springing to her eyes. This is where she *would* return, some day. It was more than a silly dream, she felt, with a determination so fierce that it startled her, it was an essential need. *It is only here that I feel complete,* she nearly said aloud, as her heart swept over the beauty and nostalgia of her childhood home. Blinking, she hastily mopped her eyes with the napkin she had clenched in her fist and returned to the kitchen.

It was Lissie, chatting cheerfully to Elaine and standing closest to the foyer, who heard the hesitant tap upon the front door. She excused herself and opened it to warmly receive her former daughter-in-law. The two women exchanged heartfelt embraces and Lissie, sensing a slight trepidation on Denise's part, took her by the hand to lead her into the living room, a gesture that didn't go unnoticed by Leigh or David. He had laughingly declined Kirsten's request for a glass of wine and looked up with a start.

Denise, he thought, had never looked more beautiful. Beneath her unbuttoned coat she was clad from head to toe in the most becoming winter white, right down to her cream suede boots. Her slightly windblown hair gave her a far more natural look than to be carefully coiffured and lacquered. She looked—he searched for the word—luminous. She tucked her purse beneath one arm and carried her gift, exquisitely wrapped in a small box, to place beside the others, threatening to spill over the tabletop and onto the floor. There certainly wasn't a dramatic hush that fell over the room, but there was a slight drop in the level of conversation as a few eyes curiously followed her trek towards the dining table, and it was Kirsten, still peeved by her failure to obtain alcohol on the sly, who asked just loud enough for others to hear, "What's she doing here?"

Chapter 12

"SHE WAS INVITED," DAVID replied tersely to his niece, then added, "And the tone you just used was pretty rude."

Kirsten glowered and said nothing while Denise, pretending not to have heard the exchange, greeted her with a bright smile.

"Hi Kirsten," she said. "You look amazing." Then she turned her smile upon her former husband. "Hello, David."

"Hello." He returned her smile and spoke without thinking, as he tended to do when blindsided by her beauty or point of view. "Talk about amazing." He felt his cheeks grow hot and deliberately focused his attention on opening a bottle of chardonnay. "I'm sorry," he said, still looking down as he began to wind the screw into the cork. "I shouldn't have said that. Would you like a glass?"

Denise cocked her head and dropped one shoulder in order to meet his gaze until, unflinchingly, he raised his eyes to hers.

"You look amazing, too," she smiled. "Never apologize for giving a compliment. It's nice, isn't it?"

"Your hair looks much better than mine," he said, returning to his familiar and far more comfortable self-effacing approach. "Mine looks like I brushed it with a chair."

"It is getting a bit long," Denise admitted. "But that's always suited you. Along with the three-day growth which is tellingly absent and only proves how much you love your mother."

"Busted," David chuckled, then added, "You must be an attorney or something."

"Or something."

"Something else, I'd say," he intoned, brave enough this time to initiate a steady gaze. He poured a glass of wine, handed it to her, and was disappointed when she warmly smiled her thanks but turned away to join his mother near the fireplace.

Kirsten, who had withdrawn a few feet to help herself to a canapé, now returned, frowning.

"I didn't mean to be rude," she began, chastened. "I just don't get it."

"Don't get what?" David gave a wry smile but had a feeling about what was coming.

"I mean—" She licked the last bit of goat cheese off her thumb, "You're *divorced.*"

"Yesss."

"So why would you invite her here?"

David eyed his niece and could tell her query was genuine in its curiosity.

"Well," he replied, "just because you're divorced doesn't mean you don't like each other."

"That makes absolutely no sense," she retorted. "Can't I have a *little* wine? You could pour it in a water glass so no one would notice."

"Get your own booze like I had to when I was your age," he countered, then added, "It makes perfect sense. Just because you don't love each other anymore doesn't mean you don't still like each other."

"Yeah, but I watch you and Denise and you guys get along better than my parents and they've been married *forever.*"

"Then they still love each other."

"Huh." Kirsten gave a snort. "Could've fooled me."

Abruptly changing the subject, David asked, "You want a Coke? I think there's a can in here."

"Would you pour some wine in it?"

"No," he said, yet grinned as he fished out the cold red can. "But if I wasn't such an awesome uncle I would pour wine into your Coke because it would make you sick as a dog, and I'd have a good laugh at your expense. Here." He popped the tab and poured the fizzy soda into a wine glass. "Now you can pretend you have a glass of some kind of crappy merlot and feel all grown up."

Kirsten regarded him for a moment. She liked David in that he had always treated her as an equal, never as a child, which was particularly appreciated by an insecure girl of sixteen. He was pretty cute, too, although she had never really thought of him in that light until a school friend had pointed to him in a family photograph and asked who "the hot guy" was. It seemed impossible that he could be related to her mother who was, especially lately, bordering on the morose. David was funny, tall, lean, and seemingly even keeled. Kirsten didn't think she had ever even heard him raise his voice. He tended to wait until everyone else had spoken their peace before slipping in some sardonic comment that either resulted in laughter—or horror—but always broke the tension.

"You're so weird," she said and left him.

Around eight o'clock, a few of the guests had retired to the sofa near the fire or various chairs, and Leigh, aware that the energy of the gathering was slightly dissipating, cocked her head towards the birthday cake on the sideboard. David, catching her eye, gave her a quick nod. Stepping over to strike a match and light the candles—a large, white 7 and 0 raised above pink sugared roses that encircled the top—David held a bottle of champagne aloft and declared, "Folks, it's time for the birthday girl to make her wish!"

Lissie, having turned with the rest of the guests, placed her hands on either side of her face and cried, "Oh, dear, I had been in such sublime denial all evening until I just saw my age on that cake." The room erupted into laughter.

Peter, his arm around Elaine's waist, was the first to proclaim, "Listen, kid, you think seventy's bad? Just wait a few years!"

Tracy, who had been dutifully assisting Leigh in the kitchen, piped up from the back of the room.

"Lissie, if turning seventy looks like you, then honey, give me seventy. Right now!"

David popped the champagne cork expertly into a bar towel and began to fill the flutes before him. "Come on, ladies and gentlemen, grab a glass to toast the best looking woman in the room."

"Hear, hear," agreed Denise, who took one and passed another to Elaine.

Leigh carried the cake on its glass pedestal towards the dining room table and nodded to Wes to dim the chandelier. In the glow of the firelight, candles flickering, she presented it to her mother as she urged everyone to sing.

"How absolutely beautiful, darling," Lissie breathed.

"Make a wish!" Peter ordered when their rousing rendition of the birthday song (tuneless, perhaps, but enthusiastic in effort) was finished.

Lissie turned to her friends and family. "I shall," she proclaimed, clasping her hands together in front of her chest. "But I believe it's already coming true!"

Taking a deep breath, she blew out the 7 and the 0 while joyfully acknowledging the applause that surrounded her.

"All right, everybody," Leigh called, "Come get your slice of cake."

David slipped his arm around his mother and before the guests could focus their attentions elsewhere announced, "But first, let us drink a toast." He pressed a sparkling flute of champagne into Lissie's hand, stepped back and declared, "To my beautiful mother, friend, and confidant. You never cease to inspire us with your boundless energy, honesty, intellect—did I mention energy?" The group chuckled knowingly, and he finished with affectionate sincerity, raising his glass, "If there's anything you can't do, we've yet to discover it. And we love you very, very much. Happy Birthday."

There was another smattering of applause, and as Leigh began to slice and serve the cake, she announced that this would be a good opportunity for her mother to open the gifts piled before her.

Tracy shouldered her way through the group and handed Lissie a gift bag, its contents wrapped in pale yellow tissue. "I promise you," she began, deliberately catching Leigh's eye. "This isn't a Leatherman."

"Oh, Tracy, you really shouldn't have gone to any trouble," Lissie said then burst into laughter as she pulled out a book titled *How to Build Your Own Garden Shed*.

"Don't try and pretend you hadn't thought about it," Tracy accused her good-naturedly.

"I have!" Lissie cried, then amended, "Actually, a gazebo. A small one."

Peter stepped forward and planted a kiss on her cheek as he placed a small parcel into her hands. "From the both of us. You only turn seventy once, you know."

Lissie carefully removed the pale blue wrapping paper and silver ribbon and gasped as she opened a black velvet box to reveal a tasteful swirl of gold enclosing a perfectly round amethyst in its center.

"What an exquisite pendant," she whispered, lifting the piece by its fragile chain, her eyes beginning to brim with tears. "And it's my birthstone! Oh, you're both far too generous."

Elaine remarked about what fun they'd had having it made especially for her, and Peter, in his usual boisterous fashion, admitted relief that she liked it. "We've only seen you in very simple jewelry," he explained. "We were worried you would think it was too flashy."

Lissie held the pendant against her cat pin and with mock despair replied, "Oh, no, I believe it clashes," before giving them each a warm embrace and assuring them she loved it.

"Mother," David handed her the book he had found for her, bound only with a red ribbon.

"Nice gift wrap," Kirsten commented, and was pleased to earn a chuckle from her father.

"I'm trying to be ecologically sustainable," David replied archly, before adding, "besides, I was out of tape."

"A book is always welcomed," Lissie said graciously, gently pulling away the ribbon and running her fingers over the green cloth cover. "*A Shropshire Lad*," she smiled, and reached up to kiss her son's cheek. "Especially this book. It's perfect."

"It's not exactly a first edition," David clarified. "There were only about five hundred printed, initially, and I shall get you one of those when you turn eighty," he winked, then continued. "But this is a first edition from a 1914 printing and in pretty nice condition."

"It's in beautiful condition," Lissie agreed, and carefully opened the book, letting the pages fall where they may before reading aloud,

"Loveliest of trees, the cherry now,
Is hung with bloom along the bough,
And stand about the woodland ride
Wearing white for Eastertide.

Now, of my threescore years and ten,
Twenty will not come again,
And take from seventy springs a score,
It only leaves me fifty more."

"Oh, dear," Lissie said, her eyes widening and then crinkling with amusement. "That doesn't leave many springs for me, now, does it?"

"Don't count on it," David said. "You're going to outlive us all, you know."

Leigh tentatively passed her mother a gift bag after her mother had placed the book carefully upon the table. As Lissie, bemused, extracted a leotard from the tissue paper and held it high for all to see, Leigh explained. "Knowing how you enjoy your morning yoga, we got you three months' worth of weekly classes at the studio in town."

"Oh!" Lissie exclaimed. "How very thoughtful. Thank you!"

"Their next session begins in early March, so you've got time to exchange that leotard for some actual yoga pants."

"Oh," Lissie said, suddenly remembering her undisclosed plans.

"Is there something wrong?" Leigh asked.

"Of course not," Lissie stammered. "But twelve classes...you must have spent a fortune. I know what they charge, and—"

Wes, standing behind his wife, interrupted.

"It's our pleasure, Lissie," he said. "And to be frank, I don't know if I can handle the tension of watching Leigh pull her hair out trying to find something for you that you don't already have, so for God's sake, take the gift."

The laughter that followed was particularly welcomed by Wes as his remark, as funny as it might have been, had more than a ring of truth to it. Leigh had been both prickly and alienating to live with the last several weeks. When she voiced her frustration in regards to her mother, a gift, or the party, it appeared she did so for the purpose of simply venting. Neither he nor Kirsten could suggest anything that wasn't received with scorn, if not blatantly ignored.

Lissie smiled her thanks and kissed her daughter. Denise, standing beside Peter, reached behind her to pick up the small box from where she had placed it on the dining table, and asked him to pass it forward.

"Denise, dear, you shouldn't have." Lissie murmured, upon receiving it. The box was wrapped in paper dotted with tiny, vintage roses and a pale green ribbon neatly tied into a bow. As she pulled it away, she saw that inside were tucked concert tickets and Lissie's eyes grew wide.

"Season tickets to the symphony?" she whispered. "Oh, Denise, really, it's just too much. I'm utterly overwhelmed."

Denise, well aware of Leigh's stare fastening upon her and desiring to alleviate any feelings of attempted upstaging, hastily explained. "In all honesty, these were given to my boss by a grateful client and, well, Richard isn't exactly a fan of classical music, so he kindly offered them to me and, voila." She smiled, making a small flourish with her hand. "I am re-gifting them to you." Glancing at Leigh, she continued lightly. "So after you take your yoga classes, you'll be nice and limber to sit comfortably all night."

Lissie placed a finger to her lips and remained silent.

"Unless you don't enjoy the symphony?" Denise joked, but noticed Lissie's expression had changed to something akin to dismay.

"She loves the symphony," David interjected. "Don't you, Mother?"

Lissie held the tickets in her hand and stared at them for a few moments, then raised her gaze to the rest of the room before letting it settle on her son. "Of course I do," she murmured. "I just...I just don't want these wonderful gestures to go to waste."

"What do you mean?" Leigh frowned.

Feeling hemmed in, Lissie looked to David to top up her champagne, giving her a reason to retreat from the small throng. Standing next to her son, she felt relief in being able to take refuge behind the dining table. She took a small sip, for courage if nothing else, before glancing about those assembled before her. "I really hadn't planned on announcing this," she faltered, and her eyes fell upon Peter who, with a kind smile and the briefest of nods, gave her the nudge she needed. "But the reason these delightful and *thoughtful* gifts—" She looked specifically at her daughter as she spoke the word. "—won't be used is that I won't be here."

"What?" Leigh's reply sounded like a whip crack.

"Mother?" David asked, also alarmed, although his tone was far softer.

Lissie's hands flew to her cheeks and she stammered. "Oh, I'm making such a hash of this! But before anyone thinks I just received some terrible news, let me assure you that there's nothing wrong, I'm not dying, but I won't be here, at least part of the time." Exasperated, she blew out her breath then smiled at the puzzled faces before her. She was grateful to have the stem of her champagne flute to grip as she plunged ahead. "I am following a life-long dream of mine, and I am moving to England."

Her announcement was followed by a sharp intake of breath from Frances, then a murmur or two before settling into a stunned silence. Denise, who had always greatly admired her former mother-in-law and had declared more than once that she hoped to emulate her at that age, was the first to speak as she raised her glass and said softly, "Well done."

Leigh, her stomach growing suddenly hot with a wave of nausea, which tended to come upon her when she was given bad news, mocked Denise under her breath, repeating, "Well done," as if it were the most ridiculous statement ever uttered, then addressed her mother curtly. "What on earth are you talking about?"

"I suppose I've had enough champagne to help me explain," Lissie began with a tentative smile, struggling inwardly. This was not the way she had wanted to do this. Her children deserved to have been told personally, privately. And so she began with an apology.

"David, Leigh," she sighed before taking a breath and forging ahead. "Please believe me when I tell you that my intention was to tell you of my plans, privately. I'm afraid I just became overwhelmed and, frankly, felt quite guilty accepting these lovely gifts, but I am very sorry not to have told you earlier." Then turning to those assembled before her, she clasped her hands, saying with genuine sincerity, "And I'm so glad all of you are here to celebrate this new chapter in my life because it's both exciting and rather daunting to undertake such an adventure at my time of life, but it is a very cherished dream and I would love to have you all rooting for me."

"Wow," David exhaled, glancing at Denise and then his sister. He could see Leigh was churning inside and made an attempt at levity. "They've got great British beers at the pub, Mother. You don't have to fly across the pond to get them, you know."

His mother smiled but was acutely aware of the tension that remained in the air. "Well, you did say in your toast that if there was something I couldn't do, you hadn't found it yet." This was received by a chuckle or two and Lissie, eager for her guests to return to their joviality, opened her arms wide and said, "Please, help yourself to some of this delicious cake and enjoy yourselves."

Leigh stared fixedly at her mother's face, then abruptly turned on her heel and left the room.

Tracy, watching the scene unfold from the back of the room, followed her friend's retreat to the kitchen.

"You OK?" she asked, touching Leigh's shoulder.

"No, I am not OK," Leigh choked, leaning over the sink. "I am not OK." She turned to face Tracy and noticed with despair that a couple of the servers were headed towards them, their trays rattling with empty glasses and plates. "I can't talk about it. Not right now. Can you give Wes and Kirsten a lift back home? I've got to get out of here." And with that, she snatched her coat and purse from where she had hung both over the back of a kitchen chair and banged out the back door.

Chapter 13

WHETHER IT WAS HAVING mixed champagne and whiskey, or a night of tossing and turning in the sagging single bed of his childhood bedroom, David was groggily awake as dawn began to settle across his bedclothes and one particularly assertive ray of sun settled over his face. He stretched and marveled how he had found room, as a teen, to share this bed with the family Labrador, Wally.

Rubbing his eyes, he began to mull over the events of the previous evening, beginning with the palpable relief he and his mother had felt having the house to themselves after retrieving coats and scarves for departing guests and thanking the caterers. He had sent his mother to bed with the understanding they would talk things over in the morning and Lissie, grateful, didn't resist and obediently went upstairs.

He had spied Denise slipping her gloves on near the door and walked over to join his former wife. "Thank you for coming," he said. "It meant a lot to her."

Denise looked up and smiled.

"Quite the evening," she said. "How are you feeling about it all?"

"Stunned, I guess," he said. "I don't know. I think I need another drink." He strode over to the sideboard to pour himself a whiskey from the decanter. Catching her raised eyebrow, he said, "Don't worry, I'm not driving. I'm staying over." He raised an empty glass as an offer to join him. She shook her head.

"Gotta go?" he asked.

She nodded. "Yes, early morning."

"As always."

"Seems that way."

David returned to where she stood.

"I didn't believe that story about your being given the tickets for one minute, you know."

Denise shoved her hands into her coat pockets and leaned against the door frame. "Well, I didn't want Leigh to feel any competition..." she let the rest of the sentence trail away.

"Still very generous of you," David pointed out.

"She's worth it," Denise replied in a manner that was matter of fact. "And I love her. I'll always love her."

There was something about that comment, articulating what had been gathering momentum in his own heart that pained him. They were standing quite close together and it took everything he had not to gently take her face in his hands, lean in, and kiss her. Regardless of what had gone wrong between them, what had irretrievably broken down, there would always be a connection, an unspoken attraction between them.

Instead, he swallowed hard and said, "You really deserve to be made partner at the firm and when that happens, I hope you'll let me take you out to celebrate. I know I screwed up and despite all that—"

"David—" she tried to interrupt.

"Despite all that," he spoke over her, "it's important to me to let you know how proud I am of you. I've always been proud of you. You deserve everything you've been working for."

"Thank you," she said, dropping her eyes. "That means a lot." She gave his arm a little squeeze before turning to the door. He opened it for her.

"See you around," he murmured.

"See you around," she echoed, and walked briskly down the front steps towards her car. She had gotten a new one. A BMW.

Of course, he thought to himself, but without rancor. That was simply Denise. That was simply Denise moving forward into her new life. Without him.

He heard his mother come downstairs and knew in moments he would be smelling freshly ground coffee coming from the kitchen. On the rare occasions her children stayed over, Lissie enjoyed pulling out the stops and indulging them a bit. He rose and dressed, cleaned his teeth with his finger and spat into the bathroom sink, ran his fingers through his hair a couple of times, threw on his sweater and trousers, and went downstairs to join her.

"Good morning, darling," Lissie said as she looked up from setting the table. "Help yourself to coffee."

David glanced at the table. "Three plates?"

"I phoned Leigh before going to bed last night," she explained, setting down the cutlery, "and I asked if she'd join us for breakfast."

"How'd that go?"

Lissie paused. "Not terribly well. She didn't say for sure whether she would be coming."

"Awful lot of drama going on," David sighed, pulling a mug out of the cabinet.

"She's terribly hurt," his mother replied, and David was reminded of her integrity in refusing to speak negatively of one of her children to the other. "So let's have our coffee and give her a few minutes." She checked her watch. "If she's not here in a half hour, we'll have our breakfast."

They sat facing each other and David looked squarely at his mother. "I know you'd like Leigh to be here before discussing anything," he began, "but I'd like you to know that I get it. I get wanting something so badly..." He let the rest of the sentence dissipate into the air.

Lissie reached across the table and grasped her son's hand. "Thank you, darling." she murmured, then added, "And are we speaking of just me?"

Abashed, David took a gulp of his coffee and waited a few moments before replying. "I guess not."

"Was seeing Denise difficult for you?"

David set down his mug and sat slightly hunched over the table.

"The funny thing is that I was more concerned with how you might feel," he began, raising his eyes to meet his mother's. "I assumed I'd be fine because, hey, it's over. We're divorced. There's no acrimony, no hard feelings..." He struggled to reveal what he hadn't yet admitted to anyone, much less himself, and picked up a spoon to idly stir his coffee.

"Darling, do you still love her?"

There was nothing coy about his mother. No head-patting platitudes, no evasions. And as challenging as that could be, this sort of question had a comfort in it, knowing that the result would be a step towards resolution.

"I feel punched in the gut every time I see her walk away," he said, flatly. "If that's what still loving her means."

Lissie leaned back in her chair and surveyed her son for a few moments.

"I haven't asked very much about your divorce, David, because I didn't want to intrude," she began. "However, what I will tell you, darling, is that when you're the one who is left, it's very difficult."

David looked up with a start. "But you're the one who left Dad."

Lissie shook her head slowly. "Not really. With his illness, he began to leave me, leave us, week by week. And there is nothing worse than seeing the person you love begin to withdraw to a place you can't follow. It's the most helpless feeling in the world and there was nothing I could do about it. Truth be told, I was grieving the end of our relationship long before I filed for divorce." She leaned forward once more to hold David's hand. "So I do understand how it feels. It's devastating."

David nodded. It was uncanny how his mother had been able to put into words the despair that had accompanied the last year of his marriage. Denise's laser-like focus on her career, her all-encompassing compulsion for success, her desire for distractions...*God*, he thought, with a sudden clarity, perhaps he and everything he represented, the polar opposite of the world in which she lived, had been nothing more than a distraction from that.

They both looked up as Leigh, hesitating only a moment after a quick tap at the back door, entered the kitchen, looking pale and slightly crumpled in her sweats.

"I'm so glad you're here, darling," Lissie said, rising to give her daughter a kiss on the cheek that wasn't returned. "Do sit down and let me get us all breakfast. Sausage and eggs?"

"Sounds great." David added a bit of enthusiasm for his mother's sake.

"Not much for me," Leigh mumbled, taking her mother's seat and sitting across from her brother. "I'm not really hungry."

David looked levelly at his sister. He felt a twinge of annoyance. Was she going to make any sort of effort to be civil?

As the sausages began to sizzle and spit in the cast iron pan, David asked casually, "Wes and Kirsten make it home all right, last night?"

"They're fine," she replied tonelessly. "Tracy drove them home. I was in bed by the time they got in."

Lissie began to pour orange juice and placed a small glass before each of her children. She was grateful for David's lead and said, "I thought Kirsten looked particularly pretty last night."

"I was just glad to get her in something besides jeans." Leigh replied, then added, "and she'd be prettier if she worked on her attitude."

The irony of the statement did not go unnoticed by either her mother or brother, but was left untouched. Using a spatula, Lissie began to load their plates with scrambled eggs, followed by the sausages, and set them down on placemats that David remembered from their childhood. Finally taking her own plate, she sat at the head of the table and said, "Dig in."

They ate in silence for a few minutes until Lissie, dabbing her mouth with her napkin, raised the subject that was the point of their gathering.

"I would like to begin by, once again, apologizing for the way you both were made aware of my plans last night."

"It's fine, Mother," David replied. His sister remained silent.

Lissie pushed her plate to the side, folded her hands together and leaned slightly forward on her wrists. "I guess the best way is to just jump in." She gave a quick smile before continuing. "This will probably all sound a bit silly, this love affair I've had with England. I think it goes back to having an English mother and accompanying her over on my twenty-first birthday, and, really, the only way I can put this is that I felt as if I had gone home. Whether that was because she continued to keep English traditions in our household, I don't know. Even my name, Felicity, is far more common over there than here. All I know is that from the moment I stepped off the plane, the countryside— everything, really—felt surprisingly familiar and wonderfully comforting as well. And when I lost her just a few years later, it seemed to create even more of a pull."

"You don't think simply visiting more often would fill that need?" David asked.

Lissie opened her hands, palms up, and shook her head, "I don't know, darling. I've asked myself that very question. I think it's because I want to fully immerse myself in the country, the culture. I don't want to just visit. I want to *live* there. Currently, with a visa, I can only stay for six months at a time, but I'd like to give it a try, anyway."

"None of this makes any sense," Leigh finally spoke, shaking her head. "I mean, why now? For heaven's sake, Mother, you're not a young woman."

Lissie paused and looked at her daughter. She was not unprepared for the sentiment that had been expressed.

"No, I am not a young woman, darling, which is why I've decided to do it. The answer to 'why now' for me has become 'why not now?' This has been a dream I've had since I was very young. I put it on the back burner, where dreams belong, while I married your father and raised both of you. Then, of course, there was the divorce, and I had to work very hard to keep things going, and I used to think, well, *one day*, perhaps when you were both grown and out on your own. But then there were weddings to plan and a grandchild to welcome..." She let her voice trail as she relived the last quarter of her life before continuing with a boldness that had not yet been present in her explanation. "And then I got cancer. With no guarantee that I would survive. Quite frankly, I decided, it's now or never, and I began to work out a sort of timeline when I could actually make it all a reality."

"What if you get sick, again?" Leigh continued her assertion of what she believed to be commonsense.

"Leigh—" David stepped in.

"No," Lissie interjected. "That's a valid point. I can get sick just as easily in America as in England. I have very good health insurance and they have excellent doctors and hospitals over there as well."

"But what about the house?" Leigh persisted. "You can't just leave the house sitting for six months at a time. Who's going to mow the yard and water your garden and check that the pipes haven't burst in the winter?"

Lissie took a deep breath. "I'm going to sell the house. That's part of the plan."

Leigh shoved her plate away as the familiar sudden nausea took hold of her. "What?" she said, stricken. "What do you mean, sell the house?"

"I've asked Peter to list it for me. He's still with the realty company and is going to help." Lissie explained.

Leigh abruptly rose to her feet and pushed her chair to one side, its legs shrieking in protest as it skidded across the pine floor. "Oh, I see," she said, hotly. "So Peter's known all about this, too? So everyone's known all about this except for your own children?"

"This wasn't about going behind your back, Leigh." Lissie chose her words carefully. "This was about making sure I could actually make it all happen."

David watched with something like awe as his sister began to pace about the kitchen, her arms tightly folded in front of her. He had never seen her so strident since they were children. It was as if he was seeing her again as the emotional eight-year-old she had been after the divorce.

"But why *sell* the house?" She stopped and turned to her mother, her voice rising. "Why not just rent it and use the income?"

"Because I need the capital from the house, darling, to do this," Lissie tried calmly to clarify. "And I don't want to have to deal with tenants. This is a lot of house to keep up and I think what makes sense, especially as the house is paid off, is to sell it and let it finance my move, and then perhaps rent an apartment or small condo in town to live the other six months of the year."

Leigh, defeated for the moment, sank back down in her chair and buried her face in her hands. David glanced at his watch, and then his mother, with raised eyebrows. She nodded. It wasn't just that he needed to leave for the studio, they both knew, but that privacy was needed. He rose slowly. "Well, I'll miss this house," he said, taking his jacket from the back of the chair, his eyes sweeping the walls that enclosed them. "But it's your life, Mother, and it's only fair that you finally do something for yourself. I'll talk to you soon. Bye, Leigh."

Leigh didn't answer, nor did she take her face from her hands. However, with the departure of her brother, along with the opportunity to renew her battle, she slowly sat up and wiped her eyes.

"I just don't understand how you can do this," she whispered, looking at her feet.

"Leigh, darling," her mother extended her hand to try and console her daughter. "I'll be back fully half of each year." Leigh flinched at her touch.

"I'm not talking about *you*," she said, savagely. "I mean the house. I can't believe you're selling this house. You know what it means to me!"

Lissie, taken aback, struggled to understand. "Darling, I know it's your childhood home and you have many cherished memories here, but—"

"God!" Leigh cried, rising again and slapping her palm upon the tabletop. "Stop talking to me as if I were a child! It's so much more than just some memories, Mother, this house is *everything* to me, do you not understand that? The *only* time I have ever been happy, truly happy, in my life, was in this house. With my father. You were always so remote, always so damned coldly capable and self-sufficient, never sympathetic to what I was going through..." Her voice broke and she couldn't continue.

"Leigh." Reeling, Lissie rose to take her daughter by the shoulders. "You have to understand this, no, darling—" She turned Leigh around to face her. "Look at me. I will be the first to admit that I kept my emotions in check during that time. I *had* to. I had never been so frightened in my life. No one was talking about depression in those days, I had no idea what was happening. I was frightened what your father might do—"

"He would never have hurt us!" Leigh cried.

"I was frightened what he might do to *himself!*" Lissie exclaimed, her own voice rising. "I only knew your father was falling apart, and we were going to *lose* this house! I couldn't possibly let you and David, as little children, see me fall apart as well, don't you see? I *had* to be strong, that's how I managed. That's how I got my real estate license, how I paid the mortgage, and how I put food on the table. I did everything I could, Leigh, including trying to help your father."

"But don't you see," Leigh said, putting a teeth gritting accent on each syllable, "that your being strong didn't come from a place of strength at all? It's not that I don't understand your feeling the need to have put on that front, but Mother, that's all it was, a *front*. A big, impenetrable front of strength when all a scared, little girl needed

100

was her mommy." Having said her piece, she put her hands to her mouth, exhaled slowly, and raised her face, taking in the oak beams that ran across the kitchen ceiling above her. "This house is all I have," she choked, tears spilling down her cheeks. "You talk about your dream, well, what about mine? The thought of one day returning to live in this house is the only thing I've had to look forward to."

Lissie, straining to make sense of the situation, could only flounder in her reply, "But you have your family, Leigh, your *own* home, surely—"

Leigh turned away from mother with a brittle laugh, "What I have is a stale marriage to a man who doesn't understand me, and a daughter who enjoys repeatedly pointing out that I don't know anything about anything."

Perplexed, Lissie slowly shook her head and said, "But pinning all your hopes on returning to a house that once gave you a few years of happiness as a child, Leigh, isn't that going backwards?"

With a look of triumph, Leigh crossed her arms and spun back to face her mother. "And isn't that exactly what *you're* doing, Mother? Running away to England because of some solace it gave you when you were young?" she asked, angrily. "Why is it all right for you to do that, but not for me?"

Slowly, Lissie took her seat. She found she couldn't answer.

Chapter 14

THE DAYS THAT FOLLOWED found Lissie at somewhat of a loose end. Not only had Leigh's emotional outburst shocked her, but the subtext of selfishness directed towards her was devastating. Lissie looked out her bedroom window upon rising to see a heavy belly of steel grey clouds obscuring the mountains and a crisp breeze rattling the tops of the trees. She shivered slightly and dressed quickly. These were her least favorite conditions in which to walk, especially when the sky looked as if it might burst open at any moment, but walk she would. From experience she knew that no matter how much she might dislike heading out into the elements, she would always return invigorated and clear-headed. And she needed that now. After a few minutes of stretching, she zipped herself into her down jacket and sat to tie the laces of her walking shoes.

"And isn't that exactly what you're doing, Mother?" She could hear Leigh's hurtful accusation as if she were standing beside her in the kitchen. *"Why is it all right for you to do that, but not for me?"* Sighing, Lissie pulled the hood of her jacket over the back of her silvery head, thrust her hands into her gloves and started out through the back door.

A particularly robust gust of wind nearly sent her sideways as she strode down the gravel drive, causing her to pull the strings beneath her chin, tightening the fit of the hood around her face. Her eyes watered against the brittle air as well as the declarations that had been lobbed against her. *"Always so damned coldly capable...never sympathetic...an impenetrable front of strength."* Had it all been a terrible mistake, she despaired, striding doggedly into the wind, to keep her own emotions bottled for the purpose of appearing strong in those long ago days if the result caused her children anguish? Did David feel the same way? Then, as troubling thoughts tend to do, they began to multiply, tripping over themselves: Had her determination to appear calmly in control inadvertently created behaviors in her children that would undermine their relationships as adults? Did Wes 'not understand' Leigh because she wasn't capable of articulating her emotions? Had David been unfeeling towards Denise? Surely not, she reflected, with a quick shake of her head, she had witnessed her son and his wife in far too many tender interactions for that to be true.

She passed Carol's house but her neighbor's newspaper remained in the driveway as she had wisely decided there was nothing pressing enough to read with temperatures hovering in the mid-twenties. She noticed that Carol's gentleman friend still discreetly parked his car behind the house. The heavily wooded sides of the road seemed to close in on her and she picked up her pace towards the bend in the distance. The demise of David's marriage had deeply saddened her. They had seemed ideally suited in every way, she remembered, frowning. What had gone so terribly wrong?

Coming now to the bend in the road, the tree line ended as the expanse of fields opened on either side, and had it not been overcast, the opening would have allowed a flood of morning light from the east. Lissie gazed over the fields and the blanketed horses who stood immobile, their sizable rumps turned against the keen wind that swept in from the north. She stopped walking and grasped the top rail of the fence with both hands as if to steady herself, taking in this view she had seen countless times but had yet to tire of. It was too hurtful just now to think of the acute distress for which her daughter held her responsible, as well as the stinging retorts she had received, so she decided to attempt to reach her again in a day or two. What needed to be resolved was monumental and she had no clear idea how to proceed. Turning back towards the road, Lissie raised her hand in an appreciative gesture to a car that slowed to pass her. The occupant, a young brunette woman, made her think of Denise. How grateful she was to have been so close to her...closer, she admitted with reluctance, than she was to Leigh. Denise, she knew, was the sort of woman others might find intimidating, but not to her.

Lissie stopped in her tracks as the first few pellets of sleet began to bounce over the asphalt surface of the road as well as off her shoulders. Despairingly isolated, she felt a wistful desire to telephone her former daughter-in-law because she knew Denise would offer straightforward advice devoid of melodrama. Not that she had ever divulged any sort of familial estrangement to her, but Lissie knew she could count on her to be both confidential and kind, yet impassively objective. Denise was, in fact, disconcertingly similar to herself, Lissie realized with a start, as an unsettling feeling began to prevail around her heart. The saying *Sons marry their mothers* reverberated through her brain. It dawned on her that in marrying Denise, David may have (subconsciously, consciously?) married someone like her very self. And what did that mean? That he had sought a life partner either unwilling or unable to be emotionally available for him?

Just sort of coolly indifferent to everything...wasn't that how Leigh had described Denise? *But is she*, Lissie brooded, *and am I?* She had once found it a source of pride that she had never been considered a 'drama queen,' that unattractive adjudication leveled against women who became overwrought with emotion in trying circumstances. Perhaps there should be no pride in it at all, she thought bitterly, her eyes brimming with tears that stung from the sleet. Perhaps she was simply incapable of being a fully feeling human being. This thought rapidly gained validity with the realization that she hadn't even an inkling of what the house meant to Leigh. How could she have been so blind, so tone deaf to her own daughter?

The sound of a car horn being tapped caused her to start and turning quickly around, saw that it was Peter, gesturing to her from the warm interior of his Suburban.

"For God's sake, get in!" he barked out the window. "You'll catch your death!"

Normally, Lissie would have laughed and waved him on, but she felt so heavy-hearted, she complied meekly and climbed in through the passenger door.

Peter reached over to turn up the heat a notch. "I had a feeling I'd find you somewhere out here," he said. "I swung by your house with the contracts for the listing. Only you would be crazy enough to be out walking in this weather."

Lissie ducked her head and said nothing.

"Hey," Peter said, shifting the vehicle into park. "Are you all right?"

Lissie fished a tissue out of her pocket and pressed it to her eyes.

"I've only seen you cry twice in my life and each time it's been in my car," Peter declared, then added with a kind smile, "I'm beginning to get a complex."

"I think I've made a discovery about myself which isn't especially pleasant," she gulped.

"How can I help?"

"Drive, just drive," Lissie said.

"Have you eaten?"

She shook her head.

"Well, that's part of the problem. Let's go to that breakfast place in Saluda." He reached over to pat her hand reassuringly. "Now, tell Uncle Peter all about it."

In the twenty minutes it took to wind round the back way to the mountain town, Lissie slowly spilled her heart as well as a few tears, felt foolish for doing so, and this constant battle for composure left her feeling wretched and defeated. Peter nosed the Suburban into a parking spot a few doors down from the restaurant. He killed the engine.

"You know what I think?" he asked, turning to face her.

Lissie shook her head.

"I think Leigh's being a pain in the ass," he said succinctly. "A major pain in the ass."

'She's devastated," Lissie replied. "And to hear how miserable she's been, Peter, that breaks my heart."

"Look, ever since she was a little kid, she's had a black cloud over her head," Peter reasoned. "This is nothing new."

Lissie put her face in her hands for a moment. "But what if I've been the cause of that?" She dropped her hands and looked steadily at her friend. What a bear of a man he was, she thought with gratitude, what an enormous comfort he could be.

"Why, because of the divorce?"

She nodded.

"Well, hell, kid, it's not as if you had an option, right?"

Lissie leaned back and stared out the windshield. It was beginning to grow cold inside the car.

"No," she agreed. "You're right. But Leigh was clearly a daddy's girl. She adored John and he was very, very, good with her. She had no idea why he retreated for days or weeks at a time. I couldn't think of anything else to say but that he was sick."

"Which was true," Peter confirmed.

"Which was true," Lissie echoed. "But Peter, when we separated it was as if a light was switched off in Leigh. She couldn't understand why her father never got in touch, never even phoned on her birthday. How do you explain that to a child when you can't explain it to yourself? She went from being a relatively quiet, easy child to becoming difficult, negative. And the truth is, I don't think she's ever forgiven me."

"Look, Lissie." Peter squirmed slightly in his seat to find a more comfortable position. "Do you know anyone who's had a perfect childhood? I sure as hell don't. And when we were kids, no one was talking about 'dysfunctional families,' right? I mean, I got the hell beat out of me by my old man, and I hated him for it, but I got over it, because I realized, later on, that he didn't know any better. None of us knew any better. Leigh's what, forty? Forty-one? She needs to get over it. Look at David; he seems completely unaffected by the divorce."

"I'm not sure if that's true, but David was a couple of years younger than Leigh when we separated," Lissie explained. "A toddler, really. He hadn't yet developed the same emotional involvement with his father as Leigh. And you know how it is for the older child when a new baby, comes along, getting all the attention...Leigh felt very territorial in regards to John, and I let her."

Peter unsnapped his seatbelt, disembarked from the vehicle and walked around to Lissie's side.

"Let's go in and get some grub," he suggested, opening the door. "Things always feel better after a full stomach. Especially when I tell you what the house has appraised for."

Lissie gave a tired smile and stepped out to the curb. Hands in her pockets, she turned slowly to face him.

"I appreciate everything you're doing, Peter, including all your help with the listing," she said, her eyes reflecting the dejection of her spirit. "But how can I put the house on the market, now, knowing what I know? Especially since I still can't answer Leigh's question. Peter, how can I blithely run along after my dream knowing that I'm destroying hers?"

Chapter 15

KIRSTEN CUT A SOLITARY figure in the back of the school bus, the last child to be dropped off. She sat hunched over her phone, reluctantly texting back and forth to her best friend, Sophie, before stowing the phone in her backpack and looking despairingly out the window. She hated being the last kid to be dropped off. She hated that she was forced to spend an hour on the bus to be delivered to a home she could drive to in less than twenty minutes if she had a car like most of her friends. And she particularly didn't like walking into a home that seemed to be transmitting conflict each day.

If that wasn't bad enough, Senior Prom was on the tip of everyone's tongue at school, the event being a scant five weeks away. It was the prevailing topic of conversation from Sophie, who had excitedly been texting that she had received her 'promposal' from Tyler. She was already looking at dresses. Kirsten found the images of these dresses being fired in rapid succession with the same question to be annoying: "What about this one?"

Kirsten stared out at the brown wintry landscape pouring before her, as bleak as her mood. No one had asked her to the prom. No one had last year, either, to the Junior Prom. Her school didn't have an especially large graduating class and whether true or not, she felt she was the only girl without a date.

"Don't worry, somebody'll ask you," Sophie had encouraged, generously confident in her own inclusion. "You're cute, Kirsten, just stop looking so grumpy all the time."

Kirsten caught her reflection in the streaked and spotted bus window. Maybe she did look grumpy all the time. But how else should she feel? Sophie had no idea what she'd been going through at home, especially when Kirsten couldn't explain it adequately herself. Instead, she could only share, "My mom's crazy. She's just freaking out all the time."

This had been slightly exaggerated. Leigh had been sent reeling since receiving the news that her childhood home was to be sold, but she hadn't been particularly vocal about it, except to her husband. And the result of those conversations left her despondent and increasingly critical to those around her. As was his nature, Wes had remained placid and patient, but now being the target of unfair indignation, coupled with his wife's near hysterical compulsion in regards to her mother's house, had pushed him past his limit.

"If we put our house on the market, even as a fixer-upper," Leigh had impatiently explained to Wes, for the third time that week. "Surely we would have enough equity in it to use as a down payment on Mother's. We've always paid our bills on time and you've got a good credit score."

Wes, keeping his back to his wife, had been pouring a cup of coffee the morning of what had escalated into an explosion. "Even if your mother knocked a hundred thousand off the price of her house, we couldn't afford it," he replied, drily. "It's what, four bedrooms? On seven acres? It'll cost a fortune."

"Then I'll get a job," Leigh maintained. "If that's what it takes, I'll get a job and make the mortgage payment, myself."

Wes placed his coffee cup on the counter. He leaned against it as he turned to face his wife.

"You're forgetting one thing," he said slowly. "I don't want to live there."

Leigh looked at her husband in horror.

"What do you mean you don't want to live there?"

"Exactly what I said," Wes replied, sitting down at the kitchen table. "I don't want to live there."

"How can you say that?" Leigh said. "You've always enjoyed going over there. You've always commented on what a beautiful, old place it is."

"No," Wes shook his head. "*You've* always enjoyed going there. Sure, I went along and kept my mouth shut for Kirsten's sake, as well as to get some peace and quiet, but have you any idea what it was like for me, every other Christmas, when it was our turn to spend it with my folks in Ohio? To listen to you moan all the way up on the drive, talking about how it didn't feel like Christmas at my parent's house? How you couldn't wait for next year, when everything would be the way it should, at your old house? How do you think that made me feel? And *seven* acres? It's all I can do to keep the half acre we have here mowed throughout the year. How the hell would I have time to keep up seven acres? And Kirsten will be leaving for college soon and that has to be paid for, in case you forgot. The last thing I want is to take on some big, drafty house that will be a nightmare to maintain, especially when I didn't want to in the first place. For God's sake, Leigh, you're so wrapped up in that damned house that you're not even considering how the rest of us feel."

Leigh, unable to digest the criticism, found herself lashing out in desperation. She remained standing, the table between them, leaning forward, hands clenched at her sides, as she cried. "But that house means *everything* to me! It's all I've ever wanted, why can't you understand that? God!" She flung her arms into the air and gestured at the kitchen as a whole. "Look at this room! Look at this house! The whole damned place is a depressing dump and I can't believe you won't even consider moving into a beautiful, historic home, especially when it means so much to me!"

Wes, in an extraordinary move that was quite out of character, had slammed his fist down with such force on the table that half of the coffee in his cup had leapt over the brim and splashed next to it in a brown puddle.

"Not *once* do you ask what *I* would want," he said, hoarsely. "In case you don't remember, I've done plenty for you. I worked extra hours so that you could stay home. And if this place is the dump you make it out to be, maybe if you had made half the effort as you claim you will now by getting a part-time job, we could have afforded the new kitchen and bathrooms you feel you *must* have. But, by God, I deserve some say in this, too." He rose and snatched his jacket from the back of the chair and his wallet from the countertop, before turning to finish. "After busting my hump for twenty years, my say is that I don't want to move into some huge house with seven acres that we can't afford and don't need." With that, he had banged out the door into the garage.

Open-mouthed, Leigh had watched her husband slam the door behind him. She put her hands to her face and began to cry. "But I need it!" she sobbed. "I need it!"

While Kirsten had not witnessed that particular scene, she had keenly felt the after effects as she returned home from school that day. The air in the house was fraught with tension and it was clear her parents were sleeping in separate bedrooms. When she did finally ask what was going on, Leigh, making little effort to be reassuring, had sighed, "Your father's being very difficult lately." And so it was into this household that Kirsten entered each afternoon, before disappearing into her bedroom to lie on her bed, staring at the ceiling, glumly chewing on one of a stash of candy bars she had begun to hoard in the drawer of her bedside table.

Kirsten was aware of other kids in her neighborhood whose parents had divorced and she idly wondered if her own parents were on the same path. Rolling over on her stomach, she began to smooth out the foiled wrapper that had contained her second chocolate bar. She folded it into a football, as she had seen the boy on whom she had a massive crush, Derek, do in math class before sending it with a flick from his index finger through the goalpost that another boy had created by touching his thumbs together, fingers stiffly raised. Derek had never given her a second look, nor had he spoken to her, and Kirsten subjected her heart to more misery doubting he ever would.

However, if her parents divorced, she decided with very little deliberation that she would live with her father. He had done all that was required of a dutiful parent: standing on the sidelines at soccer games, glancing over her homework, saving funds for college. Although he had never particularly gone out of his way to inquire what might be bothering her or attempt more than a passing comment to bolster her self-esteem, Kirsten felt that, if needed, she could actually talk to him without fearing the repercussions that tended to come from her mother.

A divorce would probably mean moving, she realized, looking around her bedroom and the purple walls she had painted herself, adorned with posters of Justin Bieber and Harry Styles. That wouldn't be so bad. Fathers seemed to move into apartments. Thinking of one complex not far from her school, that had both a pool and a clubhouse, was appealing. She allowed herself to fantasize about throwing a pool party when the weather grew warm and inviting Derek, who would see what he had been missing when she appeared in a bikini. She had a decent bust, she thought, propped on her elbows and glancing between them at her cleavage, but there was also no denying she was beginning to develop a swell in her hips and stomach as they strained against the waistline of her jeans. This realization added further despondency and she pushed the empty wrappers onto the floor, not bothering to put them in the trashcan in the corner.

"Kirsten!" her mother had called from downstairs. "Come put your laundry away."

Sighing, Kirsten sat up and traced the letter D with her big toe into the carpet beside her bed. In the next moment, she brushed the sole of her foot over it, as if wiping the image away. Rising, she opened her bedroom door and went downstairs.

Chapter 16

LEIGH HAD BEEN IN touch with her father twice in the past week, realizing as she dialed that he would not be as comforting as she might hope, but there was a balm in simply connecting that soothed her. It was normally Libbie, his latest live-in girlfriend, who picked up the landline phone as she did this day.

"Hi Libbie, it's Leigh," she began, "Can I speak to Dad?"

"Sure, Leigh." Then a hand went over the mouthpiece and Leigh could hear a few muffled tones, followed by her father asking more than once, "Who? Who is it?" and then, "Oh, Leigh." After a few moments, he had placed the receiver to his ear and offered, in his usual vague manner, a tepid greeting.

"Hello?"

"Hi Daddy," Leigh said with more cheerfulness than she felt.

"Leigh?" he replied.

"Yes," she said, speaking a little loudly. "Yes, it's Leigh. I was just calling to say hello."

"Oh, that's nice." As usual, there was nothing he would offer, no inquiries of his own.

"Are you doing all right?"

"Yes, I'm all right,"

Leigh exhaled slowly, then tested the waters.

"Daddy, I was wondering if I might come for a visit? It's been years. How would you feel about that?"

113

There was a silence that stretched to what felt to be minutes. Leigh felt her heart begin to sink.

"A visit?" he finally asked. "What, now?"

Leigh laughed. "No, not right now, Daddy. I'm on the other side of the country. But I thought I might fly to Los Angeles for maybe a long weekend. Would you like that?"

"She wants to come for a visit," her father was saying loudly to Libbie. He then returned to his daughter.

"Libbie says that would be all right," he said.

"That's nice of Libbie," Leigh replied. "But how do you feel about it?"

"I feel fine," he said. "I've had a cough, but I'm fine."

"All right, then I'll make the travel arrangements and tell Libbie I'll send her an email with the details," Leigh explained, knowing her father no longer used a computer. She said her goodbyes and hung up the phone, feeling a sense of trepidation. In her life, she'd rarely been so impulsive and now she began to wonder how she would tell Wes. Her wariness, however, gave way to defiance as she began to consider her actions just in light of what she felt to be her husband's betrayal. Her mind flashed back to the disastrous trip to Los Angeles she had taken with David all those years ago. She only hoped that this time her father would be pleased, or at least capable, of seeing her. She was more patient than her brother, she told herself. She would have no trouble waiting should he need to retreat for hours at a time. She could get to know Libbie better. Leigh assumed they were still residing in the small duplex in West Hollywood. Her mood lightened. The idea of traveling to California was daunting, but at least she had something to look forward to.

She felt slightly wicked in the days that followed, going secretly online to check out the price of airfares, outlandish for only a weekend, and began to wonder if it made more sense to stay for a week. There was, of course, Kirsten to think of, but she was nearly seventeen; surely she could fend for herself after school until Wes came home? It might even, she thought with some satisfaction, give

Kirsten a new appreciation for how much work Leigh did around the house when her daughter would be faced with doing her own cooking and cleaning. There was still Wes to tell, and as justified as she felt in her decision, there appeared a small knot in the pit of her stomach.

In the end, she hadn't had to say anything. On Monday, she had been unloading the dishwasher when her phone rang. Recognizing the Los Angeles area code, she supposed it to be Libbie and answered promptly.

"Hi, Leigh," Libbie began, "I don't want you to worry unnecessarily, but I've taken your father to the hospital this morning and thought you ought to know."

Leigh clenched the phone hard, nausea overtaking her. "What's wrong with him?" she asked, struggling to keep her voice calm.

"Well, he's had this cough for the last couple of weeks and it's like pulling teeth to get him to the doctor, but then this morning he really sounded as if he was struggling to breathe, and I put my foot down and told him if he didn't go to ER with me, I was going to call an ambulance, so he agreed. Turns out he's got pneumonia in his left lung."

"Oh, God," Leigh breathed.

"I know it sounds awful," Libbie tried to console her, "but rest assured the doctors are on top of it. He's at Cedars Sinai and that's an awfully good hospital."

"I'm coming out," Leigh declared. "I want to be there."

After she hung up she called Wes at his office and told him plainly of her plans and to her relief, he didn't attempt to dissuade her. He didn't even mention the cost. That was good of him, she admitted to herself as she went back to her laptop and booked a ticket. She found a flight that would depart at nine the following morning, connect through Atlanta, and get her into Los Angeles nearly five hours later. She realized, as she packed, that she wouldn't be needing her winter coat or gloves. It would be cool in Los Angeles, but not as frigid as it had been in the foothills of North

Carolina. She briefly wondered what was even in fashion, then sighed as she realized that, with her figure, comfort was always a priority over style and besides she'd be sitting in a hospital most of the time. She went to her trusted elastic-waisted khakis and a few lightweight sweaters. Suddenly, she stopped and straightened her back. David. She hadn't told David. Would he even care? She considered not telling him, then decided he had a right to know. Taking her phone from the nightstand, she called him. As she had expected, he hadn't been particularly concerned.

"Well, if you feel it's necessary to go, I think you should," he replied to her news.

"Yes, I feel it's necessary," she said, somewhat curtly, "when a parent is sick enough to be admitted to hospital. I'm supposing you aren't interested in coming?"

David had hesitated a moment before answering. "Leigh, it's not that I'm being hardhearted. I don't even know the man."

But Leigh wasn't angry with her brother. She was relieved to have her father to herself. "I get that," she said, her tone softening, "I really do. Don't worry. I'll go on my own and let you know."

"Thanks," David replied, gratitude evident in his voice. "Have a safe trip, OK?"

Lying in bed later that night in the guest room in which she now resided, Leigh found it impossible to sleep. She felt pulled in two completely different directions. On one hand, she was almost giddy with the anticipation of seeing her father, yet she worried for his health, both physically and emotionally. Surrendering to insomnia, she sat up in bed and began to read a bestseller until her eyes grew heavy. Before she knew it, her alarm clock woke her at six and she was up in a flash to get breakfast for her family before leaving for the airport.

"Will he even know who you are?" Kirsten asked, somewhat cruelly, as she dug her spoon into a bowl of cornflakes.

"Of course he will," Leigh found herself retorting, but there was no confidence in her inflection.

She hadn't flown in years and felt utterly overwhelmed changing planes in Atlanta. There were hordes of people, all seemingly arriving at the same time and flooding through the terminal. It was daunting enough to deal with the kiosks at ticketing in Asheville, and, giving up, she had stood in line for assistance from a reservationist who was especially helpful when Leigh had mentioned she was taking a last minute flight to visit her father in the hospital. But in Atlanta, she felt as if she was being swept along with the tide of bodies and was relieved to find her gate wasn't as far a journey as she had feared. Glad not to be going standby, she reluctantly felt relief to have a seat even though it was in the middle, and with the assistance of a truly bad film and an inane half-hour sitcom, Leigh made it to Los Angeles five hours later.

Libbie had insisted on picking her up and was waiting for her in baggage claim, a roundish, middle-aged woman with a kind, deeply tanned face and a mass of tightly permed red hair piled on top of her head.

"I've just come from sitting with him." She greeted Leigh with a warm hug. "He's a bit groggy, but hopefully the antibiotics will start kicking in."

"Can we go straight to see him?" Leigh asked.

"Of course."

They walked over to short-term parking, climbed into Libbie's Nissan and spent several minutes snaking through traffic as they worked their way along roads with exotic Spanish names such as La Tijera, before turning onto La Cienega, passing an ugly landscape of oil wells pumping up and down like prehistoric birds in dry, brown fields. Leigh was surprised how quickly they then arrived in West Hollywood, despite the traffic and countless red lights. Before long, they came to Beverly Boulevard and Libbie negotiated the turns that led them to the parking deck of the hospital.

"I'm so glad you came to get me," Leigh said with feeling. "I never would have found this in a million years." She glanced up at the intimidating towers and added, "I wouldn't even know how to get into this place!"

"It's pretty big," Libbie agreed.

They rode in silence up the elevator to ICU and Leigh began to feel her heart pound. The uneasy feeling of being in a hospital with its unwelcoming sterile environment coupled with the nervousness of seeing her father began to make her palms tacky. She felt a rivulet of perspiration travel downwards from beneath her right armpit. Stepping out of the elevator, Libbie pointed to the left and Leigh followed her, fascinated by how she held all that hair together with one banana clip. She reminded her of a poodle. Coming to a stop outside his room, Libbie informed her that the policy of ICU was only one visitor at a time, but she would go quickly in with her to make the introduction, if Leigh would like that. Leigh replied she'd like that very much.

Entering slowly through the doorway, Leigh stifled a gasp. She had remembered her father as robust, not only from her childhood, but from her last visit, albeit twenty-five years ago: he'd been broad-shouldered, still somewhat muscular in his frame. The man that lay in the bed before her, oxygen tube inserted into his nostrils, was frail and thin with sunken cheeks and looking a decade older than his seventy-three years. "John?" Libbie touched his shoulder gently. "Honey?"

He blinked his eyes and looked at her for a moment before closing them again.

"Sweetie? You have a visitor. Are you up for a visitor?"

He opened his eyes once again and held them steadily upon her.

"Your daughter, Leigh, is here. She flew all the way from North Carolina this morning to see you."

The old man cast his eyes about the room until they landed upon his daughter.

Leigh took a step forward and sank down on the bed beside him, touching his palm, careful not to disturb the IV inserted in the back of his hand. How yellow his hand looked. With dismay, she noticed he had large, purple blotches up both arms.

"Daddy?" she asked softly. "Daddy? It's Leigh."

He nodded, then closed his eyes and sank back into a deep sleep.

"The doctor said he's going to be out of it for a while," Libbie said. "He's very weak." She stood up. "I'd like to run to the grocery store if you don't mind sitting with him, Leigh. I've spent so much time here I haven't been able to do the things I need to do at home."

Leigh waved her away. "Absolutely, do what you have to do. I'm more than happy to stay with him as long as you like."

She was delighted to have this private time with her father, even if he had only given her the briefest nod of acknowledgment. Leigh would sit with him all night, if necessary. There was no place else she would rather be. She rose, careful not to disturb him, and pulled the pale blue leatherette recliner from the corner of the room next to his bed. She made herself comfortable and before long, had drifted to sleep, still holding his hand. She was only allowed a half hour before the rattle of a meals trolley from outside his room jolted her awake. When she sat up, she also took in a tall, slender man of Indian descent whom she supposed to be a doctor, as he entered the room.

"Hello," he said and smiled, extending his hand. "I'm Dr. Patel and I'm the hospitalist. Are you Mrs. Merriman?"

"No," she said, somewhat taken aback, then leaning forward from the chair to shake his hand, she added, "I'm Mrs. March. Leigh, his daughter."

Dr. Patel touched the screen of his handheld device, then looked at her over the top of his reading glasses. He didn't look unduly concerned.

"He's stable, which is good news," he said, and Leigh exhaled with relief.

"So is the pneumonia clearing up?" she asked.

"A little early to tell," he replied. "But we're aggressively treating him with antibiotics. I don't want to create unnecessary worry for you, but there are things which are best to be prepared for.

Sometimes, when an elderly patient is admitted, we do run into other problems that crop up because of the stress of the situation: a-fib, that sort of thing, but for now, he's doing as well as can be hoped. He's going to be quite weak for a while and, unfortunately, these sort of traumatic events do tend to advance the progression of the disease."

Confused, Leigh frowned and said, "Disease?"

"Mrs. March," he replied, "your father has dementia."

Chapter 17

ONLY ONE OF THE inhabitants in the cream-colored, Spanish-inspired two bedroom duplex, quite literally identical to half a million others in Los Angeles County, was sleeping. Leigh lay on her back, her eyes traveling around the stucco walls punctuated with two framed posters of a beach. Which one, she hadn't a clue, but the scene included glassy blue skies and water and a thread of sand with two colorful umbrellas. The other was similar but its point of focus was a lone palm tree. To her left, beside the bed, was a rattan table upon which perched a hand-painted Mexican jug, crammed with silk flowers. A matching chair stood pushed into a corner and beside it, against the wall, a flimsy wicker folding screen. The entire room felt cheap, Leigh thought, as did the rest of the flat, really. The furniture in the front room facing the street was shabby and even stained, more than likely from two geriatric cats that hadn't moved from their tightly curled sleeping positions on the sofa since she had arrived. Another siren, the third she had heard since midnight, screamed through the La Brea intersection nearby, and she marveled that anyone could possibly sleep in a city with so much racket and light. Despite closing the really quite charming wooden shutters on the inside of the windows, harsh blue-white light from both billboards and street lamps found its way through the slats.

"You didn't tell me Dad had dementia," Leigh had said, not accusingly, to Libbie, but flatly, with despair, when they had arrived back at the duplex earlier that evening.

Libbie had dropped her purse on a kitchen chair before sinking down on the sofa, and sighed.

"I think that's because I didn't want to tell myself," she admitted. "And I guess I hoped you might hear what I was hearing when you spoke to him on the phone."

Leigh shook her head slowly. "He's always sounded a little vague, but I hadn't noticed anything particularly different."

"That's what I've been telling myself these last few months. It started with him asking the same question, a couple of times in an hour, and at first I just thought he was being a typical man, you know," she said as she gave a little laugh, "not paying attention. I even started getting a little irritated with him. Then a couple of weeks ago, we were watching the news and about an hour later, I asked him what he'd thought about what the governor had just announced and he couldn't remember it." She looked sadly at Leigh. "I got so scared, Leigh, because I've been through this before, so I know better than to ignore the symptoms."

"With whom?"

"My father," Libbie replied. "And, if you can believe it, later on, my mother." She kicked off her shoes and propped her comically small feet, resplendent with crimson toenails, upon the coffee table and shoved her clasped hands between her thighs before finishing. "My father had Alzheimer's and I firmly believe the stress that my mother was under, caring for him all those years, not only brought on her heart attack, but later her senility. Leigh, I'm sixty-five years old and I don't think I can go through that again."

Leigh felt a sudden chill as if her heart stopped. "What are you saying? That you won't care for him?"

Libbie shook her head. "Not that I won't care for him, Leigh. I *can't* care for him, not when it becomes advanced. I love your father and I'll certainly take care of him for as long as possible, especially when he comes home from the hospital, but he's going to get worse from just having been there and I can't cope. I've lost ten years of my life caring for my parents, and for all I know, I'm going to end up with dementia, too. Life is precious, and it's short. I'd like to live a bit more of it before I can't. It's selfish, I know, but there it is."

Leigh had digested this for several minutes before replying.

"It's not selfish. I completely understand. I'm just at a loss as to what to do."

Libbie had risen from the sofa and reached over to give Leigh an enormous hug that contained more affection than she had felt for ages. She allowed herself to be gently rocked from side to side before Libbie pulled back, her eyes moist with tears, and placing Leigh's face in her hands, said, "Honey, between the both of us, we're going to figure this out, because we both love your father more than anything else in the world." Leigh sighed and rolled over on the sagging mattress of the double bed. She was profoundly grateful for this roly-poly redhead with her huge heart in her huge bosom and her affectionate manner. If only her own mother could be so demonstrative, she thought. She frowned, thinking of Lissie, and found it impossible to connect her vibrant, lively mother with the elderly, frail man currently struggling in ICU. Try as she might, and despite having seen family photos when they were both young, she couldn't imagine them married, couldn't imagine her mother sitting with him in the hospital. True, he was older, but only by three years, and her mother looked a decade younger than she was. In fact, she looked far younger than Libbie, whose face was etched with creases across her deeply tanned forehead and along both sides of her mouth. Perhaps Libbie's face told the tale of the decade of anxiety and grief she had experienced caring for her parents. Not that Lissie, Leigh admitted, rolling once again over on her back as the box springs groaned beneath, had had it easy either, but struggles are always less daunting, she reasoned, when one is young.

But what to do? What on earth to do? Leigh closed her eyes tightly as if to force herself to sleep and put a pillow over her head as yet another siren, either an ambulance or police car, came shrieking through the intersection. She had seen the price of gasoline in Los Angeles and while sitting with her father, had picked up a day-old newspaper from the little table on wheels next to his bed and idly perused it, finding herself astounded by the price of homes as well as rentals in the classifieds. She opened her eyes again and looked once more around the dismal guest room. Clearly neither her father nor Libbie had any sort of money between them. They probably used their collective social security checks just to cover the rent on this depressing flat. He'd be eligible for Medicaid, she mused, then felt a shudder of horror radiate through her chest. She had visited nursing homes with Medicaid patients: four to a room, vacant eyes unaware of their surroundings, parked in their wheelchairs in the corridors, the faint, prevailing odor of urine...Leigh burst into tears and muffled her sobs with the pillow as the cruelty of circumstances loomed in her heart. Would he even remember he had a daughter? After all these years of trying to reconnect with the beloved father that she had lost as a child, the realization that she was losing him again was too much to bear.

Chapter 18

LEARNING FROM KIRSTEN that Leigh had flown to California had been another dart of pain for Lissie. That her own daughter hadn't felt the inclination to include her in the worrying news created another layer of grief, and she had kept her voice deliberately even and calm as Kirsten mentioned that the grandfather she had never met was in hospital, the news being only a casual aside to explain why Kirsten was phoning her to ask how to tell when a cake was fully baked.

"I always stick a toothpick in them," Lissie had replied. "And when you pull it out, if it's clean and not gooey, you know the cake is baked through. What are you baking?"

"A cake for Dad," Kirsten said. "It's his birthday on Monday and Mom didn't even remember. Or care. Anyway, she's out in California."

Which was how Lissie learned the distressing details. She inquired about the welfare of all concerned, received very little information in return, and felt unspeakably low after hanging up the phone. As trying as it might have been over the years with her daughter, the ebb and flow of their relationship had never collapsed into estrangement. She sat down at the kitchen table and stared out the window over the sink to the bare orchard, the skeletal limbs against the grey sky. Closing her eyes, she whispered a heartfelt prayer that her former husband would survive, especially for Leigh's sake. She had never wished John ill will; she had never harbored resentment towards him. There were certainly times during their marriage when, between tearfully imploring him, she had turned brutally cold towards him. But she had tried to forgive herself for this as those displays of frustration were borne from the complete ignorance of his condition.

"For heaven's sake, take a shower!" she had cried, snatching the covers from his prone body, still in bed after three days. "The whole room smells. What is wrong with you, John? Why won't you speak to me?"

So many times, she thought miserably, so many times she had punished herself, believing she had done something to turn him silently away from her.

"I didn't know," she whispered aloud, dropping her head in her hands. "I had no idea."

She imagined Leigh, now sitting tearfully next to his bedside, consumed with grief and fear. She imagined her alone, in what could only be thought of as an enormous, impersonal, dangerous city, struggling to find her way around, knowing no one, and Lissie's heart ached for her. To lose her father, as fragile as she had been, especially in this way, would do her in. And on top of that, to lose the house...Lissie now forced herself to sit up and commit to the idea she had been carefully weighing. Leigh wouldn't lose the house, she decided firmly. She simply couldn't do that to her.

She rose and walked slowly to the living room and pulled open a small drawer in her antique leather-topped desk which held an array of note cards. Nora was a proudly proclaimed Luddite and refused to have a computer in her home, so Lissie knew she would have to write to her. She could certainly telephone, but she didn't trust her ability to control her voice at present, and she knew she would be able to express herself far easier with pen on paper. No matter which direction she went, Lissie thought resignedly, she was causing disappointment. Nora had been counting the days until her cousin had arrived. With the exception of Hugh in Sydney, Lissie was the only family she had left and it had brought such joy knowing her cousin would be residing in her village, offering both comfort and companionship as well as the sort of adventures no one else would dare attempt. *That's always been you, Felicity,* Nora had written in her small and neatly precise style. *I'd have never been brave enough to even consider a weekend in Paris on my own. You're going to bring such life to my years!*

Lissie chose the first note card, featuring a delicate watercolor of an English robin on the outside, and from its interior fell the tickets to the symphony she had tucked away for safe keeping. *I guess I'll be able to go, after all,* she thought, remembering the yoga classes as well, but neither revelation stirred any enthusiasm. She bit her lip for a moment before writing. What would she say? She hadn't thought that far ahead. She began to think of an alternative plan, something to offer her cousin as a consolation, but nothing satisfying came to mind. Without selling the house, her savings would probably allow her one trip a year to England, or perhaps every other year. If she stayed with Nora, there would be no hotel or rental car fees. However, as she would need to engage someone to watch her house and tend to the property while away, she wouldn't be able to visit for too long, but perhaps she could manage two weeks. It normally took her two or three days to completely recover from jet lag and that would cut into her holiday...growing even more depressed, she put down her pen and sighed. This wasn't how it was supposed to be, she thought. She had planned her dream with such detail it was crystal clear in her mind's eye: taking the long train ride to Plymouth and from there, a coach or even a taxi back to charming Padstow where she would stay the night. The following morning, she would pack a small picnic basket and make her way back to Trebarwith and when she arrived, she would spread out the blanket as she had nearly fifty years ago, and standing in the grass near the cliff's edge, her silvery hair blown back from her face, seeking Gull's Rock in the distance, she would crack open a bottle of champagne (or perhaps just a bottle of cider), and toast her mother's memory. She had pictured this scene so many times that it was as real as was the present moment in which she lived. Returning to England was so much more than a 'bucket list' item realized, she thought sorrowfully. It was meant to be the complete fulfillment of a life that had never been easy: a life often spent in solitude, struggling up and over each obstacle that had been placed in her path and coming full circle to this moment of not only a personal triumph, but of an unabashed communion with the spirit of her mother, taken far, far too young. Lissie had survived the very thing that had claimed her mother and she wanted—she needed— that sacred moment of ascendancy. She wanted to feel the sea air pass through her very fingers, holding her arms aloft and declaring with a heart bursting with gratitude, *"I am here. I am here in the memory of everything you held dear. And I'm all right."*

But as with everything else in her life, her plans were now turning out to be something different, something difficult. Despondently, she thought of her age and the handful of years she could only hope would provide her with good health. She was approaching the end of her life and from all accounts, she had left it too late. Perhaps, she considered wryly, her heart sinking further, dreams were marked with expiration dates and weren't meant for women whose next decade would be their eighth. How she would break it to Nora, she didn't know. She would just begin to write and, as always, tell the truth. She took a deep breath and spoke sternly aloud to herself, as if the tone itself would pluck her from her misery and spur her towards resolution. "Right, old girl, that's long enough for a pity party." She picked up her pen and began to write.

Chapter 19

HAVING ENDURED A frustrating week owing to an assistant he both hired and fired within three days who forgot to pack up all the equipment after a location shoot as well as dropping a lens and cracking it, David accepted Eli's invitation to join him for an evening at the pub, where he presumed he'd once again be picking up the tab.

"Ha!" said Eli, slapping down a twenty on the counter as his friend arrived. "I'll have you know that I have cold, hard cash today. I got a gig!"

"Wow," David, said, impressed. "Then I'll have an IPA."

Eli frowned. "Well, actually, I don't have enough to buy yours, too, but at least I can buy my own."

David pulled out his wallet and nodded to Stephanie. "I guess that's something. So, what's the gig?"

"Next Monday at The Riff," Eli replied, rubbing his hands together. "And you've got to come."

"I think I can make that."

"I just wish," Eli sighed, "that I had someone to take." He looked over at Stephanie, "Hey, are you working next Monday?"

Stephanie was pulling back an amber tap and pouring a Guinness.

"Nope."

"Wanna be my date for my gig?"

"Nope."

"Why?"

"Because you don't wash your hands after you pee."

Exasperated, Eli swiveled on his stool to face David. "Why won't she go out with me? You know what? I think she's gay. Hey, Stephanie," he called, purposely raising his voice so that most of the patrons could hear. "Are you gay?"

Stephanie slid the beer to a customer, flipped a curtain of dark blond hair over one shoulder, and turned to Eli. "If you're the one asking, then yeah. Yeah, I'm gay, Eli. Sheesh."

David laughed appreciatively into his beer. It was the first time, he realized, that he'd laughed all week.

"So, anyway," Eli continued, as if his self-esteem hadn't been thoroughly trounced in public. "I've got this gig and it's going to be great. You wanna know why?"

"Can't wait."

"Because the band is made up of four little pricks. Total attitude, lots of hair gel, doing mostly indie covers and a couple of original tunes. Like barely in their twenties. But one member is out, sick, and they've gotta play because it's an audition set for The Riff to see if they can get some work up here. So they asked around for someone who can step in and play rhythm guitar, and end up getting in touch with yours truly."

"So, you're slamming them instead of being grateful?" David asked. "This might explain the trajectory of your career."

"Hell, no, I'm not grateful," Eli spat, and then leaned in, conspiratorially. "You know what the lead singer says to me when he meets me and sees that I'm a balding, middle-aged, fat guy? He gets very condescending, even though I'm saving their ass, and says, 'just make sure you stay at the back of the stage, by the drummer.' Like I'm an embarrassment to them."

"You are an embarrassment," Stephanie observed, walking past him with a handful of dirty glasses.

"Why does she say those things to me?" Eli asked, following her departure with his eyes.

"Because you ask for it. You've got this weird, masochistic streak in you," David explained, then added with some confusion, "But I'm not following. Are you going to play with them or not?"

Eli nodded with slow satisfaction.

"Oh, I'm going to play, all right. That's why I want you and everybody I know to be there. And get this." He opened his wallet to show a few more twenties. "I even asked to get paid in advance, which really pissed him off, but I told him, hey, I'm in demand, and either you pay now, or find somebody else."

"And are you in demand?" David asked hopefully, having drained his beer.

"Oh, hell, no," Eli replied. "But at least now I can cover rent this month."

They watched a knot of college kids come in. Eli sighed and said dolefully, "I'm beginning to feel too old to hang out here, anymore. Next thing I know, they'll start calling me Gramps."

"You're as young as you feel," David replied. "That's what my mother says, anyway."

"Hey," Eli asked, with genuine concern. "How's she doing these days, your mom? I always liked her. How was the party?"

"It was good," David said slowly, as he debated whether or not to give further details. Finally, he shrugged and added casually, "Denise came."

Eli's eyes, a bit bloodshot, widened considerably. "Did she? How'd that go?"

"It went fine," David replied. He raised his hand to get Stephanie's attention. "It was good to see her."

"I don't know how you do it," Eli said, shaking his head. "Staying on such good terms, I mean. None of my ex-girlfriends will even talk to me."

"They didn't talk to you when you were going out," Stephanie remarked, setting down a couple more bottles.

131

"Why are you so mean to me all the time?" Eli wanted to know, beginning to sound serious. "And why do you have that purple crap dyed into your hair?"

Stephanie leaned back against the cash register and crossed her arms. "You know, I was actually going to give you an honest answer, but then you slammed me, so let's just say you're an easy target."

"Well, I think you just hate men."

"Oh, no," said David, in a low voice, as he waited for the wrath about to fall upon his friend.

Without missing a beat, Stephanie countered. "I only hate men named Eli. I have a kid, so I can't hate men that much."

"Yeah, well," said Eli, waving his hand dismissively, "you don't need a man for that, these days, you know. Just a turkey baster."

"Oh, no..." David repeated, grimacing.

"Which would be more satisfying than you." Stephanie shot back.

"So, you won't go out with me?" Eli incredibly tried again.

"That would be a no."

With a curl of his lip, as if testing her, he asked, "Huh. Would you go out with David?"

She didn't hesitate. "Sure." She looked candidly at David. "Want to go Monday?"

Unprepared, David put down his beer and cleared his throat. "Uh, OK. Sure."

And to his complete surprise, he realized he had a date.

Chapter 20

LISSIE HAD LEARNED EARLIER in life that the best way to work through disappointments or even depression was to follow her late mother's advice: *"Think of others. Bring joy to someone else and you will find yourself feeling joy as well."* Admittedly, these days it was difficult to imagine feeling lightness in her heart, so heavy with despair. However, she knew from experience that simply making herself available to others did indeed bring a sense of peace. With this in mind, she telephoned her granddaughter Sunday evening to see if she would like her help to arrange a birthday dinner for her father.

"That's a nice offer, Nan, but whenever Mom doesn't cook, honestly, his favorite thing in the world is pizza, so I thought I'd just order one for us. If you'd like to come and join us, that'd be great."

Touched, Lissie said that she'd love to and if Wes would like beer or wine, she'd be happy to bring it.

"Oh," Kirsten said, lowering her voice in case her father should overhear. "I have another idea, if you could help? I baked him a cake and kept it hidden in the fridge, but I made some cupcakes, too, and I thought it would be nice to surprise him at his work with them. He told Mom he's been working through lunch, lately, and it might make a nice treat."

"Kirsten, that is such a thoughtful thing to do," Lissie replied. "How can I help?"

Kirsten lowered her voice to a whisper. "If you could take me to his office tomorrow morning before school, I could give them to him as a surprise."

"But won't that make you late for school?"

"A little," Kirsten admitted. "But I feel pretty bad for him with Mom not even remembering his birthday. I just wanted to do something a little more special than having pizza when he gets home."

Lissie smiled into the receiver. "I think it's all a lovely idea and I'll be happy to help."

Between them, they conspired for Lissie to stealthily pick up her granddaughter after Kirsten had left the house in the pretense of walking to the top of the drive to await the school bus. From there, it would be a forty-five minute wait until her father arrived at the office, twenty minutes away. Hanging up the phone, Lissie felt warmed by the inclusion. It had been ages, she thought, since they had done anything together, just the two of them. Not since childhood had Kirsten sought out the companionship of her grandmother, particularly when Lissie, who didn't believe in ignoring bad behavior, didn't hesitate to gently reprimand her. Now approaching seventeen, she was far more inclined to seek out friends her own age, which was only normal. The flicker of an idea began to ignite in the back of Lissie's brain. Would it do that much harm if she treated Kirsten to a lovely self-indulgent breakfast in town afterwards before driving her back to school? She smiled at the thought of sausages and pancakes with lashings of syrup and the two of them sharing conversation as well as a meal. There had certainly been more than a little turmoil in both households, she supposed, and Kirsten might be grateful for a little pampering.

The following morning Lissie pulled her car out of the driveway, two tall travel mugs of hot tea with lids firmly in place rooted in both cup holders. It would be a long wait in the parking lot of Wes's office and on this blustery winter morning, hot peppermint tea would be a nice way to remain warm. She made two turns in six miles before she reached her daughter's street. Winding round the first curve, she saw Kirsten zipped snugly into a puffer coat, leaving her post near the mailbox and walking hurriedly towards her carrying a small plastic container. Her cheeks were pink and, most refreshingly, she was wearing a smile as she flung open the passenger door and scrambled in.

"Hi, Nan," she said a little breathlessly, securing both her seatbelt and the container of cupcakes in her lap. "I don't think he suspected a thing. He was still dressing when I left."

"Excellent," Lissie said with a grin. "I feel like we're on a spy mission!"

"Yeah." Kirsten nodded enthusiastically. "He doesn't have a clue."

Cleverly, Lissie put the car into reverse so as not to pass the house and take the chance of being seen, but instead backed into a neighbor's drive to turn around. As she drove back to the intersection, before turning onto the main road that would take them into town, she looked at her granddaughter with mischief twinkling in her eyes and said, "Kirsten, what is your first class this morning?"

"English."

"And how are your grades in English?"

"Good. It's easy. Why?"

Lissie declared her breakfast scheme and Kirsten's face lit with happy anticipation. "That would be great, Nan. I didn't get a chance to eat anything this morning and I'm starving!"

They drove in companionable silence until they arrived at the offices of Benson and Company, CPA.

Lissie put on her blinker to turn into the parking lot, but Kirsten had another idea.

"Nan," she said, laying her hand on her grandmother's arm. "He'll recognize your car if we park there. Can you parallel park? We can park on the street, behind that truck, and watch from there."

"I can certainly give it a try," agreed Lissie and tucked into the space on her second attempt. Turning off the engine, Lissie looked at her watch and asked, "What time does he usually arrive?"

"The office opens at nine, but he likes to get here earlier, especially with April being almost a month away. He'll probably come along in about half an hour." She placed her container on top of the dashboard and picked up a mug of tea, warming her hands.

"What kind of cupcakes did you bake?" Lissie asked.

"Carrot cake," Kirsten replied with satisfaction. "His favorite. I even made the butter cream icing instead of getting the ready-made kind."

"That's always the best." Lissie smiled, and asked which ingredients she had used.

Far earlier than either expected, Wes's Taurus was seen slowly approaching the office and Kirsten sat up with a start. "He's really early," she said.

From their vantage point they watched him pull in and park at the back of the lot, well away from the building.

"I sort of want to wait until everyone else gets there so it's a bigger surprise," said Kirsten, looking at Lissie. "Do you mind if we wait a bit longer?"

"Not at all."

They had expected Wes to get out of his car and use his set of keys to enter the building. He didn't. He remained inside.

"Wonder what he's waiting for?" Kirsten mused.

Before long another car, a cranberry colored SUV, turned into the lot and pulled alongside the Taurus. Open-mouthed, Kirsten watched while her father stepped out of his car and into the passenger side of the SUV.

"What's he doing?" she asked, a tinge of annoyance evident in her voice.

Lissie frowned with concern. "Darling, I don't know."

Her heart beginning to pound, Kirsten's eyes followed the car as it passed directly in front of them and stopped at a red light. In horror, she watched as the driver, a woman with dark curly hair and sunglasses, leaned in and kissed her father.

"Oh, my God," she breathed. "Oh, my God. Nan, he's having an affair!"

Suddenly, the intimacy of their environment, their tickled anticipation of a shared plan, shattered before their very eyes, and it felt to Lissie as if someone had thrown a bucket of ice water over her, she was shaking so. She grabbed her granddaughter's hand.

"We don't know that," she said, and fighting to keep her voice steady, repeated, "We don't know that."

Kirsten snapped her head around and, having lost all control, shrieked, "Of *course* we do! We both saw him, they were *kissing* and drove off in her car! Don't talk to me like I'm a baby, I know what I *saw*!"

"Darling," Lissie began with no idea of what to say next.

Kirsten snatched her hand away. Grabbing the container of cupcakes, she flung open the door.

"Kirsten?" Lissie asked with alarm. "What are you doing? Kirsten?"

Ignoring her, the girl climbed out of the car and hesitating only to look both ways, jogged across the street towards the parking lot. Terrified, Lissie opened her own door and stood trembling, watching her over the roof of her car. She tried calling after her to come back and found her throat so constricted she could barely utter a sound.

Having made it safely to the other side, Kirsten strode towards the back of the lot and her father's car. Once next to it she whirled around, and yelled to Lissie, "I want to give him his cupcakes!" and the brief moment of relief that Lissie felt was quickly replaced with incredulousness as she watched Kirsten open the container and, one by one, smear the frosting of each cupcake across, first, the windshield, then each window of the car before stuffing the last one into the tail pipe. She threw the container on the ground and ran back to her grandmother, sobbing hysterically.

"Oh, Kirsten!" Lissie cried, her own eyes filled with tears as she took Kirsten into her arms. "Oh, darling!"

Chapter 21

EVERY GRAVE CHALLENGE THAT Lissie had squarely faced and surmounted in her life still left her woefully unprepared for what was before her as she sat with her granddaughter in the chilled interior of her Volvo that Monday morning. She switched on the ignition in order to warm them both and slowly shook her head in disbelief. What on earth was she going to do? It was impossible for Kirsten to be taken to school in this state—she was inconsolable. And because Lissie herself was still in a state of shock, she was at a complete loss of what she could offer. She gave in to the moment and continued to hold her granddaughter while she wept.

It was Kirsten who finally pulled back, giving Lissie an opportunity to do something by opening her purse and pulling out a packet of tissues.

"Every grandmother has a limitless supply of these, you know," she said with a jerky smile.

Kirsten didn't reply as she blew her nose repeatedly. To Lissie's horror, she watched her granddaughter pull out her phone and begin typing.

"Kirsten, darling, what are you doing?"

"I'm texting Sophie," she muttered, not looking up.

"About what just happened?" Lissie asked, alarmed.

Kirsten nodded.

Instinctively, Lissie snatched the phone away, imploring, "No, no, Kirsten, please don't do that!"

"Nan," she cried, "what are you doing?"

"Kirsten, if you send that, it's out in the world. Everyone could find out. This is a private family matter."

"Why are you protecting him?" her granddaughter raged. "Everyone should know what he's doing!"

Lissie put her hand to her mouth, reeling between two generations as she realized what she had suggested was considered archaic in this new world where emotions and events were vented publicly for the world to see.

"I'm not protecting him," she said, in desperation. "I'm protecting your mother. Oh, Kirsten, imagine how humiliating it would be for your mother!"

Kirsten froze. She was torn between the compulsion to share her anger online and an allegiance, as tenuous as it felt these last several weeks, with her mother.

"And as convincing as it might have looked, we still don't know the facts," Lissie added.

"OK," Kirsten said limply, resigned to her choice. "I won't. What should we do?"

"What do you want to do?" Lissie asked. She had no idea of her own. "Shall I take you back home?"

"Home?" Kirsten's eyes widened with alarm. "I'm not going back home! I'm never going back home." She looked at her grandmother with desperation. "I want to go back to your house."

Lissie nodded and carefully pulled into the street, driving south. Every possible grave scenario whirled through her brain. When they returned to her house, eager to find something to do with her hands, she seated her granddaughter down at the kitchen table and began to heat a small pot of milk on the stove.

"I think hot chocolate, don't you?" she said, forcing a lightness into her voice. "Hot chocolate makes everything better. And how about some pancakes and eggs?"

Kirsten nodded forlornly, still zipped in her jacket, hands in her pockets.

Lissie pulled a carton of eggs from the fridge, her hands still trembling. What was she going to do? It would be a matter of minutes, she knew, before the school phoned Wes, or, dear God, probably Leigh, to report Kirsten's absence. She glanced at the clock on the back of the stove. California was three hours behind and the thought of her daughter being awakened by such a call was unthinkable. She was making a dangerous decision, Lissie knew, walking quickly to her desk to find her phonebook and call the school, but she could only believe that keeping this from Leigh was for the good of all concerned, at least for now. And she would get in touch with Wes later.

It wasn't long before breakfast had been cooked and Lissie placed a rather full plate in front of her granddaughter.

"I'm not really hungry anymore," Kirsten said miserably.

Lissie paused to squeeze her shoulders and said, "Me neither, but we do need to eat and it will help us figure things out." She returned to the counter to take her own plate to the table.

They ate slowly in silence for several minutes.

"I just can't believe he did that," Kirsten said, laying down her fork, tears welling once more in her eyes. "Why would he do that?"

Copying her granddaughter, Lissie also put down her fork and said, "You know what? I wish Denise was here."

Kirsten frowned. "Denise? Why?"

"Because," Lissie began, carefully, "Denise is an attorney and she would say when someone is accused of something, it doesn't matter how we feel, what emotions we feel, what matters is the truth. The facts."

Kirsten looked at her. "The fact," she said with scorn, "is that I saw him kiss whoever that woman was."

Lissie gave a brief nod, but countered, "What we actually saw was that woman kiss *him*. Maybe he didn't want to be kissed. Maybe it was just a friendly kiss. Maybe, Kirsten, it was even his sister."

Kirsten shook her head with a snort. "Nan, both his sisters live in Ohio. They never come down here. That so wasn't his sister."

140

Lissie fanned out her fingers and looked at them. "All right, point taken. But it could have been a friend. Nearly everyone has friends of the opposite sex."

"But they don't kiss each other."

"I don't know about that," Lissie replied. "Look at my old friend, Peter. He's married, but we're still very good friends and when we see each other, we always kiss hello and goodbye."

"On the mouth? At a red light?" Kirsten wanted to know.

Lissie shook her head, admitting, "No, not on the mouth. On the cheek."

"And it was a long kiss, Nan," Kirsten pointed out, drawing on memory. "It wasn't some little peck on the cheek. C'mon, the whole thing is so obvious—parking his car at the back of the lot, getting into her car, leaving together. Oh, God." She stopped, her expression changing to disgust. "Do you think they were going to a *hotel?*"

Feeling it was a distinct possibility, Lissie nevertheless swatted the suggestion away on pretense of it being ludicrous. "Oh, certainly not. Absolutely not," she retorted, then made another weak attempt at an explanation. "You know, darling, your mother has been going through such a worrying time with your grandfather, maybe, just maybe, your father was going with a friend to buy her a gift for when she returns."

Kirsten sat back in her chair and laughed. "Oh, come on, Nan, even you don't believe that one. Besides, they're barely even speaking at home."

"Oh, dear," Lissie murmured.

Kirsten finally unzipped her jacket and hung it on the back of her chair. "They're not even sleeping in the same bedroom, anymore."

"I don't know if you should be telling me this," Lissie said, her heart breaking anew.

"Who else can I tell?" Kirsten looked at her. "You're the only one I can tell."

Lissie reached across the table and grasped her granddaughter's hand. "I promise you I won't tell a soul. Whatever is said won't go past this kitchen."

Kirsten nodded glumly. "Nan, it's been so awful at my house, for*ever*," she said with feeling. "Dad's always been pretty quiet, but now he just stays in the back of the house, or the guest room, working, and only comes out to eat or watch TV. And Mom," she continued irritably, "is just being a bitch, Nan—sorry for using that word."

"It's all right," Lissie remarked. "But maybe try and find a better word to describe her behavior."

"She's just been horrible," Kirsten exhaled with exasperation. "She nags at Dad, she nags at me, and when she's not nagging at us, she's complaining about everything: the house, the yard." She hesitated, then looked apologetically at her grandmother before finishing. "And you."

Lissie folded her hands together on the table and replied with sadness. "I'm not too surprised by that."

"She keeps going on and on about this house," Kirsten explained, her eyes sweeping around the room as if taking it in for the first time. "She's mad that you want to sell it. She thinks you should stay here forever and then she and Uncle David would inherit it."

"But even if I didn't sell it now, I would have to eventually," Lissie explained. "I won't be able to manage it in a few years. It's all I can do to keep up with it, now."

"I know that, and you know that, and Dad knows that," Kirsten replied. "But Mom won't let it go. And Dad finally laid down the law and said it's not going to happen, and now she won't even speak to him. If I ask her anything, she bites my head off, and—" She stopped suddenly, as if struck by a realization and looked frankly at her grandmother. "You know what, Nan? If Dad *is* having an affair, I don't blame him. I really don't."

"Oh, dear," Lissie sighed, unable to contribute anything else. Finally, she rose and said, "Darling, I think I'm going to take a nice hot bath. If you'd like to read or watch television, please feel free. We'll talk more about this a little later. I just need to think some things through."

She picked up her handbag and trudged up the stairs. Once in her bedroom, she closed the door, sat on her bed, and opened her handbag to retrieve her phone. She called her son-in-law.

"Wes," she began, "I hope you have a few minutes because we need to talk. It's important." On the other end, the stark request was received with tentative agreement. "I have made it a point never to intrude in my children's marriages," she continued, firmly, "but you need to know something. This morning I drove Kirsten to your office where she had planned to surprise you with cupcakes she had baked for your birthday. And while we waited for you, we saw—well, I think if you've looked at your car, you are probably aware of what we saw. Now, I don't know what's going on with you and that woman and it's none of my business, but I have Kirsten here at my house and she is obviously very upset and refuses to come home. She can stay here as long as she likes, but this needs to be sorted out, Wes, and I'll leave it to you to tell Leigh."

On the other end, at his desk, Wes put down his phone silently, grateful to be alone in his office. The state of his car had shocked him and he had put it down to vandals. Then he remembered putting his coffee mug into the dishwasher earlier in the morning and seeing a dirty muffin tin, wedged into the back. It all began to make sense. Desperately, his mind began to race. He clasped his hands together into a fist and pressed it to his mouth, leaning on his elbows.

"Oh, my God," he murmured. "Oh, my God."

Chapter 22

LEIGH ENDED HER CALL to Wes with relief. He hadn't batted an eye when she telephoned to say she needed to stay at least another day before flying home. He'd been particularly supportive, which pleased her, and filled with the relief that her father was steadily improving, she was kinder to her husband than she had been in some time. She had had a positive if quick consultation with her father's doctor, and after a discussion with Libbie, she was trying to wrangle a legal appointment so as to be granted power of attorney.

"It's a good idea, Leigh," Libbie had agreed. "This way you're both protected. It's obvious to me you have his best interest at heart. I'm supposing you haven't got siblings that would object?"

Leigh thought fleetingly of David. "No, just a brother and he's pretty much washed his hands of Dad."

"That's too bad," Libbie said, sympathetically.

It had been both comforting and revealing to spend the extra time with Libbie. Despite the scruffiness of their surroundings, Leigh found she was beginning to grow fond of the duplex with its one car garage, the pull-down door emblazoned with a spray of graffiti. She felt comforted sitting in her father's favorite chair in the front room, its arched window facing the street and partially obscured by tendrils of purple bougainvillea. Outside, it was crisp in the evenings but warm enough for short sleeves during the day. They had gone for a walk down the leafy street, and Leigh was startled that when they encountered the next intersection, Beverly Boulevard, there were a number of restaurants from which to choose as well as a tire store and a retirement home.

"You'd never think all of this was just a few hundred yards away," she marveled.

"It's wonderful, isn't it?" Libbie enthused, her head not quite reaching Leigh's shoulder despite the mound of hair twisted up to spill over her crown. "You can see why your father gave up his car years ago. We can walk to everything. Even the old folks' home!"

Leigh turned to her with apprehension in her face. "Oh, Libbie," she began, "I just can't let him end up in a nursing home. What am I going to do?"

"Leigh, honey," she said, placing her arm around her waist. "We've got a lot of time. Before he went into the hospital, we were actually beginning to look at places to move."

"Why would you want to move?" Leigh asked, baffled.

"Oh," Libbie said with a wave of her hand, "our new landlord is a developer and bought the place last year to tear down and build a big new home on the lot—this happens all the time in Los Angeles, but John asked him if he'd be willing to let us stay for a few months to give us time to look around. Turns out the guy is having a little problem with the bank, so he gave us a full year before we had to move out."

"So Dad's been clearheaded enough to deal with that?" Leigh asked hopefully.

"Oh, yes," Libbie replied with a smile. "John's just a bit forgetful right now and so far he's been very compliant. Oh, he gets a little frustrated now and again, but I think he's going to remain the same gentle personality he's always been, which is a blessing. My own father became very combative and it was a nightmare." She beckoned Leigh to follow her as they negotiated the crosswalk and Leigh was astounded that the moment they stepped off the curb, every car on the intensely busy street came to an immediate standstill to allow them safe passage.

"This would never happen in North Carolina!" Leigh exclaimed. Not truly trusting her own power as a pedestrian, she continued to look both left and right as she hurried after Libbie.

Their destination was a local coffee shop popular with musicians who had stayed up all night, dozing into their coffee, and a young group of the avant-garde with a smattering of hipsters self-consciously dressed in a way that looked, while carefully considered, as if there had been no thought to it at all. In the back, one or two hopeful actors were hunkered over a script with whatever breakfast they could afford.

"What a place," Leigh declared upon entering. She felt completely out of her element as well as suddenly frumpy and aged.

"Welcome to West Hollywood!" Libbie laughed and slipped into a booth, her bosom resting on the top of the table. "I've lived here nearly my whole life, so it all feels very normal to me." Her eyes took in the occupants. "Aren't they great?" she whispered. "I love being around all these young people. They're so brave, following their dreams, and taking a chance in this big ol' town. I just love their energy."

Leigh remained silent and followed Libbie's gaze. No, she thought, she wouldn't have attached 'great' or 'brave' to any of them. And she certainly wouldn't allow Kirsten to wear what some of the girls were wearing, or frankly *not* wearing. She had been horrified enough when she had first spotted Kirsten wearing black nail polish. She glanced back at Libbie with her crimson nails and nearly burgundy frizzy hair and for the life of her could not imagine this woman with her father. Is this what he found attractive?

"Libbie," she began, after they had ordered their omelets and coffees, "how did you meet Dad?"

Libbie leaned forward and proclaimed, "Honey, I was his housekeeper."

Leigh's eyes popped open, shocked. "His housekeeper?"

"Now, this was several years ago. I had divorced husband number two and was doing whatever it took to pay the bills. I was waitressing at night and during the days, I was cleaning houses. And let me tell you, that was good money. I had a system. I could scrub down a place the size of your Dad's in under a couple of hours: bathroom, kitchen, dust, vacuum, and I charged fifty bucks, which wasn't half bad for two hours' work." She looked up to thank the waitress—adorned with four silver hoops pierced into her eyebrow—for delivering the coffee, and Leigh watched in amazement as she stirred in three packets of sweetener. "Hot and sweet, just like me," she giggled, catching Leigh's eye. She went on with her story. "Your father would always stay while I cleaned. Most folks would go out, because they knew me well enough to trust me to lock up when I left, but John would hang around, and at first I thought maybe he didn't trust me, but after a while I could tell he sorta liked the company, you know? Like he was lonely."

That last remark filled Leigh with sadness. She could imagine her father, isolated and alone in the dank little flat.

"So, we get to talking—well mostly me talking, but he was really kind and interested in my life," Libbie sat back in the booth, her eyes tracing upon the memory from another time. "In fact, he seemed to be the only person interested in my life, and trust me, honey, the *last* thing I was looking for was another relationship. I'd pretty much had it with men at that point."

"Maybe he felt you both had something in common?" Leigh suggested.

"Ha!" Libbie laughed, slapping the tabletop with her plump brown hand. It was impossible not to notice the large diamond flashing on her third finger. "We had nothing in common, outside of both being divorced. Your dad was educated, an architect. I had been a backup singer with a few bands in the sixties and, don't be shocked, a bit of a groupie. I think he was fascinated by that."

Leigh was glad the omelets had arrived so that she could avert her eyes. She picked up her fork and speared a small cluster of grapes at the edge of the plate. It was interesting to her that whatever she ordered in California always came with lovely fresh fruit on the side, unlike the obligatory twist of a tired orange slice resting on a piece of wilted lettuce back home. She tried to conceal her shock as she glanced back at Libbie, trying to imagine this rather cartoon image before her as a desirable young woman. And had Libbie seduced her father?

"Now, don't be thinking I was some kind of slut," Libbie said, reading Leigh's thoughts and making no effort to lower her voice. "It was a special time, then. It wasn't about sex, you know, although that was wonderful," her eyes began to twinkle. "It was about being around and absorbing all that creative energy and talent, being a part of that whole scene. The entire world was being shaken up and I was smack dab in the middle, loving every minute of it." She put down her fork and leaned over the table, her knitted top, already strained by her ample bosom, now in danger of being stained by the food remaining on her plate. "Honey," she whispered, "for a time, I used to hang out with *Jim Morrison*. Can you believe that? And he was beautiful. *Beautiful*. The most beautiful man I have ever seen. He used to brush my hair and tell me that I had hands like little white doves."

Looking quickly at those same brown freckled hands, Leigh began to regard Libbie with unease, wondering if the comfort shared between them had been nothing more than a ruse, and that the woman before her was possibly a pathological liar. She'd heard about Hollywood being filled with misfits, unable to release dreams of stardom and believing their own fantasies. She squirmed a little in her seat as she took another mouthful of coffee.

"Honey, your face!" cried Libbie, bursting into laughter. Sobering, she reached across the table and patted Leigh's hand companionably. "You were looking at me like I was crazy, and yes, I have certainly been a little crazy in my life, but Leigh, you need to know that I love your father very much and I think he might love me. He's certainly been very good to me." She noted Leigh glancing once again at the enormous ring on her finger and held it up, letting it the catch the light and sparkle impressively. "It's beautiful, isn't it? But don't worry, we're not married. We're not even engaged. Your father bought this for me one Valentine's Day years ago, and that was funny, because it was the first time he'd ever bought me anything for Valentine's. He said it was a sort of thank you gift for saving him." She cocked her head and stared at the ring for another few moments before adding poignantly, "but he didn't realize he'd saved me, too." She looked at Leigh, her small brown eyes like raisins blinking back tears.

Leigh felt both relief and disconcertion. Her faith in Libbie restored, her attention was drawn back to the ring and she wondered how on earth her father could afford such a thing, unless of course it was a fake. Then her mind returned to the question she had been desperate yet frightened to ask since arriving.

"Libbie, did Dad ever talk about me?"

Libbie looked at her frankly. "No, honey, he didn't." Upon seeing Leigh's face fall, she added quickly, "but then, he never talked about anything from his past. I didn't even know he had been an architect until a couple of years later. When I had asked him early on what he did for a living before he retired, he'd say, 'Oh, this and that.' So I figured he'd been like me, you know, working different jobs, no real career. It wasn't until we were walking in Beverly Hills one day that he pointed out the city hall and starts telling me it was a beautiful example of Spanish Revival from the early thirties and who designed it—I can't remember their names now, but I stopped and turned to him and said, 'How do you know all about that?' And he said he had been an architect! Had designed a couple of governmental buildings in Garden Grove and even a Montessori school in San Francisco. He'd done pretty well for himself. You could have knocked me over with a feather, I was so surprised. But that was then, and I think as the years went on, he just sort of lost interest or was burned out, because when I met him, he'd been retired for years. And he didn't seem to care much about anything."

"But he never talked about his family?" This had been a blow.

"Not on his own. I had to drag it out of him one day, when I asked if he'd ever been married or had kids. He said he'd been married briefly when he was young, but it was pretty clear he didn't want to talk about it, so I left it alone."

Leigh nodded, trying to hide her disappointment. "Maybe he was embarrassed. Or maybe he felt that, once he'd moved across the country to California, he wanted to start over."

"Maybe," Libbie replied. "And I didn't want to push him, so I just took it all at face value, although I used to kid him that for all I knew he was in the witness relocation program. But in the end," she sighed, expanding her bosom to its maximum, "we look after each other. He makes sure I have a roof over my head, food to eat, and is so kind to me, while I make his favorite meals and make sure he takes his meds one of which is for depression." She eyed Leigh closely. "Did you know about that?"

Leigh felt a little lurch in her stomach. "Yes," she said. "It's why my mother claimed she divorced him."

"Were they very young?" Libbie wanted to know.

"Not very," Leigh replied. "I mean, not kids. They were in their thirties."

Libbie sucked her back tooth and was silent for a moment.

"What kind of woman is your mother?" she asked at last.

Leigh leaned back and contemplated the ceiling. The restaurant had embraced an urban industrial feel by exposing stark metal pipes that ran from end to end. She sighed and repeated the question, as if rhetorically. "What kind of woman is my mother? Well, right now, we're not on the best of terms because she's made some decisions that seem pretty selfish to me, but it's been said she could have been one of those pioneer women, you know? Savvy, self-sufficient, doesn't suffer fools..."

"That's a shame," Libbie remarked, and then surprised Leigh by adding, "because that's exactly the kind of woman I think your father needed."

Leigh gave a little snort. "Well, she didn't seem to care much about that. She left him."

"You know, this is all beginning to make sense," Libbie said slowly, a revelation dawning. "Leigh, I'm not going to pretend every day with your father has been a bed of roses, because it hasn't. We've had our ups and downs like everybody else. But I will tell you this: your father, to the best of my knowledge, has always taken his medications. It was the one thing that he was open about after we had gotten together, because I had found them in the bathroom and asked him about it. He told me that he had to take them, and I was to *make* him take them no matter what, because he said that when he hadn't, it had cost him an awful lot in his life."

Leigh felt her chin begin to tremble and couldn't prevent the tear that splashed down upon her plate.

"So you see, honey," Libbie said, kindness radiating through her face. "Don't be too hard on your mom. I'm pretty sure if she hadn't been strong enough, especially with two children, to make some sort of ultimatum and divorce your father, he might not be with us now."

"Are you saying," Leigh gulped, struggling with the thought, "that he would have killed himself?"

"I don't know," Libbie admitted. "But I do know that you can't make somebody change when they're ill. You can't, no matter how much you love them. My first husband was a drinker, so trust me, I know. It has to be their decision, and I'd bet the rent that when your father lost all of you, that was the incentive he needed to try and change."

Leigh blotted her eyes with the napkin she had kept wadded in her hand and sighed. "There's so much I don't know about him, Libbie. It breaks my heart. I just wish I knew why he never got in touch with my brother and me. Not once. Why do you think that was?"

Libbie shook her frizzy head. "Honey, I don't know. But I think you touched on it before when you said maybe he was embarrassed. I mean, I don't want to speak for him, but maybe he thought you'd all be better off without him in your lives. That's not an unusual feeling for people who suffer from depression."

Leigh nodded slowly and absorbed this possibility. She suddenly felt compelled to leave the restaurant and walk, if necessary, to the hospital several blocks away. She needed to be with him.

"I feel like I never really had a father," she said miserably. "And now that I've found him, I feel like I'm losing him all over again. I'm so scared, Libbie. What are we going to do when it gets to the point that you can't care for him any longer? I can't afford to pay for him to live in a nice facility, like the ones in my area of North Carolina. They're thousands per month and I can't even imagine how much they cost out here. He's going to wind up warehoused, in some Medicaid wing of a nursing home, and I can't bear it."

"Why would you say that?" Libbie said, frowning. "Honey, he can well afford to be taken care of."

"How is that possible?" Leigh asked, thinking of the worn shabby furniture and the grimy exterior of their duplex. "Especially when you're probably going to have to come up with even more rent when you move?"

Libbie, wearing the mischievous expression of someone about to proclaim wondrous news, crossed her arms in front of her bosom and leaned across the table, her weight on her elbows. "Leigh," she said, dimpling her overly rouged cheeks, "we don't rent. Honey, your father *owned* that duplex. He bought it back in the late seventies, before the real estate crash, and rented out the other unit in it, which was a pretty smart way to pay off the mortgage. He only sold it because it's on a big corner lot and the developer bought the lot next to us and kept pestering John until he came up with an offer, as they say, that he couldn't refuse."

Leigh's mouth fell slightly open.

"Honey," Libbie, lowering her voice so that only the two of them could hear, continued, "Your father has over six hundred thousand dollars sitting in CDs at the bank."

Chapter 23

AS ARRANGED, DAVID MET Stephanie at The Riff Monday night, although he felt so ill at ease that he nearly called to cancel until he remembered he didn't have her phone number. He felt thrown by her invitation and very much put on the spot. But in the end, as he went out of his way to put no effort whatsoever into what he wore before leaving his apartment, he told himself that they were no more than friends. He and Eli had been regular customers of Stephanie's for a couple of years, so it wasn't a date at all, he reasoned as he buttoned a faded grey and black flannel shirt with a frayed collar that he'd had for ages. They were all going out as a sort of group. He ran a quick comb through his hair—he had actually had it cut and was annoyed that one side wouldn't lie down properly, not because he was worried what she might think, but because he thought it looked stupid. He put on his jacket and headed out, bounding down the stairs and out the front of the building, before getting into his Jeep to drive the two miles to the club.

God, he thought, switching on the ignition, *what if she wants to sleep with me?* Still deeply wounded by the end of his marriage, he remained attracted to and even longed for Denise. He hadn't even entertained the idea of being with another woman. Simply the thought of kissing Stephanie, he pondered while backing out of his assigned spot in the complex before changing gears and pulling into the street, was unsettling. Not, he admitted, that she wasn't relatively attractive: she was peppered with freckles over the bridge of her short, slightly snubbed nose and had a wide mouth with a slight overbite that broke easily into a broad grin when she wasn't being harassed by Eli. From what he could tell on his side of the bar, she even appeared to have a cute figure. If he had to describe her, he would say she looked all American, the kind of girl who played, and indeed was, on the pub's softball team during its informal springtime charity league with the other saloons in the area. But it would be like kissing his sister, he frowned, not because he knew her too well, but because he was simply used to her in nothing more than a casual friendship. He had been so intensely connected to his own wife, he'd never even noticed who else might be around him. He wondered with a dart of pain what it would be like when word got back to him, if it ever did, that Denise had embarked upon a new relationship. The thought of bumping into her in town, arms linked with another man, was more than he could bear, especially now when he still felt raw and especially vulnerable. And so his intention this night was to behave no differently with Stephanie than he did at the pub. He would be a good foil, funny when it occurred to him, but most importantly, he would be indifferent. It was imperative, he decided as he waited at a red light, to give no indication that he was interested in pursuing anything else than what the night was meant to be: getting together to support, and probably laugh at, Eli.

He pulled into the club and had little problem finding a parking lot as it was still early and since it was a Monday as well as 'open mic' little in the way of a crowd was expected. He immediately spotted Eli's vehicle, a battered Chevy Luv pickup still, incredibly, on the road. He had no idea what sort of car Stephanie drove. Locking his Jeep, he walked in through the front doors of the venue, paying the cover charge, and ordering the first of the two drink minimum.

Eli, of course, was chatting up a waitress who stood looking as if she was desperate to escape, her tray firmly clasped in front of her as a sort of protective buffer. With an attempt at gallantry, David waved his hand to get Eli's attention. It worked, and his friend ambled over before depositing himself on the nearest barstool.

"How are you feeling?" David asked.

"About tonight?" Eli asked. "Fine. It's easy. I had to learn a couple of songs, but it's easy." He pulled out his phone to check the time. "They need to get here pretty soon, we're up first tonight."

"How long do you play?"

"Every band does a twenty minute set. So, basically, three or four songs?" He gave a wicked smile. "I can't wait. By the way, where's Stephanie, you bastard? I can't believe you took my girl."

"Yeah," said David. "I could see how depressed you were as you were hitting on that waitress. She doesn't even look old enough to work here. And Stephanie's not your girl. Or mine."

Eli smirked. "Dude, don't try and tell me you don't want to hit that."

"Stop saying, 'dude,'" David suggested. "You're almost forty. It's embarrassing."

"Speak of the she-devil," Eli muttered. "She just walked in."

David turned his head to see Stephanie, duly paying her cover charge and looking up with a raised eyebrow at her date. He debated for a moment whether or not to intervene, then realizing he would look like a lout if he didn't at least pay her admission, hastily rose to his feet and walked over to her, reaching for his wallet.

"I'll get this," he said, somewhat lamely. "Hi, Steph."

"Thanks," she replied. "Hi."

An awkward few moments followed.

"D'you want a drink?"

"Sure," she said, pulling a bill from her wallet and pressing it firmly into his hand. "Anything but beer. How about a vodka and tonic with lots of tonic." She looked at him pointedly before adding, "I don't want to get drunk."

"And I don't want you to get drunk," he said feelingly. "OK, I'll get it."

He bought her the drink and handed the tall glass to her as they moved over to where Eli was seated.

"So, are you ready?" she asked Eli.

"Oh," Eli looked up with feigned surprise. "You're talking to me now? I figured you'd be all over lover boy here."

Had the lights not been dimmed, both men would have seen a faint blush creep into Stephanie's cheeks.

She recovered in time to counter, "Eli, you're such a putz."

Eli turned to look at David.

"Did you hear that? I can't believe you're going out with her. She's like a praying mantis—she's going to bite your head off by the end of the evening, and you won't even see it coming. Mark my words."

David nearly said, "We're not going out, we're hanging out," but for reasons unknown, didn't. Instead, he echoed Stephanie by saying, "Eli, you're such a putz."

"Oh, very nice," said Eli. "So glad both of you came to support me tonight. Did you bring tomatoes, too?" And with that, he drained the rest of his beer and stood up, hiking his jeans up over his sagging backside before setting off to corner another waitress.

They both watched his departure. Stephanie turned to David.

"Can I ask you something?" she said.

"Fire away."

"You seem like a decent guy," she began, "well-spoken, polite, successful...so why do you hang out with Eli?"

David chuckled and stroked the stubble on his chin, "Old habits die hard, I guess. He was my roommate in college before he dropped out and busked his way through Europe. He was quite the lady killer."

"But he thinks he still is."

"Yeah," David shrugged, raising his beer to his lips. "He still does. And that's a source of endless amusement."

"Oh, I get it," Stephanie realized. "He's comic relief."

"Something like that," David confirmed.

There was another pause, this time slightly less awkward, that was broken by the emergence of assorted musicians entering from the back of the club. Three unkempt young men with various tattoos and an air of insolence each carried a cumbersome piece of equipment before setting them down near the stage and heading back the way they came in for another load.

"I'll bet that's the band Eli's playing with," David pointed out. "What are they, twelve?"

"That might be pushing it," she agreed. "I think the drummer's wearing Oshkosh."

David found himself laughing in spite of himself.

"You're funny, Steph," he said. "You've got a good sense of humor."

"Yeah, well, it keeps me from killing people. Like Eli."

They fell silent once more and David began to feel slightly more at ease.

"OK," Stephanie said, suddenly smacking her hand for emphasis on the bar. "A couple of ground rules. Number one, I don't sleep with anybody on a first date."

"That's actually kind of a relief," David replied.

"Number two," she continued, ignoring him, "while on the first date, we arrive and leave separately, so there's no awkward, 'do we kiss goodnight,' worries at the end of the night, and thirdly, on this same first date, I pay my own tab so that I'm under no obligation for anything else."

"Hey, Steph?" David asked.

"What?"

"Do you ever get asked out on a second date?"

"Sure I do," she said, somewhat offended, then admitted, "Not really. Actually, I haven't been on a date for a while. Which is why I asked you."

"Gee, thanks."

"What I mean, is," she hesitated, then flipped a lock of her thick hair, the ends tinged with purple, over her shoulder. It was a youngish sort of gesture, David observed, but as there appeared to be no affectation about it, was also somewhat appealing. "What I mean is that I've been really busy with school and work and being a mom, and you've been...married."

"Yes," said David, a bit stiffly, wondering about the subtext at the end of her statement before adding, "I was." He was relieved to have the appearance of Eli, exiting the bathroom in an outlandishly loud Hawaiian shirt, as a diversion. As his friend began to approach them, he was stopped in his tracks by one of the band members, electric guitar slung over his shoulder, standing uncomfortably close to Eli and appearing to be talking loudly as he gestured angrily.

"Oh, man," David said. "This doesn't look good."

"What the hell is he wearing? I've never seen him in a Hawaiian shirt," Stephanie said. "Is he going to put on shorts with socks and sandals, too?"

"All I can say is, it's a good thing he got paid up front," David replied, raising his beer towards Eli in a salute. Eli caught his eye and flashed a huge grin.

A voice from the sound booth suddenly boomed over the loudspeakers.

"Ladies and gentlemen, welcome to open mic night at The Riff. Put your hands together for *The Skinny!*"

Stephanie looked at David and silently mouthed, "The Skinny?"

A smattering of applause rippled through the audience that appeared to number no more than a dozen patrons, leaning against the bar or seated at a couple of tables a good distance away from the stage. The band members leapt up the side steps, trailed by Eli walking sedately and lifting his guitar strap over his head. The drummer seated, the bassist doing a last minute tuning of his instrument, the lead guitarist and vocalist posing himself behind the mic, his legs—indeed skinny—sheathed in leather and stretched in a defiant stance. He shook the hair from his eyes and shouted, "One, two, three, FOUR!" before exploding into a cacophony of chords and turning once to look threateningly at Eli who remained obediently stage left, well behind the drummer. With a raspy voice that shredded the notes, he screamed the repetitive first verse in rapid succession, like a jackhammer: "She don't love me anymore, she don't love me anymore, she don't love me anymore, more, more, more," and spun on his heels to play his guitar facing the drummer and Eli, before swinging back around and working the front of the stage.

"She don't love him anymore," yelled Stephanie into David's ear.

"Probably because of his grammar," David yelled back, and Stephanie laughed.

The rest of the song was just as bombastic and deafening and, despite the wildly theatrical antics of the singer, they received only polite if not indifferent applause at the end.

"Thank you!" he bellowed into the mic, wiping his face on his sleeve as if performing for a packed stadium. "This next song is called, 'Bye, Baby, Bye,'" and launched into another clanging performance. Again, attitude trumped ability, and Stephanie grimaced as she cut another look at David. "They're awful," she mouthed, to which he nodded, cringing. Suddenly, the performance took an unexpected turn as Eli, looking straight in their direction, gave a campy wink. As the lead singer screamed into the microphone, Eli began to do an impression of him, leaving his position behind the drummer and stepping directly into the spotlight where he began to fling his head repeatedly up and down to the beat, then jerk his paunchy, garishly attired body around in rapid, uncoordinated movements, unabashedly ridiculous for all the world to see.

David, about to take a pull from his beer, froze, the bottle stopping inches from his lips and said, "What is he *doing?*" Stephanie, whose mouth and eyes popped open, stared in disbelief until they caught each other's eyes and began to convulse with laughter. It was achingly hysterical and Eli, determined to commit completely to his character, flung himself sideways, knocking the singer off balance and crashing the standing mic to the floor, creating ear piercing feedback to squeal throughout the club. Stephanie, getting into the spirit of the thing, pumped her fist in the air and gave an encouraging show of support, shouting, "Go, Eli, go!" while David, not to be outdone, pressed on the bright light of his cell phone and held it aloft as if demanding an encore. The other members of the audience, recognizing this as theatre of the absurd, began to join in, a few of them dancing wildly and purposely off beat, while two of them went as far as to bang their heads on the side of the stage.

"Oh, stop!" Stephanie, doubled over and weeping with laughter, grabbed David by the shoulder, crying, "I'm going to pee my pants, stop! Stop it!" which only resulted in David laughing harder and, losing his balance, grabbed at Stephanie's arm until they were using each other for support. They begin to sober a bit until Stephanie looked over at the stage again to see the lead singer screaming obscenities at Eli who continued his manic performance, this time in a flailing circle around him. Stephanie, her knees buckling with a renewed fit of giggles, collapsed into David's arms. He didn't stiffen— he was laughing too hard—but he was immediately aware of the warmth of her body, and how it fit so well against his, and that this sudden physical intimacy wasn't disturbing. There was even an odd comfort to it, despite how little he actually knew Stephanie. She pulled back and looked at him, still laughing, a section of her hair spilling over her face, tears running down and her mascara beginning to melt. Without warning, she kissed him impulsively on the mouth and yelled in his ear, "I've been wanting to do that for a long time." Reeling, David gave her a weak smile in return, but stepped back and grabbed his beer from the bar, fighting for composure. From stage, the lead singer gestured wildly to the sound booth to kill the audio and the stage went silent while Eli took lavish curtain calls with a flourish of both arms.

"Did I just freak you out?" Stephanie asked calmly, and David found he couldn't reply immediately. He began to stammer. "It's not— it's not that I don't find you attractive."

Stephanie cut him off, abruptly, saying, "Look, David, it's no big deal, OK? Tonight was just about getting you out, dipping your toe into the dating pool. It's all right. Really."

"It's just that I still haven't even come to terms with my divorce and, really, Stephanie, you're great, but, do you mind if we just stay friends?"

"Of course not," she lied stoutly, and unconsciously flipped away a lock of her hair. "Listen, the last thing I'm looking for is some kind of relationship. I haven't got time for that, anyway. Just thought we might have some fun, that's all."

"Oh, it's been fun all right," he said, wiping his eyes. "Honestly, I can't remember the last time I've laughed that hard. Thank you, I really needed that."

"Now I know why you keep Eli around," she said with a smirk that was not unkind. "I'd pay twice the admission just to see that again. That's the funniest thing I've ever seen."

Eli, red-faced and panting with the grass-skirted hula dancers on his shirt drenched in sweat, joined them, pouring an ale down his throat. "So, what did you think? Think they'll take me on tour?"

David nodded slowly. "You've outdone yourself," he complimented his friend. "Although I can't believe you didn't get punched in the face."

"I would've snapped his bony spine like a twig," Eli retorted and glanced at Stephanie. "See what you're missing by not going out with me?"

"True," Stephanie admitted, "but at least my self-worth is still intact."

"I saw the kiss," Eli teased, drawing his voice out like an obnoxious little brother. "So where are you two headed now, hmm? Your place or mine?"

"Actually, I have to be up early in the morning," David said, not being completely untruthful. "I need to get going. You coming, Steph?"

Stephanie took a long drink and looked around the club, deliberately evading his eyes. Casually, she replied, "I'm going to hang out for a bit then head home. See ya, David."

"Bye, Stephanie. I really had fun."

Despite the sincerity in his voice, he felt a twinge of guilt, but turned to leave. Eli was on his heels, still boasting about his performance.

Stephanie waited a few moments before turning to watch David leave. She saw his lean frame shoulder through a small group of girls who turned and looked his way appreciatively. Stoically, she unzipped her purse to rifle for her car keys, taking her time. When she was quite sure he was long gone, she slung her purse over her shoulder and, sighing, exited through the back door.

Chapter 24

KIRSTEN SPENT LATE TUESDAY morning doing two things that would not only have never occurred to her, but also would have resulted in strident resistance: taking a walk with her grandmother and leaving her phone behind.

"March is certainly coming in like a lion!" Lissie gasped as another icy gust caused them to pull their collective scarves further up their faces.

"This is crazy, Nan," Kirsten grumbled, head down into the wind, trudging forward with the air of an overburdened cart horse.

"Isn't it just?" Lissie laughed, but she shuddered and began to walk faster. "Pick up the pace, Kirsten, and you'll warm up faster."

"*Why* are we doing this?"

"Because," Lissie stopped and turned to her granddaughter with a wink. "It's fun!" She resumed her march, beginning to pump her arms, and admitted, "All right, it might not be fun today, but it's wonderful to be outdoors. Clears the head and haven't you heard the saying, 'a body in motion, stays in motion'."

"No," Kirsten said somewhat petulantly, then added with a groan, "I wish I'd gone to school, now!"

"By the time we get past the bend," Lissie explained, relieved to have heard Kirsten's retort, "we can turn around and then the wind will be at our backs, which will make it far more comfortable. And when we get back, we'll bake cookies. How does that sound?"

"Like I'm five," Kirsten replied, but the idea briefly warmed her. She had read about forced marches in history class at school and as they continued on in silence, she began to imagine herself as a prisoner. That slowly morphed into a fantasy in which she would be rescued by Derek, except for the fact that he would never notice she had been taken captive as he didn't know she existed. She sighed with the angst of being nearly seventeen and without a boyfriend.

"Are you really hating this that much?" Lissie asked, taking note of the sigh.

"I'd rather be inside," Kirsten replied, and then, her face falling further, added, "but it's not about that."

Lissie turned and searched her granddaughter's expression before saying, "I hope you feel you can talk to me, Kirsten, about anything. Anything." And as if to reinforce her heartfelt offer, she slipped her arm around the girl's shoulders as they continued their trek.

It seemed to Kirsten that it had been a very long time since she had felt a kindly hand or an expression of physical affection, and unconsciously, she moved closer to her grandmother. Because her arm was now wedged between them, she found herself slipping her own arm around Lissie's waist, which felt ridiculously trim regardless of being encased in the thick insulation of her down coat. Before long, they had come to the bend in the road and as if cued by the heavens, the early spring sun made a valiant effort to break through the clouds, sent three shafts of light that sparkled across the remaining frost on the fields, and danced over the hides of the horses, excited to be turned out from their stalls, trotting briskly up the hill with twin streams of steam coming from their flared nostrils.

"This is my favorite view in the world," gushed Lissie, holding fast to Kirsten. "Isn't it just beautiful?"

Even Kirsten nodded. She had been driven past this bend more times than she could count on the way to her grandmother's house, but usually had her eyes on her phone or wasn't taking notice. She hadn't any particular attraction to nature. She wasn't remotely athletic or interested in sports, and as with many from her generation, tended to find her entertainment indoors in front of various screens. Now, as she gazed across the landscape before her, she shivered with appreciation as well as the cold. The horses were funny, cantering in circles only to approach one another again, rearing.

"Are they fighting?" she asked.

"No, just playing," Lissie explained. "They're kept up in the barn at night, then go out in the fields in the morning, so they're full of energy, especially in this weather. A couple of them are pregnant and there is nothing more adorable than when the foals are born, running around with their mothers, kicking up their heels. And the mothers are so patient with them. Sometimes you'll see them trying to doze in the sun and the foals are just all over them," she chuckled.

Kirsten thought about her own mother and fear flooded through her chest.

"Nan," she said, "what are we going to tell Mom?"

Lissie gave Kirsten's shoulder a little squeeze and said, "Well, your father is going to have to tell her what happened and if she feels the need to talk to either of us, then telling the truth as we know it is always the best thing to do."

"She's coming home tonight," Kirsten said. "And just thinking about it makes me scared. You know, Nan, before this all happened, it had gotten so bad at home that I figured they were probably going to get a divorce, and that I'd live with dad just because he's, I don't know, easier. No drama. But now, even though I know Mom's been really awful to him, I'm so mad that he would do this that I wouldn't want to live with him, because now I know he's a liar." She looked up at Lissie, tears beginning to well in her eyes. "I don't know what to do, Nan. I don't want to live with either one of them." Her voice broke, and she slumped her shoulders as she added, genuinely defeated, "And I don't even feel that either one of them wants to live with me."

Lissie's heart broke into pieces at this forlorn declaration and she instinctively gathered her granddaughter into her arms, letting her cry into her shoulder, her own eyes blinking back tears. Never had she seen Kirsten so anguished, so bleakly desolate. It was a moment of such raw vulnerability that a new intimacy between the pair began to take root. Kirsten, no longer weeping but keeping her face pressed against her grandmother, felt safe enough to whisper, "I just want to be happy," as if the thought was both as desirable and remote as a sunny, warm clime.

Lissie continued to hold her close and murmured, "And I want you to be happy, darling. You deserve to be happy. Things have a way of working out, no matter how bad they seem. You can trust me on that."

Kirsten pulled away and gazed into her grandmother's eyes, remarkably clear and kind. "Did you go through a lot of bad things, Nan?" she asked.

"Oh, yes," Lissie replied, then added with an air of nonchalance, "but here's the funny thing. When they're happening to you, especially when they sort of snowball and come rolling, one, two, three in a row, you're not even sure if you can survive them. But you do." She looked penetratingly at her granddaughter. "You just keep moving forward, Kirsten. That's what you have to do. Then when you become old, like me, you look back, and all those bad times almost seem like a movie that happened to someone else, because they're so distant, you don't even remember them that well. And the strangest thing is that those bad times help mold you into becoming the person you end up being, and you might even feel grateful for them."

"That's hard to believe," Kirsten said, dolefully, then looked up with the sweetest smile Lissie had seen from her in years, as she added, "and you're not old, Nan. I don't think you'll ever be old."

"From your mouth to God's ear," Lissie replied, smiling in return.

Kirsten pulled carefully away from their embrace and turned to look back at the fields, but inclined her head so that it rested, ever so lightly, upon her grandmother's shoulder.

"Nan?" she asked, tentatively.

"Mm?"

"Did you get along with your mother?"

As she watched the horses beginning to pick at the few dormant tufts of grass within the brown stubble of the fields, the scene before her slowly began to dissolve, as did the frost from the gradually warming sun, into the green and wild beauty of the Cornish coast, windswept grass between her toes, wildflowers nodding and scattered before her like a living tapestry. In her mind's eye she saw her mother, arms outstretched, as if touching the very sky, and pirouetting, as if in slow motion, near the cliff's edge, her girlish face turned up to the sun, the breeze rippling through her hair. And laughing, always laughing. Gulls were screaming overhead and the diminutive white sails of boats dotted the sea beyond. She watched her mother turn towards her, a beckoning smile in her warm and affectionate eyes. This memory, making up the very core of her being, was what had sustained her through every difficulty in her life, and now seemed as distant as the opaque indigo swell of mountains, rising beyond the fields.

"Oh," she breathed, aware of the melancholy that began to seep into her heart. "We were very, very close." Then slipping her arm around Kirsten once again, she said, "But I lost her so early. We had a thousand things that we wanted to do, just the two of us. And then she was gone..." She looked at her granddaughter and said, "You're so lucky to have your mother, Kirsten. I know you may not feel that way right now, but life can change in the blink of an eye."

"But she's so mad all the time," Kirsten pointed out.

"I believe that's because she's been sad for a long time," Lissie replied, softly. "But I'm hoping I can help with that."

"You're not going to sell the house, are you?" It was less of a question and more of a statement.

Lissie shook her head slowly. "No, I'm not."

"But that means you can't move to England."

Lissie's eyes swept once more over the fields, her vision evaporating.

"That's right."

"Nan," Kirsten said, suddenly articulating the sadness that swept over them both. "That's not fair. You should go. You need to go." She tugged at her grandmother's sleeve as if she were a child. "And I want to visit you there. I want to do all the things you never got to do with your mother."

Lissie looked at Kirsten in astonishment. This plea, this desire for inclusion, that had eluded her with her own daughter, was now coming from her granddaughter, and from a place of such complete selflessness that Lissie was moved beyond words. To think Kirsten had somehow intuitively grasped what had resided so powerfully in her heart, was overwhelming. She embraced her granddaughter and held her for what seemed ages.

"Come on," she said, forcing brightness back into her voice. "Let's go bake those cookies."

Chapter 25

ONLY NOW BEGINNING TO feel vaguely familiar with her surroundings, hours before she was scheduled to leave, Leigh walked the hospital corridor towards her father's room with faint trepidation. He was much improved, Libbie had reported when Leigh returned from a rather frazzled couple of hours sitting uncomfortably in the back of a cab amid the morning rush hour snarl of traffic after attempting to secure power of attorney.

"I'm afraid if your father has dementia, you are past that point," she was told rather breezily by the attorney suggested by Libbie. He had been a friend of her family and hopefully not nearly as expensive as those in a revered zip code. "In order to have power of attorney, the principal, your father, would have to be of sound mind and agree to the conditions. If he is incapacitated, then we are looking at conservatorship, which means you will have to complete a petition and file it with the court," the man continued, rattling off the requirements so quickly Leigh was struggling to keep up. "And then, of course, your father would have to receive notice, followed by a court investigator who checks into the claim, and interviews the both of you before reporting their findings back to the court. Finally, you will have to return to California to attend the court hearing along with your father, and it's up to the judge to determine whether or not to grant you petition for conservatorship."

"But I've been told he's just in the very early stages of dementia," Leigh countered, completely overwhelmed. "What if he's

169

just a little forgetful here and there, but is still living independently, still going about his business?"

"Then I would suggest speaking to your father's doctor for that evaluation," came the reply.

Now, as Leigh walked slowly towards ICU, her rubber-soled shoes squeaking with each step along the polished floors, she was thinking less about the idea of a drawn-out legal commitment and more of how her father might meet her. He hadn't seen her since she was barely out of her teens, and although they had conversed relatively regularly over the phone prior to his pneumonia, she wondered: would he have any idea who she was? Would she be able to stand it if he didn't? It had already been such a shock to have seen him looking so gravely ill, so frail, she wasn't quite sure she had the courage to withstand what might await her as she crossed the threshold into his room. She passed the nurses' station, placed strategically in the center of the unit for observation, and nodded to a couple of faces she had come to recognize over the three days of her lengthy visits. As she approached room 117, a male nurse was just coming out carrying a tray of partially-eaten lunch.

"He's doing much better," he commented upon seeing Leigh. "You'll notice quite a difference."

"It doesn't look like he ate very much," Leigh said, eyeing the plate.

"He ate a good breakfast and was still feeling pretty full. Plus, it's not uncommon for irregularity to be a problem, especially with elderly patients," the nurse went on, passing his hand over his abdomen as if to illustrate. "So it's not too unexpected. Anyway, he's sitting up, reading. Enjoy your visit."

Leigh thanked him for the update, feeling a palpable relief. Surely sitting up and reading was a good sign, wasn't it? Taking a deep breath, she walked through the doorway and greeted him in the way she thought would be less unnerving.

"Hello, John."

Her father looked up from his paper and peered at her over the top of his reading glasses.

"Yes?" he said. "I've just eaten, they took the tray away."

Leigh swallowed and came closer to his bed, but not as close as she had been when he had been lost to her in his sleep. She found herself feeling stiffly formal, unable to sink down next to him or even in the recliner in the corner. He did look better, she thought as she regarded him for a moment, less yellow. Now, sitting upright in his bed, he looked far less sunken about the eyes and cheeks. Yes, he still looked older than his years and had no resemblance to the muscular, athletic man of her childhood, but he certainly no longer looked as if he were at death's door.

"I don't expect you to recognize me as it's been years," she said, feeling her heart begin to pound. "But we have spoken quite a few times in the last several weeks over the phone. I'm your daughter, Leigh."

"Leigh," he said flatly, as if digesting it. He folded his newspaper neatly and placed it down on the wheeled table that reached over his bed. "Leigh. You're my daughter, Leigh?"

"That's right," she said, as casually as possible. "From North Carolina. Libbie told me you were ill and in the hospital, so I flew out to see you."

"Is Libbie here?" There was hope in his voice.

"She was here earlier," Leigh replied. "While I was—" She caught herself, then continued, "while I had to go out. So I told her that I would come and keep you company. Is that all right with you?"

Her father raised his hands, the left one trembling slightly as he removed his glasses from behind his ears, and with the same precise movements he used with the newspaper, folded them slowly and placed them next it. "That would be all right. But I'm not much company. I get tired quickly."

There was something about the delivery of his speaking pattern that felt familiar to Leigh. She remembered it from her childhood: succinct, nearly monotone.

"You used to call me 'Bunny,'" she found herself saying. "When I was a child."

A flicker of recognition went through his eyes. "Yes, I remember that," he said, to her great relief. "A very quiet child," he added after a pause, then looked at her as if he were trying to put the two images together. "Bunny. And you're Leigh?"

She nodded.

"And Libbie's here?" he asked.

Her heart broke a little. "No," she said, repeating herself. "Libbie was here earlier, but she needed to run errands and I wanted to spend some time with you before I have to leave in the morning."

"You're leaving?" he asked, slightly perplexed.

"Not until tomorrow morning." She tried to sound reassuring. "I've got all day to spend with you, if you'd like that. There's so much I want to—" She stopped, not wanting to overwhelm him. "I'd love to learn a bit more about you and tell you about me, so we can get to know each other better."

John folded his hands over his lap and watched her steadily. Still not feeling relaxed or even welcomed enough to sit next to her father on his bed, Leigh tugged the reclining chair, cumbersome as it was, from the corner so that he could look at her comfortably without craning to turn his head. She sat down and kept her purse in her lap, feeling the need to be holding something.

"I'll bet you can't wait to get out of here," she said, feeling him out, "and go home."

"Yes."

"I've been staying in your house with Libbie. I understand you've lived there for a long time."

"Yes, I've lived there my whole life."

"Have you?" she asked, carefully. "Didn't you used to live in North Carolina?"

"No."

"When you called me Bunny you used to live in a big white farmhouse in North Carolina, do you remember? You restored that house all by yourself."

His eyes traveled from her gaze, though the doorway and back to her face. "Farmhouse," he said faintly, as if searching for something. "There was an orchard."

"Yes!" Leigh said, her heart lurching with hope. "That's right. An apple orchard, and a little barn down at the bottom for a pony."

He nodded slowly and looked away again.

"We used to live in that house," she said, swallowing hard. "Many years ago."

Her father's mouth began to work slightly, as if trying to form a thought, and his eyes returned to hers.

"You're Lissie?"

Crushed, Leigh bit her lip and shook her head slowly. "No," she said, fighting to keep her voice steady. "Lissie is my mother. You are my father. I'm your daughter, Leigh."

The old man closed his eyes. "I'm tired," he said.

Leigh remained silent and watched him fade into sleep. Only then did she reach slowly for his hand and press it softly into her own. "Daddy," she whispered, "I love you."

His eyelids fluttered opened and he intoned, "I love you, too," before drifting from her once more.

She couldn't process the moment. He had spoken the words she had craved to hear her entire adult life, but she had no way of knowing if they were meant for her. *But I'll hang my heart on it,* she thought, choosing at last to believe he recognized that it was her, at least in the moment. *I'll hang my heart on it because it's all I have.* She looked up as a nurse, different from the one she had seen earlier, paused in the doorway, cleaning her hands with hand sanitizer dispensed from a small box mounted on the wall just on the other side.

"How's he doing?" she asked pleasantly.

Leigh took a moment to compose herself then tried to reply, but faltered.

The nurse, a middle-aged African American woman with a name tag that read *Jacqueline* smiled kindly and said, "It's hard not to worry when we see our parents in hospital, but he's really responded well to treatment." She looked at the monitor to which he was connected. "His oxygen saturation is at ninety eight," she said approvingly. "That's really good. That's better than a lot of people walking around."

Leigh nodded and sighed. "It's just that I haven't seen him in a long time and didn't know until a couple of days ago that he had dementia."

"Oh," Jacqueline replied. "I see. Well, don't let anything you hear while he's in here scare you too much. It's pretty much a given with our elderly patients that they become disoriented when they're admitted. It might be because they're not sure if it's day or night, but it's not unusual at all."

"You're very kind to be so reassuring," Leigh said. "But it's more than that. He's been showing signs of dementia over the past several weeks."

Jacqueline nodded. "I see," she said. "But just remember that his simply being here will make it appear worse than it might be."

"The strange thing is that he was getting me mixed up with his girlfriend, and then even my mother, but he remembered living in North Carolina forty years ago and even that we had an orchard."

Jacqueline waved a hand. "Oh, that's kind of par for the course. For sure you'll want to talk to his doctor about it, but if he's anything like my father was, he'll be able to remember the street address from his childhood but not what he had for lunch." She paused and gave a chuckle, "Shoot, these days, I can't even remember what *I* had for lunch."

"It seems like everyone I talk to has a family member with dementia," Leigh frowned. "It's so prevalent."

"Yes it is," Jacqueline sighed. "And they say we're going to see a big wave of it with the baby boomers." She stooped over the bed and arranged the pillows beneath John's shoulders before turning to Leigh and asking, "Do you want me to lower the bed so he can rest more comfortably?"

"I think he's O.K. as he is," Leigh said. "It's been a long time, but I used to be a nurse, so I'll make sure he's comfy and doesn't try to get up, or anything."

Jacqueline smiled and said, "Oh, he is blessed to have a daughter who will know how to care for him. I wish all my patients did." She turned to leave.

"Jacqueline?" Leigh was nearly afraid to ask what was on her heart.

"Yes?"

"With your father," she began. "How quickly did his dementia progress? I mean, I guess I'm asking how long will my father have before he can't," she lowered her voice to a whisper, "function on his own?"

Jacqueline crossed her arms and pursed her lips as she thought back and replied, "Well, I'll tell you what my father's doctor told me when I asked that same question. You know, there's all kinds of dementia and some affect different parts of the brain. Does your father have Alzheimer's?"

Leigh shook her head. "When I spoke to his GP, he didn't think so, because when he last saw Dad, he felt his mental state and coordination was pretty good, but couldn't confirm it without doing some more tests."

"Well, my father had plain old age-related dementia," Jacqueline said. "But his advanced pretty slowly, so that when he actually died at eighty-seven of a heart attack, he still knew who I was and could eat and drink and watch football. I remember asking his doctor earlier on how fast it would go and he said that, while there's medications that help slow down the progression, there's no way to really tell. He did say that you can have an idea by comparing how they are now to the previous year, so if he's not too much different from last year, that might be a really good sign. But if he's radically different and you're seeing a rapid deterioration..." She didn't finish.

"Thank you so much," Leigh said, taking it all in. "You've been so helpful. As I said, I did meet with his doctor, but it was such a quick consultation because he squeezed me in before his first patient that I forgot half the things I was going to ask him. It's been such a hectic couple of days."

"It's never easy," Jacqueline said and patted her on the shoulder before leaving the room. "It's never easy."

Chapter 26

DAVID WAS RELIEVED TO see a busy week shaping up before him. There was an intriguing as well as flattering offer to shoot an engagement portrait of the mayor's daughter, and it had been implied, when speaking to the mayor himself over the phone, that David would be needed for an innovative creative approach in the mayor's re-election campaign for all print media.

"What I'm looking for," the mayor had articulated, "is something fresh and different. My platform has increasingly become more about sustainability for our area and how to carefully balance that with growth."

"I am all about that," David had replied sincerely, "which is why you've had my vote in the past. Are there any particular ideas that you'd like to discuss? I'm thinking the last thing you want is the obligatory shot in shirtsleeves, one finger supporting your suit jacket hanging over the back of your shoulder?"

The mayor burst into a good-natured laugh. "Exactly. I know exactly what you mean. No, I certainly don't want that. Or a photo of me wearing a hardhat mingling on a jobsite with the other hard-hatted workers, looking as if I have a clue of what they're talking about. Something earthier, more approachable."

"Maybe something like hiking with your family or a local kids' group in the woods," David suggested, "illustrating your record and commitment to the environment."

"Without looking too much like the tree hugger I actually am," the mayor agreed.

Their conversation turned back to the engagement portrait, a price estimate, scheduling availabilities. David hung up the phone, grateful for the commission, and the fact that he had been the only photographer considered. He had pointed out to the mayor that he wasn't a wedding photographer, but this wasn't a wedding. This was to be a singular portrait, simply a keepsake of an only daughter with her diamond ring on display, beautifully captured in a way that wouldn't look amiss next to the generations of framed representations of women hanging in the living room of their home. David had seen the daughter, alongside her father probably, on a televised charity event and she was lovely: a strikingly tall brunette with a porcelain complexion and enormous dark eyes. *Someone's a lucky guy*, he thought, sitting at his desk with his loupe in hand to check the focus on a series of experimental shots he had taken earlier. He was reminded of his own wedding and the failure of his subsequent marriage. Everything felt as if it had happened yesterday. Everything seemed to happen so astonishingly fast, and he had become painfully aware that the numbness he had felt shortly after the finalization of his divorce had ebbed into an abiding sense of sadness which seemed to close in on him daily. Ironically, he could manage to keep it away—or at least at arm's length—by the very things that contributed to his divorce: detachment and distraction. Work had been particularly useful and he tried again to think about the engagement portrait, but it only served as a reminder of the photographs he had taken of Denise with the black and white film he had insisted on using, the light and shadow so powerfully capturing her finely sculpted features and expression. Funnily, his favorite image of the both of them remained on his phone, and he found himself scrolling down to (of all things) a 'selfie' of the both of them after he had grabbed her by the hips during a walk in the fall and hurled both of them, together, into an enormous pile of leaves. She had been shocked, angry, flustered, and finally laughing when he pushed his face up against hers and snapped the photo, both of them covered in leaves and autumnal light. She used it (he'd wished she hadn't, as it felt to him intensely personal) as a cover photo for her personal social media account, and dismally, he found himself pulling up her Facebook page, reading that she had, of course, changed her relationship status to 'divorced.' He felt like a stalker, especially since she had trusted him enough to not block him from her list of 'friends.' But here he was, looking to see if she was sharing any photos that he knew he wouldn't want to see.

He disliked social media not only because it had become yet another thing to compete against for his former wife's attention, but because he could see no point in what he regarded to be inane comments ("so much traffic at the mall," and "great check up at the dentist's!") posted throughout the day, coupled with pious 'memes' or self-righteous social outrage. He admittedly had a page for his business, as well as a Twitter account, however he visited them begrudgingly. Denise had changed her cover photograph—no surprise—to an image of a sunrise over the mountains and captioned inside the comment box, "A new day." Meaning *what?* he thought. A *new life? A new relationship? A new beginning?* Her profile photograph was thankfully taken not by herself inside her new car, but by someone else, showing her leaning against a building somewhere in Asheville, looking almost pensive. He scrolled down the comments, reading, "You're so beautiful, Denise," from a couple of girlfriends. He hesitated upon reading, "I know that look," from Spencer, the associate he vaguely recalled from the ill-fated Christmas party. David only remembered him because he had thought Spencer was an interesting name and it stuck in his memory. He clicked on Spencer's name to pull up his profile photograph. He was as David remembered, blond and athletic.

"For God's sake," he said aloud, disgusted with himself. He tossed his phone aside. This was exactly why he should never have gone to her account, never read anything, because now his mind was beginning to whirl with incriminations that weren't even relevant to his life anymore. It was bad enough to feel the murkiness in his heart day after day, and the last thing his exceedingly bruised ego was in need of was a wave of insecurity thinly disguised as jealously. It stood to reason that Denise would be moving on. Why wouldn't she? Unless, he dared to entertain the impossible thought, she also felt wounded and vulnerable and possibly missed him. His mind raced back to when he saw her at his mother's party. The memory of her saying goodbye, leaning against the door, hands in the pockets of her winter white coat...surely he knew her well enough not to have misread that look of wistfulness, possibly even regret? It had carried him for days with a sort of buoyancy. And the only thing that had brought him back to earth, in a shattering but not altogether unpleasant way, was Stephanie's audacity in both asking him out and boldly kissing him amid fits of laughter.

Stephanie, he thought with a flinch of discomfort. How was he going to deal with that? It was another reason he was profoundly grateful for his workload. It made an excellent excuse to dodge Eli's persistent texts from the pub, to join him, and presumably pick up his tab, but mostly to avoid seeing Stephanie. As adamantly as she had declared herself relieved to remain just friends, he couldn't shake the feeling that she wasn't being entirely truthful. Had she not yelled into his ear *"I've been wanting to do that for a long time"* afterwards? Surely she hadn't had a crush on him all this time—she never showed the slightest interest in him and, besides, she knew absolutely nothing about him with the exception that he particularly enjoyed wheat beers. He shook his head and smirked at his own ego. If he actually had a clue of what a woman was really thinking, he wouldn't be divorced. Picking up the loupe to return to his work, it occurred to him that, alternatively, he might never have married.

Chapter 21

IT HAD BEEN A relatively uneventful flight for Leigh as she returned to North Carolina. She had rarely flown in her life and sighed with relief when the pilot announced the descent for her connecting flight from Atlanta. She had purchased a bestselling paperback for the long journey which departed Los Angeles at the ungodly hour of six that morning, but had nodded off promptly after takeoff. Only when the rumbling of the drinks trolley came down the aisle was she jerked awake, with the slightly panicked reaction of not realizing where she was. She ordered a coffee, had difficulty opening the tubs of creamer without her elbows poking into the passengers either side of her, and tried to read the book but found it impossible to concentrate.

There was much to consider with no room for error, be it conscious or unconscious, as the decisions before her would greatly impact the very wellbeing of her father. When she said her final goodbye the evening before with Libbie present, he had given every indication that he indeed understood who she was. He politely thanked her for going to the trouble of leaving her family and coming to see him. He even seemed pleased that she and Libbie had become firm friends. There was a conference with a doctor present where it was decided that he would not be returning immediately home to their shared duplex, but rather that he would be transferred to a rehabilitation unit for the interim as he had lost strength and was at risk for falling. This was understandably met with both annoyance and resignation by her father, however it warmed Leigh's heart to see

Libbie gently encouraging the decision with common sense and promising to visit each day. "There's no sense in you getting hurt and ending right back here in hospital, is there, Sweetie," she had murmured to him, sitting next to him on the bed where Leigh longed to be, holding his hand in both of hers and leaning affectionately into him. And when it came for Leigh to say goodbye, she desperately wanted to give him an enormous hug that would last forever and a kiss on the cheek, but his manner towards her, while kind and courteous, remained formal. She dared not risk a kiss that might be only stiffly tolerated, so instead she pressed his hand quickly and released it as she bid him goodbye with declarations of hoping to return to see him soon. He nodded, thanked her, and gave a brief smile.

Intellectually, Leigh knew she couldn't be surprised by his lack of affection. It was only normal after seeing her for the first time in years. Sadly, she also knew only too well that the reason he was now aware of her physical presence was because she had initiated everything. Her father could easily have gone to his grave having made no effort to renew the relationship with his own children. She wondered if he would think of her at all in the coming days. She wondered if the formality she felt with him could possibly be borne from deeply-embedded guilt he perhaps felt. As she departed the plane and walked slowly towards baggage claim, she was surprised at how tired she was, relieved Wes and Kirsten wouldn't be there to meet her, and glad she had driven herself to the airport. She wasn't yet at a place emotionally where she could explain how her visit actually went. Describing their home and Libbie's effervescent personality would be easy enough, but the feelings she was experiencing in regards to her relationship with her father were tumbling through her brain. It would take her thirty minutes to drive home and, at last comfortable in a seat large enough to accommodate her with the familiar landmarks flashing by, she would use that time to allow herself just a chance to...be.

By the time Leigh pulled into the driveway of her house, she surprised herself by thinking, when compared to where her father lived, her own home wasn't perhaps that bad. *Lord,* she thought, in amazement, *who knows what this place would go for in Los Angeles?* True, it still looked like something out of a 1970s television show, but at least the trim was freshly painted and it looked presentable. The lights on either side of the front door suddenly illuminated, and Wes stepped out with an offer of assistance with her bag.

"You must be tired," he said, giving her a quick kiss when she didn't offer one. "Good flight?"

"A long flight," she replied. "But all right. Not too much turbulence."

"I picked up some Chinese that I can warm up," he suggested as they crossed over the threshold and entered the house. "I didn't know if you'd eaten or not. But if you're not hungry, that's fine too."

"Actually, I haven't eaten since lunch," she said, "so that'd be great, thanks."

Wes said he would carry her bag upstairs, which he did, while mentioning it was good that her plane got in on time as there were strong storms predicted later in the night. Leigh couldn't remember him being so chatty, almost rambling. She glanced around the kitchen. It was immaculate. That was a surprise, as well as quite touching. By habit, she opened the door of the fridge and immediately saw the birthday cake in a plastic container tucked well into the back on the middle shelf.

"Oh, Lord, Wes, I completely forgot your birthday," she apologized, feeling truly mortified when he stepped back into the kitchen. "I'm sorry."

"Don't worry about it," he said quickly. "You've had a lot on your plate."

"Well, yes, but I'll make it up to you, I promise." She hesitated a moment. It had been so long since she had given a compliment to her husband that the words, even the rhythm of the sentence, didn't come easily. Raising her eyebrows she managed, "The kitchen's so nice and tidy. I should go away more often. Where is Kirsten, in her room?"

"She's actually at your mother's," he said, stepping slightly ahead of her as he reached into the fridge.

"What's she doing there? It's a school night."

Wes turned around, a small white carton of cashew chicken in each hand. "She didn't feel up to going to school Monday or today."

Alarm flared within Leigh's breast. "She must be really ill, then. Why didn't you tell me? And she should be here, in her own bed, not at my mother's."

"Well, with me being at work," he stammered, beginning to feel distinctly unwell himself, "it seemed like a good idea."

Leigh reached into her purse for her phone. Wes, his heart pounding, said, "She's been in bed all day. Probably finally asleep. Let's not disturb her—" He hesitated, wondering why the back of his mouth suddenly had an almost metallic taste. "We'll both go over to get her in the morning. I can go into the office a little late."

Leigh considered the idea and nodded her consent. "But you should have told me," she repeated.

"I actually called your mother earlier and she offered to cook us breakfast in the morning," Wes said, hoping to sound neutral in the circumstances.

Leigh flicked the idea away with a wave of her hand. "That's ridiculous. We won't have time for that. Either Kirsten's still sick, and I take her straight to the doctor, or she's fine, in which case we drive her straight to school."

"You don't think your mother might want to hear about how you've been?" Wes asked. "How the trip went?"

Leigh gave a little snort. "I really doubt my mother would be that interested in my father's wellbeing," she said, then gave a heavy sigh. "I'm really tired. I think I'm just going to turn in early."

Wes watched her walk down the hallway and was flooded with relief when she opened the door of the guest room and went inside.

The following morning, after a sleepless night, Wes was uncomfortably aware that his mouth felt so dry that even two glasses of water couldn't moisten it. He dressed rapidly, gave a quick polite smile when he saw Leigh enter the kitchen, and offered her a cup of coffee.

"No, thanks," she said, "I'd rather we just get going."

It was surprisingly balmy out and Wes found himself wondering if it was the temperature or the fact that he was wracked with tension that led to the perspiration already forming under his arms. He gently inquired over the health of his wife's father only to be given rather short, although not unkind replies. As they pulled into the drive of his mother-in-law's home, he turned off the ignition, swallowed hard twice, and reached for Leigh's arm to detain her as she tried to open her door.

"I need to tell you something," he said, his throat constricting.

Leigh frowned at him. "What?"

"I don't even know where to begin, but you're going to hear about it when we go inside, and I want you to know—"

"Kirsten?" her eyes flew open in horror. "It's Kirsten, isn't it? Oh, God." She flung his arm away as she pushed open the door and bolted towards the house.

Wes followed pathetically in her wake and when he reached the wide open front door, he saw his wife standing near the staircase, flummoxed, amid her mother, Kirsten, and David.

"What on earth is going on?" she wanted to know. "What's David doing here?"

"Nice welcome," David observed drily. "I actually just dropped by to have coffee with mother. Don't worry," he added in a tone which did little to belie his irritation or reveal that his mother, for once going against her principals, had telephoned him the night before requesting his assistance for moral support without going into details. "I won't be staying long."

Kirsten looked first at her grandmother, then her uncle. "Could you maybe stay a little longer?" she asked.

Sensing something not quite right, he nodded and replied, "If you need me to, sure."

"I do," she said.

"Why don't I get us all coffee," Lissie offered. "Come into the kitchen, everyone."

When they had gathered around the table with Leigh and David taking the same seats they had throughout their childhood and Wes sitting between his daughter and Lissie, Leigh observed sardonically, "This feels like some kind of intervention."

When there was no answer, despite an anemic chuckle from her mother as she tried mightily to elevate the tension into lightness, Leigh looked pointedly at each face before her and asked, "What's going on?"

Lissie glanced swiftly at Wes, who sat hunched and rubbing his hands together as they rested on top of the table. He shook his head slowly, not daring to look at his daughter whose eyes he could feel boring through him, and cleared his throat.

"Monday morning, your mother and Kirsten arrived at my office early to surprise me for my birthday," he began, haltingly, and allowed a brief glance at his daughter along with a weak smile. "They were bringing me homemade cupcakes. They waited in your mother's car for me to arrive and they saw something that looked pretty bad. Disastrous, really, but at the risk of sounding cliché, it's not what it looked like."

Leigh looked at him steadily, expressionless.

"What they saw..." He gave a slight cough before continuing. "Was me in a car, driven by another woman, and I'm afraid some conclusions were jumped to—"

"You *kissed* her!" Kirsten interrupted hotly.

"*What?*" Leigh asked, the color draining from her face. For a moment she thought she had not heard correctly and repeated, "What?"

David froze across from his sister. He knew in a flash he would never forget the open-mouthed disbelief she wore, her hands gripping the edge of the table. As annoyed as he had been by her brusqueness earlier, he was filled with devastation, humiliated for what he could only suppose was coming for her.

Lissie, who had remained near the sink, felt compelled to contribute for the sake of fairness. "That's not exactly true, Kirsten."

Wes held up his hands. "What they saw was her kiss me. What they also saw was that I allowed it."

Leigh placed both her hands over her stomach, lurching with nausea. "I think I'm going to be sick," she said and left the table. No one said anything. Kirsten looked shattered, David thought, and he was tempted to hold her hand, but her father should be doing that. The trouble was, he wasn't. In a few minutes, Leigh reappeared, holding herself stiffly, defiance beginning to burn in her eyes.

"This is all making sense to me, now," she said, and didn't sit down. Instead, she pulled herself up to her full height, which was not considerable, and pointed to her husband. "You were very supportive, even eager of my going to California and now I know why: so that you could continue whatever affair you've been having on the sly without my being around. God, what a fool I was," she spat, furiously. "Coming home, the house all nice and clean, actually thinking you cared enough to not saddle me with housework as soon I walked in, but now I see that was all just to try to butter me up because you had been busted by your own daughter and mother-in-law!"

"It's not what it looked like." Wes attempted his defense, but was sharply cut off.

"So what *was* it, Wes?" his wife asked, wringing sarcasm from every word. "What was it? You arrive at your office before work and sneak into some woman's car and, against your will, she begins kissing you? Had you just changed her tire and she was thanking you? Or maybe you were choking and she was giving you mouth to mouth?"

Wes looked at his daughter, who had now dropped her head in tears. "Can we not do this in front of Kirsten?"

"Oh, you're worried *now* that she's being affected?" Leigh asked, incredulously. "She's the one who saw you, so go ahead, Wes, tell your daughter that it's not what it looked like."

Wes tried to slip his arm around Kirsten's shoulder but she shook it off. He glanced up at Lissie and asked tonelessly, "Is that coffee ready?"

"Yes," Lissie replied quickly, and came over to press a cup in his hand.

Wes made no effort to even blow on the coffee to cool it. He took a sizable gulp and looked squarely at his wife, then his daughter.

"What she saw—what they both saw—was me being kissed by a woman who has become a friend."

"A very *good* friend, I should think," Leigh interrupted bitterly.

Wes placed his coffee down and looked at her calmly. "Do you want me to explain, or condemn me now?" When no answer other than an icy stare was returned, he continued. "Yes, she has become a good friend. She—I'm not going to tell you her name—works for one of our clients, and I had to talk with her several times on the phone, and then she would come by the office now and then. I'm not going to lie to you, Leigh, we hit it off and became friends. But we have never gone down the road you're thinking. And we had never even kissed. What Kirsten and Lissie saw was her kissing me, for the first time."

"Liar!" Leigh hissed, between clenched teeth. "Do you really expect me to believe that?"

"Darling," Lissie murmured, trying to assuage the rising anger before her.

"And *you*," Leigh turned to cut her mother off in a voice that was deathly cold, "How dare you decide to take my daughter out of school without my permission?"

"Leigh, it wasn't like that," Lissie began.

"I see," her daughter replied, with a bitter laugh. "Wes says being seen kissing another woman isn't what I think it is, and now you're telling me that what you did, which was to secretly keep my daughter out of school without calling me, her *mother*, to ask permission, also isn't what I think it is? I guess I look pretty damned stupid to all of you!"

"Leigh, calm down," David spoke up.

Ignoring him, Leigh took a step closer to her mother and whispered savagely, "This is what happened after I flew across the country to sit with my deathly ill father in the hospital. This is what I've had to come home to. And it all could have been avoided, at least for Kirsten's sake, had you not decided to take it upon yourself to keep my daughter out of school. She is never going to forget what she saw, she may never get over what is happening, because of *you*, you meddling old woman!"

"Mom, stop!" Kirsten cried, upon seeing her grandmother's face crumple before her eyes, stricken.

Wounded beyond measure and struggling to regain her composure, Lissie stepped back to the sink and began to rinse her mug, but her trembling hands betrayed her and she dropped it, the mug breaking upon impact. She took a deep breath and turned around slowly, before addressing her daughter succinctly.

"Leigh, you're my daughter, and I love you. I realize you are hurting, but I've needed to say this for a long time, and I'm going to say it now. I am *not* the person you need me to be to justify your anger. I'm *not*." With that, she left the room and both David and Kirsten rose from their chairs to follow her.

Chastened, Leigh followed her mother with her eyes before turning them angrily back upon her husband.

"How could you do this to me?" she choked, fighting back the tears. "How could you? My world has been falling apart, my father almost died, and you, you—" She couldn't continue.

Having fought a valiant fight for self-control, Wes suddenly gave in and raised his head, looking at his wife with a fierceness she had never witnessed.

"Let me tell you something," he said, his voice low and strained. "You can believe what you want to believe, but here's the truth and you'd better get ready, because it's ugly. For years, I have worked as hard as I can to provide for you, and for as long as I can remember, I have received nothing but criticism and abuse in return. You make it known pretty much daily that you hate our house, you hate how you look, and you sure as hell act as if you hate me. For God's sake, Leigh, you've become the most miserable woman I've ever known. And no matter what I say, you dismiss me like I'm an idiot for even trying to suggest a way to help. You're obsessed—" His eyes left hers for a moment as they flashed across the walls around them. "—with this damned house and have made my life, as well as Kirsten's, as miserable as your own because you can't have it, even bullying your own mother over it. Now, you may not want to believe this, but I have *not* been having an affair. I will admit I have been attracted to another woman and allowed myself to be kissed in a moment I should not have allowed happen, but I have not slept with her." He stopped, took a deep breath and delivered his final blow. "But I have *talked* with her, and *confided* in her, for hours and hours, and if our marriage means anything to you, Leigh, *that* should scare the shit out of you far more than any one night stand, because *that* is an intimacy I haven't had with you for years."

Leigh's mouth fell slightly open as the words, ringing with truth, began to invade her. Unwilling to accept blame as was old habit, she stammered, "That's not true, I do talk to you."

"That's right, you talk *to* me," Wes shot back, "you sure as hell don't talk *with* me. When was the last time you showed the slightest interest in anything that I do? Or anything that I'd like to do? Did you notice I'd bought a pair of hiking boots, because it's something I'd like to start doing on weekends? So that my life might stop revolving around working forty to fifty hours a week and coming home to hear how crappy your life is?"

"You never said," Leigh attempted feebly.

"You never *asked*. You never cared," Wes replied, rising from his chair, "and it's gotten to the point, actually well past the point, that I don't, either."

Chapter 28

IT HAD BEEN DIFFICULT for David to put the scene he had witnessed in his childhood home out of his head as he undertook the projects of his work week. His own upbringing had been nearly devoid of emotional confrontations with the exception of the occasional bursts of teen angst, particularly from Leigh. On the whole, their home had been a quiet one. He had been completely unprepared for what had played out in front of him and deeply disturbed by the impact on everyone. His mother had been terribly hurt, but displayed, at least outwardly, her trademark resilience as she sat on the edge of her bed with Kirsten on one side and David on the other, his hand on her shoulder. As always her concern was not with herself, but with others, especially Kirsten, whom she was especially worried had been traumatized by the event.

"I'm OK, Nan," Kirsten had said, even allowing a smile that David found heartbreakingly brave. "I think my generation has been exposed to a lot more than when you were my age. I mean, it still makes me sick to think about my Dad, but none of this is a surprise, really."

David couldn't imagine the atmosphere inside Wes's car when the family finally departed. Despite his sister's effort to convince Kirsten to stay home one more day, her daughter surprised everyone by insisting to go to school, and David didn't blame her. It was a clear attempt at some sort of normalcy and to get out of what could only be imagined as a household fraught with tension. And from simply observing the family for years, he wasn't surprised Wes had sought emotional refuge elsewhere. He could never describe his sister as warm, David reflected. Dutiful, yes, and organized, absolutely. But warm or encouraging, rarely. He wouldn't be surprised if things ended in divorce, he sighed, and that might be best for all concerned.

By the time Friday afternoon rolled around, normally with a gaping weekend to be filled before him, he was relieved to be kept busy with his Saturday shoot. He checked his phone before leaving the studio for messages. Two were from the mayor. He returned the call immediately.

"Hi Scott," David said, addressing him in the informal manner in which he had been encouraged. "What can I do for you?"

"It's about the shoot tomorrow. I just wanted to give you a heads up that my daughter, who is as stubborn as I am, has her own ideas about her portrait and won't be talked out of it."

David chuckled. "What is it? Does she want to wear jeans or something instead of a gown?"

"She wants to be photographed with her horse."

"Her *horse?*" David repeated. "I'm thinking this isn't going to be done in studio."

"That's right," Scott agreed, sighing. "She wants a whole outdoor feel to it. Casual. Her mother's having a fit, but there you are."

David wrote down the particulars as they were further discussed, including the address of the stable.

"And David," mentioned the mayor, before hanging up, "another heads up."

"Which is?"

"The horse bites."

With a wry smile, David ended the call. It was a pretty comical conversation, really, the sort that he couldn't wait to share with Denise at the end of the day. He suddenly remembered hearing Wes's voice, as he had followed his mother from the kitchen, accusing Leigh of the complete lack of emotional intimacy in their marriage. It had left him cold. As much as it bothered him to admit it, he found he could relate to it. On one hand, he could, and did, share funny details of his day with Denise, who in return would listen and laugh along with him, but over time her replies seemed perfunctory as once again she was more focused on her own concerns. It had left him slightly deflated, unsatisfied. For the first time since his divorce, David began to feel a needling of irritation towards his former wife. He had been shouldering the self-appointed guilt of the collapse of his marriage with the acknowledgement that he had been the one to continue to push the issue of having children, betraying the agreement on which their relationship was based, and humiliate her in front of her boss in the process. He believed he had been the one to push her unwillingly away. But as grains of truth about his marriage began to revisit his brain in idle memories that seemed to pop up, unprovoked, day by day, he was confronted with the realization that Denise had put very little effort into their marriage. The unfairness of this revelation stung. The resoluteness that she displayed in ending their marriage had devastated him.

As Saturday dawned, David, eager to begin the shoot during the golden hour of early morning, had thrown on a hooded sweatshirt, as spring in the mountains of North Carolina often arrived with brisk winds. After a swallow of coffee and half a bagel, he got into his car, carefully packed with his equipment, and drove north towards Weaverville, where he would meet Nicole, the mayor's daughter, and her horse, already preceded by his own aggressive reputation.

Within minutes, the green-shingled stable complete with copper-topped cupolas was visible from the road, and he drove slowly down the graveled drive lined with crepe myrtles, coming to stop and parking between two horse trailers.

"Hi," said Nicole, striding out the stable's entrance to meet him, formally attired in breeches and boots. "I'm Nic."

"David," he smiled, shaking her outstretched hand. She was a beautiful girl, he thought, a model if she chose to pursue it, but a shame that she was wearing a heavy foundation of make-up. He knew right away that despite the soft lighting, she would lose a certain translucence because of it, a shame, really, because she had beautiful skin.

"Do you want to walk around and see where you might like to shoot?" she asked, waving for him to follow as she returned to the stable. "There's a fence on the other side of the barn with a field behind it that might be nice."

"If it's not facing the sun, that could work," he agreed. "Let me unpack my gear and have a look around."

The spot Nicole had suggested indeed was perfect for a pastoral serene setting, punctuated with oaks not yet leafed out. Before long, she brought out her horse, fully tacked in saddle and bridle, and led him to the fence. "This is Stanley," she introduced the dark bay hunter with a wary, cocked ear, to David. "I was thinking I could be sitting on him," she said.

David crossed his arms and carefully regarded his subjects, now massive in scope, as well as the background. "The only thing with that is you want to be able to see your engagement ring, right? I just wonder, with your holding the reins, if we'll be able to see it?"

"Good point," Nicole agreed.

"What about if you sit on the fence and just hold him?" David asked. "Could look really nice and natural. Less like a hunting print."

"I like that idea," Nicole enthused, and stepped deftly on the bottom rail, lifting herself with ease on to the top.

"So, how did he get the name Stanley?" David wanted to know, as he pulled his reflector from its case.

"I think from Laurel and Hardy," she replied. "Stan Laurel, Because he's sort of cartoony and a worrier. With a long face."

"What would a horse worry about, his hay being late?"

Nichole chuckled. "No, sometimes when we go to horse shows, he gets really worked up in the atmosphere and kind of freaks out. New things make him nervous."

David stood back at a short distance, the reflector balanced and leaning against his legs instead of secured in its stand. "That's nice," he said, as Nicole sat up straight and both girl and horse looked at him. "I just wonder if we can look a little more informal by maybe you putting your hand on Stanley's neck or something."

Nicole complied and David took a few test shots. He looked to see what had been achieved, and, pleased, continued. Stanley, nearly dozing, lay his head across his owner's thighs and Nicole, laughing, threw her arm over his neck, balanced her chin on the top of his head. Her hair fluttered in the breeze, and her diamond ring glinted in the light.

"Ah, that's beautiful," said David, "love it."

"I'd rather he prick his ears forward so that he doesn't look like such a carthorse, though," she said.

David pushed the reflector slightly forward so that the sunlight bounced back toward his subject and Stanley, suddenly alert, raised his head, pricked his ears and snorted at it.

"Perfect!" David laughed, clicking a dozen shots in rapid succession. Suddenly, a gust of wind lifted the circular, golden reflector off the ground and sent it sailing towards the horse who half-reared in fear and plunged backwards several steps, yanking his owner off the fence.

"Whoa, whoa, you're OK." Nicole, on her feet and calm with a lifetime's experience, kept the reins and spoke soothingly to her horse as he trembled with terror from the reflector now resting in front of him.

"So sorry," David apologized, jogging over with the lack of experience that would have taught him not to make sudden movements in front of a nervous twelve-hundred pound animal. As he reached down to snatch up his reflector, a savage pain suddenly tore through his left shoulder and right arm as Stanley, in a flash, not only sunk his teeth through his sweatshirt and into his flesh, but struck out with a foreleg, his steel-shod hoof hitting David so hard in the upper arm and chest that he was knocked over backwards.

"Oh, my God!" Nicole cried, jerking Stanley backwards with a firm, "No!" and well away from David. "I'm so sorry—are you all right?"

David, unreasonably embarrassed, rose quickly to his feet while holding his upper arm with his left hand. The pain was intense, as if he'd been hit by a cinderblock. "The good news," he said, trying to make light of the situation, "is that even though I only got off about a couple of dozen shots before Jaws here tried to eat me, I think we got some good ones. The bad news is I'm right-handed and there's no way I can hold a camera. We're going to have to bag the rest of the day."

"Seriously, are you all right?" Nicole asked again, her face filled with concern. "Do you need your arm looked at? Let me put him back in his stall and I can drive you to the hospital."

"No, no need for that," David, still embarrassed, declined, but added, "Although I could use your help in loading my gear back in the Jeep."

Nicole nodded and led Stanley away, his head hanging low like a scolded child. She was back in five minutes, and still apologizing profusely, she helped pack away the equipment, including the reflector. "I'll just chalk it up to experience," David said before inching slowly into his car, trying not to show his discomfort. "Horses really don't like light bouncing around in front of them."

He drove slowly down the graveled drive, gritting his teeth over each shallow pothole and swearing aloud when he tried to change gears. He was in agony. He drove as long as he could in second gear. Feeling the stickiness that was blood seeping through his sweatshirt and clammy perspiration break out over his brow, David pulled over a few miles down the road, twenty minutes from home. He could have telephoned Nicole since he had her number, but he felt grudgingly emasculated in doing so. Wincing, he reached for his phone and hesitated, having no real idea who to call. The last thing he wanted to do was to worry his mother with all she had been through, and he couldn't handle whatever drama might accompany his sister. He could try Denise. However, he was trying mightily to make a clean break in that respect. His finger hovered over the list of names on his phone. It suddenly occurred to him with despair that the only emergency contact he had at present was Eli. With distaste, David touched his name on the screen and let the phone ring. Eli answered, slightly out of breath. For an awful moment, he feared Eli had finally found a waitress that would fall for his pitch, but then he heard people yelling in the background. Eli was at the park and began to explain he was coaching, but David, feeling worse by the minute, cut him off abruptly and gave an abbreviated version of what had happened before requesting help in being driven home.

"Man, I don't know if my truck will make it up the grade," Eli said on the other end. "Want me to call a cab? Uber?"

"That'll cost a fortune and they'll never find me out here. Damnit, Eli, just get in your truck and give it a shot, will you? I feel like I'm about to pass out." Eli knew the area and realizing the situation was far more serious than he originally thought ended the call by saying he'd find a way to get there.

David tried to lean back in his seat but the wound in his shoulder was so severe he couldn't bear it. Instead he hunched over the steering wheel and closed his eyes. His arm was throbbing so badly he could feel shooting stabbing pains past his elbow. Feeling blood beginning to trickle down his back, he blanched. As masculine as he'd like to think he was, the sight of blood—even the thought of blood—made him nauseous. Then the alarming realization shot through his brain that he hadn't had a tetanus shot in years. He had to consciously slow his breathing as he felt a rising panic in his chest. *I'm going to die here,* he thought grimly, *I'm going to die here in my car because Eli has a piece of shit truck that won't make it up the grade.* He turned on the radio to take his mind off his plight, and listened to a classic rock station until it played a break-up song which made him think depressingly of Denise, so he turned it back off and waited. Another fifteen minutes passed. Now aware that his peripheral vision was waning, David squinted as saw a late model red Subaru slowly approaching. He was so desperate that he decided to flag it down and struggled to get out. The car pulled up alongside and Eli jumped out of the passenger seat while Stephanie stepped out the driver's side.

197

There appeared to be someone else in the backseat, but he couldn't turn his head far enough to see

"Steph?" David croaked, feeling as if his knees were giving way.

"I'm coaching the tavern league this year," Eli, walking towards him, proclaimed with pride. "We were practicing when you called. Steph's on the team, and she sucks. But her car runs."

"Shut up, Eli," Stephanie ordered. She looked closely at David, and he could see alarm in her eyes. "You don't look good. We're getting you to the hospital. Can you scoot over?"

David shook his head.

"All right," she said, then commanded Eli, "Help me get him into the backseat." Between them, they managed to support him beneath each shoulder, David, giving a shout of pain, and when they settled him into the back seat of his own car, Eli did as he was told and elevated David's legs, while Stephanie jogged to her car, opened the back, and brought out a blanket.

"I think you're going into shock, David," she said, draping it across him. "Stay with me, OK?" then over her shoulder, she yelled, "Buster! Come on, you're riding with me."

David opened his eyes and said, "Buster. Buster?"

A boy that looked to be about eight with red hair that stood up like a hairbrush all over his head peered through the back window and said, "Yeah, Buster," before scrambling into the passenger seat. He turned around and looked at David and his eyes grew wide. "Mom, he's got blood all over his back."

"Eli, the keys are in my car. Throw me my purse." Catching it expertly, Stephanie ducked into the driver's seat and started David's car.

"Can you drive a stick?" David asked, weakly.

"Of course I can drive a stick," Stephanie retorted, the gruffness in her voice concealing the very real fear vibrating through her. "What idiot can't drive a stick?"

David felt himself crack a wan smile at her remark. There was something so frank, so unabashedly forthright in Stephanie's manner that somehow instead of being intimidating, she managed to be comforting. He relinquished all control and let her take over. She found the way back to the interstate in three turns and instructed her son to phone the hospital and tell them she was bringing in a patient who appeared to be going into shock. It was the last thing David remembered hearing.

Chapter 29

ELI, PUTTING STEPHANIE'S CAR into reverse, paused for a moment to light a cigarette. As he began to turn the Subaru towards the hospital in pursuit of David's Jeep, he suddenly saw a cell phone on the side of the road. Throwing the car into park, Eli leapt out to retrieve it. It appeared to be David's, and Eli, his nerves still on edge from seeing the state of his friend, began to punch every familiar name he found in a desperate attempt to inform the family.

Stephanie was met at the hospital by a male nurse and an EMT with a gurney. She cried, "I don't know if he's breathing," as she watched David being expertly lifted and rushed inside. She was shaking uncontrollably and couldn't even attempt to feign calmness for the sake of her son as she jerked the car around to the closest parking space and told him to hurry as they both ran back into Emergency.

"Can you give us his information?" asked a woman at the check in desk.

"Only that his name is David Merriman," Stephanie replied. "I don't know anything else. His wallet is probably on him. If not, I can run back to his car and look for it."

"Any idea if he's allergic to any medication?"

Stephanie shook her head.

"So, to be clear, you are no relation to him?"

"No," Stephanie said, then added, "just a friend."

She put her arm around Buster and led him to the waiting area. Her son wanted a Coke out of the vending machine and she opened her purse and gave him a handful of quarters. "Get a water instead, OK, Buster?"

Stephanie scanned the waiting room and took in an elderly man in a wheelchair and a young couple, one of whom was holding an icepack to their swollen cheek. There was a wide screen television turned on too loudly with Saturday morning cartoons blasting throughout the area. Buster returned and pleased, settled down next to her to watch TV while Stephanie wanted to scream out loud in protest that such inane triviality shouldn't be allowed while people were in pain and frightened to death over the sake of loved ones. She got up and paced a couple of times within sight of her son. It was surreal to even be here, she thought, surreal when Eli had yelled for her across the field. The day had started out beautifully: she and Buster had a lot of laughs as she worked to improve her game so she could assist him with his, her son being passionate about baseball. He had been standing just behind the fence, fingers entwined through the chain link, egging her on and laughing so hard his elfin face was pink, which made her crack up in return and completely miss the ball that rolled between her legs. It was then that Eli had yelled at her and she purposely ignored him, thinking she was getting reamed for her error. Having never seen her paunchy customer exert any physical effort whatsoever since she had known him, she frowned when he began to run towards her, and she saw from his expression that something was wrong.

Leaning against a wall with her arms crossed, she thought how uncomfortable she'd initially felt by Eli's request. It wasn't that she wouldn't come to David's aid—of course she would—but it was awkward, really. His unusual absence from the bar felt like an avoidance of her. She'd blown it, she thought, scuffing the tip of her running shoe back and forth along the polished floor. She'd been such an idiot to completely misjudge everything she'd been feeling, and he'd been feeling, the night she had impulsively kissed him. What was she thinking? After so pompously informing him she didn't want to get drunk, she couldn't even blame her actions on alcohol. No, she thought, still cringing from the memory, she'd allowed every bit of the school girl crush she'd had on him that had been bottled up for as long as she could remember to come bursting out the night she had fallen, laughing, against his chest, effectively horrifying him. No wonder he had been in such a hurry to leave; he was probably mortified. She knew he was freshly divorced and she had seen how it had affected him. *Hell,* she thought, recalling his behavior over the preceding months, she had witnessed the change in both his demeanor and posture when he came in to meet Eli each week, and while she couldn't say she could tell his marriage was in trouble, she knew something was seriously wrong.

She had seen Denise, just once. She was good-looking and smart and chicly put together. Stephanie even remembered that she had politely asked what the house white wine was, warily ordered it. When it arrived, she took one sip and left the rest. She remained courteous and quiet but seemed uncomfortable, electing not to join in with David and Eli and a couple of other friends. And she never returned. Stephanie figured that a scruffy pub off Lexington Street wasn't terribly alluring to someone like Denise, but she didn't hold it against her. She couldn't really see Denise and David as a couple, although she couldn't deny that David appeared gutted in the weeks before his divorce, rarely speaking, everything about his manner strained and defeated. As strongly attracted to him as she was—and just as disappointed to learn he was married—her heart never leapt at the knowledge she'd gleaned in pieces of conversation overheard while serving him drinks: his marriage was over. In fact, she had ached for him. He had such a cheeky smile that she hadn't seen in ages, and even Eli hadn't been quite as obnoxious as usual. Slowly, especially after Christmas, which must have been excruciating for him, he began to regain a little of his old self, jibing back at Eli's taunts and casting an occasional smile in her direction when he ordered yet another round for his friend. She told herself firmly not to read anything into those smiles, but her heart melted with each, and she was determined not to let on that she felt anything differently for him than for any of her regulars.

Stephanie returned to sit next to her son whose eyes remained firmly fixed upon the screen, his bottle of water unopened. She picked up a magazine next to her and flicked through it, then put it back, unable to concentrate. She dropped her head and clasped her hands together at her knees and began to pray, her request rapid and insistent. She looked towards the broad automatic doors that separated her from the emergency room and began to tremble as each scenario played through her head. David had looked frighteningly pale, his skin clammy. She hadn't seen his wound but the amount of blood had terrified her. She had no idea the extent of injury to his arm. Suddenly she caught sight of Eli, trundling in and approaching the woman at the admissions desk who Stephanie had spoken with earlier. He seemed to be gesturing angrily before turning away with frustration. Spotting Stephanie, he came over, reeking of nicotine.

"What the hell is going on? They won't tell me anything, won't let me back there because I'm not family," he said.

Stephanie shook her head. "I don't know anything more than you do."

"How was he when you got here?"

"I kept trying to look at him in the rearview mirror to see if he had lost consciousness, because I would have pulled over to do CPR, but I couldn't really see. When I got here and jumped out, he wasn't responding." She looked at Eli and her voice broke. "I don't know if he was breathing."

Eli frowned and then asked, "But passing out isn't that big a deal, right? You don't just stop breathing if you pass out."

"If you go into shock you do," Stephanie replied, tears springing to her eyes. "Your blood pressure drops and you can go into cardiac arrest."

"How do you know all that stuff?"

"I have a kid, you learn all that stuff. Plus, I used to lifeguard when I was a teenager."

Eli digested the information. Peering at her, he said, "You've fallen for him, haven't you?"

Stephanie shook her head violently. "We're friends. I'd be torn up if this happened to any of my friends."

"You wouldn't be acting like this if it was me in there. And I'm your friend."

Stephanie looked at Eli, blankly. "No, you're not."

"That's only because I don't tip as much as David," he pointed out. "By the way, the ashtray in your car doesn't work. It won't pull out."

"Dammit, Eli," she hissed, mindful of her son. "Have you been smoking in my car?"

"No," Eli lied, "I just thought you would like to know it doesn't work." He looked up. "David's mother and his ex just walked in." He got to his feet and looked back over his shoulder at her. "You coming?"

Stephanie shook her head. "No," she said. "They're going to be worried enough as it is. We don't need to gang up on them."

She knew, however, and suspected that even Eli knew, that she would find it difficult to stand amongst the women who had deep relational ties to David while she alone had none. She sat against the wall of the waiting room, feeling frightened and isolated, and absentmindedly began to stroke the spiked red hair of her son. Buster had always looked as if he'd stuck his finger into an electrical outlet. He lifted his face, his nose and cheeks sprinkled with freckles as fine as grains of nutmeg, and smiled at her. He was old enough to understand that what he had seen had been alarming and serious, yet young enough to be quickly distracted by what appeared on the screen in front of him. Stephanie suddenly felt a wave of gratitude towards the cartoons continuing to blare from the television. She glanced up and took in David's mother, seeing the resemblance in the shape of the face, and her slender, elegant frame that was tall for a woman of her generation. She watched as the woman stood transfixed, speaking with Eli, one hand pressed to her mouth. She was being supported more emotionally than physically by Denise, who stood tense and still, taking in each detail, her arm around the elderly woman's shoulders. Denise walked confidently to the admissions desk and after a few moments, turned and spoke with David's mother. Within minutes, a nurse appeared from the other side of the automatic doors and ushered his mother inside, holding up her hand to illustrate only one person allowed at a time. Denise, Stephanie noted, sat down at the admissions desk to give David's vital details. She would be able to do that, of course, Stephanie thought. Despite being grateful, she suddenly felt overwhelming sadness. This beautiful woman, so cool, so collected, the longtime object of David's intense desire, would know every facet of his being: "Is he allergic to any medication?" "No." "Does he have insurance?" "Yes." "Can you fill in his address?" "Yes." "Social Security number?" "Yes." "Next of kin?" "Yes." "Does he have a living will?" "No."

Stephanie looked at Denise's slightly broad yet still feminine shoulders and erect back clad in a beautifully fitted cardigan and immediately became woefully aware of her own sweaty appearance, having come straight from the baseball diamond: her hair greasy with perspiration, slicked back in a ponytail beneath a baseball cap with the monogrammed logo of a beer mug emblazoned across the brim. She looked self-consciously at her ripped jeans, one bare knee stained with red clay as she'd tried to nab a grounder, her sweatshirt grass-stained. Eli had stepped outside, presumably to have another smoke, and he reentered just as Lissie burst back through the door, her face emanating joy with arms outstretched to embrace Denise. With the experience of silently observing others at a distance, Stephanie could feel the relief that swept through the small group.

That was all she needed to see, she thought, giving a silent and heartfelt prayer of thanks. Rising, she took Buster's hand. She wasn't needed here. David had those that he most loved gathered near and they would be the first faces he saw when he opened his eyes. Picking up her purse with her other hand, she ushered her son around the group, giving them a wide berth as she left the hospital unseen.

Outside, there was a dilemma. She nearly turned around to exchange keys with Eli, but after a quickly reconsidering, she reasoned that David's car and his equipment, worth thousands, would be safer with her. Eli lived in a dicey neighborhood and couldn't be entrusted to care for his own things, let alone someone else's. However, as she made sure Buster had fastened his seatbelt as she clicked hers closed, she was only too aware of a deeper truth. Feeling as isolated as she was from David, she chose his car as some sort of solace: to sit in his seat, to listen to the stations he had programmed, to place her hands in the same place where he gripped the steering wheel. She chewed her bottom lip to control her emotions and put the Jeep into first gear. It was pathetic, she knew, but it was all she had.

Chapter 30

LEIGH HAD PICKED UP her phone and put it back down three times in the past half hour. What a nightmare her life had become, she thought. She was still reeling from her husband's infidelity and had yet to assume any responsibility for her actions towards all involved. *Dammit, I'm the one who's been screwed here,* she frowned as her mind continued to revolve around what she considered to be betrayals from both her mother and Wes. *So why should I be apologizing to anyone?* Yet her hand hovered over the phone once more.

It was Tracy who had put this idea into her head to call her mother after Leigh had emailed her friend the following morning in floods of tears and a rambling plea for help. Tracy, as expected, had responded immediately, saying she would be over in minutes. And also as expected, she brought a bottle of wine.

"It's pretty early for that, isn't it?" Leigh mentioned, glancing at the kitchen clock and allowing herself to be tightly embraced by her friend.

"When you find out your husband's been fooling around, it's always wine o'clock," Tracy replied and sat down promptly at the kitchen table with a corkscrew. She had listened attentively to Leigh's sorrowful saga, from her father's illness to being blindsided by Wes's affair, ending with what she felt was a betrayal of trust from her own mother. What Leigh had glossed over, however, was Wes's subsequent accusation of her long term negative behavior, as well as the circumstances revolving around her mother's actions.

Tracy, not unacquainted with this pattern of behavior from her friend of thirty years, had begun to gently nudge Leigh towards what she suspected to be the truth.

"So you think he's having an affair?" she had asked, pouring her friend a generous glass.

"Of course I do," Leigh sniffed. "I mean, does he really think I would buy some 'it's not what it looked like' excuse? That's almost more insulting than his actual infidelity."

"But of all people, Wes?" Tracy asked, frowning with disbelief. "I mean, granted I don't live with the guy like you do, but I've never known him to be untruthful about anything."

The comment chafed because Leigh knew it to be accurate. However, she was kept from nodding in agreement by the grudging knowledge that Wes's truthfulness must then also be applied to her own behavior, which she wasn't ready to accept. So she simply shrugged.

"Did he say if it had been going on for a long time," Tracy pressed, "or just started?"

"Oh, all nice and innocent for evidently several months," Leigh smirked, warming up to the wine after a few ambivalent sips. "He *says* they were just friends, that she was nothing more than a business contact. Then, he said, they began talking for *hours*—can you believe that? Hours and hours, with nothing happening, just confiding in each other, and then *she* initiated the kiss in the car when Kirsten and my mother saw them. Just leaned in and threw herself at him, because, as you know, Wes is such a hunk she couldn't resist."

Tracy squinted an eye. "Wes said that?"

"No," Leigh admitted. "He didn't say that last part, but really, it's so ridiculous."

"What did he say they talked about?"

Leigh looked down at her wineglass and traced a finger around the rim. "He didn't say. Who knows? Who knows what the hell Wes wants to talk about?"

Tracy hesitated, absorbing the gravity of the moment.

"You should," she replied after a few moments. "You should know what he wants to talk about."

Leigh rose abruptly and opened a kitchen cabinet.

"I can't drink on an empty stomach," she muttered, returning with a package of potato chips. She ripped open the bag, took out a handful and offered the rest to Tracy, who took her share.

"I'm not really that interested in what Wes has to talk about," Leigh retorted, deliberately averting her eyes. "As far as I'm concerned, he hasn't been interested in anything I've had to say for months. And he certainly hasn't had my back lately, in regards to my mother, or the house. I'm sorry, Tracy, but all of a sudden it feels like you're beginning to side with him and everyone seems to forget that *I'm* the one being shit on, here. I mean, for God's sake, how the hell could he cheat on me? Destroy everything we've had together?"

Tracy looked at Leigh, soberly. She reached across the table and squeezed her friend's hand.

"I've known you since we were kids," she began, "so you know you can count on me to be straight up with you, right?"

Leigh nodded, fighting the tears that were welling up in her eyes.

"Leigh," she began, drawing courage. "I don't think you've been in love with Wes for years."

Leigh's mouth fell open.

"How can you *say* that," she cried. "How can you? Who do you think cooks and cleans and irons his shirts? Not that other woman, I can tell you. *Me*, that's who!"

"That's obligation," Tracy countered. "That's not love and you know it. Listen, this is not about me attacking you, so don't get defensive, OK? You and Wes and Gary and me, we used to have a good time when we'd all have a night out. I remember Wes as a pretty chatty guy and more importantly, I specifically remember him being courteous and attentive when you would speak or tell a story or whatever. But I've got to say, in recent years, it seems to have deteriorated into you sort of picking on him and Wes hanging back, not contributing anymore."

"I suppose your marriage is a bed of roses?" Leigh sniped, bristling with resentment.

Tracy smiled kindly at her friend.

"Nice try," she said. "But we're not going to derail this conversation, although I will answer your question. Hell no, my marriage isn't a bed of roses but it's pretty comfortable, like an old pair of shoes, you know? Does Gary still shake my cage? Oh, Lord, no. And if you asked him that same question, I'm sure he'd say the same thing about me, especially after having three kids and stretch marks that look like a topographic map. He leaves his wet towels on the floor in the bathroom and his dirty underwear a foot away from the laundry hamper. In twenty years of marriage, he still hasn't learned to open that lid. Drives me nuts. But you know something, Leigh? We talk. We talk a lot and even better, we listen to each other. We still crack each other up. He's somebody who thinks puns are funny, bless his heart, and maybe I'm laughing at him more than with him, but we still laugh. And most importantly, there's not a day that doesn't go by that I'm not glad he's in my life," she sobered suddenly and asked Leigh point blank, "So, tell me, if Wes was no longer in your life, would it make that much difference to you?"

Leigh sat frozen and rattled. She had never considered the possibility and couldn't immediately answer. She looked past Tracy and began to shake her head very slowly back and forth. After a very long minute or so, she looked directly at her best friend.

"I don't know," she whispered. "Tracy, I don't know."

"It's a tough question," Tracy replied. "But maybe worth considering."

Leigh nodded, then sighed. "I feel like we're together out of habit. I've been so angry at him because he refuses to see what my mother's house means to me—"

"I don't think that's true," Tracy interrupted. "I think he knows *exactly* what the house means to you, but that doesn't mean he wants the same thing. A house is a huge deal, Leigh. It's not like one of you wanting to go to the beach for vacation and the other wanting to go to the mountains. You're talking about the biggest investment there is for a couple. And I wouldn't be surprised if it doesn't scare the hell out of him. Try to see it his way: what if you guys were able to scrape up enough to come up with the down payment and buy it from your mom? And let's not even talk about the cost of property taxes and utilities...but what if you moved in and then Wes lost his job or the economy crashes into another recession? There you would be, underwater, this giant house around your neck..."

"It's the only thing I've ever really wanted in my whole life," Leigh cut her off sharply, tears freely flowing down her cheeks. "You know, I've never asked for designer clothes or jewelry. I've never owned a new car. None of that matters to me, but Tracy, the thought of that house going to some new owner who would probably gut it, rip out the kitchen and turn it into some bullshit open-plan living space with granite countertops and a 'media room'...I can't stand it." She looked imploringly at her friend, and repeated, beginning to sob, "I can't stand it, I just can't stand it."

Tracy stayed silent for some time and let her cry. Finally and as gently as she could, she asked, "Is it worth ending your marriage for?"

With a new defiance beginning to flare within her, Leigh suddenly sat up straight and blew her nose. She looked Tracy straight in the eye.

"Yes," she said with complete conviction. "Yes, it is."

Tracy felt a physical chill creep up her spine but said nothing. She did glance at her watch and mention there was no rush, but she'd promised to drive an elderly neighbor to the dentist in an hour's time. It was a rare thing for Tracy to lie, however she was feeling desperately uncomfortable and very sorry for Wes, whom she'd known and liked for years. And then there was their daughter.

"How does Kirsten seem to be handling things?" she asked, tentatively.

"She's not really speaking to me," Leigh shrugged, "since I had that scene with my mother." Glancing up at her friend, she added, "I guess that's another thing that's all my fault?"

"Lord, Leigh," Tracy sighed, leaning forward to top up Leigh's glass. "I don't know. I mean, are you asking my opinion?"

"Does it matter?" Leigh replied, tartly. "You're going to give it to me, anyway."

"You're right," Tracy replied, "I will, and remember, this is tough love, OK? I have never known your mother to do anything deliberately behind your back. Ever. I think maybe what happened with Kirsten was that your mother sensed things weren't quite right at home, and when Kirsten wanted to do something nice for Wes on his birthday, she said yes, less for Wes's sake and more to help Kirsten. Should she have asked your permission? Absolutely, but given the fact that you were in a different time zone and Kirsten was feeling sorry for her father, I'd say she was really trying to do the right thing. I'd also guess no one is feeling worse about it than she is."

"Kirsten said she was trying to hide it, but she was crying," Leigh admitted, sighing heavily, "and I can count on one hand the number of times I've ever seen my mother cry. But even if her intentions were good, look at the results. I guess I would have found out about Wes's girlfriend at some point, but Kirsten would've been spared from actually seeing it. So it's really hard for me to be forgiving right now."

Tracy, who had barely touched her wine, picked up her car keys from the table and began to rise to her feet. Leigh looked up.

"You're going?" she asked, surprised.

"Yeah," Tracy replied, pulling on her jacket, then joked, "my work here is done."

"How do you figure that?" Leigh retorted. "Everything's still a mess."

Tracy leaned over and gave her friend a long, firm hug.

"Yes, it is," she agreed. "Everything *is* a mess. And everyone seems very unhappy." She zipped up the front of her jacket and looped her purse strap over her shoulder. "But the good news is that it'll only take one person to make everything better. Stop being a pain in the ass, Leigh. You might hate me for saying that, but I love you too much not to say it. I'm standing here, watching your marriage and your relationship with your family go down in flames and it's all so preventable."

"So, I give up my dream, and ta-da, everyone will be happy?" Leigh scoffed. "And then I'll just keep my little self content sitting in a corner and knitting somewhere? Is that it?"

"If you see it that way, sure," Tracy replied, refusing to take the bait. "But let me just say this and I'll get out of your hair. I get how much you love that house, I really do. I know what it means to you. But Leigh, that house won't be standing next to you when Kirsten is walking down the aisle with the man she marries. That house won't be presenting you with your first grandchild. And that house won't be holding your hand when you're old and in your last days. Your family does—if you're lucky enough to still have one." Tracy leaned forward and gave her friend a peck on top of her head while Leigh sat, unmoved.

Now she sat by herself and contemplated the phone, lying screen up next to her on the table. She had not yet decided if Tracy was being entirely fair. She trusted her enough to know that everything she said had come from a place of good intentions, but Leigh couldn't help thinking that no one seemed to understand the *depths* of her feelings, and if they did, surely they would realize it was necessary to help her in any way they could. The problem, she wanted to shout, was that everyone—her mother, Wes, Kirsten, David, even Tracy—all thought of the house as nothing more than bricks and mortar. They failed to see it as it was to her: a living, breathing museum of everything she held dear—an essential part of her very being. To lose the house would be tantamount to losing a limb. Except, she thought bitterly, people who lose their limbs seem to go bravely on, forging ahead. *Not me,* she thought, shaking her head ruefully. *If I lose the house, I'll lose everything.*

She began to think of her mother, so eager to sell up without a backward glance for the sole reason of financing this ridiculous fantasy of running away to a country Leigh had never visited nor had a desire to. She could only think of the age-old stereotype of bad food, bad teeth and bad weather. Only her mother, she sniffed, who would walk out every morning despite the elements could find anything romantic in that. Now, if it was California, Leigh considered, she could almost understand wanting to move there. The weather had been just about perfect, and yes, the traffic was insane and the people pretty odd, but everyone she met had smiled and been helpful. Especially Libbie, with whom, she reflected sadly, she felt closer to than her own mother.

"Don't be too hard on your mom," she grudgingly remembered Libbie advising. *"I'm pretty sure if she hadn't been strong enough, especially with two children, to make some sort of ultimatum and divorce your father, he might not be with us, now."* There was truth in that, Leigh knew, no matter how much she wanted to deny it.

Sighing, she picked up the phone and dialed her mother.

Chapter 31

DAVID SAT EXPECTANTLY ON the edge of his hospital bed, waiting to be discharged and for his ride home. It had been without a doubt the most bizarre two days of his life. *"Proximal humeral fracture,"* the ER doctor, a weary-looking woman, had informed him, *"as well as a cracked rib."* Both diagnoses came after a lengthy examination and X-rays, which had been excruciating. *"Can you move your arm a little more forward?"* "Hell, no!" he had shouted, trying to will himself not to vomit. He knew there had been a gap in his memory from being driven by Stephanie straight up to Emergency, and came to with a woozy jerk, suffering the worse pain he'd ever known as his blood pressure was elevated chemically and fluids administered. The entire back of his sweatshirt, cut free from his body as he lay on his back, was soaked in blood and the back of his shoulder had required no fewer than twenty-five stitches with talk of a possible permanent indention at the site. Stanley had evidently taken a bit of muscle with his bite, and just the thought of it made David queasy.

He recalled seeing the color drain from his mother's face, when she was allowed in to see him after he had been stabilized. Recognizing the very real fear in the eyes of the woman who had always held her emotions quietly in hand had made him suddenly frightened of his own situation. He was aware of a tube connected from the back of his hand to a drip and a machine that monitored his heart and blood pressure. She couldn't embrace him, he was in such pain, but she sat next to his bed and stroked his forehead and spoke soothingly until the morphine eased him away from her. When he next opened his eyes, he was so shocked to see Denise that he was speechless. She, too, had initially appeared frightened, but smiled and held his hand. He remembered being profoundly grateful for her presence, yet strangely uncomfortable in his vulnerability. As feminine and delicate as she might appear, Denise oozed an aura of strength, and somehow with her simply standing over him, the insecurity that had plagued him during the last two years of their marriage now seemed to swell into an odd sort of emasculation. It made him feel like a child in her presence. The feeling began to dissipate as she relayed to him what the doctor had told her, how he was in excellent hands, how she hoped he knew she would be happy to help in any way she could. And, as always, she looked beautiful.

"Very kind offer," he had murmured, "but I know how busy you are."

"Some things are worth making priorities," she had replied with genuine warmth in her eyes.

He closed his own, sadly aware of the irony that he had waited to both hear and feel that sort of selfless sentiment from her for their entire marriage.

And then when he was finally admitted to a room four hours later to be kept overnight for observation, Eli had shuffled in and told him that it was Stephanie who had, both figuratively and quite literally, saved the day.

"Some nurse in the ER told me you need to thank whoever thought to elevate your feet," he said, opening a packet of crackers David had left untouched from his dinner. "Seems it kept your blood pressure this side of the grave. That would be Steph."

"Steph?" David had asked with surprise, fighting for coherency amid his pain medication.

"Well, it sure as hell wasn't me. I took one look at you and just about lost my cookies. She was cool as a cucumber. Knew exactly what to do: get a blanket, get your feet up. She was on her game."

"Yeah," David mused, thinking back. "I remember that. And I remember a redheaded kid staring at me through the back window."

"That's her kid, Buster."

"Perfect name. He looked like a Buster."

Eli had returned David's phone and mentioned, before departing, that Stephanie had kept his car because she claimed she would look after his equipment far better than Eli would. David sighed with relief.

"I've been worried about my camera all day," he admitted.

After Eli left, and with his phone in his hand, David found Eli had programmed Stephanie's name to his contacts list. He hesitated before calling her. Yes, he wanted to get his car back, but at the same time, with his right arm immobilized and strapped to his side, he couldn't drive it. And yes, he wanted his equipment back, safe and sound in his studio. But most importantly, he wanted to thank Stephanie profusely. Stephanie, whom he had been avoiding and yet, who had actually saved his life. It would have been a straightforward sincere call to make had Eli not tossed one last observation to him before leaving.

"By the way, dude, she was crying in the waiting room. She was scared you hadn't made it."

Strange, he thought, because he never saw Stephanie after he was admitted. Perhaps, he considered, somewhat chauvinistically, she was simply overcome with emotion from the entire ordeal. It had been pretty frightening for all concerned. Even the mayor had called, beside himself, offering whatever assistance necessary and rambling wildly about using David for more work than he could ever wish. Whether he was being genuine or trying to avoid a lawsuit or both, David didn't know, but he was grateful for the call and told him he would be fine.

He closed his eyes and replayed the morning, flinching at the memory of the sudden, searing pain of being bitten as well as the shock of the blow upon his arm, and, as it later became evident, his rib from the horse's hoof. He'd never been hit so hard in his life and it left him breathless. Had Nicole not been present, he would have been writhing in pain on the ground. Certainly it had been ridiculously foolhardy to decline the girl's offer for help, and had it not been for Stephanie...everything swam before him...

"Stay with me, OK?"

Was that what she'd said? Ordered, actually, her frank brown eyes filled with apprehension. He wondered if she would consider coming to pick him up and drop him off at his apartment. His mother had pleaded for him to let her take him back to her house to look after him, but he fielded her protestations by pointing out she lived over half an hour from the city and he wanted to be near the studio. He knew Denise would come but he still felt intimidated in her presence—why, he wasn't sure. Looking at his bare legs below the hospital gown, he realized with a start he had nothing to wear. His sweatshirt had been trashed, his jeans grass-stained and dirty from his fall in a plastic bag next to the bed. Besides all this, he felt grubby as hell. It was a lot to ask from Stephanie, he knew, regardless of their pact to remain 'just friends,' but perhaps he could count on her once more. He pressed her number.

She sounded surprised to hear his voice and, sure, she said, she could help him out if he didn't mind waiting until her mother returned home *to* look after Buster. He was embarrassed to mention he had nothing to wear and awkwardly suggested that as his key to the apartment was on his car key ring, might she consider, if he gave her his address, picking up a pair of sweatpants and a shirt with buttons as it wasn't possible to pull anything over his head. The thought of her seeing the state of his apartment—he hadn't made his bed or washed dishes in a couple of days—was one thing. Stephanie going through his underwear drawer was quite another. She must have sensed his discomfort because she immediately launched into the casual banter to which he was accustomed.

"Look, Merriman," she began, "I'm not really comfortable going into your bachelor pad and rifling through your things, so why don't I just swing by the store and buy some sweats for you to wear? What are you, a large?"

"Yeah, large. That would be great, Steph, thanks. I'll pay you back."

"You bet you're going to pay me back. You're also going to pay the hazmat crew I'm going to have to hire to scrub out the smell of smoke Eli left in my car."

"Oh, man," David said, beginning to laugh. He immediately regretted it as the pain from his ribs stabbed across his chest like a knife. He gasped and said, "Ow."

"Only hurts when you laugh?" Stephanie cracked.

"Big time," he replied.

"All right," she said, ending the call. "I'll be there as soon as I can, probably about an hour."

He put down the phone. With his left hand extended very slowly owing to the soreness of that shoulder, and not wanting to pull the stitches, he scratched his stubble. No way was he going to be shaving anytime soon. He thought about Stephanie and realized with an amused lift of his eyebrows that the reason he liked her was that she wasn't unlike the male friends he had. Sure, she was kind of attractive, certainly not a knockout, but she had a ready grin and her expressive brown eyes disappeared into merry slits when she laughed, which was often, but there was nothing overtly feminine about her. Unlike many of the women he knew, Stephanie wore very little make-up, and with the exception of having the ends of her hair dipped in purple dye (perhaps a last ditch effort to cling to rebellious youth as she appeared to be in her early thirties), she presented herself as she was in an open, 'one of the guys' sort of way, although, he reminded himself, with a nicer bum. And she was funny, wickedly funny. Compared to Denise, she was also forthright and bold, however offering seemingly none of the hidden, enigmatic layers that he had found so irresistible about his former wife. Denise was cool, charming, smart, a quick wit when so inclined. When they began seeing each other, there seemed to be something new he discovered each week: she spoke French, she could make a soufflé, she had turned down a tennis scholarship, she had studied the piano...in short, she had benefitted greatly from a privileged upbringing and intended to continue living that heady lifestyle. She was also intensely competitive and David was all too well aware of its effect.

It was an hour and change when there was a crisp knock on his door and Stephanie poked in her curious, freckled face. She wore a smile and her hair hung loose, swinging well below her shoulders. She held up a yellow plastic bag and proclaimed, "You know you're special when your friends shop for you at the Dollar Store."

"Hey, there," David smiled, finding himself immediately at ease. "I'm assuming you bought the entire spring collection for my wardrobe?"

"Don't be greedy," she retorted and pulled up a chair to sit next to him. Opening the bag, she pulled out a pair of men's sweatpants in a camouflage pattern, to his horror.

"Oh, nooo," he groaned.

"Sorry, it's all they had. This stuff was leftover from winter and on their clearance rack. They didn't have any other sweats. It was either this or a tiger print. But wait, there's more!" With that, she whipped out a button down faux Hawaiian shirt.

"You're killing me!" he said. He began to laugh, then did his best to stop, holding his left hand across his ribs. "I can't wear this!"

"But Merriman," Stephanie insisted, opting to use his surname as a new term of friendly endearment, "with the camouflage bottoms, no one will see you, right? So all they'll see is the shirt as you get wheeled out of here."

"Eli wouldn't even wear this," he pointed out ruefully.

"Oh, yes he would," Stephanie countered, "and he'd save it for Sunday best."

David, despite himself, was shaking silently with laughter and grimaced with pain.

"OK, I'll stop." Stephanie controlled herself, taking note of his discomfort. "But one more thing. It felt way too weird to be buying underwear for you, so I didn't. You're going to have to go commando, *capiche?*"

David was relieved when a nurse came in with his discharge papers and before discretely stepping out of the room, Stephanie mentioned cheekily that David would need help dressing. Once outside in the corridor, she stood opposite his door and leaned against the wall, exhaling slowly. Her chest had felt tight with expectancy. She had been both unprepared and surprised to receive his call and simply hearing his voice on the other end, sounding both warm and apologetic if not a bit uncomfortable, requesting help, felt terribly intimate, and her heart had leapt with gratitude for his recovery and the opportunity to see him. She had already chastised herself a thousand times for having initially pushed him away and was determined to remain as casual as possible. She told herself firmly on the drive up that he had no romantic interest in her, and she could handle it. What she couldn't deny was that her heart continued to pound in his presence, but she would find a way to muffle it as it was better to remain simply friends with David than not see him at all. Even addressing him by his last name was crafted as an attempt to further distance herself.

After a few minutes, a nursing assistant with a wheelchair arrived and tapped on the door. As the nurse verbally consented, the door was opened and Stephanie, biting her lip to prevent both of them laughing, watched as a ridiculously attired David was eased into the wheelchair.

"Is this necessary?" he asked the nurse. "I can walk. Slowly, but I can walk."

"Sorry," she smiled, with a shake of her head. "Hospital policy."

Stephanie looked up at the nursing assistant, a hulking man with enormous forearms. She nearly offered to push David to his car, then realized that might feel embarrassing for him under the circumstances, so she trailed behind, carrying the bag that contained his personal items. As they exited the elevator taking them down to the first floor, Stephanie mentioned she'd bring the car around so he wouldn't have to wait and jogged ahead. David watched her from behind and thought she even ran like a guy: athletically, not a trace of feminine self-consciousness.

Mindful of his rib, she reclined the passenger seat back a couple of notches so that he wouldn't be sitting painfully upright. The assistant methodically lowered David into the seat and even lifted each of his legs from the ground and gently bent and swung them slowly around and into the car as if he were a child. David's right upper arm, encased in a short cast, was strapped to his side for stability and he was unable to even fasten the seatbelt. The assistant pulled the belt from high above the seat and passed it over his body, clicked it closed, then pulled the wheelchair away and closed the door gently. Stephanie climbed in the driver's side. It felt intimate, yet Stephanie felt slightly ill at ease and imagined David felt the same.

"Are you comfortable?" she asked.

"As much as I can be," he replied. "Just don't hit any potholes."

"You got it," she said, feeling a bit more confident in that she felt an inviting sense of responsibility.

She didn't initiate any conversation as she carefully maneuvered in and out of traffic, but he began to chuckle when she grimaced as she was forced to brake rather too hard when someone stopped abruptly in front of them.

"Your face," he said. "Stephanie, each time you step on the brake you look as if you're hurting worse than I am. And then you hold your breath each time you let off the clutch. It's funny."

"Seriously, with what you're wearing, you're saying I look funny?"

"You look like you're sitting on ice cubes."

"And you look like you went shopping at Boy George's yard sale."

They were stopped at a light and, gritting his teeth through his laughter, David suddenly remembered he was going to need his pain medication prescription filled at a pharmacy.

"Can do," Stephanie said, "although you know what they say about laughter—"

"What they should say about laughter is that it freaking hurts like hell," he countered, then he looked at her soberly and touched her lightly on the arm with his left hand. "You're pretty great, you know that? I'm really grateful for everything you've done."

"Yeah, well." She tried to toss it away.

"Eli said you probably would have left him to die."

"That's because with Eli, it would have been a mercy killing."

"Oh, God," groaned David in his laughter, holding himself with one arm. "Uncle. Seriously, uncle. I can't take it."

Two minutes from home with David feeding Stephanie directions, it suddenly occurred to her.

"Can you sleep lying down, flat?"

"No way."

"Do you have a recliner?"

"No," he replied, frowning, her train of thought dawning on him. "I didn't even think about that. I have a couch, and I might be able to sleep on that if I prop enough pillows on the end."

Stephanie drew to a halt in front of his complex and looked at him.

"But then how will you get up, when you need to? You can't roll over, not with your rib and your arm." She went back and forth, internally debating while David sat quietly thinking, until she found the courage to suggest as casually as possible, "Look, I have a recliner at my house. I can call Eli, and if he hasn't already sold my car, get him to meet me, and we'll load it up and bring it to your place."

"No, no, that's way too much trouble," David shook his head. "I've already ruined enough of your weekend."

"Or, alternatively—" She took a deep breath to find the courage to make fun of herself at her own expense, so to offer, "You can stay with me this first night. I know you want to be in your own man cave, doing your own manly stuff, but at the end of the day, Merriman, you're going to need help getting up, or getting something to eat, and I promise I won't throw myself at you again, OK? What d'ya say?"

David smiled at her generosity but couldn't prevent the unease that began to pump within his chest at the suggestion. He desperately wanted his privacy. He needed a shower, wanted to be under no obligation to be anything other than completely self-indulgent with his first, considerably painful night of healing.

"Nah, I'll manage," he said, yet was sincere when he added, "but I really appreciate it."

She nodded and pulled in close to the front steps of his unit and got out, opening his door. As slender as David was, his weight was still considerable for her five and a half foot frame, and she had to really struggle, as did he, to not only walk to the curb but to mount the first step. Anything that caused his waist or chest to move, despite being taped, caused him to grunt with pain, and he was incapable of using his right arm to pull himself along with the railing. After three attempts, Stephanie stopped to catch her breath and looked at him, raising an eyebrow.

"Yeah, sure you'll manage."

"We've got to go up a flight of stairs, too, to get to my place," David said, accepting defeat. "All right, I give. I'm sorry, I had to see if I could do it."

It never occurred to Stephanie to jokingly rub it in with an, 'I told you so.' She simply nodded and said, "I get it. I would have, too. Nobody wants to stay at some stranger's house when you feel miserable; you want to be on your own."

Slowly, painfully, she helped him back into his car and got back in to drive. "It's only a few minutes away," she said encouragingly.

Had his pain medication not been wearing off, it might have piqued David's interest to see where the girl he knew only as the local bartender lived. For now, he simply longed for a comfortable place to rest and was therefore only mildly surprised when she got on Highway 25 and headed south for little more than five minutes, turned right off the exit onto a quiet road before taking the first left, little more than a country lane winding through an invitingly rural area. He had supposed she would have lived in some tiny studio in town, never in the country. They passed a couple of trailers of which he assumed either might easily be her address, and was quietly surprised as she pulled into the paved drive of a handsome log home that sat impressively on top of the hill.

"Don't get your hopes up," she grinned, reading his thoughts. "I live in the guest house around back."

As promised, there was a miniature version of the home directly behind on its own half acre, enclosed by a split rail fence. The house was rustic, charming—exactly the kind of place David might like for himself should he not be firmly planted in the city.

"This is really nice, Steph," he commented, taking it in.

"The daffodils are about to open," she said, pointing to a border that ran in front of the house. "You should see it then. Like a blanket of gold." She looked dreamy when she said it, then came back to the present, popped out of her side of the Jeep and with the same painstaking process as before, they made their way to the front door.

"No stairs," she said. "Just a couple of little steps, here." She struggled to help him ascend them, then unlocked the front door with one hand, while supporting him with the other.

"No stairs," he agreed feelingly, beginning to really ache.

She shoved open the door with her shoulder and joked that she felt like a cop doing a drug bust. When he didn't reply, she realized how his sense of humor was deteriorating with pain and gently encouraged him to a mahogany brown leather recliner pulled near a stacked rock fireplace.

"Can you lean against it for just a second," she asked, "so I can grab a couple of pillows to put behind you?" Hearing his grunting assent, she disappeared for a moment and returned with two large goose down pillows in hand, and guided him gently down so that he could finally relax in comfort.

"So, here's the plan," she said. "I'm going to run to the drugstore to get your prescription filled, then I'm going up the hill to my mom's house and hang with Buster." She saw his expression of confusion and explained. "My mom lives in the house on the hill. I rent this place from her and she and Buster are 'bffs,' so he's always happy to stay over. Anyway, that gives you this place to yourself, just to chill out and sleep. I'll be back in about half an hour with your meds, all right? Need anything?"

David shook his head briefly. He wanted nothing more than to sleep forever, but the pulsing pain throughout his shoulder and ribcage was persistently interfering. The strap that bound his upper arm against to his body, and ran across his upper chest certainly assisted the healing of the fracture, but the strap must have been lying across a nerve because every couple of minutes, he would feel a sizzle of pain running diagonally across his ribs. Despite his discomfort, he began to doze, and only awoke when he was gently prodded by Stephanie to take his pain pills, then he began to feel as if he was floating, like the ebb and flow of a tide, and was lulled into a dreamless sleep.

Chapter 32

NOT THAT DAVID WOULD remember any of it, but Stephanie, sleeping with one ear open, had heard him stir just after midnight and found him, attempting to push himself out of the recliner, struggling and cursing softly with pain.

"Hey," she said quietly from the open door of her small bedroom, clad in a pair of sweat pants and an over-sized T shirt, barefoot. "Let me help you. You need to hit the bathroom?"

He nodded. She walked behind him and put a hand under his left arm. His right arm, clamped against his side, couldn't be used, and David had been trying to get up by pushing on the left arm of the recliner solely, causing his upper body to torque. He gasped with the ensuing pain.

"Poor baby," she said without thinking, and immediately despised herself for doing so. It had been nothing more than an honest, heartfelt reaction, but she had been trying diligently not to make any emotional missteps which would create any extra awkwardness between them, particularly while sharing such a small place.

"Here," she said, offering her left arm and shoulder, "if you push on me, does that give you enough leverage?"

David put all of his weight on her shoulder and she had to fight to keep her knees from buckling, but he managed, with a sizable grunt, to lift himself unsteadily to his feet.

"Thanks," he croaked.

"Obviously, you're a big boy and can go by yourself," she chided him, finding that the more matter-of-fact she was about things, the more he seemed to relax, "but you are loopy on opioids, so I'm going to station myself outside the bathroom door and you keep the door unlocked, OK? Just in case you get dizzy."

David nodded once more and leaned on her as they walked the half dozen steps to the little room just inside the hallway. He had been able to find comfort sleeping in one position, however the rest of his body felt stiff and cramped and he was utterly miserable. Stephanie remained dutifully outside the door and after he relieved himself, she gave him her shoulder on which to rest his hand but he surprised her when he slipped his arm around her shoulders instead and gave her a small squeeze.

"You're a good nurse," he said, companionably.

She smiled and felt flooded with warmth. It was far easier for him to sink back down on the recliner than to get up, and she arranged the blanket she had put over him earlier, so that he would feel neither cold nor restricted.

"I think it's time for you pain meds," she said. "Want me to get them?"

"Please."

Everything in her house was nearly within reaching distance and she walked over to the tidy galley-style kitchen, poured a glass of water, shook out a pill from the bottle, and returned.

"Here you go," she smiled. "That ought to knock you out for a while. Can I get you anything else?"

He declined and then, as she extended her hand to pat his shoulder before going back to bed, David took it and held it for a moment.

"You're the best," he said and closed his eyes, beginning to drift.

"Yeah, yeah, that's what you say to all the girls," she joked softly.

David opened his eyes again, briefly, and when he murmured, "And if things were different..." he appeared completely lucid, before falling back into a deep sleep.

Stephanie backed up slowly and leaned against the mantelpiece, staring at him. If what things were different? Meaning? She didn't know about mind-blurring opioids, but she had been around enough drunks in her profession to know that alcohol never made anyone say anything, but it did loosen inhibitions as well as the tongue. She regarded his face, completely unlined in his sleep, and savored the opportunity to stare at him unseen. His hair was tousled and flecked with grey, and his beard, should he continue to let it come in, reflected the same mottling of colors. As he slept, his lips parted and she stared at his mouth and jawline, still youthful in its firmness, and his slightly bony nose.

"Whew," she breathed and shook her head, smiling, before returning to bed.

The guest house was south facing, and when the watery early spring sun began to seep in through the east side of the house, tentacles of beams stole through a window to David's left. He opened his eyes, not quite sure where he was. He began to look searchingly around the room and everything in it had a calming effect on him: the rustic log walls, the rock fireplace with a mantle that consisted of a rough cut and he supposed hand hewn timber beam with a couple of silver framed photographs glinting atop it, the pine boards beneath his feet covered with an oval area rug in a vintage pattern of flowers upon a cream background. His eyes, trained to appreciate light and color, took in each soothing item and he fell briefly back asleep. Within a half hour, he stirred, aware of a crushing pressure that began in his abdomen and reached straight up his chest. The pressure created a stabbing sensation from his rib and he began to panic. When he opened his eyes, he found himself face to face with an orange cat with an enormous head and pinkish, piggy eyes, staring directly at him.

"Jeez!" he yelped.

"Bub!" Stephanie bellowed, from somewhere behind him, "Get *down!*" and when the cat blatantly ignored her, she strode over, picked him up—the length of him was endless—and pulled him off, depositing him outside the front door.

"I'm so sorry," she apologized. "He had been sleeping with me last night and I didn't realize he had gotten down. Are you all right?"

David blinked and passed his left hand over his chest.

"I think so. Sorry I yelled, I'm not really a cat person."

"Which is why he sat on you." Stephanie smiled. "They know that, you know."

"So, Bub, as in Bubba, I'm guessing?"

"Actually no," she replied, going into the kitchen. "Bub stands for 'big ugly bastard' which was the only way to describe him when he started showing up outside the window."

David chuckled. He tried to stretch with his arm and winced.

"Hey, Steph," he asked, tentatively. "Is there any way I could take a shower?"

Stephanie appeared from around the corner, skillet in her hand.

"Sure," she nodded. "I was going to make some breakfast. D'ya want to wait?"

He shook his head. "It's getting to the point where I can't stand myself," he said, "but I don't want to stop you from having your breakfast—"

"Don't be silly," she said, setting the skillet back down on the stove behind her. "You're past due for a pain pill, do you want one?"

"Nah," David declined, beginning to push himself out of the recliner with effort. "I'd like to start weaning myself off that stuff," he stopped abruptly as the pain took hold of him. Stephanie started over to assist him.

"No," he said, a slight edge to his voice. "I can do it," and with a massive effort along with considerable teeth gritting, he hoisted himself up and over to his left side and stood, unsteadily, with his left hand on top of the recliner.

"There's fresh towels in the bathroom," Stephanie said, then looking at his right arm, added, "You've got to keep that cast dry, and probably the bandage over your stitches. Hang on a minute." She ducked into the kitchen and reappeared with a trashcan liner and handed it to him. "Wrap that around your cast and don't worry about the bandage because it probably needs to be changed, anyway."

"Thanks," he mumbled and made his way painfully to the bathroom.

Stephanie returned to the kitchen and began to warm the skillet, breaking eggs and dropping bread slices into the toaster. She worked quietly, keeping an ear attuned for any unnatural noise coming from the bathroom, but as she heard the shower turned on and subsequent quiet, she relaxed and returned to task. In a few minutes, the water was turned off and the groan of a floorboard revealed he was returning.

"Hey Steph?"

Stephanie turned her head and saw David leaning against the entrance of the hallway. He had a towel wrapped around his waist. Flustered, she tried to regain her composure and replied, "Yep?"

David rubbed his chin with his left hand and looked embarrassed.

"I, uh, can't wash under my left armpit."

Stephanie, despite her embarrassment, chuckled and said, "I don't think that's a sentence that's ever been spoken in this house," before walking up to him. He looked on the edge of humiliation and she touched him on the arm and said, "Hey, Merriman, just because you might need some help doesn't make you any less strong, you know?" He nodded with a smile that appeared as quickly as it disappeared. He wondered what it was about Stephanie taking charge that allowed him to acquiesce with dignity. He followed her back into the bathroom, which was cramped at best.

"So," she mused aloud, appraising his dilemma. "I'm thinking that maybe if you turn around and face the sink, and, if it doesn't hurt, rest your right hand on it, and move your left arm away from your side—" She turned and soaked a washcloth in warm water and soap, then stood behind him. "I can stand behind you and get up in there."

David, careful not to strain the wound on the back of his shoulder, pulled his arm away from his side inch by inch. He stared at her reflection in the mirror, and when she caught his gaze, they both began laughing.

"You're not going to tell anyone about this, are you?" he pleaded, wincing through the pain.

"Why?" she shot back. "You're nothing special. I wash all my friends' armpits." She tried to remain as casual as possible, even attempting to adopt a clinical approach as her hand glided over his chest and gently washed, but her body began to betray her as her legs suddenly felt unsteady.

"There," she said, quickly patting him dry with a hand towel, wanting to make her exit. "That wasn't so bad, was it?"

David shook his head and said, "One more thing, I desperately need a toothbrush."

"Oh, sure," Stephanie said, pulling open a narrow drawer. "I think there's one in here that Buster got from his last dental appointment." She retrieved it, squeezed on the toothpaste and handed it to him, then filled a glass with water for him to rinse. "If you don't mind a purple dinosaur on the handle. But you did say you were desperate." She waited for him to rinse, then reached to take back the glass and asked, "Anything else?"

David placed the glass on the edge of the sink and took her hand, instead. "Just this," he said, and pulled her close. Stephanie, her body pressed gingerly against his chest, raised her eyes to his and whispered, "You sure you want to do this? Friend?"

"I don't know, I don't know," he stammered, then despite the protestations of his rib, bent down and kissed her, softly, his left hand gently caressing the back of her head, through her hair. He kissed her again, this time with urgency, and Stephanie, quaking from head to toe, kissed him back, raising her arms and threading her fingers together behind his neck. He pulled slightly away from her with a slight gasp and said, "Ow, that really hurts," as he straightened his body, but continued to hold her, and neither of them could prevent softly chuckling at the situation.

"Are you OK?" Stephanie asked, raising her face to look up at him.

"Steph," he began as honestly as he knew how, "I'm all over the place, you know? I don't know where my head is." He stepped back and dropped his arm slowly. "And I really shouldn't have done that. I'm sorry. It's not fair to you."

Stephanie lowered her eyes, digesting his statement. Her lips still felt soft and warm from his kiss and when she raised her eyes to meet his a second time, she managed to engage the familiar banter that was comfortable to them both, but that she didn't feel.

"You know something," she said, with a bright smile that he would never know the difficulty it required for her to express, "it's been a long time since I've been kissed and that was really nice, but let's just leave it at that." She gave his chest a perfunctory pat, as she would a dog, and added, "So let's eat. And then you can decide if you want to stay here a little longer, or I can call Eli to bring my car back and have him drive you home in the Jeep."

She wanted to keep it light, give him an easy way out and as she turned to make her way back to the kitchen, she fought back the despair that threatened to reveal itself as her eyes grew moist and she kept herself busier in the kitchen than she needed to.

David followed her slowly back to the den and remained standing, his eyes wandering around the room, now fully drenched in light. Below the window to the east, there stood a small workbench with a chair. His eyes were drawn to the collection of tools, each tucked into its own hole, drilled into a raised stack of miniature shelves. Something glittering caught his eye and he picked up a silver ring, with an intricate woven design that appeared to be tiny tendrils of ivy, and in the center a sparkling yellow stone.

"Ah, you've spotted my other livelihood," said Stephanie from behind him, setting down a couple of placemats on a tiny table for two, just on the other side of the fireplace.

"Did you make this?" David said, turning his head and looking at her with surprise.

"C'mon, Merriman," she replied with a grin, before stepping back into the kitchen. "You didn't really think that tending bar in my thirties was my first career choice, did you?" She reappeared with two plates piled with scrambled eggs and toast and ducked back in to retrieve mugs of coffee. "I managed to get one of the shops on Lexington to carry a small range of my pieces, but that's not going to pay the rent. Come get something to eat," she invited.

"I never turn down food," he said gratefully, and was glad the oak chair had sturdy arms as he lowered himself and picked up a fork. "So what's your story, Steph? I don't even know your last name."

"Briggs," she replied, taking a bite and then a swallow of coffee before continuing, "and my story is that I moved here for a new start, because there was a nearby school to study metalwork and jewelry design, as well as thinking it would be a great safe place for Buster to grow up." She gave him a quick smile and added, "He's a free range kid. Crazy about being outdoors." She looked up and out the window to her right and said, "Brace yourself for impact, Hurricane Buster is coming down the hill."

David followed her eyes and watched with amusement the sun illuminating her son's head so that it appeared as if on fire as he hurtled down the hill, his knapsack bumping his shoulders with each stride, his short denim-clad legs pumping like pistons. Within moments, he had burst through the front door and, out of breath, yelled, "Mom! I'm going to be late for the bus." He stopped as he noticed David and added, "Hi."

"Hi," David returned.

"I like to wait with him for the bus," Stephanie explained, then turned to her son. "Did you have breakfast?"

"Grandma made me eat oatmeal," he said, screwing up his face in distaste.

"Good. All right, let me grab a sweater," Stephanie said, rising. "It's in my bedroom. Be right back."

Buster stood sturdily in front of David, as if sizing him up.

"Buster Briggs," David said, attempting to break the silence. "You ought to be a boxer with a name like that."

"I'm gonna be a baseball player," the kid shot back.

Stephanie returned from her bedroom. "That's not his birth name," she explained, shrugging into the sweater, "but he was a one-man wrecking crew as a toddler—"

"So my dad started calling me Buster." Her son jumped in to finish the story.

"I see," David nodded. "What does he call you, now?"

"He can't call me anything," the boy said, flatly. "He got shot. And he's a hero."

David, taken aback, glanced up at Stephanie, who kept her eyes on Buster.

"Yes, he is," she agreed, ruffling the top of Buster's head. "A huge hero." Her eyes flickered to David and she succinctly filled in the gap. "He was a cop. Routine traffic stop."

Buster, remembering the blood he had seen on David's sweatshirt, asked, "Did you get shot?"

It took David a moment to follow his meaning. "No," he said, glancing at his left shoulder and then back at the boy. "I'm not nearly brave enough to get shot. That's for heroes."

His remark, off the cuff, and yet instinctively so meaningful to her son, brought profound gratitude to Stephanie's heart, and she swallowed, feeling overwhelmingly emotional.

"Let's go, Buster," she said, and then, not trusting herself to look at David, tossed "be back in a few" over her shoulder as she shepherded her son through the door.

David nodded and watched through the window as Stephanie sauntered alongside the boy up the driveway, her arm resting around his shoulders. They were chatting and he could tell by her profile that she was smiling. He exhaled slowly, and considered what he had just heard. Slowly, not bothering to filter a curse, he raised himself out of the chair and stood so that he could see them crest the hill and disappear on the other side. He turned around and, facing the fireplace, now realized the first of the two silver framed photographs on the mantle were of what appeared to be a happy family. *That's where he gets the hair*, David thought, leaning in and seeing a strawberry blond man with an approachable face, arms wrapped around Buster, thetwo of them wearing broad grins for the camera. Stephanie was leaning against her husband's shoulder and smiling, her eyes warm with affection.

"A young widow with a kid," he murmured aloud, feeling like a heel and deeply regretting leading her on, regardless of whether or not it was intended. He put the photo back and moved to the second one, smiling as he looked at Buster sitting on Santa's lap and laughing, his hair like a flame against the green corduroy coat he wore. His heart stopped. He'd seen him before. He was sure of it. He took the photograph from its place and for what seemed ages, stared at it, frowning, the memories that began to swirl around his brain making him feel hollow, unwell.

The door opened and Stephanie reappeared, rubbing her hands together.

"Chilly out there," she announced and then seeing him standing with the photo in his hand, said, "that's my favorite picture of Buster."

"When was this taken?" David asked.

"Two Christmases ago," she replied, and stepped up next to him, taking it gently from his hand. "It was the first Christmas after he lost his father and we had just moved down here from Rhode Island." She smiled at him as she continued, "I have the best mother in the world. My parents split up when I was a kid and she remarried a great guy and they retired here to the mountains. He suffered a massive heart attack, not long after they bought this place and, well, where better for me to start a new life with Buster? We're company for each other and Buster adores her." She looked back at the photo and added, "I wanted to make some new traditions for Buster. He's almost nine and not completely sure if there really is a Santa Claus, but this was taken that first Christmas. We had hot chocolate at home, then went to see him."

"Was this taken at the mall?" David asked, his mouth going dry.

Stephanie nodded. "I have this year's picture, too, in my bedroom, but I like this one better. It was such a special evening for us." She started to say something else, but the look on David's face gave her pause.

He looks like he just stepped out of a Norman Rockwell painting, he remembered saying to Denise, as they waited in line behind the children a little over two years ago.

"I was there, too, with my ex-wife," he said, limply. "I remember seeing him and pointing him out to her."

"You're *kidding*," Stephanie's eyes grew wide. "That's unbelievable!"

David nodded. "It's pretty amazing. Listen, Stephanie, if you wouldn't mind, I'd like to call Eli to see if he can bring your car back and then drive me home in mine. I'm going to need to get in touch with quite a few clients, and I should probably start figuring out how I'm going to get around on my own."

Stephanie gave a brief nod, giving no indication of the disappointment she felt.

"And I don't know how I'll ever thank you," he said, pressing her hand with a quick squeeze. "I've never had to thank anyone who's saved my life before."

"You can give me an extra big tip the next time you come to the pub," she said, giving it everything she had.

He laughed and indicated he was going to step outside to get a better signal to make his call. But once outside, as he stood in her front yard and scrolled the screen of his phone to find Eli's number, the truth of his need to draw away from her became apparent with the sudden sense of isolation that came over him. The memory of Stephanie's special evening with her son had collided directly into the same night his marriage began to fall apart.

Chapter 33

LISSIE HUNG UP HER phone and remained sitting at the kitchen table, one hand lightly against her stomach as if to soothe the lurch that she had felt upon hearing Leigh's voice at the other end of the line. It had been such a difficult week. She had been terrified by David's accident, and her daughter's rebuke, *You meddling old woman,* continued to ring over and over in her ears. She had been wounded beyond words, not only with the name-calling, an occurrence that had never before happened, but the icy contempt in Leigh's expression combined with the accusation of creating a permanent trauma for her own granddaughter—it was more than she could bear.

In the past, when encountering uneasiness in the relationship she shared with her daughter, Lissie had found comfort in the assurance of knowing her own truth: that she meant well, she always meant well, and that she was as open and honest as she could possibly be. However, as she now watched the afternoon shadows grow longer across the orchard from the kitchen window, she began to question her own intent.

For the first time in months—and only because the time before last she had been down with a bad cold—did she not take her morning walk. Perhaps it was because of the painful accusation directed at her, but she suddenly felt old, very old, as well as foolish. Lissie had lived long enough to know that careful introspection began with emotional purging. That lesson had come, funnily enough, from her mother, when she had grumbled about the length of the Anglican church service she had fidgeted though as a child.

"Why do we have to say the confession prayer?" she had asked her mother on the drive home.

"So we can empty our hearts before we take communion." Her mother, taking her eyes briefly off the road, had smiled at her.

"Why do we want to be empty?"

Her mother laughed. "So we can be filled with love."

Lissie had digested that as well as could be expected at ten years of age.

"So we empty ourselves and then God isn't mad at us?"

"I don't think it's about God being mad at us," her mother replied. "I think it's about emptying our hearts of anything that's too much about ourselves so we can then fill it up with love and loving thoughts for others."

That memory, as clear as if it were yesterday, remained with Lissie, and made her acutely aware of the capability of children to retain things never expected by adults. As she now absorbed the phone call from Leigh with what felt like a rather reluctant apology as her daughter had qualified the admission by repeating, more than once, that Lissie should have been granted permission regardless of circumstances, Lissie felt no real comfort at all.

It wasn't that she was interested in spite or holding any sort of grudge against Leigh. In fact, had she not called when she did, Lissie would have attempted the first line of contact, so much was her desire to smooth out what seemed to be the constant creases in their relationship. It was just, she thought while bowing her head and looking down into the bottom of her empty mug, that no matter *what* she thought or said or did in regards to her daughter, it somehow always ended up being received as offensive. So as she thought back to that brutal morning, right here in this very kitchen, her eyes moved slowly around the table, seeing each bewildered face that had been before her, especially Kirsten's. And as she considered the charges leveled against her, no matter how cruel, when Leigh had angrily risen to her feet and confronted her, she would, as was her habit, accept the pain in the necessary search for truth and comprehension.

Lissie knew all too well that Leigh would always hold her responsible for the divorce from her father and she had accepted that despite the inequity. However, in her quest for stability within her family, particularly in those early angst-ridden days when she dared not allow her children to see an iota of weakness less they suspect how close they all were to destitution and homelessness, had she worn that mantle of what she perceived as strength too rigidly, with too much pride? Yes. She found herself accepting this unpleasant truth as it began to settle uneasily upon her. Yes, it *had* given her a rather prideful air—oh, she hated what she knew was following closely on its heels—of subtle superiority. And as it had lifted her over each hurdle that had been put before her, she relished the feeling of self accomplishment that came with it, as well as the fear of letting it go.

But was she not allowed to experience *any* pride, Lissie wondered, unconsciously turning over both palms on the table as if questioning the universe. Was it sanctimonious of her, after years of scrimping and saving and worrying, to sit again at this very table and savor the achievement of writing the final check of the mortgage, tucking it carefully inside and sealing the envelope? Was it not a physical relief to be able to buy her children proper winter coats instead of driving into the city, where she wouldn't be seen, to search among the racks at the Salvation Army for something not noticeably worn or shabby? Or have substantial savings put away for their education? Surely not, but somehow, in so doing, she had managed to become a figure that was remote and unsympathetic to her daughter.

And also, perhaps, to herself. An inkling of a revelation, as painful as the last, began to flicker in the back of her brain. All those years after the divorce she had kept herself bound so tightly in self-perceived strength and capability that any thought of vulnerability was eschewed, and along with it, any chance for romance, for love. Peter would have given her anything she needed or desired. He was a good man aching to provide for them all, but she wouldn't consider it. She had already suffered the frustration of complete inability to help her own husband, as well as the humiliation of not having even recognized the mental illness that was staring her right in the face, and she simply would not—*could not*—put herself in such a position of unguarded accessibility ever again.

Each revelation seemed to link with a new one. She found herself considering Leigh carrying this unintended legacy and how it had pained her, when Kirsten was both an infant and later a toddler, that Leigh had not been a natural mother. Dutiful, yes, in every regard, but missing were the spontaneous displays of affection that Lissie remembered receiving so plentifully in her own youth. She was unable to see this in her own daughter: the unbridled joy of the attachment to one's child. And it was this natural attachment to Leigh despite all circumstances that led Lissie to the only solution she could think of not to render her daughter lost to her forever: she would keep the house.

She sat stoop-shouldered, a rare occurrence, as she came to the saddest realization of all. Had she only been capable of seeing the tracks she was laying earlier in her life, how much healthier might her family be. How natural it would have been for them to nourish their own marriages, their own relationships, and in return, perhaps her own dream wouldn't have held nearly such an intensity. In fact, it may never have revealed itself to her at all. She would bid it goodbye, although she would have to, for the time being, return to be indebted to the steely resolve to see her past the disappointment. But, she reckoned, if it resulted in the healing of her daughter's marriage and family, no price was too dear.

Chapter 34

WHEN DAVID RETURNED TO his own apartment, relying on the inadequate shoulder and wheezing lung capacity of Eli to make it up the flight of stairs to his front door, he wasn't surprised to find a voicemail of gentle concern from his mother, but raised a brow as his phone showed three attempts to connect from Denise. With Stephanie's guesthouse tucked at the bottom of a sizable hill, it made sense that the calls had gone directly to voicemail. Considering the amount of opioids he had consumed, it was probably not a bad thing. Fittingly, he returned his mother's call first, and found her sounding slightly depressed, unusual for her. Rationalizing it as motherly concern, he did his best to persuade her that, quite untruthfully, he was feeling much improved and getting around quite well.

He allowed himself time to open the mail and one-handedly prepare a cup of strong coffee before listening to the messages left by Denise. It was a not-so-unconscious attempt to tamp down any attempt his emotions might make in rising with the anticipation of speaking with her. She was calling to check on him, he reasoned, which was a kind and decent thing to do. Trying to find a more comfortable position on the couch, he stuffed a cushion behind his back with his left hand, took a deep breath and listened to the first message.

"Hi David," she began cordially enough, "it's me. Just checking in to see how you're doing. Talk to you soon, bye."

The second was similar, and the third gave away a bit more concern in her voice as she repeated that she would appreciate hearing from him, that she was worried. She deserved a prompt reply, he felt, and returned the call.

"Oh, I'm so glad you called," she said, the relief evident in her voice. "I was having all sorts of visions of what might have happened. I even drove by, but you weren't home."

"Yeah, sorry about that," he said, feeling unreasonably apologetic. "I stayed at a friend's the first night, because they—" He found he couldn't say *she*. "—had a recliner and it was the only way I could get any sleep."

"Poor thing," she replied sympathetically. "Listen, how are you for food?"

He hadn't really thought of that.

"OK, I think."

"Tell you what," Denise said, the briskness he knew so well returning to her voice as she began to take charge. "Let me bring you a few things that'll be easy to manage with just one hand. I've actually made something that is already frozen, and all you have to do is pop it in the microwave."

It was incredibly decent of her, he said, and thanked her. "*Some things are worth making priorities,*" he recalled her saying to him in the hospital, and this was a rather lovely illustration. He was soon struggling to his feet and having a quick wash and an obvious change out of his ridiculous bargain sweats, as well as running a comb through his hair.

He certainly hadn't expected her as quickly as she arrived, and as he had left the door unlocked to save him the effort of struggling to his feet—for some reason, he didn't want her to witness that—it was easy to casually call "Come in" when he heard her tap on the door.

"Hi," she said softly, and approaching him rather quickly, she surprised him with a sudden yet careful embrace that left him warmed, and offered her a lopsided grin in return.

Denise, he knew, would never consider even looking at such a place in which he now resided, yet she showed no notice or distaste for the bare walls or mismatched furniture. He had wanted the cleanest, least difficult break possible when he moved out and took nothing from the pleasant arts and crafts home in which she remained on Blossom Street. He had yet to think of the apartment as a home and had therefore put no effort into it, and it showed.

"Kitchen through here?" she asked, not stopping, holding a woven bag containing the frozen lasagna she had made for him.

He nodded and sat as quickly as he could back down on the couch so she would be unaware of his grimace.

"So," she said, returning and delicately sinking down next to him, "tell me what happened. Eli said something about being attacked by a horse?"

He chuckled. "I can't say I wasn't warned. I was doing a shoot for the mayor's daughter and he warned me the horse bites. He never mentioned a word about the karate chop, though."

Denise frowned with genuine concern and glanced at his cast.

"How long does that have to stay on?"

"Because I'm still relatively young with the strength of ten men," he joked, "about eight weeks."

"Oh, wow, that's tough, especially with your not being able to work. Are you all right with income?"

That query unsettled him and he replied with more conviction than he felt. "Of course, no problem."

All of these questions, he would readily admit, came from a place of sincerity, but the pacing of them made him feel slightly defensive, as if she had slipped into her role as prosecutor. At the same time, this assertive characteristic of Denise, now being applied to him with her full focus, was as intriguing as it was unusual.

Denise cast her eyes downward as if debating whether or not to proceed.

"I know this may sound a little unorthodox, given our circumstances," she said at last, "but would you consider letting me pop in now and again to look after you? Would that make you uncomfortable?"

She was careful not to sit too close, he noted, as if weighing each nuance in his behavior.

"That's very generous of you, but the last thing I want to do is interfere with your work."

She cocked her head and with a small smile, as if mustering courage, she confessed, "I've been able to arrange some time off work."

"Denise." He was stunned. "I can't ask you to do that."

"David," she said, taking and pressing his hand for a moment, "What I said in the hospital, I meant. I don't want to go into it right now but let's just say I'm grateful to have the opportunity."

The first day or two he was slightly guarded with her, courteous and respectful, but by her visit on the morning of the third day, there arrived an ease of familiarity. David was surprised by how loose he felt in her presence, how naturally casual. And when she mentioned popping back by that same evening, he found he was impatient for the time to arrive. By mid-afternoon he decided to take a cab into town and swing by the studio. He found as long as he kept his posture straight, his right arm strapped firmly to his side, he managed quite well. The pain from the rib was an immediate reminder should he slouch or twist in any way. It was good to get his feet back onto Lexington and stretch his legs. Normally active, it had been depressively confining to remain resting in his apartment. He glanced in the windows of a fair-trade clothing shop, then a florist, as he carefully walked along, until something caught his eye in the front of a woman's boutique and he stopped suddenly in his tracks. In the window was a display of summery prints. Hanging from a tiny, copper stand was a necklace that seemed familiar to him. When he looked closer, David saw the design continued in three rings in a copper tray: delicate vines of ivy that would wrap around a finger, each punctuated in the center with a different gem stone: agate, garnet, and the one he had held in his own hand, yellow citrine.

245

It wasn't that he hadn't thought of Stephanie in the time that he had been on his own, but with each appearance of Denise, Stephanie's significance and how that might relate to him had diminished to the point that he hadn't even thought about the pub a few blocks up the road. Now, he stood mesmerized, and was glad to see her creations prominently on view. With an amused smile, he thought of Buster barreling down the hill to her house, and he thought of Stephanie at her workbench, working by the light of the small window above and tending bar at night. David was all right with money presently, not enough to be reckless, but flush enough to want, in some way, to give her the sense of accomplishment he thought she deserved, and he stepped inside the shop and bought the citrine ring. He didn't know who he might give it to, and for a fleeting moment he considered Denise, but he had never seen her wear silver. Nor was it appropriate because really, the only person he had purchased it for was the single mother and her redheaded boy who hadn't had the easiest last couple of years. He slipped the ring into the pocket of his jacket and was relieved as he turned left at the next intersection and saw the familiar awning of his studio.

Everything appeared in order, Eli having carried his gear to the backroom which remained locked. David tentatively attempted to sit in the office chair behind his desk, but it swiveled and wouldn't remain still, so he gave up and leaned against the desk instead. It was a fine if brisk day, and if he would actually get around to cleaning the windows in the back of the studio, even with the attached security bars on the outside, he would have an impressive view of the undulating landscape of mountains behind. His cell phone doubled as his work phone so any messages that would come in had already been seen at home. There was little to do or that he could do here, but still it was a comfort just to be surrounded by the familiar. He considered changing the framed photographs across the exposed brick walls to the side. They hadn't been changed in ages and he still displayed the magazine cover that Denise had remarked upon the first time they met. It was as if all his thens and nows were blurring together, yet it wasn't unnerving. He checked the time on his phone and, eager to get back before Denise arrived, turned to leave.

When Denise arrived, she appeared sober and quiet, with none of the breezy nonchalance that had accompanied her during her last visits. It was immediately evident to him that something was troubling her. Comfortable enough in her presence, he pointed it out.

"You all right? You seem a little down."

She put her bag on the kitchen table and pulled out a couple of sealed portions of chicken and glanced at him briefly.

"Would you like a glass of wine?" she offered, retrieving a bottle of pinot at the bottom.

"Like I've ever turned down wine," he joked.

She poured them each a glass and carried it to the couch where he sat.

"How are you feeling?" she asked, her eyes serious.

"Fine," he replied, puzzled. "Pretty great, actually. Still sore, but you know."

She cast her eyes down to her glass a moment before raising them to meet his.

"How are you feeling," she paused, then added, "about us?"

He hadn't been prepared for this, and yet he wasn't thrown.

"I feel," he hesitated, gathering his thoughts. "I'm not quite sure, but I feel pretty comfortable."

He waited to follow her lead.

"David," she said, tossing her hair out of her eyes and searching his face. "I've had a couple of epiphanies the last month and I'm not even sure if it's fair to proceed, but I feel the need to share them with you."

He became distinctly aware of his heart thudding beneath the strap that ran across his chest. "Go on," he encouraged quietly.

In the endearing way that always touched him, she cocked her head so that her ebony hair spilled just over the back of one shoulder and she continued. "I've come to the realization—" She gave a short laugh. "—that the earth doesn't actually revolve around me or my career. I've also come to the realization that my reason for even being in Asheville was to strike out on my own and not join my father's firm in Boston. And I'm pretty sure that comes from some relational competitiveness I've felt with my brother, you know, to prove that the little sister would show them all. But I know now that I've proved my point and having spoken to my father this last week, well, he's made it very clear he would love to have me back home in Boston at his firm." She watched David closely for his reaction. There was very little; he was stunned.

"Are you saying you're moving?" he asked, feeling his throat constrict.

She nodded. "I want to put the house on the market and I know you were adamant about just walking away with nothing, but you contributed ten thousand to the down payment as well as half the mortgage payments—"

"You know I don't care about that," he interrupted.

"I know you don't, but fair is fair. When the house sells, I want you to take your share back, please."

David shrugged. "If it makes you feel better." He felt the return of the hollowness that had only in the last few days begun to dissipate. Sensing it, Denise leaned forward and placed her hand against his cheek.

"When I realized the earth didn't revolve around me, I recognized that I had made some pretty rash decisions and that's been agonizing to accept."

"What are you saying?" David asked, his gaze penetrating into her own. "Are you saying what I think you're saying?"

"I'm hoping," she smiled, then shook her head to correct herself, "I'm *praying* that you'll consider giving us another chance. Come to Boston with me."

Chapter 35

DAVID LAY IN HIS bed, propped up by pillows, having sunk mercifully asleep amid a swirl of emotions that began with Denise initiating a kiss, then another, and when he joked that he wasn't sure if he could manage physically considering his injuries, she had whispered in his ear before her lips began to trail down his neck and onto his chest, "You don't have to do anything."

Her side of the bed still warm, he watched her now as she wore one of his shirts that hung loose over her slender frame and smiled over her shoulder at him as she began to tidy his room.

"Oh, now, this is very attractive," she laughed as she picked up the dreaded camouflaged sweats and Hawaiian shirt. "Are they dry clean only?"

David laughed, hiding his embarrassment. "They were useful that first day home. You can trash them."

She gave the bathroom a quick wipe round before coming to the side of the bed and offering her hands.

"Need help getting up?"

"Need help lying down?"

She kneeled beside him and kissed him. "I'm starving," she said, then winked. "Let me make you breakfast and then we can work it off." He took her right hand in his left one and she helped pull him to a sitting position. Once on his feet, he enveloped her with his good arm and rested his chin on top of her head. Everything in his life had turned upside down because of Denise, and now, with her having returned and giving herself totally to him, it was almost more than he could fathom. He nearly vibrated with longing, gratitude, and relief. Oddly, he even thought of his mother and had a flash that suddenly he knew exactly what she meant when she'd said that when she returned to England, how she felt as if she had returned home. He held onto Denise tightly. He was home.

She pulled away slowly and mentioned she had brought a cinnamon raisin loaf from an artisan bakery in town and declared it to be the best she'd ever had. "I'm thinking French toast," she offered. "What about you?"

"I'm thinking that would be great," he said and kissed her once more before releasing her completely.

He followed her into the living room just off the kitchen, and she paused to pick up her shoes and put them to one side as well as his jacket that had fallen from the back of a chair onto the floor. As she picked it up, the citrine ring tumbled out and fell to the floor.

"What's this?" she said, picking it up. "Isn't it pretty?" She glanced at him, her eyes questioning.

Thrown off balance, his awkwardness obvious, he stammered, "I bought that yesterday."

Suspecting what she considered to be the implications, Denise hesitated before sliding it on her finger.

"David, did you buy this for me?"

He couldn't commit to the whole truth and instead, replied weakly, "Actually, I didn't think it was your style."

She slipped the ring onto her finger, the stone glinting in the light. "Normally it wouldn't occur to me that I could wear something like this, but it's beautiful." She looked up, her eyes moist. "And touching." She walked over and placed her hands on either side of his face and kissed him, softly. "Thank you. How incredibly thoughtful."

David stepped back and ran his fingers through his hair, a gesture he felt compelled to do when uncomfortable and at a loss for words. The ring looked beautiful on her delicate hand, yet it hadn't been meant for her. But in this moment, it meant everything to her.

His integrity defeated, he murmured, "I'm glad you like it," and remarked he was going to take a shower, glad to have a reason to recover his thoughts in privacy.

＊　＊　＊

Even Eli's presence couldn't dampen Stephanie's mood as she arrived early to work her shift at the pub. She'd received a boon in the form of an email from Linda, the proprietor of the boutique, stating, *"Thought you'd like to know you've had a great month so far! We sold a pair of your earrings Wednesday, and one of the rings yesterday. Commissions paid at end of month, but definitely interested in carrying more of your line!"* This was such a timely validation for her, not just to have landed her work in an upmarket shop, but to have already sold some of the pieces. The success sent her somewhat deflated spirit soaring into the clouds.

"You're early," Eli commented, never one to miss the hour-long happy hour that began at five o'clock, and waiting to place his order. If he consumed enough nuts, he also found he felt full enough to skip dinner.

"Yep," she concurred, and felt light enough to be playful with him. "I couldn't tear myself away from seeing you again."

"Huh," grunted Eli, checking his watch. "Tearing yourself away from lover boy is more like it."

"It's not what you think," Stephanie said firmly, leaning against the bar and crossing her arms.

"Yeah, him staying over at your house, right, not what I think. Next you're gonna tell me nothing happened," he muttered. Eli was delighted to see a flush creep into her cheeks. "Aha!" he crowed, victorious, "I knew it! Tell me all the lurid details of how you attacked a disabled man."

"You're such a pig, Eli," she snapped angrily. "David slept in the recliner and was in a lot of pain. We're just friends, get it? And that's all we're ever going to be. Now stop being such an ass, or you can go drink somewhere else."

In the two years they had sparred, Eli had never truly gotten under Stephanie's skin. He felt no triumph in the fact that he just had. He realized immediately that he had landed a blow that had hurt, which had not been his intention. He remained silent for a few moments and saw that she had turned her back on him to busy herself with setting up for her shift.

"You might *say* you're just friends, but you shouldn't be," he said clumsily.

Stephanie spun around, her eyes narrowed.

"What's that supposed to mean?"

"You should be a couple," he shrugged, as if it were the most natural thing in the world. "You and David. You're good together."

"He's barely divorced," she mumbled, reaching for a bar towel and avoiding his eyes. "You don't put that kind of pressure on someone who just got divorced. Even if I was interested."

"Which you are," Eli stated flatly. "Even if you end up just being a rebound relationship, you'd still have fun."

Rolling her eyes, Stephanie gave a snort of laughter. "Yeah, that's what I'm looking to be, a rebound girlfriend. Thanks a lot."

"I think he likes you." Eli baited his hook. "He may not realize it, but he likes you."

"Meaning?" she asked, trying to sound disinterested.

Eli stretched and twisted his neck, cracking it from side to side. He enjoyed dragging it out.

"I'm too thirsty to continue."

"You're *such* an ass," Stephanie declared, and grabbed a beer from the cooler, popped off the cap and set it down with such force that a portion of foam spewed out the neck.

Savoring his prize, he grinned. "Look, I've known David since he was eighteen and he's a good guy, but he's an idiot with women. When we were in college, he'd always go for the ice queens, you know? Bitchy girls that always left him second-guessing himself. And I'm not saying

Denise is like that, but I have never seen him as relaxed with her as he is with you. That night at the club—I haven't seen him laugh like that in years. Every time he's around you, he's laughing. And when I drove him home from your place, he was pretty quiet, so I figured something had gone on with you two, because you could tell he was thinking pretty hard."

"He was also in a lot of pain." Stephanie attempted to brush off Eli's statements that were going straight to her heart. She thought of David right before he said he needed to go home, looking at the photo of her with Buster and her late husband, Ross. How vulnerable he must have thought she was, even needy. How much pressure that would add to a man who was already leery of taking a step forward towards a relationship. But he didn't know the truth and she hadn't had the chance to tell him.

"I was thinking about seeing if he'd come hang out tonight," Eli mused, pushing the issue. "But he still can't drive and he's probably pretty depressed holed up at his apartment." He glanced up at the bar clock above them both. "You've got time to run over there before your shift starts. Take him a beer and tell him it's from me. Except you're gonna have to run me a tab."

Stephanie stood, mulling it over.

"I just don't want to go crashing in and make us both feel uncomfortable," she said warily.

"Look, Steph," Eli said, exasperated. "It's as plain as day that you're crazy about the guy. Pisses me off, but there you have it. And it's as plain as day that he really likes you but he's just been using the hand brake on his emotions, you know? You want to wind up like me, middle-aged and hanging around bars trying to pick somebody up? Get over there and tell him how you feel. And then you can thank me by having an open bar at your wedding."

Stephanie's face broke into a broad grin but she remained standing with her arms crossed, unconvinced.

"I can't believe I'm even *considering* taking relationship advice from you," she said, then impulsively grabbed a bottle of David's favorite wheat beer, shoved it into her purse, and headed to the exit. She pointed a finger at Eli and declaring, "You'd better not be wrong."

"I'm never wrong!" he shot back.

"You're *always* wrong!" she shouted, opening the door and departing. She darted out to the street where she had parallel parked her car, leapt in, and drummed her fingers on the steering wheel with impatience as she waited for a break in the line of cars before her in the street. One elderly gentleman—he would never know her gratitude—ushered her in with a wave of his hand and she pointed the Subaru south towards David's apartment. Red flags raised all around her brain as she knew her impulsiveness had not served her well in the past, but it wasn't as if she was going to steamroll him, she told herself. She planned to remain neutral, casual, the very essence that allowed him to relax with her in the first place. And, she thought, putting on her blinker and pulling into his complex, she knew exactly what she was going to say. There had been no time to rehearse, but she was going to tell her truth.

She unzipped her purse and pulled out the beer, still cold, so that it would be the first thing he saw when he opened the door. She got out, made sure she was in front of the right building, then trotted up the front steps through the entrance and up the flight of stairs outside his door. She wondered, her heart warming, if he had actually seen her from the window because as soon as she knocked, he called from inside, "You don't have to knock, c'mon in!"

She opened the door tentatively, saw him widen his eyes as he looked at her and stuck out her hand, clasping the beer in front of her.

"Care package from Eli," she announced, grinning. "Except it's not really from him because he can't pay for it until next week."

"Steph!" David was sitting on the couch, answering emails on his laptop, and felt his heart stop and panic pump though his chest. "Wow...how are you?"

She stepped just far enough inside his apartment, wary of appearing the slightest bit intrusive, to place the beer on the coffee table in front of him. She remained standing on the other side of the table and shoved her hands in the back pockets of her jeans.

"I'm all good," she said, and because she had a sense of his unease, added, "I'm not staying. I just wanted to swing by and drop that off and say I hope you're feeling better."

David, covering his nervousness, gave her a smile that he hoped didn't look as forced as it felt.

"That's really sweet of you, Steph," he said, and his sentiment was genuine. "I was just surprised. How's Buster?"

"Being a Buster," she replied, and they both laughed at the thought of her son. She took a breath and plunged in, "David, I have to get to work, which considering what I'm about to say is probably a good thing for both of us. I haven't really been honest with you, and I just wanted to throw this out if it was something that bothered you."

David stared at her, trying to will away the knot forming in his stomach. He gave a brief nod for her to continue.

"When Buster's father, Ross, was killed, we weren't getting along. Our marriage was in big trouble and we were headed for divorce. I found out that Ross was having a second affair and I had already contacted an attorney." She paused for a moment, her eyes sweeping over the floor as if being pulled back by the memory, then looked squarely at David and finished. "But I will never let Buster know that. Ever. It's so hard to give a kid any kind of innocent childhood in this world, and it's really important that I give something to Buster that he can believe in forever."

"I get that," David replied, his mind flicking to his own fatherless childhood. "I get how important that is."

"So." Stephanie let out a long exhale of relief. "I just didn't want you to think that I was presenting myself as some fragile frightened widow, all alone in the world and looking to be saved by anyone." She hesitated, then added, "Or you."

Absorbing what he had heard, David smiled. "There's nothing fragile or frightened about you, Steph," he said. "You're as tough as they come."

The sound of the door opening behind her made her turn around.

"Oh!" said Denise, genuinely surprised. "I'm sorry, I didn't realize you had company."

David made a massive effort to rise quickly to his feet. He felt excruciatingly awkward, floundering for an explanation.

"This is Stephanie," he said a little louder than he had intended. "Not only is she the one who drove me to the hospital, she actually saved my life, knowing what to do before we got there."

"Oh, my word," Denise gasped, walking over to put down the grocery bag she was carrying and place herself next to David. "I can't tell you how grateful we are." The personal plural she chose made it very clear to Stephanie that she had unwittingly invaded her territory.

"Would you like to sit down?" she added cordially. She never stopped smiling.

"No," Stephanie replied quickly, searching for a graceful exit. "I actually just dropped by to give David a beer from the gang at the pub."

"How sweet is that?" Denise said, chuckling softly. She turned to David and asked, "Shall I get a glass?"

Denise touched his arm, and when she did, Stephanie at once recognized the ring on her finger. She went suddenly numb for what felt to be an age, and found she could do nothing but continue to stand transfixed with her hands remaining in her pockets and staring at it, drowning with the mortification that she had gotten it all wrong, so terribly wrong. She had never experienced such an all-consuming humiliation in her life. With Denise having stepped into the kitchen, Stephanie turned her gaze to David and he would never forget the look in her eyes as she stood before him, her heart splintering into shards. He shook his head slowly, unable to articulate the circumstances behind what she had just witnessed. Grasping for what little dignity she had left, Stephanie took a slow breath and attempted to be audible as she murmured "Bye, David," then struggled to walk slowly to the front door, which she opened and closed softly behind her.

Once on the other side, desperate not to make a sound, she covered her mouth with her hands as if about to be ill and fled down the stairs out the front door of the building. When at last she was in the privacy of her car, nearly losing all control, she glanced up at the front window of his flat to make sure he wasn't watching her. She would not cry in front of him. She would not. She backed out of the space and when she turned her car around, she began to shake with sobs. She wept, agonized: when would she ever learn, how could she have misread everything? She pulled over on the side of the road, crying so hard she couldn't see, and holding herself, she hunched over the steering wheel, wretched, embarrassed by her naiveté and completely broken. She couldn't go back to work—the thought of seeing Eli sent her into another flood of tears—and she knew in an instant she couldn't return. She would never put herself in the position of seeing him again. She pulled out her phone and texted her boss, explaining she had an emergency. Then she pulled up David's number and blocked it, rendering further telephone contact impossible. She reached into her console for a wad of napkins she tended to keep whenever she and Buster went for fast food. Normally they came in handy to wipe off the stickiness or abrasions that came with a rambunctious eight-year-old, but now she used them to wipe her eyes and blow her nose. She regarded her reflection in the rearview mirror with dismay and smirked at her running mascara, the skin beneath her freckles splotched and the tip of her nose red. It was bad enough to feel pathetic and even worse to look it. This was something she would never forget, this evening, she fumed at herself. The recklessness, the lark of bounding over like a bloody Labrador, high on the belief that her jewelry was desirable enough to be purchased, eager to clear up any pretense of who he might think she really was, only to be blindsided by the truth that was devastating on every level.

She put her car in gear and found herself driving to the park. She remained sitting, staring at the empty baseball diamond. She thought of how badly she had misjudged Ross, believing the monogamy he preached, the jealousy he displayed should he feel she was being observed by another man. She thought of the nights she had lain in bed when Buster was an infant, unable to sleep until hearing the key in the door signaling he was safely home from his shift. When he began coming home an hour later, she had been beside herself with fear and implored him to call her so that she wouldn't worry. And when she had found the telltale receipts from a florist, coupled by his sudden insistence to walk the dog at all hours with his hand firmly clutching his phone, all was revealed a month later when his girlfriend began calling their landline and hanging up each time Stephanie answered. She had been left reeling, and short on years and experience with an infant to raise, had believed his self-condemnatory apologies, his actual tears of remorse, and had taken him back. The month Buster turned five, she had been at the grocery store, her son sitting in the cart, when she was confronted by a girl who looked no more than eighteen, declaring her love for Ross and belittling her in the middle of the dairy aisle. Stephanie was proud that she had confronted her husband with neither tears nor anger when he arrived home. She had told him, remaining completely calm, that she had contacted an attorney. He had paced and sworn the girl was a liar while she moved into the guest room and telephoned her mother. Two weeks later, he had been shot in the head while pulling over what he suspected was a drunk driver.

But all during that time, Stephanie had maintained a clear sense of who she was. She *knew* she was a good wife, a good mother. She had worked hard to get her figure back after the birth of her son and remained physically attentive to her husband. And while she had been shattered to learn of his first lover, not once did she ever question if she was in any way to blame for his wandering eye. She allowed that the stress of his work had led him to a regrettable mistake. When the second affair was revealed, she was grimly determined not to allow him to take her dignity or question her self-worth and remained remarkably collected and firmly unyielding as she retained an attorney and began to make plans for her life that didn't include him. She felt empowered and wonderfully strong. However, she realized sorrowfully that her misjudgment of David had left her desperately vulnerable.

"There's nothing fragile or frightened about you, Steph," he had declared, just minutes ago. *You have no idea* she thought, and despite the wreckage of her heart, she felt no animosity towards him. She wished she could. But the truth was he hadn't lied to her, she reminded herself miserably. He had told her the truth as he knew it, each time she asked. *"Are you sure you want to do this?"* she had asked him that morning in her tiny bathroom. *"I don't know, I don't know,"* he had replied, but she had allowed him to kiss her and she had kissed him back. She could have stepped away. She could have simply said, "Then let's not do this," but she didn't. She had so hoped he might stay with her, not be frightened of her, and yes, she dared dream, fall in love with her. How could she have possibly entertained such a fantasy when she had seen his face so many times over the weeks leading up to his divorce and the desolate expression he wore, defeated and broken. She had carefully observed him from behind the bar as he ignored overtures from flirtatious woman who had approached him both before and after his marriage. It had been plain to anyone except, evidently, herself, that this was a man still desperately in love with his wife. This undeniable realization was nothing less than humiliating for her as she remained in her car, wiping away fresh tears. In a few moments, she seemed to gather strength, for as she blew her nose a second time she suddenly sat bolt upright and switched on the ignition. She needed to compose herself and get her act together, she told herself firmly. She had a young son that depended upon her, and if nothing else, for his sake, she would not allow her heart to run wildly down such a destructive path ever again.

Chapter 36

IT WOULDN'T BE UNREASONABLE to describe the atmosphere inside the March household as an uneasy truce, although truthfully no compromise had been made or even discussed. Whether Wes continued to see his female friend, Leigh had no idea, although the thought of it pricked at her pride. However, she still couldn't bring herself to discuss the state of their marriage. She knew her headstrong insistence upon obtaining her mother's house would be seen as the underlying issue that had created the fissure through the very foundation of their marriage.

The memory was still unsettlingly painful. In the two weeks that had passed since the scene around the kitchen table, Leigh had in her view done her part by phoning her mother to apologize. Her mother had been quiet in response, not saying much, although she politely thanked her for the call, which Leigh regarded as emotionally stingy. While she did still feel a sense of guilt for the name-calling, Leigh remained feeling justified for her outburst as she had been confronted with as much as any wife and mother could tolerate. She decided to take her version of the high road: remaining curtly polite while she managed the household. She continued to prepare meals and keep the house of which she despaired tidy. She even kept the vase on the kitchen table overflowing with the daffodils from the front garden, now nodding in the sun outside the living room window. While she didn't bid Wes good morning upon coming out of the guest room at the beginning of each day or ask after his welfare when he arrived home each evening, she inquired what he might like for dinner or if he had a clean shirt for the morning. With Kirsten, she exhibited more patience. Regardless of whether or not she received a reply, Leigh made sure to ask daily how school had been. She was admittedly disappointed that her daughter hadn't immediately rallied around her when Wes's affair had been revealed. Sensing Kirsten's festering annoyance in both of them led Leigh to tread lightly around her daughter. Knowing it was a difficult subject, she touched briefly on the upcoming prom on a Friday, if, for nothing else, than to show concern.

"Not going," replied Kirsten with feigned indifference. "It's stupid, anyway."

Searching for a way to change the subject, Leigh suddenly had an idea.

"I was thinking about your senior photographs," she offered. The idea was still odd to her, having only experienced waiting in line at the same age to pose for a half dozen photographs where she wore the same moldering strapless green velvet drape over her bust that every other girl had worn at Blackburn High.

"I thought you said we couldn't afford them?" Kirsten frowned.

"I said we couldn't afford the ones you were thinking of," Leigh replied carefully, "but I was thinking perhaps we could ask David if he'd be willing to do it?"

"I don't know," Kirsten mumbled. She remained lying on her stomach on the bed. "It feels weird to be posing in front of David, and besides we don't even know if he can hold a camera yet."

"Let me ask him," Leigh suggested lightly, "and even if he can't, maybe he'll have a good idea. It's not that your father and I don't want you to have nice photographs, Kirsten. It's just that the package you were looking at was hundreds of dollars."

"How do you know what Dad wants when you don't even talk to him?" Kirsten asked pointedly.

Leigh had remained silent for several moments before answering stiffly. "Regardless of whatever is going on between your father and me, you are still our priority." She rose from sitting on the edge of Kirsten's bed and left the room, hurt that she once again felt under attack.

In the end she had put in a call to David, and David, having been forced to move all his scheduled shoots (at least those willing to be inconvenienced) well into May when his cast would come off and his physical therapy had ended, was eager to have something to do. And frankly, he thought as he hung up, not only was it a timely opportunity to spend more time with his niece, especially considering what she had been through, it would fulfill his much needed desire to be occupied. Because the shoot was a favor, he smiled, he would have no trouble getting her to pack up and unload his gear as well as carry it all, and more than likely, he would use a tripod as he couldn't count on his arm to remain steady, but there were benefits to that as well.

Having been asked to select an area that she felt represented her personality, Kirsten was in a quandary. Her friend Sophie had been photographed at the local botanical gardens, sitting prettily among a swath of wildflowers which Kirsten thought made her look like some hippy folk singer and told her so, which resulted in Sophie not speaking to her for three days. Kirsten hadn't really thought of a place having much significance to her. She wasn't at all outdoorsy, and the only place she could think of that made sense to her in recent memory was past the bend on her grandmother's street where she had stood in the freezing cold, comforted by someone from whom it felt very natural. Her own mother was startled when informed of the request by David, who would depend on Leigh to pick him up and deliver him to the spot with Kirsten. When she suggested to Kirsten that perhaps the front porch of her grandmother's house might be more appropriate, she was firmly rebuffed, the anguish of that terrible morning when they were all gathered together still fresh in her daughter's memory.

They arranged to shoot in the late afternoon one Saturday, and Leigh, departing with a sigh after being dismissed by Kirsten who was too embarrassed to have her hanging around, decided to swing by the house unannounced to visit her mother. She was nearly to the top of the street when her phone rang, and glancing at it, she recognized Libbie's area code and number. With sudden apprehension, she pulled into her mother's driveway and remained in her Toyota while she answered the call. She had been telephoning Libbie periodically to check on her father, but it was unusual for her to receive a call. However Libbie, in her savviness, sensed the potential for concern, and as soon as she heard Leigh's voice laced with tension, she said, "Don't be worried, your father's fine."

Leigh wasn't aware she'd been holding her breath until she released a lengthy exhale.

"Libbie," she sighed. "How are you?"

"Gorgeous as ever," she laughed, and Leigh could just imagine her, brown eyes crinkling and smile creasing each side of her mouth in deep crescents. "I've got quite a lot of news for you, so are you at a place where you can sit down?"

"I'm sitting now," Leigh replied a little nervously.

"I've got some good news and some great news, and some, well, I won't say bad news, but maybe inconvenient news."

"All right," Leigh said. "Go ahead."

"The good news is that John has been released from rehab. The staff there were very happy with how motivated he was to work on regaining his strength and he was actually released a little early."

"That's great to hear," Leigh replied, beaming at the thought of her father whom she had last seen looking terribly frail exercising doggedly with self-discipline.

"And the even *better* news," Libbie began, "is that he hasn't shown any significant decline in his memory loss."

Leigh closed her eyes with gratitude and said, "Libbie, you just made my day."

Libbie paused as if gathering her thoughts and said, "OK, Leigh, here comes the inconvenient part. Once we got home from rehab, I had a long and careful talk with your father about his health. I didn't tell him he had dementia, just sort of glossed over it as age-related memory loss, but he knows exactly what I went through with my parents and he's no fool. He straight up asked me if the doctors said it would get worse, and I told him over time it would, but that he absolutely did not have Alzheimer's. Then we began to discuss the future and I think it's because he had very little memory from being so ill in the hospital that when I brought up that he really needed to arrange a power of attorney with someone he trusted, he saw the sense in it and agreed. He also was very firm in saying when he begins to decline, he didn't want me to go through what I had gone through with my parents with him, and I thanked him for that." Her voice broke and Leigh could hear her struggling for composure. "I also told him I loved him and I would always make sure he was all right, that I would never just walk away."

"But can we even get power of attorney?" Leigh wanted to know. "Because when I spoke with your attorney friend in California it was so convoluted, and I was told if he had dementia, that wasn't possible."

"That's another part of the good news," Libbie replied, her voice suddenly regaining its brightness. "I spoke privately with your father's doctor and he was very confident in saying that if we met with an attorney soon John would be fully capable of understanding exactly what was being executed on his behalf. The law states that he would have to have to be sound of mind and agree to it. But the problem, Leigh," Libbie hesitated, then taking courage, plunged ahead, "is that your father only wants to give power of attorney to me."

"Did you tell him I had trained as a nurse and was completely committed to looking after him?" Leigh asked, hurt.

Libbie sighed, and tactfully replied, "Honey, I did, and don't take this personally, all right? John said it was very kind of you to offer, but he just doesn't know you well enough."

For the first time in her adult life, Leigh felt a sudden surge of anger towards her father and had to bite her tongue to prevent herself from saying, "That's not my fault, is it?" She remained silent for a few moments before murmuring dispiritedly, "I guess he just doesn't want me in his life."

"Well, you're wrong there," Libbie told her, gently. "Because he does want to know you better. You've got to understand that seeing you was a huge shock to him and he's dealing with a lot of residual memories and emotions. But we talked about when he lived in North Carolina and even about when he was married to your mother. Really, Leigh, in a weird way his getting sick has been a blessing because he simply wouldn't talk about any part of his earlier life before, and now he is. And what he has proposed, if it's all right with you, and only if I tag along, is coming to visit you in North Carolina."

Leigh grasped her phone in both hands, disbelieving, her mouth working silently, unable to speak.

"Honey, are you all right? I didn't make you blow a gasket, did I?"

"No, I mean, yes," Leigh said, now laughing with an unfettered joy she hadn't felt in years. "Seriously, Libbie? He wants to spend time with *me*?" Her eyes filled with tears that flowed freely down her cheeks, as if quenching the agonies of abandonment that had cloaked her very being since childhood.

"Yes, he does, and as you know, we've got to move out of this place at the end of this month. So I thought it might be a good idea, if it works with your schedule, if we could come out sooner rather than later? Because I've got a realtor friend who's going to look for rentals for us and if I can get us packed up and ready to go before we visit you, she's promised to get us moved into the new place, so when we get back from North Carolina, we'll just turn the key and walk straight in."

"You mean you'd allow your friend to pick out a place for you?" Leigh asked, astonished and still wiping her eyes.

Libbie laughed, "Why not? She can take pictures on her phone and email them to me. Honey, I know this town like the back of my hand and I'm going to know every nook and cranny she sees. Anywhere in West Hollywood suits me." She dropped her voice to a whisper. "And anything will be better than this old place."

"It is a bit dark," Leigh chuckled in agreement.

"You know, your dad has always been very resistant to change," Libbie confided. "You probably noticed that from the furniture. It wasn't that he couldn't afford anything better, he just liked it and said it was comfortable and it made no sense to replace it. The duplex was paid for, and in California, that's a miracle in itself. While it might not have been the Taj Mahal, you've gotta admit you couldn't have a better location. We walk to everything and there's always something to do. But it was a big surprise to me that he was up for a flight across the country. Not because of seeing you," she amended quickly, "just the fact that he was doing something that was so much out of his comfort zone. But then again," she mused, finishing her thought, "it won't be new to him, will it? He remembers it."

"Well, I am ecstatic," Leigh breathed, smiling, "just ecstatic."

"And you have room for us?" Libbie asked.

Leigh lifted her eyes to the graceful front facade of her family home as an outlandish idea began to take shape, "Yes," she replied. "Of course I do."

Chapter 31

DAVID, IT HAPPENED, WAS quite happy to be restricted to shooting with his tripod. Even if he wasn't injured, he would have used it. With April came a softer and longer late afternoon, and as the day ebbed towards evening, he had the ability to secure his Canon atop the tripod, keeping the camera still with no danger of blurring as the shutter speed slowed to allow more light into the lens.

He had indeed been glad to get away on his own, still chafing at the sense of confinement. Denise had been superb, spending a great deal of time with him. Ironically, he thought, as he waited for Leigh to pick him up, they had spent more uninterrupted time together during his recovery than they had in their marriage. It was only on their honeymoon and vacations that they had been together one on one for any stretch of time. And while he remained deeply grateful for her presence, coupled tenderly with her affectionate assistance, he had not had an extended time to himself to resolve the guilt, which had become quite palpable, of his sizable part in the decimation of Stephanie's trust. Even with his eyes closed, as he had tried the night of her unannounced visit, he could still see her face, the very light seeming to drain from her eyes. It couldn't be compared to the women in his past who had anguished when he had declined to make commitments, because what had been painfully exposed by her broken expression was that her very faith in *him* as a decent human being had been smashed into pieces all within the period of five minutes.

How he had wanted to go after her, to tell her that he had purchased the ring simply to give her business the leg-up it deserved, that he had never intended to give it to Denise. Would she even believe such a story? That he would not, could not, ever be so unfeeling as to have done what had appeared to her. Yes, it was awkward when she arrived at his door, but only because he knew Denise would soon be—he paused before considering the word to himself—home.

He had been so consumed with self-loathing after Stephanie's departure that he had remarked to Denise that he thought he might be coming down with something and went to lie down. Ever supportive and gently attending, Denise had laid down beside quietly him as he agonized over the trust he had just annihilated. This girl, this wise-cracking and effervescent girl with the open heart and candid gaze that he had called his friend—who *was* his friend—had allowed him to muddy the waters by kissing her until he—dare he admit—was frightened by the feelings struggling to gain a foothold within him about this girl he had left in shreds.

There was nothing he could do. He could only watch as she recognized her own ring on Denise's finger. He stood mute, impotent in his inability to explain, feeling worse by the hour and knowing he hadn't the privacy to even try to phone her and apologize. All the while, as he lay beside Denise he pictured Stephanie believing him to be brutally indifferent. David was unable to right the wrong. When finally the morning came and Denise went to check the mail back at the house on Blossom Street (after gently testing the waters by questioning if he might be more comfortable in what was "his home, too, after all") he had seized the opportunity to call Stephanie. He found each time he tried, it went directly to voicemail. He realized she would never be notified of his call and he had been blocked. She had effectively closed the door to everything they had meant to each other, and he didn't blame her. Nice way to thank someone who had saved his life, he told himself with disgust.

Things deteriorated further in the early afternoon when, with Denise in his presence, Eli called and blithely accused David of kidnapping his bartender for his selfish desires and leaving him high and dry. Replying in stilted sentences as Denise prepared lunch in the kitchen, David learned that not only had Stephanie failed to return to work, but from all appearances, she was no longer employed at the pub. Guilt ebbed into panic as he worried for her welfare. He wasn't conceited enough to think she would do anything rash on his account, but he needed to know she was safe, that she wasn't struggling to provide for herself or her son. He would go to her house. It was a risk, but he would go alone, though that would take longer than he desired. He had just begun physical therapy, only painfully managing a very small range of motion in the affected shoulder of his fractured arm. He still found it impossible to change gears in his Jeep.

Kirsten stood self-consciously in front of the fence.

"D'ya want the horses in the background?" she asked.

David, crouching to look at the shot through the lens, straightened, and said feelingly, "As long as they stay in the background. I don't want a single one of those bastards anywhere near me."

Kirsten, having never heard her uncle curse, burst into laughter. Taking advantage of an authentic expression, David clicked away, firing off a dozen shots.

"You better not show any of those to anyone," she gulped, wiping her eyes.

"Why?" he asked. "You look great."

Kirsten's face clouded over, unconvinced.

"I don't look great," she muttered, "and I hate my thighs."

David, remaining behind the tripod, replied, "I've never met a woman who doesn't hate her thighs," then added, "Kirsten, for these photographs, tell me what you want them to say about you."

She shrugged.

"I mean, if you just want to look like a cute high school senior, we can do that, but if you want to appear to be something else, tell me."

Kirsten faced him. "I'd like to appear to be anything else than who I am."

"Why would you say that," he said, his heart breaking a little, "when you're such a cute girl?"

She gave a little smirk and stepped backwards so that she was leaning against the fence, the evening light gilding the sweep of hair that spilled over one shoulder. David managed to capture it before she realized and stiffened.

"Yeah," she said. "I'm so cute nobody's even asked me to Senior Prom."

"If it makes you feel any better, I didn't go to mine, either."

Kirsten raised an eyebrow. "How come?"

David lifted the camera and tripod a foot forward and bent down to position the reflector, this time immobilized by its stand, and replied, "I was too embarrassed. Couldn't dance, acne." He grinned at her. "A real chick magnet."

"But at least you *could* have gone, if you wanted," she pointed out. "Nobody asked me."

"Well, then they're idiots."

"Which means the entire graduating class of guys are all idiots?"

One-handed, David unfastened his camera from the tripod and carried it over to where his niece stood and turned it around so she could see the images he had just taken. She looked lovely.

"If the entire graduating class of guys can't see how pretty this girl is," he said, "then, yes, they're all idiots."

Kirsten glanced at the digital images briefly out of curiosity, not prepared to like what she would see. She stared at them. "I didn't think I could look like that. Even my skin looks good."

"It's all you," he smiled. "All I did was add a little light to what the sun was already giving us. Now, we're not going to have this light for much longer, so let's do as much as we can. Tell you what," he handed her the camera as he carried his tripod and set it up in the middle of the road, "if we can prevent getting hit by a car, walk in front of me and when I say 'now' look at me over your shoulder."

Kirsten was game for this. As she began to walk, David yelled "Now!" and giggling, Kirsten flashed a grin over her right shoulder, a soft breeze lifting her hair. He had her repeat the effort several times, adding comical orders like "Look out! Rabid horse behind you!" and "Look! It's Justin Bieber!"

By the time Leigh returned, herself looking surprisingly cheerful, David and Kirsten were wrapping up and David was savoring what he enjoyed the most about his profession: giving a boost of self-confidence to an insecure subject. Her entire attitude had changed, he noted with a smile, as Kirsten asked to show the results of the shoot to her mother, carefully taking the camera and jogging over to the car as Leigh pulled over onto the shoulder. He could see Leigh's animated response, the excited chatting between them. He had needed this afternoon, he thought, folding the tripod and tucking it beneath his left arm, his hand free to carry the reflector. God, he had needed this.

Chapter 38

LISSIE HAD DECIDED TO give the kitchen a good scrub down when Leigh tapped on the back door unannounced. So surprised was Lissie to see her daughter, and her subsequent news, that she now stood staring through the kitchen window with sponges and cleanser unused on either side of the sink.

She placed her hand against her chest, as if to will her heart to stop thumping as she tried to take in what she'd just heard. *"Daddy actually wants to fly out and visit me, get to know me,"* Leigh had gushed, almost as a child unable to contain her excitement, *"and he's coming with his girlfriend, Libbie."* It momentarily struck Lissie as being funny that at an advanced age, a romantic interest would still be referred to as 'a girlfriend' as if they were all teenagers. However, she was so grateful to see her daughter nearly alight with elation that as shocked as she was by the announcement, she made a point of adding brightness to her voice when she replied, "That's lovely, Leigh," and "What a wonderful opportunity for you both!"

Leigh, in turn, assuming her mother's supportive response had laid the ground work for her hitherto proposal, added, "And it would be so good for him to come over, Mother."

Lissie had a sharp intake of breath and stared at her daughter, caught between championing her news and struggling to comprehend Leigh's meaning.

"Here?" she asked, rather weakly. "You mean come over here, to the house?"

"Yes," Leigh replied with a light laugh as if it were obvious. "Over here to the house. That's not a problem, is it?"

"I don't know," her mother had stammered. "I'm not sure—I think I need to think about it."

Leigh, still buoyed by the euphoria from the phone call with Libbie, for once didn't immediately lose patience with her mother. Neither did she think her request any big deal. Surely it would be recognized simply for what it was: allowing an elderly man the opportunity to see the house he had resurrected forty years ago.

"Why do you need to think about it?" Leigh frowned, genuinely puzzled. "After all, it's been decades. It's not like you both haven't moved on."

Lissie gave a small smile and to busy her hands in preparation for the tension she feared looming on the horizon as always, turned on her coffee maker. "Shall we have a cup and talk about it?" she suggested.

Leigh nodded, but found she couldn't sit down at the table, not after what had occurred around it recently. "Let's take it in the living room."

"That'll make a nice change, what a good idea," Lissie replied, her back to her daughter as she spooned the coffee into the filter. "We so seldom use that room."

In minutes they were seated opposite one another in front of the fireplace, Leigh on the sofa and Lissie in her favorite wing chair, recently reupholstered in a neutral wheat with a subtle flourish of floral crewel embroidery across its high back.

Leigh stirred her coffee and glanced down at the sofa upon which she sat and said, "It wasn't this same sofa, but this is where Daddy and I used to sit in the afternoons when you were out with David."

It had not gone unnoticed to Lissie that in all these years, Leigh had continued to address her as 'mother' while girlishly referring to her father with the far more affectionate 'daddy.' She supposed it was just a reflection of the way she was viewed in her daughter's eyes, but it disturbed her in that she was unable to explain why David, with whom she shared a closer relationship, chose the same moniker for her as well. Now she observed her daughter who had just two weeks before been painfully unkind, then apologized begrudgingly, then not been in touch until this moment. Leigh perched on the edge of the sofa, her countenance radiating happiness, and all of this was taken into consideration by Lissie as she endeavored to put her own thoughts into words.

"I'm glad you have such happy memories of this room, darling," she began, wanting to recognize the significance of Leigh's recollection. "I know they're important to you."

Leigh took a sip from her cup, noting that her mother had chosen to use her better china, and placed it back in its saucer before setting both on the coffee table between them.

"Do you have any happy memories in this room?" Leigh asked, her question sincere.

"Oh, my goodness, yes," Lissie replied with a forcefulness that caught Leigh off guard. She had frankly assumed that with her mother's original decision to sell the house, she had little emotion invested in it.

"We had some lovely Christmases in this room, do you remember?" Lissie asked, seeing the eight-foot fir tree that stood sentry, bedecked with lights and tinsel before the front windows each December. She still erected a tree there, but on her own, she used a much smaller one.

"Of course," Leigh replied, dreamily, "and big family occasions around the dining room table. I remember an Easter Egg hunt where you had to run to the Cunningham's to get more eggs because the ones you had put out the night before had all been carried away by raccoons."

Lissie smiled at the memory. "Yes, and neither you nor David were well pleased to have scoured the property for hastily-colored hardboiled eggs." As her daughter continued to chuckle, Lissie injected, "I wish those days could have gone on forever. I certainly assumed they would."

"But they didn't," Leigh said flatly, coming back to earth.

"That's right, they didn't, and darling, the other memories are what seem to be troubling me in regards to having your father come here."

"What if you weren't here?" suggested Leigh as if her mother's feelings were merely an inconvenience that could be easily remedied. "What if you went out for a long lunch with Frances or David? He's certainly had cabin fever; he'd probably love to go."

Lissie inclined her head toward her daughter and asked quickly, "David doesn't know about his father's visit?"

There was something about the phrasing of question that needled Leigh. Prior to hearing her mother say 'his father's visit' she hadn't considered their relationship. David was uninterested, as he had said time and again.

"I don't think David cares. He knows I've been in contact with Daddy, but he told me he wants no involvement."

"He might find that he's changed his mind," her mother suggested, treading lightly. "It would be a shame if he were denied that opportunity, don't you think?"

Leigh remained silent, unreasonably annoyed in her selfishness. With effort, she left it alone and repeated, "What if you weren't here while Daddy came over?"

"Darling." Lissie held up her slender hand. "All of this has happened so quickly. The thing is, I just don't know yet how I feel. Even if I weren't here...it's difficult to explain how it might feel to have someone I was married to forty years ago walking through my house, regardless of if I were here or not. Can you understand that? Imagine if you were in my shoes." She stopped as she quickly caught herself and realized the implications of her explanation with Leigh's marriage in peril.

However, it mattered little to Leigh. She had been so indifferent towards Wes for years that the thought of him suddenly gone from her life then reappearing years later bore little consequence to her emotions. "I wouldn't really care," she shrugged, and it broke Lissie's heart to hear it.

"Well," Lissie sighed, covering her despair and valiantly striving to be understood, "I think for me, it's about the other memories we've acknowledged, because those years, Leigh, and the subsequent struggle, nearly did me in." She leaned forward to pick up her coffee before it went cold.

"But you've always been so strong, and you've survived all that. You're the tower of strength everyone raves about," Leigh countered, bewildered. "If it were me, I'd want to stand there, hands on my hips, just to show my ex-husband that I didn't crumble, that in fact I thrived."

Lissie stared at her daughter, speechless. After a moment, she gasped, "Leigh, I *loved* your father. I *adored* him. There was never any inclination of my wanting to get back at him in some way. Losing him was like a death."

Leigh's eyes widened. Because she had never asked, she had no idea of the ardor her mother had felt for her father. In her eyes, she had always assumed that her mother had made the brisk and determined decision to break cleanly from the marriage for what she had claimed to be the good of the children and a fresh start. She had never heard her mother speak in almost poetic tones.

"When I met him—it sounds silly coming from an elderly lady, I know," Lissie continued, seeing her daughter was allowing her to explain unheeded. "I was infatuated with John. He was the most handsome and fascinating man I'd ever met, and terribly kind. I was like a lovesick puppy, I couldn't eat, I couldn't sleep..." Her words trailed off as for the first time in ages, she allowed herself to remember the sublime golden days of their early marriage. Leigh was astounded. Not only had she never thought of her mother as being even capable of such girlish giddiness, she also suddenly realized she'd never felt any of those things for her own husband.

"Oh, the plans we had," Lissie sighed, finished with her coffee and clasping her hands together in her lap. "And when we found this house, derelict and falling down, actually given to us as a sort of bonus with the purchase of the land, it was as if every dream I'd ever had was coming true. And when his illness made itself known, darling, I was so frightened. I thought he was physically recoiling from me, from all of us. That I had done something to drive a wedge between us. My heart was in pieces every single day. The divorce was terribly difficult. We came so close to losing this house." She stopped and took a long, affectionate look around the room. "And it's all *those* memories that I'm frightened will come back with a vengeance with your father's visit."

"But he's on medication and he's nothing like that anymore." Leigh persisted softly, although she remained quite moved by her mother's story. "In fact, Libbie thinks he probably feels pretty ashamed by it all."

"He shouldn't be ashamed because he was ill," Lissie said. "But memories are a very powerful thing and they do remain, even when we think we've left them behind. I know you must understand that, Leigh, because we share the same memories: wonderful times, and indescribably painful times. The memories of asking my beloved husband to leave are just as devastating as the memories of your beloved father leaving."

Leigh looked down at her hands, lying open and cold in her lap. She had never allowed that her mother could have experienced such depth of feeling, and, incredibly, had only thought of her father as her father, and not the intensely handsome complex man with the slow smile that had swept young Felicity off her feet and into a passionate marriage. But her heart remained heavy.

"I understand," she nodded slowly, "and I can see why you're uncomfortable with it." She raised her eyes and looked at her mother. "I was just hoping that seeing the house again would give him a boost. He's in the early stages of dementia, Mother, and I don't know how long it will be before he doesn't recognize any of this," she said, close to tears. Raising her hands, she gestured to the room in which they sat. "Or me."

"Oh, darling," whispered Lissie, springing from her chair and embracing her daughter who, for as long as either could remember, had rebuffed such sentiment. She allowed herself to cry in her mother's arms as Lissie kissed the top of her head and smoothed her hair.

"You bring him here, Leigh," she murmured, determined to distance her own fears for the sake of quelling her daughter's. "You bring your father home. I'll manage."

Chapter 39

AFTER LEIGH HAD DROPPED David off at his apartment and helped him carry his gear up the stairs, she found herself so warmed by the pleasure of the afternoon that it was easy to talk to her brother. Instead of the residual envy she had directed towards him for years based on his seeming rapport with their mother, his slender frame and a life that had certainly appeared from the outside as exciting as it was completely devoid of responsibilities, she found herself concerned for his welfare and touched by his growing relationship with Kirsten.

"So, everything's all right, then?" She had carefully broached the subject of the reunion with his former wife, handing him the last duffle bag of equipment from her car.

Unused to anything but the most superficial concern from his sister, David didn't follow.

"Well, I've got about another six weeks in the cast, but apart from that," he replied.

"I meant with you. And Denise. Everything all right?"

This both startled and unnerved him as he'd never confided in Leigh regarding anything, actually, since they both became adults. They had very little in common and very much led their own separate lives.

"Yeah," he allowed, nodding slowly. "It's going in a good direction."

"Do you think a reconciliation is in the cards?" she pressed.

"It's been a crazy year." He had no intention of speaking his heart and remained courteous, yet vague. "We shall see. By the way," he added, before she started the engine, "when's Kirsten's prom?"

"Couple of weeks," she replied, and her face fell. "Poor kid."

"Yeah," he agreed. "I don't know how anyone survives high school. Should be abolished altogether," he went on, making a joke, but it was lost on Leigh. "Anyway, glad she likes the photos."

"David, thank you," Leigh replied, earnestly. "You can't imagine what it meant to her today."

"Actually," he said, thinking hard, "I can. See you around."

When he walked up the stairs, he found Denise waiting for him, dressed as if for an evening out. She looked enchanting in a simple, black knit dress that swept over her body, with black pumps and no jewelry with the exception of the ring. He tried not to look at it as he breathed, "You look amazing. Too amazing to be with a sweaty photographer like me."

She smiled enticingly and sauntered over to him, wrapping her arms lightly around his neck.

"A little surprise for you," she teased, then kissed him deeply. "But if you wanted to shower first..."

"Intriguing," he replied, smiling slowly. "Be right back."

"Want me to scrub your back?" she offered, trailing a finger down his chest. "You don't have the biggest shower, but I think there's room for two?"

His mind suddenly flashed to the little guesthouse.

"Actually, with the way you look, I think I'd rather wait for what's in store later," he murmured, "and not cut straight to the chase."

Denise chuckled deep in her throat. "Good plan."

When he returned, wearing the cashmere sweater she'd given him and the easiest pair of jeans he could get into, she stood waiting by the door, jingling a set of keys. He raised his eyebrows, questioningly.

"Dinner at one of the best places in town," she smiled, "with your own personal driver."

"I'm not sure I'm dressed appropriately," he said, tentatively. "I'm not even wearing socks."

"Oh, this place is so exclusive, nobody will care," she winked. "Follow me."

They descended the stairs and she gestured to her car, the black BMW he had seen the night of his mother's party. She even opened the door for him, saying, "After you."

As she drove, she kept one hand on his upper thigh and he felt slightly uneasy as he tried to focus on relishing the attention. They crossed under the freeway and he immediately recognized the residential neighborhood he knew so well.

"Blossom Street," he stated the obvious. "You're taking me to the house?"

She nodded, flashing him a flirtatious smile, and pulled into the drive. They got out and David looked around, as much as he could see as twilight had stretched into nightfall.

"Place looks great. When do you have time to keep up the garden?"

"Oh, I get a crew in twice a month for that," she replied breezily, continuing to jingle her keys and glancing over her shoulder at him. "Come on in."

He walked up the familiar front steps to the craftsman porch and waited between two enormous urns overflowing with heart-shaped leaves of Brunnera while she unlocked the front door. Following her into the house, he noted the floors gleaming underfoot.

"Refinished?" he asked.

"Mm hm," she said, "they needed it, and as I'm putting it on the market..." She didn't finish but continued to beckon him forward, crooking her finger and leading him into the darkness, not stopping to light their way.

He followed her blindly, joking he didn't want to walk into a door.

"Wait there," she said, and positioned him in the front of the dining room. The air was laden with wondrous aromas. He could hear the strike of a match and suddenly Denise could be seen, smiling through the spherical glow of each candle she lit on either end of the table. The tabletop was covered in white linen and before him was a decadent feast. Denise took his left hand and led him around, giving him a tour of the gastronomic fare before him.

"Oysters." She began her list, pointing. "Lobster rolls, white truffles, caviar, strawberries dipped in dark chocolate..."

"Good lord," he said, astonished.

"And, naturally..." She ran her fingertip around the lip of a silver wine cooler chocked with ice. "Champagne."

"I'm blown away," he laughed. "You're spoiling me."

Denise slowly backed him into the wall and wrapped herself around him. "Actually, I'm seducing you."

David would remember that evening as the beginning of most hedonistic night of his life. Sometime during the early morning, he awoke needing to visit the bathroom, and fumbling his way from the bed in which he hadn't slept for well over a year into the bath, he switched on the light and chuckled, not without embarrassment, at his reflection as he caught sight of smears of chocolate across his chest and stomach. He took a quick shower before returning to spoon with the woman that had returned to him body and soul. She stretched lazily and rolled over to face him, entwining a leg over his thigh.

"Have you thought anymore about Boston?" she murmured.

"Mm," he responded, "it's a compelling idea, but..."

"But?" She nudged him forward, her palms resting against his chest.

"To give up my business here, and start all over in Boston," he replied, gently, "it's tricky, you know?"

"Oh, baby," she smiled. "You will have *so* much work up there. Asheville is so small-town compared to Boston."

"That may be true, but there's also a lot more competition in Boston," he reasoned. Seeing her face fall, he didn't continue. He had always enjoyed Boston: it was a hell of a city and a photographer's dream. However, he felt connected to Asheville in the way that the Blue Ridge mountains were connected to the earth. He loved the accessibility of the city, the beat, the vibe. He felt planted there.

"I suppose there's alternatives," she mused, not giving into defeat and pressing her hips against his. "There's lots of couples that have commuter relationships, even marriages."

He eyed her. She stared back, candidly.

"What are you saying?" he asked.

"I'm saying," she said in a voice as soft as it was determined, "that I love you. And I don't think I ever stopped loving you."

David pulled her firmly against him. It was too much to take in. She was giving him everything he had desired from her for years. Everything. It was if he had managed to catch a hummingbird in his hands and marveled over the jewel-toned colors of the creature, the iridescent ripples of light over its body. Yet David was not quite sure what to do with it, especially when it had pursued him. He was so intensely aroused by her, their physical dynamic unaltered by divorce, that he believed the slight disquiet he was feeling was the unfamiliarity of finally having her unconditionally.

They made love, ate breakfast, and from all appearances they seemed to have picked up the pieces of their broken marriage. David found himself wandering around the home they had shared while Denise showered. It was surreal. Everything was the same, unchanged, in the previous place yet different. Was it simply his perception from not having been in the house for so long? There was something that prevented him from thinking of it as his house, their house. It was the house he had left, shed like a heavy coat, given to her his share, without ire or resentment. He had been so shattered by her steely resolve to quickly end their marriage that he couldn't bear further contact to iron out any remaining legal details. "Here," he had said, arms raised, emptied of emotion, standing in this very room fifteen months ago when he had returned to collect his belongings before moving out. "Take it. Take everything. I don't care."

She had observed him icily, saying nothing, her training as an attorney compelling her not to voice her thoughts.

Standing here now he felt a small shiver run up his spine, the smallest of disturbances pricking in his brain. Too many conflicting emotions tied to this house, he finally determined. He wasn't sure where they would end up, but they could never live here again.

She was disappointed, after dressing, that he requested to return to his apartment.

"You seem to rest so much better here," she said.

He put his arm around her. "That's because you're wearing me out! But there are some things I need to see to, emails, and I think I can reschedule some of my shoots earlier than I thought."

"That's great," she smiled. "All right, let me get my purse."

He was further surprised when she reminded him she was available whenever he needed her. He couldn't get over that she had continued to take this lengthy not to mention expensive amount of time from the firm. He gave a justified smirk at the thought of Richard, more than likely supremely annoyed that his star associate had chosen to leave to care for the former husband he considered to be a plebeian photographer.

After she kissed him through the open window from the driver's side of her car, she returned both hands to the steering wheel and he saw the sparkle of the citrine on her finger. It gutted him. Everything that had been heady and magical between them the night before now seemed a tarnished sham. He gave her a forced smile and headed up the stairs to his flat, knowing the ring didn't belong on her hand and feeling laden with the cowardice that plagued him. Denise had no knowledge of the intention behind the ring. Neither did Stephanie, but she had been the one who suffered, and it couldn't be allowed to stand. Enough, he resolved. Today he would see her.

Chapter 40

IT WAS NOTHING LESS than mortifying for David to come to the depressing realization that he had no other choice but to rely once again on Eli for another life-altering event. Unable to pilot his own car (or even be a passenger in it once he discovered Denise had taken his keys by mistake), he had reached for his cell phone to call his shambling friend. Even worse, he now found himself in the passenger seat of Eli's 1980 Gumby green Chevy Luv pickup. They were inches away from turning into the drive towards the hill on which sat the large mountain home of Stephanie's mother, the guesthouse well out of sight on the other side.

"Stop," David said in despair. "Wait a minute."

Eli looked at him, his cigarette hanging out of his mouth.

"Will you put that out?" David added, fanning the air with his left hand. "You're making me stink of nicotine."

"Yeah, but I'm smoking this so I don't smell like weed," Eli reasoned.

"Oh my God," said David, putting his face in his hands.

"So what's the deal?" Eli asked, reluctantly stubbing out his butt in the overflowing ashtray. "Why are we stopping?"

David leaned back in the broken seat of the truck, looking upwards and imploring the heavens. His mind was spinning; he hadn't yet decided exactly what he was going to say to Stephanie. He didn't know if she was even home or how unfair it was to invade her privacy. Would she even look at him? Listen to him?

"Because I'm freaking out," David replied. "I don't even want to have to pass her mother's house."

"I can go hang with her mother," Eli offered, "and create a diversion."

David looked at him. "Please don't do that," he said. He drummed the fingers of his good hand on the dash and continued to weigh his options.

"Look," said Eli, checking his watch. "It's not like I have all day, and at some point, David, you're going to have to shit or get off the pot. Like Stephanie did."

"What are you talking about?" David frowned.

"When she came to see you. I essentially told her the same thing: you like him, he likes you, so go see him."

"You *told* her that?" David said incredulously. "Why the hell would you tell her to do that?"

"Well, how the hell was I supposed to know you were back with your ex-wife? I was doing it as a favor!"

David put his head back in his hands and hunched over until his unhealed rib forced him to straighten. This recent revelation casually mentioned by Eli in his usual offhand manner had only further complicated matters. He shook his head. "Can't do it," he said defeatedly. "Turn around."

Eli slapped the steering wheel with both hands in exasperation and turned to his friend.

"David, for God's sake, just man up, will ya? What are you afraid of? She's only, what, five and half feet tall? What do you think she's going to do, throw a brick at you? Now I'm going to drive you up to the top of this hill and you're going to get out and damn well talk to Steph." He put the truck in gear. Sputtering, the truck limped its way to the crest where Eli then shoved it into park, reached over his friend, and pushed open the passenger door himself. David hesitated, then climbed out.

"You have to slam it really hard or it won't close," Eli told him.

David obliged and slammed the tinny door. It bounced back open. He had to slam it twice more, cursing, before it remained shut. He pointed at Eli. "You stay here. Don't you dare get out."

"No way I'm getting out," replied Eli, lighting up another cigarette. "Stephanie's mean when she's mad."

David looked at him.

In the front yard of the guesthouse, Stephanie had her fidgeting son sitting on a stool with a towel draped over his shoulders. She was attempting to cut his hair. Bub, the cat, was stretched luxuriously in the sun.

"Are you making it stick up?" Buster kept asking. "I want it to stick up."

"Yes, it's sticking up," she replied. Hearing the sound of a door being repeatedly slammed, she mistook it for gunshots and looked up. Eli's truck was unmistakable, and she knew it well. But to see it perched facing her, across from her mother's house, made her gasp. She shaded her eyes against the sun. Was that him standing on the passenger's side? He was walking towards her. Then she saw another figure getting out of the driver's side, following the first figure down the hill.

"Dear God," she said, her scissors freezing in midair. It was David, Eli discreetly ambling behind.

"Seriously?" she said aloud when they were within earshot, her heart pounding. "Both of you? Seriously?"

David turned in surprise to see Eli tagging along. "Dammit, Eli," he said.

"Just providing back up," Eli shrugged, peeling off to lean against the fence. "She's armed."

"I tried to call you," David began, looking at Stephanie, his mouth going dry. He glanced down at her son. "Hi Buster."

"Hi," Buster replied, looking up and squinting his eye.

"Have you got a few minutes?" David asked.

"Actually, I don't," Stephanie said, then, annoyed that she had sounded petulant, amended, "I mean, I've got a lot of things to do before I go to work and I need to finish Buster's hair."

"Oh, you got a new job?"

"Yeah, I got a new job."

David shoved his hand in his pocket and made an effort to sound conversational, "I didn't know you cut hair."

"There's a lot of stuff about me you didn't know," she said without looking up, the tip of her tongue pressed against her upper lip as she focused on the clip of the scissors. She began to notice she was feeling unsteady in her knees. David's appearance felt like an ambush.

"She's making it stick up," said Buster.

"It looks good," David said.

"I know," Buster replied.

Stephanie finished as slowly as possible solely for the opportunity to collect herself. He would not see her cry, she vowed, grittily determined to remain in control of her emotions and give no indication he had meant anything to her. She removed the towel from Buster's shoulders, shook it out and blew on the back of his neck to rid him of ticklish bits of clippings.

"Can I go rolling?" he asked.

"You just had lunch," his mother replied, "you might want to wait."

"No, I'm OK," he declared, and jumping off the stool, he charged up the hill beside Eli's truck, threw himself into the grass, and began rolling back down.

David watched him for several moments and remarked, "I'm kind of feeling like that right now."

Stephanie looked at him.

"All over the place," he explained, then nodded toward her front door. "Can we go inside?"

Stephanie glanced quickly at Buster, now engaged with Eli, whom he knew from softball, and demonstrated his throwing arm.

"You've got five minutes," she said, not taking her eye off her son. "Because if I leave him with Eli for more than that, he'll come back with a two pack a day habit." She strode into the house, not looking back, and when David followed her in she remained standing and turned to face him, her arms hanging loose by her sides.

David took in the room and noticed the workbench was cluttered with tools—for what purpose he had no idea—and made the mistake of politely asking, "Been working on your jewelry?"

"Wow," Stephanie looked at him. "You just asked me that?"

"Jeez," David muttered and ran the fingers of his good hand through his hair. "That was unbelievably insensitive, sorry. Look," he blurted out nervously, "can we sit down?"

"Sure," said Stephanie, holding her own, and gesturing to the corner. "Want the recliner?"

Defeated, David took a beat then held up his hand. "OK, I can't do this. I'm sorry. I made a big mistake coming here." He turned to leave, walked through the door, then turned on his heel and came back in. "But I can't leave without at least saying I'm sorry. I'm sorry for everything."

"What are you apologizing for?" Stephanie asked, her tone having lost its edge.

"Steph," he said, "I just wanted to explain about the ring. I saw it in a shop and I bought it. I bought it because I knew you were hoping to have a career in making jewelry and I just wanted to sort of give you a boost, you know? I wasn't planning to give it to anyone. I stuck it in my pocket, and later that night, Denise picked up my jacket, it fell out, and she assumed it was for her, and I couldn't tell her it wasn't."

"Why?" Stephanie asked.

"Because I didn't want to hurt her feelings."

"Why?" Stephanie persisted.

"Because," he stammered, exasperated, "we're getting back together."

Stephanie left the room to return the towel to the bathroom. "And isn't that what you wanted?" she asked as she walked past him.

David nodded limply, then realizing he needed to articulate replied, "Yes."

"OK," Stephanie said upon her return. She leaned against the fireplace and looked at him for a moment. "Then there's no problem. You've gotten what you always wanted and that means you're happy. And because I'm your friend," she added, her heart feeling very full, "I'm happy."

David returned her stare and inclined his head quizzically to one side as he asked, "So, you're not, you know..."

"What?" she asked.

"Hurt, or anything?"

"Oh." The meaning of his question now clear, she asked, "as in heartbroken?" She paused a few moments, debating with herself over whether to reveal her feelings for him or not. It occurred to her that this was probably the last time she would ever see him, so she tossed aside the vow she had made earlier, straightened her shoulders and spoke her truth.

"So, here's the deal," she began in the frank patter that David considered an unsettling yet endearing attribute. "When I first saw you at the pub a couple of years ago, I was fascinated by you in a science project sort of way because I couldn't figure out why you were hanging out with somebody like Eli. Then I learned you guys knew each other from school, so that made sense. And then I would notice women hitting on you but you ignoring them, so then I thought, oh, OK, maybe he's gay. Finally, I see Denise the one time she came in and put it together that you two were married and yeah, I developed a crush on you, David, because I thought, wow, here's this good-looking professional guy who is so in love with his wife that he doesn't even *notice* other women." She paused and glanced out the front door to check on Buster, then continued. "And I remember leaning back against the bar and thinking *so that's what a happy marriage looks like.*"

David shook his head slowly. "I had no idea you knew all that about me."

Stephanie found she was relaxed enough to give him a quick smile, and as she did so as she sat down on the rock hearth of the fireplace and wrapped her arms around her knees. She flipped her hair back behind one shoulder before raising her eyes to meet his.

"When you work behind a bar, you do a lot of observing," she said, "and what I thought I saw with you was a really good guy, a funny guy in a hang dog sort of way, but you always seemed at least to me, I don't know, a little wary? And then when your marriage was ending, you looked like the walking wounded. I hurt so badly for you that I couldn't even hang around the end of the bar where you would sit. You never said anything. You rarely ever even looked up. It was so sad." She sighed at the memory and blew out her breath. "And then, in the last couple of months, you sort of started coming up for air, metaphorically-speaking, and I could get you to laugh at some of my jokes. Even Eli could get you to laugh, and then when we were together, we laughed a lot. But now Denise is back in your life and that's great because that means you'll be happy and I won't have to worry about you anymore."

David, stirred by her simple recitation, unmarked by either anguish or exaggeration, stared at her, slightly pained. She caught his look and rocked back a little bit as she wondered aloud dreamily, "And one day, maybe I'll meet a guy who really knows what he wants, and what he wants is me. Because it would be nice to know what that's like, and for my son, who's already had enough drama in his life."

As if by cue, Buster came in, his T-shirt stained with large swatches of green and struggling beneath the weight of Bub, who appeared to be grinning as he held fast to a small rodent.

"He's got a chipmunk in his mouth and he won't let go," Buster announced, and lifted the cat onto the kitchen counter.

Stephanie shot David a look and said, "Nobody tells you about this stuff when you start thinking about having a kid." She stuck a finger in each side of the cat's mouth to pry it open. The chipmunk, eyes bulging, was kicking with its back legs, and Bub was growling at the indignity of giving up his dinner.

"Want any help?" David asked, hoping his offer would be declined.

"Cup your hands in front of Bub's mouth because I've almost got it."

Wincing slightly, he complied.

Stephanie managed to force the cat's mouth apart and the chipmunk fell squirming into David's hands as Buster yelled, "He's bleeding!"

David closed his hands around the creature, shuddering at the feeling of its tiny body wriggling against his flesh in a panic, clawing frantically. He looked questioningly at Stephanie.

"Well, don't just stand there," she said. "Go put a Band-Aid on it. Buster, show him how to clean it up before you turn it back loose."

David found himself being led back to the tiny bathroom he had shared with Stephanie a little over two weeks ago and wondered why the oddest things that he had ever experienced seemed to happen in her company. He opened his hands just enough so that Buster could wipe away the blood with a bit of dampened tissue and then gently apply antibiotic ointment with his finger. He looked up at David.

"Have you ever saved a chipmunk before?" he asked.

"No. No, I haven't."

Buster nodded. "Thought so. Give it." David let the creature roll from his grasp into Buster's small, cupped hands, and the boy left the room, holding his patient close to his chest.

"Make sure you hold on to Bub, Mom," he ordered, taking the chipmunk outside into the grass.

Stephanie picked up the cat and his pink eyes greedily followed Buster as he went out the door.

"He's just terrible," she said, speaking of the cat. "He's fed twice a day and he still has to go out and kill things."

"Terrorist," agreed David. They stood for a moment, feeling slightly awkward, until Stephanie said, "I'm glad you came over."

"I'm glad I did, too."

"It was good to clear the air."

"Yes," he said, nodding, "it was. Thank you for being so understanding." He took a beat. "And for being who you are."

She ducked her head and replied, "Anytime," and then, as she watched him turn to walk out the door, as well as her life, she added, "Hey, David."

He stopped and turned back to look at her.

"I'm glad Denise thought you bought her the ring because it really should be worn by the woman you love."

David nodded briefly and said, "Bye, Steph."

He walked outside and joined up with Eli, who had lit his third cigarette.

"You didn't throw your butts in the yard, right?" David asked as they mounted the hill towards the pickup.

"I covered them with dirt," Eli replied. They walked on in silence until they got into the truck and Eli asked, "So, what went down?"

David stared through the cracked windshield. "Just drive," he said.

Chapter 41

LEIGH, WHO HAD BATTLED insomnia on and off for years, found herself lying awake in what she no longer termed the 'guest' room but instead 'her' room in the early hours of the morning mid-week. Instead of feeling the usual drain from broken sleep, she was tickled, anticipatory, nervous...all the emotions that had flooded into and taken control of her brain since she heard the subsequent news from Libbie detailing travel dates and flight numbers.

They would be arriving the following week on an 'open jaw' arrangement for "a nice, long, break" as Libbie had put it, "as long as we don't overstay our welcome."

"You can stay as long as you like, we're delighted to have you with us and get to meet the family." Leigh had smiled down the phone without having spoken to Wes or Kirsten first.

She had felt so light on her feet, so breathlessly excited, that she had simply assumed her happiness would emanate throughout the rest of the household. Chores had lost their sense of mundanity because she was eager that their modest home appear immaculate to her father. Cooking dinner was an opportunity to experiment with new recipes; a weeded front garden would be far more welcoming. It was as if in this past week, having come to an understanding with her mother—along with Kirsten's mood lifting dramatically and now the dates of her father's travel confirmed—Leigh felt, for the first time in years really, as if she was being propelled along by a joyful wave.

Wes had witnessed the ebullient change of mood, as had Kirsten, but it was Wes who found himself at odds with the current agenda despite the overall lightness within the house. He found himself sitting up alone in their bed in the master bedroom, carefully placing a not particularly interesting new book on the bedside table. Removing his glasses, he rubbed his eyes. Blinking, he looked around the familiar surroundings: the cream-painted walls, the pine dressers, his tall, hers horizontal, the matching mirror hanging above. At first glance—at every glance, the room was tidy, organized. The house was built well before walk-in closets were commonplace and they each occupied a relatively small one, Leigh utilizing extra space with a rack that hung over the door to store the half dozen pairs of sensible shoes she owned: one pair black, the rest neutral.

Wes was under no illusions regarding his marriage. He was aware that the staleness that had pervaded for—he tried to pinpoint a time reference—at least ten years was not unexpected. Children, finances and responsibilities all have a way of taking the bloom off the rose, but he had not been prepared for the steady increase in his wife's moroseness, and certainly not the pronounced indifference that had arrived when he had put his foot down regarding upending their life for the sake of acquiring her mother's house.

What had been the most jarring was the result of their conversation yesterday evening following dinner while Kirsten was studying in her room. He had expected indignation, tearful accusations of unfeelingness. He had not expected an almost blasé shrug of the shoulders regarding the disintegration of their marriage. And while he himself would also admit it would have been an arduous endeavor to uncover feelings of unfettered affection towards one another once again, he would have been willing to make the attempt.

"I think we have some things to discuss, don't you?" He had broached the subject of the upcoming visit by her father and Libbie as he had quietly assisted tidying the kitchen after dinner.

Leigh had turned her head to face him, her eyebrows raised. "They arrive next week," she replied.

Wes had pulled back a kitchen chair and sat down, regarding her. "Were you going to talk to me about it? Kirsten?"

"I did," she said, folding a tea towel she had finished using. "I told you as soon as Libbie called with the travel dates."

Wes folded his hands together on the table before answering slowly, carefully. "You *told* us. You didn't *ask* us. Don't you think this qualifies as a discussion that should be had as a family?"

Leigh's mouth set into a tight thin line and without looking up, she asked, "Are you saying I need to ask permission before inviting my own family to our house?"

Her husband exhaled wearily. He was by nature a patient man, but he was not in the habit of accepting what felt like blithe injustice directed towards either himself or his daughter.

"That's not what I'm saying at all. What I'm saying is that this goes far deeper than an ordinary family visit."

Leigh didn't sit. She stood on the other side of the kitchen with her arms crossed in front of her chest, irritation seeping into her expression.

"Since I seem to be completely unaware of the depths of this ordinary family visit, Wes, why don't you tell me?"

"This is not meant to be an attack, Leigh," Wes replied calmly. "But it is something I think deserves to be *talked* about."

And when he stressed the word *talk* her mind flashed back to the assignation of blame he had leveled at her in her mother's kitchen: "*You talk to me, you sure as hell don't talk with me.*" In order to prove his portrayal of her as false, she immediately drew up a chair opposite and, keeping her tone neutral, said, "I agree. Let's talk."

Her willingness had both surprised and relieved him. It was a good first step. Aware of how easily defensive she could become, he picked his way carefully through his thoughts.

"Tell me how you feel about your father and his girlfriend coming to stay," he began, knowing she was eager to declare her point of view.

"All right, but I think this will sound a bit redundant because I was pretty certain you knew that reconnecting with my father, particularly after he nearly died, was pretty much the most important thing in my life," she said plainly.

Wes nodded in agreement and waited for her to continue. She sat silently, aware of the empty air between them, waiting for him to fill it. He did.

"I am aware of that," he began. "I'm also aware that this relationship for you has happened very quickly and I'm worried, Leigh, because I see you hurtling towards all of this at top speed, and I don't want you to be crushed if everything you hoped might happen between you and your father, doesn't."

Leigh gave a quick smile as if dismissing him and replied, "Well, Wes, since you haven't been involved with that part of my life, and, quite frankly, have been completely unsupportive in most other areas, I'm not surprised you would think that."

"When did I become the enemy?" he asked, stricken. He leaned back, opening his hands in a gesture of futility. "When did asking to have my voice heard become unreasonable? I am stating my concerns for your welfare, as well as for our family, and seeing that I wasn't even given the common courtesy to be asked whether or not two guests could stay in my own house for God knows how long, I think my response has been pretty measured, don't you?"

"Your idea for my welfare is to deny my dreams at every turn," Leigh retorted, "and now I see it's extending to my father, as well. If I didn't know better, I would almost think you're jealous that I have found things in my life that have given me happiness that don't include you, just the way you've found that with your new *friend.*"

The comment stung like the flick of a whip. Wes remained quiet for several moments. The consequences he was willing to propose were grave and he made one last attempt before defeat.

"Leigh, everything that has been going on between us for the last several years has been going on well before I ever sought outside companionship," he said, adding, "*platonic* companionship. Please hear what I'm saying because I'm going to give this everything I've got. I am very happy that you're developing a relationship with your father, because I think it has the potential to be wonderfully healing for you. My frustration is the consistent lack of communication from you, the lack of interest, really, to involve me in any of these plans that you are making that will in the end affect us all."

Leigh leaned back in her chair and looked at him with what he perceived as resignation.

"Wes, when you put up roadblock after roadblock to stop me from even attempting to keep my mother's house from going on the market, I knew then there was no real use in trying to communicate with you. You kept talking about a *house*, I was talking about a *home*. My *home*. You acted as if I were a child crying for the moon and it was then that I realized that you weren't the least concerned with the true depths of my feelings."

Wes bristled. "That's a cheap shot. Of course I know what the house means to you. But because I point out the impracticalities of it, the ramifications of it, I'm the bad guy, and I resent the hell out of it. The hard truth, Leigh, is this: that house is not *your* home. It is your mother's home. I have stood by while you bullied—actually bullied— your mother to the point where she caved in, sacrificing all her own plans and dreams, just so you can have what you want." He shook his head slowly. "I don't know how you can rationalize doing something like that."

"She knows what it means to me," Leigh shot back, but her voice was hollow.

Wes rose to his feet, slowly, and stood in the wreckage that surrounded them both.

"Your mother is a good and selfless person," he said, his face expressionless in defeat. "And what is so sad is that you seem to only think of her that way now because you've gotten from her what you've wanted. And what a shame, what a damned shame, that it never occurred to you to even try and understand what *her* dreams meant to her, especially with everything she's gone through in her life." He shoved his hands into his pockets and looked at Leigh in silence before delivering what had dominated his thoughts for several weeks. "And I don't think I want to remain with a person who is comfortable justifying that sort of greed."

Leigh took a deep breath and let out an expansive sigh as if tired, showing no sign of distress or pain. She looked at her husband and replied flatly, "Fine. If that's how you feel, that's fine with me."

"It's not fine with me," he said, tonelessly. "None of this is fine with me. I was hoping you'd feel that nearly twenty years of marriage might be worth fighting for. But now I see it's not even a consideration." He left the room and she heard him walk into the den and turn on the television.

Leigh stiffened, yet held firm to her conviction that her husband's obstructions had been the undeniable source of friction between them. Unwilling to be in the same room as him or even pass him on the way to her bedroom, she remained in the kitchen and turned on the small television set on the counter, watching a game show from her chair.

Wes turned on a basketball game, his eyes absorbing the action yet seeing none of it. He was experiencing the numbness of isolation on which he hadn't counted spreading thinly within him.

Nothing so profoundly illustrated their lives more than the glow that emanated from three different screens, from three different rooms, inside the tidy split-level house on Benson Street.

Chapter 42

WITHIN A COUPLE OF weeks, David had fallen into the routine of taking up residence with his former wife, largely based on the fact that while he remained severely limited with the use of his right arm, he didn't want to inconvenience Denise by asking to be driven to places he could easily walk. She had already done so much, he felt: the shopping, the tidying up, the cooking. He had his physical therapy appointment on Friday afternoons and he had apologized as he requested her assistance once again.

"Baby, you know that I'm happy to do this," she reminded him as they stood in the kitchen putting away the groceries. "Please don't think you're putting me out. And if you want, feel free to use my car. It's an automatic."

David hesitated. He had yet to feel at ease inside her new BMW for the sole reason he had suspected it to be a gleaming representation which trumpeted her new life as a successful single woman. Not entirely sure if his thoughts were unreasonable, the car somehow rankled him.

"That's generous of you," he replied, "but then that would leave you stuck with my Jeep and you can't drive a stick shift."

"Oh," she said, and furrowed her delicate brow. "I hadn't thought of that. But it shouldn't be a problem, really, especially as I've cleared my schedule. All I have going on is a realtor lined up to come see the house this afternoon, so if you want to use it, feel free."

David smiled at her thoughtfulness but declined. "I only need to go to the studio today, and that's just up the road. I feel like I lost a lot of fitness since I got hurt, so I'm going to stretch my legs and head over there."

Denise reached over and kissed him. "You feel very fit to me," she purred mischievously.

"And if I don't get going now, I'll never get out of here," he grinned. "You're insatiable."

"Only with you," she winked.

He was relieved it was a mild day, allowing him to remain in shirtsleeves and not struggle into a sweater or jacket. Whistling, he scooped up his keys and after descending the front steps, turned right at the end of the drive and followed the leafy sidewalk downhill, taking a right on Lexington and passing beneath the freeway before reaching his favorite stretch of the city. His path to the studio took him past the shop where he had seen Stephanie's jewelry displayed, and he slowed as he took note that there were still only two rings on offer in the copper tray. This time he didn't stop. Another two blocks before turning off onto the side street on which his business was located, he was seduced by the smells of the coffee shop on the corner and fancied a cup. He had been a regular for some time and it was a comfort to not only see the staff, but to be told he had been missed. He patiently gave the litany of details surrounding his accident, as he found was expected of him by anyone who had not seen him in some time.

He ordered a dark roast with a splash of milk and thought he might spend a few minutes glancing through the local free publication he noticed had been left on a table. It was good to catch up with the goings-on in town. He checked the music listings and saw that a couple of friends were playing in the neighborhood the following Saturday. He wondered if Eli would be accompanying any of them. Seeing the dates listed, he was reminded of the prom to which his niece had not been invited. He seemed to remember Leigh being invited to hers, and somewhere there were photographs of her standing stiffly in something frothy and pink with a corsage tethered to her wrist, next to a skinny guy with a buzz cut, glasses, and an ROTC uniform. He chuckled softly at the memory and was relieved not to have attended his own, having been excruciatingly shy and insecure about both his appearance and abilities. However, he had been unaware how painful it could be not to be asked, until he had heard Kirsten's simple declaration of being too unappealing to be considered. He felt for her because it really was a night of paramount importance to any young girl, particularly one whom hadn't had the happiest of times recently. Suddenly, to his surprise and irritation, because he had never been fond of being physically invaded particularly when he was incapable of resisting, two plump hands obscured his eyes and a voice from behind him chirped, "Guess who?"

"No idea," he said brusquely, hoping his tone would project his desire to be left alone.

"Oh, go on, try," she persisted.

"Lady Gaga," he said, tonelessly.

"Wrong!" he was needlessly told as a vaguely familiar face popped around his shoulder wearing glossy pink lipstick. "Mia!" she announced, flipping both hands in the air as if prepared to take a bow.

"*Oh, God,*" he groaned inwardly, recognizing the receptionist from Denise's law firm he only had to bear once a year at the Christmas party. He feigned pleasure in seeing her and said, "Hi, Mia, how are you?"

"More to the point of it," she began, plopping herself uninvited on the chair opposite and eyeing the cast encased around his upper arm, "How are *you*? What on earth happened?"

"Long story," he replied.

"I'm all ears," she persisted. Knowing she wouldn't leave until she had all details, he recited the details of his injury as succinctly as possible with little if any inflection in his voice.

"Oh, my gosh, are you all right?" she asked, her heavily made up eyes bulging. "Do you have anyone looking after you?"

He caught himself before divulging the slightest detail and answered flatly, "I'm fine." Realizing how curt his reply was, he added for the sake of civility, "how about you?"

Mia settled herself back into her seat, a sure sign that she intended not to feel rushed and rolled her eyes. "I'm just here doing the coffee run for the office, but oh boy, has it been crazy."

"Huh," said David, specifically not pressing for details.

"Do you ever see Denise?" she asked impertinently, searching his face.

The inappropriateness of the question caught him off guard and knowing her penchant for gossip, he replied, simply, "Nope."

"Well, I don't miss the drama, I'll tell you that," she breathed with the air of someone bursting to reveal scandal. "For the longest time, everyone was on eggshells."

"Is that so?" David sighed, wondering on earth what this had to do with him, his eyes flicking to the review he had been reading in the paper before being interrupted.

"I mean, Denise is divorced, of course, and can do whatever she likes, but it's funny because I guess she and Spencer thought no one in the office knew what was going on," she said, spilling the particulars with the triumphant aura of self-importance. "But of course, everyone did."

David felt as if he'd been sucker-punched and kept his eyes deliberately averted from the prattling creature who was now leaning forward towards him. He would not give her the satisfaction of showing any interest in her breathless details, and it was excruciating knowing he needed to hear them.

"Denise is free to do whatever she likes. It's her life," he managed, somehow sounding perfectly natural.

"Oh, of course!" Mia agreed. "Of course she is, but it was like a soap opera because Richard had separated from Monica, and—"

"Richard?" David cursed inwardly for allowing himself to blurt out the name in his shock.

"Oh, yeah, Richard separated from Monica and really, everyone wondered if it had to do with the timing of you and Denise splitting up, because we've all known he's had a crush on Denise for years. He was following her around, cow-eyed, but naturally, she wanted nothing to do with him, and Hannah, one of the paralegals, had seen Denise and Spencer getting very chummy at a restaurant on the other side of town. Her husband owns the place, so Hannah's over there all the time. Anyway, all of a sudden, Spencer, I guess, went for someone a little closer to his age because Denise must be, what do you think, five or eight years older than him?"

"No idea," David replied dully.

"Well, Spencer starts seeing this cute young blonde in the office down the hall from ours, and the next thing you know, everything becomes really tense between Denise and Spencer, and tense between both of them with Richard, then I guess Denise decided just to bail from all the drama. She handed in her resignation and I guess she's been gone about a couple of weeks."

"Good for her," David said, rising to feet, his legs feeling suddenly shaky. "Good for her for moving on." Grasping his cardboard cup of coffee, he started for the door after tossing, "See ya," over his shoulder.

How he got to his studio, he couldn't remember, and once inside, he closed and locked the door. His coffee, cold, had been left forgotten on his desk as he paced slowly, feeling as if everything inside him had been excavated. He wasn't someone to fly off the handle. Very much his mother's son, he thought through his emotions, weighing them, digesting them. Presently he became too numb to travel this methodical path and he found himself revisiting the scenario of Denise and Spencer, all the while trying to wave it away with the rationalization that she indeed was single to do as she pleased.

It was her resignation that plagued him most. In the six years that he had known his former wife, not once had he ever known her to be dishonest. To the best of his knowledge, she had always been straightforward with him, no matter how badly it bruised. "*I've arranged to have some time off,"* she told him, immediately following his accident, and, really, he had to admit even that wasn't entirely untruthful. But nothing in her approach towards him, nothing in her affectionate countenance had given him even an inkling what had clearly occurred just days, if not hours, before she had arrived at his bedside at the hospital.

However, had anything actually occurred? This was, after all, he thought as he ran his hand through his hair, the meddling chatter of Mia, the office gossip. Had she not made it quite obvious during their last meeting at the ill-fated Christmas party that she still harbored a crush on him? He couldn't remain in the studio with nothing to do and no way to avoid the flitting thoughts that were saturating his brain. He opened the front door, unlocked his mailbox mounted on the wall directly outside, and retrieving what looked to be a circular and a bill, deposited them back into the mailbox, locked it, and began walking back to Lexington and turned towards College Street. He had no clear idea where he was going, and he stopped for a moment on the sidewalk, decided to turn back towards Blossom, then stopped again, to the irritation of a grizzled man behind him trying to walk his dog. He sidestepped, apologized, and leaned against a building, thinking hard. He had an overwhelming urge to get back to his apartment on Coxe Street and wished he lived closer. He considered walking. It would be a hike, but it would give him time to think, because the only thing he presently knew was that he couldn't see Denise.

He headed south, his stride long, and he found after ten minutes that he had been able to walk determinedly without thinking of anything, which was exactly as he had hoped. He kept his eyes moving, purposely distracting, sweeping along shop fronts and parked cars, gave the change in his pocket to a homeless man and stopped somewhere to grab a sandwich. He tried to eat it as he walked, which took quite a bit of focus. Frustrated, he sat down on a bench outside a bar and finished it. When he was nearly home, slightly winded from jogging painfully across intersections as well as having lost fitness, he could see the familiar brick building two blocks ahead and he sighed with relief. Through the entrance and up the stairs he was soon comfortably inside. The first thing he did was open a beer, and the second thing he did was open his laptop.

He took a long pull on the beer, swallowed hard and pulled up the website for King, Dean, Harrison and Shaw, scrolling through their roster. Denise's profile page had disappeared. So that part, he thought somewhat uncomfortably, was true. He took another long swig from the bottle and feeling cringingly sophomoric, went to Denise's Facebook page. He clicked on her list of friends and searched for Spencer. His name no longer appeared. David held his breath and clicked on her profile photo, the one where she was leaning against a building with what he remembered thinking was a pensive expression. Spencer had commented, he remembered. What had he said? David strained to remember, scrolling past remarks by female friends complimenting her beauty. *I know that look*. That was it. That was the comment Spencer had typed when David had looked at her page weeks ago. He scrolled through the comments, twice. It had been deleted. He sat on the edge of the couch and rubbed his hands together. There was a current of jealousy he felt that couldn't be denied. He had been so quickly and nonchalantly replaced in her life by another man, as well as an acknowledgement that her departure from the firm had not been altogether truthful. In fact, David thought, with more despair than irritation, she had deliberately made it sound as if she had specifically taken time off to care for him, to put her career aside for him. Because, as she told him, leaning over him in ER, *"Some things are worth making priorities."*

But what caused the chill that seeped into his chest were the ramifications that far exceeded an office affair and the muddied truth of her departure. It was what resided within Denise, so deeply ingrained that he suspected she wasn't even aware, and with profound sadness, he realized, motivated her to return to him.

Chapter 43

LEIGH HAD ADVISED LIBBIE to book her flight making Charlotte, North Carolina, their final destination, saving them a two hour layover for the sake of a thirty-minute connecting flight to Asheville. Although arriving in Charlotte meant just over an hour and a half in the car to her home in the foothills of the Blue Ridge, she wanted to shield her father from the tumult of yet another terminal, check in, and flight. She also specifically chose to take 74 towards her home because of its bucolic vistas on each side of the road once they were well past Shelby and into the countryside.

Libbie had insisted on putting John in the front seat because, as she said, "Honey, I can fold up anywhere, but he's got long legs." It felt odd still and not at all familiar to have her father in such close proximity as they drove along the beautiful stretch of highway that was nearly empty of traffic. From time to time, she would steal a look beneath her sunglasses at his hands placed quietly in his lap, free from calluses or anything that would ever indicate a working class life. He had the hands of an artist or, as he was, an architect. Frankly, Leigh thought, his hands were nicer than hers: tapered fingers of an elegant length where her own felt so unattractively stubby.

"I have never seen so much green in my life!" Libbie proclaimed from the back seat. She leaned forward between them and tapped John on his shoulder. "Have you ever seen anything look so lush? And it's all so clean...you know, in Los Angeles, they have to sweep the freeways every week because people throw so much trash out the window. I'll just never understand that."

Leigh nodded, "People litter here, too, but this is an awfully nice highway." She glanced at her father who had left the Carolinas well before this freeway had even been built, and wondered if he would recall any of the mountains that began to rear before them. The last thing she wanted to do, after being subtly coached by Libbie, was to ask at every turn, "Do you remember this? Does that look familiar?" It had a way of implying fragility as well as putting a struggling person on the spot. Instead, when she met them at baggage claim in Charlotte, after receiving an enormous hug from Libbie she offered her hand to her father and said, "I hope this isn't all too overwhelming to you. It's good to see you again. I'm Leigh." He had clasped her hand and had even given her an affectionate pat on the back, as one would a family pet, but for Leigh it was the first demonstrative display of affection from the man in over thirty years, and she was quietly delighted because of it.

"This is really quite a lot like northern California," Libbie remarked, not taking her eyes off the rolling and verdant countryside. "I really had no idea what to expect from North Carolina. It's so beautiful."

"They say it's one of the top retirement destination areas," Leigh filled her in, "after Florida, of course. But people like having four seasons and being surrounded by nature."

Libbie gave an impression of shivering and replied, "I can understand that, but I've got to have the sun. I just can't take the cold. Give me a scorching, hot day and I'm as happy as a clam."

"You say that," John suddenly quipped, "but on the scorching, hot days, you send me out to do the errands because you say it's too hot."

Libbie cackled, "That's another reason I love it!"

Leigh laughed along softly, her heart full to overflowing in the realization of the moment. She stole a sidelong look at her father but he was staring straight ahead, a soft smile curled on his lips. Suddenly he held up both hands, as if framing the view before him and said, "The blue wall. That's what we called these mountains, the blue wall, because they seem to go all the way around."

"They're almost an indigo blue this time of day," Leigh contributed, "and in the winter, when all the leaves are down, you can see so much more of them. We actually have a winter view from our house, which is something to appreciate when it gets cold and wet."

"Where are we staying?" John asked, frowning. He had asked this once before in the airport.

"We're staying at Leigh's, honey," Libbie replied, giving his shoulder a squeeze.

"So not a hotel?" he clarified.

"We have a guest room at our house," Leigh said, "and there's nothing I look forward to more than cooking you a nice dinner tonight."

The sleeping arrangements had been a delicate subject in her home as it didn't go unnoticed that she would be moving back into the master bedroom.

"Of course, I can always sleep on the couch," she'd mentioned airily to Wes, who felt distinctly validated in nearly giving his assent, thereby allowing her to experience the lower back discomfort he would end up feeling being turned out of his bedroom. He had simply said, "I'll take the couch," and Leigh had to do some fast thinking to concoct a story that Wes often fell asleep on the couch while watching basketball and remained there so as not to wake her, lest they feel they were creating an inconvenience by their presence.

"Now, that'll be a treat," Libbie sounded pleased, "because it's an awful lot of trouble to cook just for two and I'm afraid we tend to sort of graze at night instead of a proper dinner."

"But she makes a world class pot roast," John remarked and reached back to pat her hand.

"That's because we can eat on that for days," Libbie chuckled. "If I can figure out how to make one meal a week that lasts all week, I'll be in like Flynn!"

When they exited the highway onto the smaller roads that wound around the countryside, her father remarked, "See the size of the lots, here, Lib? You wouldn't see this in California."

"Goodness, no," she agreed. "You couldn't afford them, either."

And when Leigh finally pulled onto Benson Street and into her driveway, Libbie gushed, "Honey, this would be a million dollar house in Los Angeles, wouldn't it, John, at least a million dollar house!"

Leigh could have never imagined such an outlandish figure lavished upon her house and felt momentarily warmed, almost embarrassingly so, as does a new mother whose baby is admired. She even found herself modestly explaining it away: it had been the least expensive house in an improving neighborhood, the outside style was dated and undesirable hence obtained for a low price. Between them they unloaded the luggage with Leigh pointing out that should they want to stay longer, besides having a washer and dryer, there were local outlet stores where bargains could be had for more clothing.

They entered noisily through the kitchen and, being late into the evening, Leigh knew her daughter as well as Wes were home. The introductions that she dreaded, because she wanted to keep this happy little unit to herself, had her stomach tied up in knots. Wes, having heard the kitchen door open, came in, showered, presentable, and amiable, extending his hand in a warm welcome and asking if he could help carry their bags. Leigh watched him closely, said nothing, and was relieved that he had behaved congenially, when in fact she had never known him to behave in any other way.

Kirsten was waiting as they stepped into the den en route to the guest room, not observing Leigh's raised eyebrow as an indication to rise from the sofa and greet her grandfather. She remained sitting on the couch, one leg tucked beneath her, although she did mute the television as she looked up and said, "Hi."

"John," Leigh began, feeling quite nervous, and as yet unable to call her father by anything else than his first name, "this is my daughter, Kirsten, whom I've told you about, and she is your granddaughter."

It was as if the introduction suddenly gave realization to Kirsten that this elderly man was connected deeply to her, but because she had expected nothing from him, her casual greeting was organically authentic in nature to which he responded.

"You might have to give me a few minutes to wrap my head around the fact that I have a grown-up granddaughter," he said plainly, then turned to look at Leigh. "I remember you mentioning your daughter..." His voice trailed in wonder before he found it again. "So many discoveries to be made."

"It must feel really weird," remarked Kirsten candidly, missing the tact that would accrue with age.

"It *does* feel weird," he agreed, and suddenly tired, he looked at both the women and said, "May I sit down, or are we going somewhere?"

"Please make yourself at home and sit where you like," Leigh offered. She caught Libbie's eye, quietly gesturing to be led to the guest room.

Leigh showed her down the hall and into the room with its queen-sized bed. Libbie was delightfully appreciative of her surroundings and made a point of complimenting how light and feminine the room was, what a nice, green view over the backyard and the stand of poplars. She heaved her suitcase onto the bed and sat next to it, patting the space beside her for Leigh to sit.

"The reason I wanted to leave your dad alone with Kirsten was because he is not an effusive sort of person, you might have noticed," she giggled, then added, "it's up to me to provide that part. He's shy and the thing you will learn about dementia, Leigh, is that as it progresses, a person will often withdraw from things they used to do, as their world begins to get a little smaller. For example, my mother never missed a church service in her life, but as it began to take hold of her, honey, there was every excuse in the book of why she wouldn't go: she was too tired, she needed her hair done, it looked like it was going to rain..." Libbie shook her head sadly at the memory. "She had been such a social butterfly, Leigh, which is where

I get it from. So when I saw John actually engage Kirsten, I thought, let's clear off and let this happen, because it's a rare thing that he makes the first move."

Leigh, her eyes damp, took Libbie's plump brown hand in her own and squeezed it. "You can never know how grateful I am for your help. It breaks my heart you had to go through this with both your parents and now my father, and yet here you are, helping again, sharing your experiences so that I can be prepared for what's ahead."

Libbie squeezed Leigh's hand in return and patted it in motherly fashion. "Oh, but aren't I the lucky one," she laughed, her raisin eyes disappearing into a web of crow's feet, "because I feel I have another daughter!" And with that she leaned forward to give Leigh a hug and kiss her cheek. Leigh was so moved by the display of physical affection she thought she might sob, so she bit her lip and smiled warmly and said she'd begin dinner.

"Now, don't you go to a lot of trouble, honey," Libbie admonished, "especially with your dad because he eats like a bird and very L.A., you know? Lots of fresh fruit, maybe some eggs, granola, but me, well, you can look at me and tell I haven't missed too many meals."

"That makes two of us," laughed Leigh, for the first time poking fun at herself and patting her backside on the way out the door.

Having gotten both of them fed and her father quite happy with a chef salad, it wasn't a surprise when they decided to turn in early. As Leigh mounted the stairs to say goodnight to Kirsten, she was surprised to see her daughter without a screen in front of her face, but lying on her back, staring upwards at the ceiling.

"Penny for your thoughts," Leigh said from the doorway.

Kirsten turned her head and said, "He's nice, Mom. It's funny because the only grandfather I've had is on Dad's side and he's nice, but so is this one." She frowned for a moment, then said, "But what's really weird is trying to picture him with Nan, you know?"

Leigh stepped inside the room and sat down on the bed beside her. "In what way?"

Kirsten pulled herself up into a sitting position and tried to explain. "It's just that Nan is so energetic. Always marching down the road or out in her garden and now going to her yoga classes. Then I look at him and he's thin, but he doesn't look active at all. He looks kinda frail."

"He's been quite ill," Leigh reminded her.

"I know, but when I look at Nan, I can sort of imagine her when she was young, but when I look at him, he looks like he's always looked old," she mused, then looked at her mother directly. "What do I call him? Grandfather? Grandpa?"

"Why don't you ask him?" Leigh suggested. "He seems very comfortable with you."

Kirsten nodded. "He was funny, asking me things that you'd ask a little kid, like, what I want to be when I grow up." She laughed outright. "I almost said I wanted to be a fireman just to see his reaction."

Leigh smiled, "I think he's really out of his comfort zone being around young people, but there is something you need to know, Kirsten, and that is that your grandfather has dementia and is slowly losing his memory."

"You mean like Alzheimer's?"

"No, not that, he doesn't have that, but he does have memory loss. The good news is that it doesn't seem to be progressing very quickly, but just be mindful of that should he ask you the same question a couple of times or maybe forget where something is."

"That's so sad," Kirsten said, looking at her. "You just found him again. That's so sad."

When Leigh took herself to bed shortly afterwards, she was still so filled with the warmth of her extended family gathered around her that she approached Wes, who was making up the couch.

"There's really no need for you to sleep out here," she said. She was surprised by how natural and easy it felt to say, "and if you're not terribly uncomfortable about it, there's no reason we can't share the same bed. You need a good night's sleep with tax day upon you at work."

Wes straightened and looked at her, holding a pillow in one hand. "I appreciate that," he said, and with a brief nod, picked up the blanket he had laid over the back of the couch in his other hand and returned down the hall to the master bedroom. She didn't change in front of him—she hadn't done that in years—and when they lay down, they kept their backs to one another, but there seemed to be less tension and awkwardness. They both slept soundly.

Leigh was careful over the next few days to allow both her father and Libbie ample rest as well as loosely scheduling short excursions to give them both the feel of the area. She drove them to Lake Lure, where to her delight, as they descended the hill and the view of the lake framed by the mountains behind, her father suddenly appeared before them and said, "Ah, yes, we used to bring the kids here, weekends, in the summer." When they found a place for lunch overlooking the water, he turned to Leigh and asked, "Wasn't there a dock you could swim to?"

"Yes." Leigh, her heart brimming, pointed and said, "Just over there. It was a sort of rite of passage to finally make it to that dock. Tracy and I used to just collapse and lie on it."

"I don't know a Tracy," he said.

"She's my oldest friend," Leigh smiled. "You might recognize her if I showed you photographs."

Libbie was shaking her head back and forth, very slowly, as she had done much of the trip, saying, "I just can't get over how beautiful and green everything is. When you live in Los Angeles, you get used to it because basically it's a desert with the exception of little green lawns in front of everyone's home, and during the winter the hills turn green, but this is just so *lush*. You must love living here, Leigh. It would be like being on vacation all year long."

John nodded in agreement.

"I'm so used to it that it's good to hear you say that," Leigh replied. "It makes me look at it all again with new eyes."

"And I can't get over how little traffic there is," Libbie continued to enthuse. "You know, when John and I would go to Santa Barbara for a weekend now and then, we'd have to sit in traffic for over an hour before we even got out of the city to drive the two hours to get there. But here, I mean, we just zipped right down the road. Amazing."

Leigh speared a wedge of tomato and popped it into her mouth, chewing silently. She had been waiting for what felt to be an appropriate moment to offer her idea for another destination. She took a sip of iced tea, sat back and carefully proceeded.

"John, the home we used to live in isn't far from here. Would you be interested in showing Libbie the farm house that you restored from a ruin?"

"Oh, I would *love* to see that," Libbie fairly squeaked, pressing his arm. "I've never seen any of the buildings he's designed. What do you say, honey?"

Leigh's father gazed out over the water, his eyes focused elsewhere, but after a few moments, he began to nod slowly. "It's been a long time," he said. "Does anyone still live in it?"

Leigh glanced at Libbie as she replied, "My mother, your former wife, Felicity, still lives there. She was actually going to sell the house until deciding against it."

He seemed surprised and raised his faded brows at her. "Felicity? Felicity lives there?"

"Yes, and I spoke to her about us coming for a visit and to see the place, and she said we are all welcome."

"I can't," John started, then dropped his eyes to his half-eaten salad. "I can't think she would want to see me."

"Things change after forty years," Leigh smiled, "and she is completely comfortable with all of us coming over."

John looked at Libbie. "It was a big house. Quite a bit of land..." He glanced back at his daughter. "And she's selling it?"

"Not anymore," Leigh repeated.

"Well, I'm not going to push the issue," Libbie smiled back at him, "but I would just love to see the house you restored, honey, if you're all right with it."

John returned his gaze back over the lake. "Do you see the turtles sunning themselves on that log, Libbie? Over there to the right?"

Leigh's heart fell with disappointment and she made one more subtle attempt. "Actually, John, one of the ways back to my house is to drive past your old house. How would you feel about that? Not stopping, just driving past it."

The elderly man considered the suggestion as he wiped his mouth with his paper napkin. He looked at Leigh for some time and then nodded faintly, "I suppose that would be all right."

When Leigh asked for the bill, John insisted on paying and gave his wallet to Libbie. "I can't see without my glasses, you pay it."

"For heaven's sake, I can't believe how little this cost," Libbie exclaimed. "You couldn't get breakfast for two in L.A. for what they charged all three of us for lunch." She pulled out his credit card and placed it on the bill, awaiting the server, and adding, "Although that sweet tea takes some getting used to, I'm afraid that's too sweet for me."

"It is pretty sweet," Leigh concurred, chuckling at the memory of Libbie stirring three packets of sweetener into her coffee in Los Angeles. "Southerners love their sweet tea."

Having paid the bill and climbing into the Toyota, Leigh took an equally appealing route towards her mother's house, winding through the foothills.

"There used to be a cider mill somewhere around here," her father mentioned faintly, looking out the passenger window.

"Yes," Leigh assented. "We're a bit too early in the year for them to be open with cider, but they do sell all kinds of jams and apple butter."

"Now, what is that?" Libbie wanted to know from the backseat.

"It's basically a fruit spread, but with added spices like cinnamon."

"That sounds like heaven," Libbie sighed. She leaned forward and rested her chin on John's shoulder, "Honey, it's all so pretty, I can understand why you lived here."

John raised his left hand and held it gently against her cheek for some time as Leigh continued to drive. The tender connection between the two of them caused her to blink back tears and she decided to take a couple of detours, not long in length, so the couple could take in local horse farms with endlessly rolling green fields dissected by streams, then later on, marvel over the river that ran alongside the road, prompting more rapturous sighs from Libbie.

As Leigh turned left upon the road that would take them to the quiet intersection where she would then turn right to go to her mother's house, she felt her heart begin to pound and she reached for her father's wrist, pressed it, and said, "All right, we're almost there." Libbie, catching her eye, winked encouragement.

The house of her childhood, still hidden as they came around the bend—the very bend where Lissie would pause each morning of her walk to drink in the view—became visible after the half-mile of woods enveloped them on either side of the road. The white clapboard exterior became recognizable through the trees, and Leigh took her foot off the gas, allowing her car to coast to a crawl. John turned in his seat and placed his right hand on the dash for support.

"Is that Felicity?" he asked, and Leigh suddenly realized she had not noticed her mother squatting in the flowerbed to the side of the house.

"Yes, yes, that's her," replied Leigh, feeling tension manifest in her stomach. "Do you want me to stop?"

Lissie, hearing a car idling behind her on the street, turned her head to look. Recognizing Leigh's car, she rose to her feet and waved her garden trowel in acknowledgment.

"Looks like an invitation to me," Libbie chirped.

"We can stop, if you like," John murmured.

Leigh put her car into reverse and backed up in order to turn into the drive. She opened her door to step out while John and Libbie remained inside.

"Hello, Mother," she said, walking towards her. "We were actually going to just drive by the house, but Dad spotted you in the garden, so we thought we'd say hello."

Lissie, her serene demeanor effectively covering the sudden thumping of her heart, nodded with a small smile and she tugged off her garden gloves as she approached the car alongside her daughter. John opened his door to step out, followed by Libbie.

She had wondered idly over the years how he might look, but as her former husband stood before her, she searched his face to recognize a single feature. How much smaller he appeared! Where were his swimmer's shoulders and chest? His eyes had been deeply set and, yes, they were somewhat the same shape but appeared hollow, beneath. His hair, always wispy as was his daughter's, had far receded and gone white, not unlike her own. He looked at her steadily with faint apprehension.

"Hello, John," she said, smiling gently and extending her hand in what felt to be such a formal gesture to the man with whom she had shared her early life and children.

"Hello, Lissie," he returned. His grip was light.

"I guess we're the three *Ls*," Libbie laughed, taking a step forward with her arms open wide, "Because I'm Libbie, and honey, I'm a hugger," with that, she embraced Lissie. Taken aback, Lissie laughed good-naturedly and said, "Welcome."

Leigh would remain eternally devoted to the small brown woman with the mass of frizzy red hair, an unstoppable force of kindness, joy incarnate, bringing levity to the situation as she stood between Lissie and her former husband and said, "Well, I have to say, from one gal to another, I was kind of hoping you wouldn't be as beautiful as you are, but it looks like I lost out on that one." She laughed heartily and continued, "and you're awfully nice to just let us show up like this."

Her effervescence had the desired effect, as Lissie took a deep breath, and felt far more at ease. She stepped to one side so as not to block anyone's view and, gesturing to the house, announced, "This is the house John restored from a complete derelict to what you see now. Would you like to come inside?"

John nodded tentatively and said, haltingly, "It's good of you, Lissie, thank you."

They mounted the old stone steps and John stood on the front porch, his hand resting against a column as he hesitated a moment. He turned to face the road. "Lots of summer evenings spent on this porch," he remembered, glancing at Leigh before turning back and crossing over the threshold, his daughter following him, too overcome for words.

"Oh, Lissie," Libbie followed her across the wide plank floors of the foyer as they approached the staircase, her crimson tipped hands pressed against her mouth in admiration. "It's like '*Gone With The Wind!*'"

Lissie smiled appreciatively and replied, "Well, not quite that grand, but it had been the farmhouse of a successful farmer and merchant. The land was sold off before we found it, with only seven acres remaining-"

"*Seven acres?*" Libbie was incredulous. "Honey, that might not sound like much property to you, but where I live, if you had seven acres, you'd be a billionaire!"

John stood, his eyes taking in the staircase, then the ceiling. "We could see daylight through this roof," he said, as if seeing it for the first time, "And bats. Do you remember the bats, Lissie?"

Lissie nodded and grimaced, "Oh, goodness, the bats in that attic." She gave a little laugh. "I've tried to forget that, John,"

"Bats!" shuddered Libbie.

"The living room is through here," Leigh remarked, pointing to the left, "and Dad—" She caught herself. "John and I used to spend quite a lot of time here when I was a little girl." She led the way into the large airy room, the elegant fireplace gracing the north wall.

He walked towards it and ran his hand along the mantle. "Chestnut," he said. "Built by a cabinet maker," he added, then frowned. "I can't remember their names but it was a family business. Are they still around?"

Lissie shook her head. "Sadly, no. The father died, the son retired, and his children weren't interested in continuing."

"That's a shame," John said, glancing at her before directing his attention back to the mantle. "That's a shame." He stood with his hands in the pockets of his khakis, his chest slightly sunken, and turned to stare out the front windows. "Same oak tree?" he asked, surprised. "How old is it, now?"

Lissie walked up and stood next to him and they looked at it together. "I had a fellow who came to cut away a couple of broken limbs after an ice storm, and he guessed it to be about sixty years old."

"Isn't that something?" he said, shaking his head. "Hard to believe."

The group moved into the kitchen and Leigh watched her father's face lighten with recognition as he stood and stared at the cabinetry with a faint smile.

"This whole wall was rotted," he said to Libbie, waving his hand in front of them both. "All of this had to be replaced and when I met with the cabinet maker, he actually remembered this house from before it had been abandoned, when he was a boy, and was able to reproduce it for us." He turned to Lissie, "Are they still around?"

Lissie shook her head, reminding him, "I'm afraid he died and the business closed."

Her former husband passed his hand over the cabinetry and said, "I wish I could talk to him again. It's sad when people go."

"Yes," said Leigh, "it is."

"Would you like to walk the property?" he suddenly said to Libbie. "I'll show you the little barn I built for Leigh's pony." Then he stopped, remembering. "And David. What did David keep in there, Leigh?"

Aware that this was the first time her father had spoken to her directly, complete with addressing her by name, she stammered, "A bike. A mini-bike." She remained behind with her mother, as the couple departed through the kitchen door and carefully descended the broad sweep of land that ran downhill, banks of daffodils bordering either side.

"How are you feeling?" Lissie asked, passing her arm around her daughter's shoulders.

Leigh blinked at her, astonished. "How are *you* feeling?"

Lissie laughed softly and said, "I won't deny that it felt a bit strained at first, but now I'm fine, I'm just fine. Libbie is a darling."

"She is," Leigh nodded, "and she's devoted to Dad," then realizing that might have sounded ungracious, quickly amended, "He's very lucky to have her."

"I'm glad he has someone to look after him," Lissie murmured.

They could still see the top of Libbie's red head as the couple poked about the one horse stable, now converted into a toolshed with a little round table and chairs in front of it, serving as a favorite summertime spot for a glass of lemonade. John led her through the old orchard, the original trees long replaced with generations of heirloom saplings, now mature and displaying tiny green spheres which would grow into Newtown Pippin, Golden Russet, and Carolina Red June apples. They remained outside for well over half an hour and Lissie and Leigh took the opportunity to make a jug of cold unsweetened—especially for Libbie—iced tea, and when John could be heard scraping the dirt off his shoes at the kitchen door, Leigh thought both of their faces looked quite animated as they entered.

"A lot of memories out there," her father volunteered, waiting for Libbie to join him. "You've kept the place up beautifully, Lissie. All by yourself?"

Lissie nodded and replied, "Mostly, although a farmer friend down the road does the mowing for me with his tractor every couple of weeks in the summer, otherwise I could never keep it up. It's all I can do to mow the front lawn, which is why I put in such wide flower borders."

"It's absolutely enchanting, honey," Libbie said, putting her arm affectionately around John. "We had such a wonderful time wandering around out there. I have to say this is the most beautiful home I've ever seen. Ever."

"Goodness," replied Lissie. "What a lovely compliment."

"Leigh said you wanted to sell," John remarked.

"Well, I had considered it," she began.

Forgetting his daughter had told him Lissie had changed her mind, he pulled back a chair at the kitchen table and slowly sat down. Libbie remained standing, placing a hand on either side of his shoulders, giving him a gentle squeeze, beaming.

"We'd like to buy it," he said.

Chapter 44

BY LATE AFTERNOON, DAVID'S phone rang. He picked it up.

"Hi, Baby." Denise smiled down the line. "Just checking to make sure you're all right. You've been gone a long time."

"I'm good," was all David could think to say. "I'm at my apartment."

Denise was astonished. "Your *apartment?* Don't tell me you walked."

"I did," David said, aware his voice sounded businesslike and flat. "I needed to do some stuff."

"Do you want me to come get you when you're finished?"

"If you could, I'd appreciate that," he said, knowing that he wanted to talk to her in his own environment. He couldn't face returning to the house.

"My pleasure," she replied, then asked, "About what time?"

"Actually, now is good," he said, then thanked her and hung up.

He got to his feet and walked to the window that looked over the parking lot and out onto the street. It was nearing the end of rush hour, yet the traffic remained considerable. He leaned on one side of the window frame as the soft spring evening light began to descend and let his thoughts take him where they may. He felt in turns naïve, hollow, and disconsolate, but with no sense of anger. Had there been animosity, perhaps the wave of sorrow that now engulfed him wouldn't have taken such a hold. He thought of his age with a sardonic smile. It was crazy, he thought, that he was in his late thirties. Things ought to be clear, he should have an understanding of who he was and what he wanted out of life, yet he felt as floundering as he had a decade earlier. He had managed, he realized, to avoid the unpleasant return of second-guessing himself where affairs of the heart were concerned, throughout his twenties and early thirties by deliberately keeping himself at a distance. And then he fell in love with a woman who did the same thing.

During his marriage, he had turned cynical in terms of those he had heard declare that they didn't really know what love was. Once you were in it, he was certain, there was no mistaking it. He remembered his all-consuming desire for Denise after their first night together. The physical intensity burned so feverishly that it left little room for anything else within him except for the insecurity that had dogged him when he realized he never wholly had her. It had taken until now for him to recognize that he had mistaken that insecurity— that constant longing for more of her, to gain her full attention—for love. It had been the impetus of everything: how quickly they had become exclusive, the rapid ascension towards the wedding altar, and, of course, the disintegration of their marriage.

How long he stood there, he couldn't say, but his eyes were drawn to the black BMW that moved into the center lane and signaled to turn into his complex. He was aware of a quickening of his pulse but felt relatively calm. His mouth did not go dry like it had in the past, nor did his throat constrict. When Denise tapped on the door, David opened it. She met him with a kiss he did not return, but so caught up was she with excitement, she seemed not to notice and remained standing close to him, her hands resting on his hips.

"Do you remember my telling you a real estate agent was coming by to the look at the house?" she said, her eyes alight. "Guess what?"

"What?"

"Patty says, and you'd love her—really professional—anyway, she says the house should list for at least another fifty thousand over the last appraisal. How great is that?"

David offered her a quick smile before stepping back and walking towards the kitchen. "That really is great," he said. "Great for you. Would you like something to drink?"

"Great for *us*!" She stressed her reply and followed him to the kitchen. She leaned against the counter. "You feeling OK, Baby?"

David had become quite deft at popping the tops from his bottles of beer by using the drawer pulls from the cabinets and he did so now, much to Denise's amusement. "Learn that in therapy?" she chided him.

David looked at her and reached for her hand. "Come sit down," he said, and led her into the living room where they both sank down onto the couch.

"You're making me a little nervous," she said, widening her eyes theatrically.

He suddenly had the awful thought that she might think he was about to propose, so he took the time to take a long drink, placed the bottle carefully down on the coffee table and sat back, looking at her.

"When were you going to tell me what happened with your job at the firm?" he asked gently.

Thrown, Denise's eyes retreated from their comical stare to glancing away. She nodded slowly, as if gathering her thoughts, and replied, "I didn't mean to mislead you. When I first told you I had arranged for time off, you were in the ER and I felt you would have been upset if I told you I had quit."

"Why did you think that?" he asked, puzzled.

"Because—" For the first time since he'd known her, she seemed to falter, unsure of how to proceed. "Because when you tell someone you've quit your job in order to be with them, to care for them, especially when you're not sure how they feel about you, that's piling on an awful lot of pressure."

"But Denise," David said, his statement bare of inflection, "you didn't quit because of me. You quit because of your breakup with Spencer."

Startled, Denise looked at him and managed, "What are you talking about?"

"I ran into Mia who was only too happy to share office gossip."

"Which is exactly what it is."

"So you weren't involved with Spencer?"

Denise rose to her feet, and standing before him, said, "I think I'll have that drink after all." She walked into the kitchen and poured herself a glass from the half-empty bottle of pinot David had left in the door of the fridge. She remained standing for a minute or two, seemingly unsure where to settle, then returned to the couch, only to sit slightly further away from him.

"I'm not going to lie to you," she said clearly, cradling the bowl of the wineglass in her palm. "We did have an affair, but David, you and I were divorced. I was a single woman."

"What your involvement with Spencer was or wasn't doesn't matter to me," he said. "What matters to me is what happened afterwards."

Denise frowned. "I don't understand. Baby, it was when I heard about your accident and saw you again, I realized how wrong I had been about things."

David took a deep breath and reached for her hand. She gripped his, he felt, as if from fear.

"Denise," he began, "as long as we've been together, there always seemed to be a part of you that was somewhere else, and when I sat down and really thought about it, I recognized this sort of pattern that when things are steady and relaxed, it seems to make you restless. It's almost as if you thrive on chaos." He went on to explain, looking at her levelly. "And then when the chaos ends up in an explosion, you find a way to detach yourself from it and move on to something else and then it happens all over again."

"Do you really feel that way?" she asked, hurt.

"It's less that I feel that way and more that I know that way," he said, his voice tinged with sorrow. "Denise, when our marriage was in trouble, and I'm not for a moment saying that I didn't screw up, but it was as if you couldn't wait to get divorced. There was no interest in fighting for what we had, and that hurt me more than you will ever know. It was as if you simply didn't want to be married anymore and maybe even felt relieved to have an excuse to leave."

"David," she tried, taking it in, but couldn't continue.

"When we were together, there was this constant need for us to be on the go, to do new things, and I was just as caught up in it as you. But now I see that it was because you were bored with me, bored with *us*. And when we ended, there was the new car and Spencer, and when Spencer left you—" He hesitated because he could see she was becoming quite fragile with what he was revealing. "Suddenly you returned to me." He leaned back, keeping his gaze steady, but didn't let go of her hand. "And I can't go there, Denise. I can't go there again."

Tears welled in her eyes and she grasped his hand in both of hers. With her voice breaking, she asked, "You can't think this is all a sham? Please tell me you don't think I'd do that to you. Boston can be a whole new start for us, can't you see that?"

David shook his head and said, "Denise, can't you see that going to Boston is just a continuation of what I'm talking about? And when the chaos of moving and the novelty of Boston is over, it would leave us exactly where we were before? But no, I never thought any of this was a sham, because I don't think you're even aware of what it is you're doing any more than I was aware that what was driving me wasn't love, but a kind of desperation." He released her hand.

"So this is it?" she wept, searching his face for any chance that she was mistaken. "You want to end things between us?"

As gently as he could, David murmured, "Being together just isn't a good place for either one of us to be," and was surprised at how composed he felt. He was devastated for Denise, who hid her lovely face in her hands, that she would be feeling such pain while he himself felt only a sense of calm. He wanted to hold her, to aid with some comfort, but he found that he could only sit quietly while she cried and repeat, "I'm so sorry."

Chapter 45

LEIGH REMAINED SOMEWHERE BETWEEN being shell-shocked and giddy as she tore the leaves from a head of lettuce and prepared dinner. She was relieved to have the kitchen to herself and politely declined Libbie's offer of help, sending her back to join the others in the den in order to have a few square feet of privacy to come to grips with her father's announcement earlier in the day.

"*We'd like to buy the house,*" he had said, like a bolt out of the blue.

She couldn't suppress the soft chuckle that came with the memory of her mother's gasp, blanching, really, at her former husband's offer. It had taken her several moments to recover after asking, "What?" more than once, and she had immediately turned to look questioningly at Leigh, who didn't hesitate to reply, "If you think you'd really want to move here, then yes, I think it's a wonderful idea!"

It was Libbie's enthusiastic encouragement, they were to learn, that prodded John's decision. "I've never known him to open up so much since we've been together than when we were walking around behind the house," she relayed to them in private once John had stepped outside to explore the property again. "There were so many memories for him and at one point, I stopped and said, 'Honey, even the way you're walking is different. It's as if you need the grass under your feet, not concrete.'"

"Forgive me, but I feel I must ask this," Lissie began hesitantly. "Knowing he has dementia, do we really know that this is exactly

328

what he wants? That this isn't a spur of the moment impulse that you both might later regret?"

Libbie, with her enormous heart, reached across the table and placed her hand over Lissie's.

"Lissie," she replied, "as I'm sure you know, John has always been a very methodical man. He's by nature careful, not impulsive. But even during our first day here, when we went to bed that night he began talking about how much he missed the peace, the serenity of the mountains. He told me the Blue Ridge is a far older mountain range than the Sierras, and, what was it he said, that they had an almost 'maternal comfort' about them. Then the following morning, he said he hadn't slept that deeply in years, because it was so quiet." She paused and looked at Leigh, then chuckled. "I think Leigh knows from her visit exactly what he meant. In Los Angeles, it's just sirens all night long every night. I'm used to it—I even slept through the last earthquake!" Her smile diminished, and she looked seriously at both mother and daughter. "It was after we had been inside this beautiful house and had gone outside, John just kept repeating, 'It's as if I never left,' and I finally asked him pointblank, 'Honey, do you think you could see yourself living in North Carolina again?' He looked at me and said, 'But you're a California girl.' Well, I could see what he was getting at, so I just told him that yes, I love the sun and the heat, but as long as I can sit by that big old fireplace and drink coffee all winter long, I'd be willing to make the move with him." Looking up, she had noticed John making his way back towards the house and whispered, confidentially, "He had asked me about the house being for sale and I took the risk of not reminding you you had taken it off the market, Lissie, because I thought maybe, just maybe, if you had an offer in front of you, you might reconsider it."

"Well, of course I'll consider it," Lissie replied. "But I am concerned because it's a big place and it takes quite a bit of upkeep."

"Lissie," Libbie said soberly, her eyes suddenly glistening with tears. "John has told me that he knows what his future is. He's not in denial. After he came out of hospital in California, we had a heart-to-heart. He is adamant that I don't go through what I went through with my parents with him. He has made it clear to me more than once that when he gets to the point where he is advanced in his illness, that I am to leave him to the professionals and get on with my life." She quickly blotted her eyes to continue before John reached the door. "And when we were outside, he looked at me after I said I would be willing to move with him, and he said, 'I want to die here.'"

Leigh's hand flew to her mouth to prevent a sob. She was relieved to see her father hesitate outside the kitchen door to take another look around before scraping his shoes on the doormat.

"I want you to know that I am dedicated to caring for him, Libbie. For however long it takes," Leigh managed before he came in.

"I know that," Libbie smiled bravely, "and we're counting on you."

Leigh would have never dared hope for such an outcome. Now, in her kitchen, as she went about what had normally been the mundane task of mashing potatoes, she was well aware that with this heady dream come true there were important specifics to iron out: investigating if Libbie's power of attorney would be recognized in North Carolina, how his new residency might impact his eligibility for Medicaid, finding local doctors that specialized in dementia. She had oiled the pan and began to bread the chicken that lay thawing in the sink. She had a faint childhood memory that her father had once proclaimed fried chicken his favorite meal, and despite Libbie's cautions that he had become a very light eater, she was hoping he would allow her to spoil him this evening. Just in case, she made an extra-large salad if that was more to his liking.

Kirsten ambled in. It was a welcome surprise for Leigh that she began to set the table without being asked.

"How you doing, kiddo?" Leigh asked as her daughter rattled through the cutlery drawer.

"Fine," she said, then unconsciously let out a long sigh.

"Is Saturday on your mind?" Leigh touched upon the subject of the prom with care.

"It wouldn't be if Sophie would stop telling me how excited she is about it," Kirsten replied. She stood quietly for a moment before asking, "Why do people have to keep talking about things to other people when they know—I mean, they really *know*—that it hurts the other person's feelings?"

Leigh was about to answer when she glanced up and saw her husband standing in the doorway. He looked as if he, too, were awaiting her response. She took a moment to reply, weighing her words. "I think, Kirsten, it's because sometimes people get so caught up in being happy themselves they forget about how it affects others." She turned back to the stove and quietly added, "especially if they think the other person would want them to be happy."

"I want her to be happy," Kirsten stressed, "but I'd like to be happy, too."

Wes stepped into the kitchen and placed his arm around his daughter's shoulders. "I think a lot of people feel like you do, sweetie, and it's never easy," he said. Then giving her arm a squeeze, he finished, "One of the worst things about growing up is the realization that life is seldom fair."

When they sat down to dinner, all of them rather crowded around the table that normally saw only three, Libbie was the first to exclaim, "Heavens above, I can't even remember the last time I had fried chicken! I do believe I'm going to love living in the south."

"Honey," said Leigh, aping her with a kind impression, "and the south is going to love you living here."

John allowed himself a bemused smile and looked at Libbie. "I might just have to forgo my tuna salad, tonight."

"Mr. Merriman," Kirsten asked, boldly taking the opportunity to address what had been on her mind, "what should I call you?"

John, in the middle of slicing a piece of chicken, kept his eyes on his plate and murmured, "Well, certainly not Mr. Merriman." He then carefully put down his knife and fork and addressed her, "I don't really know. What would you like to call me?"

Kirsten shrugged. "That's why I asked you. I asked Mom and she said to ask you."

"I heard a woman in the restaurant today say something about a Me-Maw and a Pe-Paw," Libbie chimed in, laughing. "I've never heard such a thing! Would you like to be a Pe-Paw?"

John looked at her. "Probably not," he replied, succinctly.

"Good," Wes spoke up, "because I don't think you look quite like a Pe-Paw."

"What's a Pe-Paw look like?" Leigh wanted to know.

"I think overalls and fishing poles are involved," Wes replied. He was pleased to hear the laughter that rang out around the table.

"Now, wait a minute," Libbie cut in. "I think overalls might just suit you, John. And a straw hat. I think you'd look dead sexy."

"Ugh, you're talking about my Granddad!" Kirsten groaned.

John looked at her and said, "I think you've just named me. If you're comfortable with Granddad, so am I."

Later that night, after the dishes were cleared, with Libbie and her father having retreated to their room, Wes found the opportunity to speak privately with his wife as she sat quietly with a cup of coffee at the kitchen table.

"How are you feeling about everything?" he asked, sitting opposite her.

Surprised that he would take an interest, Leigh replied honestly. "Overwhelmed, but in a good way."

He nodded, "I can understand that." He paused for a moment, stroking his chin, then tentatively proceeded. "Have you thought about how you're going to manage, after everything's settled and they're living here?"

Leigh placed her cup quietly down. "I thought I might move in," she said, and without meeting her husband's eyes, continued. "It would give Dad a chance to get used to me being around, and I can help Libbie keep up the house and the property." Then she looked directly at Wes. "How would you feel about that?"

"I'm not sure that how I feel would change things," he said flatly. "But along with distancing yourself from me, it does appear that you're moving out of our marriage."

Leigh swallowed. "This is something I have to do, Wes."

He leaned back in his chair and regarded her silently for several moments. His face remained tractable as he asked, "Do you want a divorce?"

"No," she found herself saying, her stomach immediately beginning to churn. "No, I don't. But I can understand why you'd ask and I understand if you'd want to proceed with one."

"Let me ask you something," he said, leaning forward on his elbows and looking earnestly at her. "And I'd like you to be as honest as you can. Do you think living with your father and Libbie could give you enough contentment that you might feel kinder towards me?"

The bluntness of his question and its complete lack of resentment resulted in Leigh bursting into sudden tears as she acknowledged the truth. "I have been horrible to you, Wes, I know it. I know it. I have been so unhappy for so long about everything that I've put blame on you that you didn't deserve." She blew her nose on a napkin and gulped. "All I know is that with my father here, for the first time in my life I feel complete. I don't know how that might affect us. I can only hope that it would be in a positive way."

Wes dropped his head and seemed to ponder the tabletop. He then sat up straight and rubbed his face with his hand, before looking at her and replying, "I appreciate your honesty, but it makes me think about what Kirsten mentioned earlier. It hurts when only one person is happy. I've been hurting for a long time, Leigh, missing the wife I enjoyed putting first who did the same for me, and as you pursue what gives you contentment in your life, I'd like to have the opportunity to pursue the same in mine. So I'm proposing a separation, as it seems the most logical step forward."

Leigh exhaled slowly, and as she did, she could feel her marriage dissolving with her breath. There was a dullness that came over her, a feeling of such heaviness that it replaced the tears of anxiety she had shed just moments before. Perhaps it was that the feelings between them had finally been given voice. So strong was her resolve to return to her childhood home with her father, that she was unable to plead for another chance to amend her wrongs, to attempt a different route.

"Kirsten should probably stay here to finish her school year, but I don't think it would rattle her to pop back and forth between us, do you?" was all she could say. "It would be a pretense to stay together for her sake, and she'd know that."

"I agree," he replied quietly. "Might even come as a relief for her."

"She'll be pleased to finally have a reason to get her driver's license," she added with a wry smile.

"All right, then," sighed Wes, rising slowly to his feet. "I'm glad we're seeing things the same way, and of course there's no rush. It's going to be a pretty big upheaval, getting your father moved out of Los Angeles and into your old home. Let's just try to be fluid about everything and go with the flow."

Leigh nodded. She took a sip of her coffee. It had gone cold. She watched her husband leave the room.

Chapter 46

IT OCCURRED TO DAVID that as his life moved forward and away from his former wife, it somehow seemed to be proceeding in slow motion. He wasn't sure if that was because the astonishment that arrived with Denise's return had colored everything with an almost electrical impulse, or if life on his own was simply not an exciting one. It was one, however, that gave him peace. A consistent tranquility.

As he undertook the long walk to his studio that bright Saturday morning, he knew that he would remember her tears at their final parting, and he felt no satisfaction, no grubby sense of revenge in that. It was painful to him to witness her suffering because he believed, he *had* to believe, that she was a kind person at heart.

He stopped by his regular coffee shop to sample their daily special, and on offer that morning was a particularly robust blend from Nicaragua. To his surprise, he found that where his upper arm met his shoulder might have only loosened imperceptibly, it was enough that he could draw his right elbow centimeters backwards as he added a splash of milk from the stainless silver jug kept on the side shelf next to the stirrers and napkins. He made no attempt to lift it, the weight being impossible, but he managed to tip it forward towards his cup. It had been a funny if frustrating journey, this healing. His trips to physical therapy had so far resulted in a very small range of motion exercises, as well as his affable therapist, Ben, gently manipulating the shoulder joint and surrounding muscles. "It's easy for all this to atrophy," he had informed David, "but it's important that as you go about your day, you really think about the way you're moving your shoulder and upper arm. You don't want to be moving it in a way that's going to cause a secondary problem down the road." He finished by showing David which movements were beneficial and pointed out that by remaining mindful of only what he should do it wouldn't take long for it become a habitual pattern. As David splashed in the milk, his upper arm remaining in the clam-like brace that immobilized it, he was specific and slow in the movement, and this moment felt like a milestone. He found himself smiling and was amused by his own excitement.

Arriving at his studio, he found another welcome surprise in the form of a check from the mayor waiting in his mailbox. Although he had managed to take just over a couple of dozen photographs prior to being attacked by Nicole's horse, he had gone ahead and emailed the anemic bunch, explaining that he would certainly understand if there weren't enough to choose from. But here was a gracious note, handwritten by Nicole, declaring that the one of her leaning over her horse's head from the fence with her arm and ringed finger resting over his mane, was exactly what she wanted. The check enclosed far exceeded the cost of a full day's shoot, signed by the mayor along with a p.s. at the bottom requesting his services for all print material required during his upcoming campaign.

Having had to postpone so many shoots over the next eight weeks, he was grateful for the payment and idly wondered if Denise would now renege on her offer to reimburse his financial contributions for the house on Blossom Street. He didn't think so. It would be out of character for her to show that sort of spite. And if she did, he pondered, it wouldn't affect him greatly, but he would admit it would be welcomed. He further busied himself by finally cleaning the barred windows. Free of grime, he enjoyed a clearer view of the mountains, beginning to turn truly lush with green. There was little else to do, and so he began his trek homeward, thinking of the news his mother had given him over the phone days before. The father he scarcely remembered deciding to relocate to North Carolina was astonishing in itself, but purchasing the family home was inconceivable. David knew he would go over to meet him at some point. Again. Perhaps not just yet though, as it had been a difficult week and he was just beginning to settle into a sense of normalcy.

He waited at an intersection and smiled at a kid who was tugging on her mother's arm, wanting to cross before the light turned green. He thought of Leigh and how staggered she must be feeling by her father's decision. He hoped it would finally bring her happiness. And then he thought of Kirsten. It was, he suddenly remembered, Saturday, the day of the prom. He'd had an idea earlier in the week that had been percolating, but had been left untended by what had transpired between him and Denise. Now, he pulled out his phone and dialed his sister.

"I have something I'd like to run past you," he began, then told her his idea. He hadn't gone to his own prom, he explained, but he wasn't prepared to let his niece sit home alone in her room on the night of hers. He could hear Leigh on the other end, quite overcome with emotion as she thanked him.

The prospect of the evening propelled him home quickly. Once back at his apartment, he invested quite a bit of time researching area restaurants and phoned Leigh once again.

"Does Kirsten know where the kids from her school are going to dinner before the prom," he asked, "or do they eat at the prom? Or do they even eat at all?"

"It's so different these days," Leigh whispered, "but I'm pretty sure from what I've heard Kirsten say that a lot of the kids all go together in a sort of gang."

"Wow," said David. "See if you can figure a way of finding out where they might go without letting her in on my cunning plan."

"You're on," replied Leigh gratefully, "and this is so good of you, David."

Within minutes, David received a text from Leigh that read, "New place just S of Asheville called The Wren. Will pay you back."

David Googled it and found the restaurant. Upmarket and pricey, indeed. Sighing with relief, he just managed to get a reservation owing to a last minute cancellation. Hoping his luck might continue, he then called a limousine company. No, he was told, nothing available this evening. He tried two more, only to hear that both companies found it loftily amusing he thought there might be any car available on prom night at this hour. Wracking his brain, he suddenly remembered a musician friend who was an Uber driver with a black SUV, and after contacting him, found him happy to have his business for the evening. After giving his address and destination, he put down the phone and smiled. He leaned back on his couch and his eyes fell upon the citrine ring that Denise had taken off silently, placing it gently on the coffee table, before walking out of his life. His stomach did an odd little flip, but he chose to ignore it and returned to his research, searching online for a local florist.

"Mom, what is going on?" Kirsten had put her foot down, obstinately, at four o'clock when her mother had finally informed her that she needed to begin getting ready for a night out. "Where are we going?"

"We're not going anywhere," Leigh had replied with a mischievous smile, "but you are."

"By myself?" she cried. "No way."

"Not by yourself, you've got a date."

Kirsten narrowed her eyes at her mother. "Do not tell me you have paid someone to take me to the prom. Do not tell me that."

"You're not going to the prom," Leigh assured her, "but you are going out someplace really special, so you're going to want to dress up."

"Who am I going with?" Kirsten demanded. "I'm not going anywhere until you tell me."

"Trust me," Leigh said, trying her best to restore calm, "you're going to like him."

Just before six the doorbell rang and Wes answered the door. Kirsten, cowering at the top of the stairs, refused to come down.

"Hello, sir, I'm here to take your daughter to dinner," came the voice from the other side of the door.

"Kirsten," Wes called, beginning to chuckle at his daughter's stormy expression, "come on down."

"Not until you tell me who it is."

David walked through the doorway, carrying a wrist corsage. He stood at the bottom of the stairs, and looking up at his niece, said, "Stop bitching and get down here, will ya?"

"Oh my God," said Kirsten, but smiled despite herself. "It's you." She came doubtfully down the stairs in a beautiful form-fitting sapphire dress with a diagonal splash of sequins over one shoulder that she had worn just once to a New Year's Eve party the year before. She wore her hair loose in soft curls and carefully applied makeup.

"You're a knock out," David said simply. She smiled self-consciously.

"Little did I know a corsage just can't be a corsage anymore," he mentioned sideways to Wes as he slipped it over his niece's wrist. "They've got to be full of bling, the florist told me, with rhinestones or feathers, and nothing boring like roses, either." He glanced at Kirsten with a smile. "What do you think?"

Kirsten touched the citrine ring that firmly encircled and held the spray of mini Freesias. "It's really pretty, Uncle David," she murmured, touched. "You didn't have to do all this."

"I know I didn't have to," he replied. "I wanted to."

"Just have my daughter back at a decent hour," Wes said, with mock disapproval, "young man."

"David," Leigh suddenly appeared at the door, looking apprehensive. "Dad's here. He knows it's you, I told him what you're doing. He'd like to say hello, if that's all right with you."

David, not wholly unprepared for this moment, nodded but said nothing.

John, followed closely by Libbie, came slowly around the corner and stood in the doorway and looked cautiously at his son. He extended his hand tentatively and said, "I haven't any right to say it because I've had nothing to do with it, but the man you've become has made me very proud."

David swallowed hard. He would often think back about the raw honesty of his father's statement and the courage it would have taken, regardless if they saw each other again, to say it. Now standing before the man of which he had little if any memory, he managed to reply, "Good to see you," as well as shake his hand. He was also deeply grateful that Libbie diffused the moment by squeaking, "Oh, I'm so glad I got to have a peek of you two, you look adorable!"

David's Uber friend held the backseat door of the vehicle open for them and David ushered Kirsten in first, then slid in beside her.

"You're not in a tux," she pointed out.

"We're not going to the prom," he countered.

Kirsten lowered her eyes, "I know."

"Hey, Kirsten," he said, touching her arm, "what we're doing is so much cooler. Wait and see."

Within half an hour the SUV pulled into their destination. Kirsten looked out the back window and exclaimed, "The *Wren*? This is where Sophie and a ton of kids are going! We can't go in there."

"Sure, we can," David said. "And think about it. The prom is just some cheesy dance, but to go out to dinner with some mysterious, good-looking older guy—"

"You're my uncle," she protested. "It's creepy."

Her forceful honesty made him laugh, and he said, "I know it's creepy, but they don't know I'm your uncle and this way you can just sort of swan in on my arm looking so much more sophisticated than the rest of them, you know? Totally blowing off the dance by choice is very cool I would think if I were them."

Kirsten looked at him judgmentally and mumbled, "Well, you've got some gray in your hair, but your face still looks pretty young. All right, let's go."

David slid carefully out the door. "What about the good looking part?"

"I can't think about that," she retorted. "Way too creepy."

He laughed, and offered the elbow of his good arm, clad in his best suit.

"Now remember," he instructed, "attitude is everything. Walk in like you own the place."

Kirsten offered him a bright smile and threw her hair back over her shoulder and, together, they walked in through the massive twin oak doors of The Wren. They were greeted graciously by a hostess in a simple black dress, who checked their name off the reservation list and beckoned them to follow her to a table for two towards the center of the restaurant.

"Oh, my gosh," whispered Kirsten. "Derek's here, I'm going to die."

"Who's Derek?" David whispered back as he pulled back her chair with one hand.

"It doesn't matter," she replied. "He's with Hannah. She's gorgeous. Cheerleader, the whole thing."

"Which table?"

"Three tables over to the right, but don't look."

David found himself laughing, again at the fervent exchanges that took him back to his own angst-ridden teenage years. "I won't look," he said, then pointedly looked.

"Uncle David!" she hissed.

Behind them was an oaken bar, elaborately carved, and behind that tucked away to one side was the servers' station.

"Heads up," said the hostess, ducking her head around corner, and alerting a throng of young women gathered there. "I've just sat table eleven."

"Thanks, on my way," the one closest to her replied and pulled her order pad and pen out of the folded black apron tied around her waist. She left the station briskly and walked towards her table, the picture of confident professionalism, her hair caught up becomingly in a clip, and wearing the understated uniform of crisp white shirt and black slacks. Halfway there, she stopped abruptly, and whirled around, rushing back to the station and grabbing another waitress by the arm.

"Bethany," she implored, "can you take table eleven, please? Please? I can't serve that couple."

"Sorry, Steph." The other girl was in a hurry. "I'm in the weeds. I've got five tables full of prom kids, and they're already being obnoxious."

"I can't do this," Stephanie said in a panic. Looking up, she saw that the hostess was seating yet another table in her section and she could no longer delay. She gestured frantically to the bartender. He approached, quizzically.

"Marty, I know I could get fired for doing this, and I can't explain right now, but have mercy on me and sneak me a shot of tequila, will you?"

"Just don't get *me* fired," he muttered, passing her the shot from behind his closed fist. Stephanie picked it up with her back to the dining area, sidled around the corner to the servers' station and knocked it back, grimacing, then took a deep breath and approached the table pen in hand.

"Good evening, welcome to The Wren, would you care for something from the bar?" she recited for the third time that night, her face flushed and her attention fixed upon the order pad.

"*Stephanie?*" David said incredulously.

"I'm sorry," she said, flustered, not taking her eyes from the pad. "I tried to get somebody else to take this table—"

"This is where you're working?"

Stephanie tapped her pen against the pad and finally looked at him. "Well, I'm not doing this for my health."

"Of all the gin joints in all the towns in the world," David mumbled, doing an exceedingly poor Bogart impression.

"Look," she said, dropping both hands to her sides and glancing quickly around the room. "If you're as uncomfortable as I am, I can see if I can ask another waitress to take you."

"What are you guys talking about?" asked Kirsten, frowning.

"I'm your date's worst nightmare," Stephanie said.

"He's not my date, he's my uncle," Kirsten replied.

"And you're not my worst nightmare," David countered.

"Drink?" Stephanie tried again.

"I'd like a daiquiri," Kirsten replied with the affected posturing of an older woman.

"Not gonna happen," Stephanie said, pen poised, an amused smile curling her lips. "Try again."

"Coke," Kirsten sighed.

"Prom night?" Stephanie asked, glancing at the freesias on her wrist.

Kirsten nodded, stoically.

"How about sparkling water, in a champagne flute, which will look far more sophisticated?"

Kirsten's eyes lightened, "OK. Thanks."

"I didn't go to my prom, either," Stephanie leaned over and murmured to Kirsten so low that no one else could hear. Kirsten looked at her and smiled, gratefully.

"And, sir, for you?" Stephanie asked, assuming an air of professional servitude.

"Well, Miss." David scanned the wine list. "I'm not driving, but as my date's not drinking, I don't think I'd like a whole bottle. Do you offer a pinot by the glass?"

"We offer several," Stephanie replied, bending slightly over him, enough to take in the subtle hint of his aftershave, and pointing with her pen at the list. She was grateful for their byplay so that she didn't have to be quite herself. "The 2006 Australian is particularly nice, as well as reasonable."

David snapped the leather bound list shut. "Price is no object," he said with comical pomposity. "Bring me the Australian."

"Please," Stephanie said darkly.

"Oh, yeah, please."

Stephanie left them to take the order at the other recently seated table then retreated to the bar.

On their own, Kirsten studied the menu for several moments, and, puzzled, asked, "What's fennel?"

"An herb, I think."

"Would I like it? It says 'fennel-crusted pork chops'."

"Well, you won't know if you like it unless you try it," David suggested. He looked around the room. "So tell me about this Derek, guy."

"It's embarrassing," Kirsten mumbled, keeping her eyes on the menu. "And if you keep looking at him, I'm seriously going to die."

"What is it about teenage girls wanting to die everywhere?" David asked Stephanie as she returned to the table, carrying their drinks on a tray. "One little embarrassment and they're ready to lie down and die in the middle of a restaurant without even tasting their entree."

"One little embarrassment to you, maybe," Stephanie retorted, placing Kirsten's elegant flute of sparkling water in front of her, and giving the girl a wink before placing down David's wine. "Don't you remember being a teenager and feeling insecure?"

"No," David replied, and with more honesty than he had intended, added, "only being in my thirties and feeling insecure."

Stephanie looked at him for a beat, then changed the subject and inquired, "Are you ready to order?"

"How's the 'Bourbon Pecan Chicken?'" David asked.

"I don't know," Stephanie replied. "I can't afford to eat here."

David rolled his eyes. "Kirsten, what would you like?"

Kirsten, having watched their interaction with interest, said, "Well, I really want a cheeseburger, but I think I'm supposed to have something more grown up, so I'll have the fennel pork chop thing."

"One fennel pork chop thing," Stephanie repeated, jotting it down. "And for you, sir?"

"From your glowing recommendation, how can I resist the bourbon pecan chicken thing?"

"Right, excellent choices," she said briskly and departed.

Kirsten watched her walk away, then turned and looked quizzically at her uncle.

"She's funny," she observed.

David took a swallow of wine and nodded. "She is."

"And you guys are funny together," Kirsten persisted. "Did you used to go out?"

Thrown by her question, David, suddenly self-conscious, replied, "Yes," then amended, "No. Actually, we sort of ended before we started." He gestured towards her corsage. "She made that ring."

"Wow," Kirsten murmured, fingering the yellow stone with admiration. "How come you ended?"

Feeling more and more uncomfortable, David tried to shrug casually as he replied, "It's a long story, and besides, this night's supposed to be about you, not me."

"You're evading the question," Kirsten teased, leaning forward and pointing at him. "How come you get to tease me about Derek, but I can't tease you about her?"

"Because that's what you get to do when you're an adult. Sort of makes up for all the times you're on the receiving end as a kid," he shot back. He looked up to see a pretty girl, Kirsten's age, waving from the far side of the room. "I think someone's trying to get your attention," he said, relieved for the diversion.

"It's Sophie!" she whispered. "Oh my God, she's coming over. I'm going to die right here at the table."

"Can I have your pork chops, then?" David asked.

Sophie approached, and to Kirsten's horror, was joined by two more girls, leaving their dates behind, and chatting animatedly amongst themselves.

"Hey Kirst," Sophie said, glancing curiously at David. "I've been texting you, like, every ten seconds to get you to look over at me."

David, seeing his niece color in the agony of embarrassment, stepped in and said, "We actually find it a bit inappropriate to have our phones on the table during our conversations." He then rose to his feet, reached out his hand, and introduced himself, saying, "Hello, ladies, I'm David. And you are?"

Sophie, caught off-guard by the imposing masculine presence before her, awkwardly spoke her name and gestured to the other girls who flanked her as Madison and Amelia.

"Are you part of a prom, or something?" David asked, and found himself soon joined by Stephanie, bringing their salads.

"Yes, it's prom night," Sophie replied, as if begrudging the obvious. She turned her attention towards Kirsten, "So, are you going after all?"

"No," Kirsten admitted, looking down at her plate, "I'm not going."

"Thought not," Madison murmured for only her friends to hear.

"And thank goodness for that," said David, picking up on the comment, "otherwise we wouldn't have been able to enjoy our leisurely dinner without being rushed to attend something so—" He made a point of stressing the next word, "—*inconsequential.*"

Having witnessed the scene before her, Stephanie now announced, "Miss, your driver would like you to know that Mr. Bieber's manager phoned and said there will be two backstage passes for you at his summer appearance in California and if you need assistance with travel to please contact him."

Kirsten was on the verge of squirming until Sophie, her mouth popping open, said, "Are you *serious?* Oh my God, Kirsten!"

Kirsten looked at Stephanie in amazement and found herself replying, "Thank you, tell him I'll be in touch."

Stephanie nodded, catching David's bemused expression, and promptly left them, as did Sophie and her friends. They returned to their table, which suddenly became quite loud and buzzing with excitement as soon as they rejoined their group.

"I can't believe you did that," Kirsten said, still shaken. "I'm totally about to die."

"Don't die yet," David suggested, "because Derek is staring at you and you're going to want to die because of that instead."

Kirsten allowed herself a sidelong glance then returned her eyes to her uncle.

"I can't believe it, he is looking straight at me," she breathed.

"So this is when you break his heart by throwing your head back and laughing," David teased, and to his delight, she did just that, cracking herself up so that she actually couldn't stop laughing.

They remained long after her classmates left, and when Stephanie returned with their paid check, David smiled at her, warmly.

Stephanie handed him a copy of his receipt along with his credit card inside a red cloth-covered case and, returning his smile, said, "Hope you both have a wonderful evening."

David, returning to their previous byplay, complimented, "Excellent service. You're an excellent waitress."

Kirsten, grateful for Stephanie's contribution to her evening, extended her hand to thank her, and when she did, the stone of the ring in her corsage winked in the candlelight of their table. Stephanie, seeing it, looked pointedly at David as she replied, "Thank you. Waiting seems to be what I do best," then turned and left them. David watched her go in silence, then somewhat abruptly, smiled jerkily at Kirsten and said, "Ready?"

She nodded, but frowning, walked with him to the car. Not yet having the life experience to exhibit the needed tact within tension, after only a few minutes down the road, she suddenly turned and said, "That was weird."

"The evening?" he asked, deliberately misunderstanding. "I thought you enjoyed it."

"The evening rocked," Kirsten said. "It was incredible. And Stephanie, she was amazing."

David looked down and concurred, "Yes, she was."

"It just seems," Kirsten paused, deliberating whether or not to continue before blurting out, "it just seems like you both like each other and I don't get why you aren't together. I mean, you told me when you and Denise got divorced, you still liked each other, so it doesn't seem to make sense—"

"A lot of things don't make sense," David said soberly. "A lot of things seem obvious on the outside, but that's not always the way it is."

They rode along in silence for quite some time before Kirsten ventured her opinion again.

"You said you liked her, that she was funny," she pressed, her brow furrowed in confusion, "but that you guys ended before you started." Then using his own words against him, she continued, "And you were the one who said you won't know if you like something until you try it, right?"

"Stephanie's not a pork chop," he said dully as the car turned into Kirsten's driveway.

"No," Kirsten insisted, "but if she was here, right now, she would laugh at that." She looked up as the driver opened her door. "I guess I just want people to have happy endings, you know? My parents sure aren't having one, and I'm really grateful that I had one, tonight," she explained in the clumsy yet earnest manner of her age. Just before she slipped out the door, she eased the corsage off her wrist and handed it to him. "You should give this back to her, because then maybe you'll have one, too." She stared at him for a moment then reached in to give him a quick hug before closing the door with a smile and darting up the front walk into the house. David stared after her for a few moments, the corsage not yet wilting in his lap.

"Home, James," David quipped to Rufus, his friend.

"You got it, Hoss," Rufus replied and put the SUV in reverse.

Upon arriving at his apartment, David paid and tipped Rufus handsomely, and shoving his left hand in the pocket of his suit, mounted the front steps slowly, still holding the corsage with his right. He went upstairs, unlocked the door to his apartment, and sank down on his couch wearily rubbing his face in his hands.

Still in his suit, too tired to stand back up and change, he put his feet up on the coffee table and gently tossed the corsage which landed next to them. The remote was lying handily beside him, and he turned on the local news. It was the same as every night: a hold-up on one side of town, a murder in another area, a good news story of people making a difference...he turned it off, not having really listened.

It had been, he decided, the end of another particularly odd day. And unsettlingly revealing. He was pleased to have given Kirsten an evening he hoped she would always remember fondly, not for his efforts but to illustrate she was surrounded by people who especially wanted to demonstrate their love, had been supremely satisfying. He hadn't yet processed meeting his father and he knew that was going to take some time. He harbored no rancor towards him. It was simply at this point too overwhelming to fully embrace a rekindled relationship. He needed to get to the root of how it might affect him, which, as he glanced again at the corsage, seemed to be a recurring theme in his life. His relationship with his mother, as much as he admired and loved her, he suspected on a gut level had influenced his choice to fall headlong for a woman who would keep him ever so subtly at a distance. Even his chosen career, it pained him to admit, allowed him to interact quite intimately on a human level, but only safely behind a lens. His thoughts flicked momentarily back to his father and how the simple sentence he had uttered had impacted him: *"I haven't any right to say it, because I had nothing to do with it, but I'm proud of the man that you've become."* The profound truth of that combined with the heartbreaking realization of all the missed opportunities between them seemed such an avoidable waste. David frowned. Missed opportunities...he found his thoughts drawn back fondly to Stephanie and for once didn't attempt to deter them. He was immediately aware of the quickening of his pulse signaling what had always meant aversion. She had affected him greatly in a way that was simple yet complicated, straightforward yet scattered, and he realized at once it was only his reactions, his long-conditioned wounded reactions to what she offered with an open heart and frank honesty that were conspiring to assist him in making the biggest mistake of his life. He sat up, grabbed the corsage, and feeling for his keys, bounded down the stairs and came to a halt in the parking lot and stared impassively at his parked Jeep.

Taking a deep breath and placing the spray of flowers on the passenger seat, he easily rotated his right wrist to switch on the ignition. Glancing at the clock on the dash showing quarter past eleven, he wondered if she had already left the restaurant. He quickly redialed and found only their voicemail giving the days and hours of operations and that they were currently closed. He ran his hand through his hair, and, remembering his therapist's warning of how carefully he must move his arm, he took a deep breath as he extended the fingers of his right hand to their fullest, aiding in pushing the car into first gear. He nosed the Jeep out of the parking lot and into the street, practically empty. He found pulling into second gear was slightly easier, as he let out the clutch, gaining speed, but third was impossible. Taking his left hand momentarily off the wheel, he unsnapped his seat belt so he could lift his torso up and forward, requiring less range of motion from his upper arm and shoulder, but it still hurt enough to make him grunt between gritted teeth and he swore that the lights were against him. He kept his eyes on the clock as it closed in on the half hour and breathed with relief as he descended the entrance ramp and merged onto the south freeway. Bending his right elbow, he found he could hold the bottom of the steering wheel while crossing over with his left hand to shift into fourth gear, his rib still protesting sharply. He could see his own reflection in the rear view mirror as he glanced from time to time behind and beside him, speeding, changing lanes recklessly. He thought he looked like a haunted man, which, he grimly acknowledged, had been such a large part of his denial for so long that the very physicality of it remained in his expression.

Within minutes, he exited and the interior of his car filled with the low curses from each painful effort of multiple changes of gear, and he screeched to a halt in front of The Wren. It was dark. Getting out and clutching the corsage, he jogged painfully up to the front window, holding his upper right arm firmly in place with his left hand, and cupped his eyes to see inside. There seemed to be a light on, but only above the bar, and the chairs were all neatly turned upside down upon the tabletops. He knocked repeatedly but to no avail, and he despairingly wheeled around on his heels, his eyes sweeping over the few remaining parked cars in the lot. There was no sign of Stephanie's Subaru. He walked back and leaned against the side of his Jeep, defeated, shoving the corsage into his pocket. It had been an impulsive folly, taking this risk that he might still reach her tonight, but when the moment had come upon him so startlingly clear, it was as if his resolve had suddenly overpowered the decade of excuses that endeavored to prevent him from speaking his heart before morning. He had finally arrived at the place he knew he belonged. Presently, he thought he could hear soft laughter and voices coming from around the side of the building and he felt his heart stop as he caught sight of Stephanie, walking with the bartender towards a late model truck.

"Stephanie," he called out in a voice that didn't even sound like his own.

She stopped and turned in the direction of his voice, her eyes finding his slender figure leaning against the Jeep, and stared in disbelief.

"You know him?" Marty asked her warily.

"Yeah," she nodded. "It's OK, Marty. I know him."

"Is it the tequila guy?"

Stephanie glanced at him with a quick grin. "Yeah, the tequila guy. I'm all right, really. Thanks."

Marty gave her a quick nod and climbed into his truck, and as he pulled out, David saw that it had obscured her Subaru, as he drove slowly away.

Stephanie remained rooted where she stood and waited as David approached her. He stood within a foot of her, his hands at his sides, and gave voice to every fear, every obstruction that had prevented him from being where he was at this moment.

"Steph," he began haltingly. "I have been caught up in places that I didn't even know existed, and I couldn't tell you how I felt about you because I couldn't even tell myself. I was scared I was going to end up taking you along on some ride while I was trying to figure things out, and I couldn't do that to you. It wouldn't have been fair, so I backed off. But I think I'm there. I think I'm finally there, now." He stepped closer and took hold of her hands. "You once said you hoped you'd meet a guy who knew what he wanted and what he wanted was you," he paused, looking deeply into her eyes. "And, Steph, I'm that guy. If you still want me, I'm that guy."

"David," she stared back at him, and despite her heart beating wildly, said, "I can't be a consolation prize."

"You're not," he stressed. "Trust me, I know what that feels like and you're not. I ended it with Denise this time. And I'm so sorry you were hurt, and I'm sorry that I mistook being gobsmacked that she came back to me for love. Because it wasn't. Not even close." He took a deep breath and added, "I'm not normally this stupid."

Stephanie looked up at him, her candid brown eyes searching his face and said, "But you know that this is a package deal, right? I mean, I know you're in a really tender place right now, and I can't expect some heavy level of commitment from you, but I've got a little boy that means everything to me and I can't risk his losing faith in someone I think he's going to get pretty attached to."

David took her face in his hands and said, "Stephanie, I'm crazy about you, and I want to be a part of your crazy life. I want to pull rodents out of the cat's mouth with you and see what jewelry you're going to make and watch Buster roll down the hill in the grass." He swallowed, then added, "I think that's pretty much it."

Stephanie leaned into him and carefully placed her arms around his waist and looked up at him looking down at her.

"Deal," she said.

"I—I had this made for Kirsten," he stammered, suddenly remembering and removing the corsage from the pocket of his suit jacket, "so that she could have something beautiful to remember her night. It doesn't feel right to give it to you because of Denise, but Kirsten was obviously a lot smarter than me, because she gave it back and specifically told me I should give it to you for the same reason."

And Stephanie, abandoning her ever-present sardonic grittiness, dissolved into tears. She slipped it over her wrist and looked at him, unashamed in her vulnerability. He embraced her with his left arm and found that the range of motion with his right arm allowed him to advance his elbow just forward enough so that the palm of his hand rested on the small of her back.

"Another milestone," he whispered smilingly into her hair, then tilted her chin upwards and gently kissed her. After several moments, she turned her face and, sighing, pressed her cheek against his chest, feeling the beat of his heart, both of them flooded with the relief of having found, and having allowed themselves to be found by each other. They held on for what felt to be forever.

Chapter 47

A LATE MORNING JUNE sun spilled over Lissie's cotton-clad shoulders and having stretched with luxurious abandon, unseeing, only breathing in her favorite view: the sharp tang of the air, the world around and before her bathed in a glorious warmth after three days of heavy rain. She opened her grateful eyes and looked far out to sea. There were wisps of clouds overhead and shrieks of gulls encircling the great rock in the distance, appearing like a familiar friend from the past. She had found her way back to Trebarwith Strand, lucky to have found a tiny slot in which to park the rental car on the dead end lane that led to the beach. She had returned to this place after ambling along the South West Coast footpath, taking her time, exchanging pleasantries with other walkers, some committed to traversing its entire length from Somerset to Dorset. Lissie, however, was serenely content with this one stretch along the Cornish coast, and removed her shoes to feel the wild grasses between her toes as she had done as a girl.

She didn't venture to the edge of the cliff but remained several yards back, mindful of the crumbling rock, and as her pale blue eyes swept along the coastline, she marveled at how nothing had changed in this cherished spot. She didn't need to close her eyes to see her mother, playful and radiant as if it were yesterday, slowly pirouetting amongst the wildflowers tangled through the grass. But close her eyes she did, to feel the sun on her face, to feel her dreams realized, to feel her arms outstretched, the very sea air between her fingers.

"I've come back," she said to herself. Then opening her eyes, she smiled wistfully and spoke aloud, this time to her mother, "I've come back. I'm here, and I'm all right." The wind lifted her words and was carrying them skywards. At last, she turned and reached out her arm with her hand open, beckoning her granddaughter to join her. Kirsten rose to her feet and deposited a rock on each corner of the blanket to keep it from being blown away and walked over to meet her, taking her hand and joining her grandmother's gaze.

"This is a living part of your history, Kirsten," Lissie smiled to her. "This is where your great-grandfather proposed to your great-grandmother and produced the generation that would later bring you into the world."

It wasn't a description that was lost on the girl. Kirsten was romantic enough to visualize what the moment might have been like and she returned her grandmother's smile and said, "I'm so glad you brought me here, Nan. I'll never forget it."

After several minutes, they turned slowly to return to their picnic and lowered themselves onto the blanket, remaining obediently spread upon the ground. Lissie poured them both a cup of tea from the thermos.

"It's still a bit chilly, isn't it?" she said, passing the plastic cup to Kirsten. "Are you warm enough?"

Kirsten nodded, "I'm OK, I'm just glad it stopped raining."

Lissie chuckled. "It certainly rains a lot in England, but I suppose that's what keeps it so gloriously green."

Kirsten admired the landscape before her. "It's beautiful, Nan, I completely get why you would want to live here. I don't think I'd ever want to go back either."

Lissie's eyes widened in surprise. "Really? This doesn't all feel terribly old-fashioned to you?"

Kirsten shook her head slowly, and leaning back, rested on her elbows. "It feels old-fashioned, but I love that. Everything is so old, hundreds and hundreds of years old. Maybe it's because I'm getting older and my own life is changing so much, but it's comforting in a way to be a part of something that will never change."

Lissie looked at her and smiled. "I know exactly what you mean. Everything sort of slows down here, at least it feels as if it does to me."

"And it's charming," Kirsten observed, feeling her way about articulating her thoughts. "All those little fishing villages...it's like make believe." She suddenly grinned at her grandmother, "I haven't even missed having my phone. I don't even care. Part of me wishes I had it to take photographs of everything, but I can buy postcards."

"That's right," Lissie said. She stretched out her legs before musing, "And even then, they get misplaced or thrown away. Kirsten, when I was just a little older than you, sitting where we are now and watching my mother dance, I didn't have a camera, but I can tell you exactly how she looked, what we were wearing and even what we said. So no, we don't really need photographs to remind ourselves."

"Don't say that to Uncle David," Kirsten warned, and they both laughed.

"Have you," Lissie asked tentatively, "thought about what you might want to do with your life?"

Kirsten sat up, hugging her knees to her chest. "Well, I'm supposed to start at Appalachian State in the fall," she said, slowly drawing out her thoughts, "and it makes sense for me to study biology because I did really well in it in high school, but Nan—" She turned and looked with almost pleading in her eyes. "I'm not excited by that at all. I want to do something that really means something to me."

"I can certainly understand that," Lissie said. "Is there anything that particularly appeals to you?"

"Yes, especially after coming here," Kirsten replied, "but it's not going to make Mom or Dad very happy. I think I'd like to be a flight attendant."

"Do you think that would bother them?" Lissie asked.

"Well, you know they're both going to want me to have a degree, as a safety net, but it just seems to be a waste of money to go after something I'll never use, just to have a piece of paper that says I studied it for four years. I want to get out of North Carolina and see the world and travel all over. What do you think?"

"I think," Lissie replied, resting her hand on her granddaughter's knee, "following your heart is always the right thing to do as long as you're not hurting anyone along the way."

"I knew you'd say that," Kirsten smiled, softly, "and I'm glad you followed yours."

"Oh," Lissie breathed, her heart in her face. She said, "Kirsten, I'm so glad you wanted to come with me to this place. I really wanted to give you something special for your graduation present, but I was afraid you might find this all just to be the boring ramblings of an old woman."

"There's nothing boring about it, Nan, and you're not old. I'll never think of you as old." Having said that, Kirsten rose to her feet and shaded her eyes looking over the grassy cliffs, still seeing the image of her grandmother in her moment of long imagined fulfillment, her arms outstretched to the sky, eyes closed against the sun, the sparkling sea beyond. And she knew she would always see it.

Made in the USA
Las Vegas, NV
09 February 2024

85539262R00215